PRAIS

THE TERMINAL

Winner of the Science Fiction and Fantasy Writers of America's Nebula Award for Best Novel of the Year

Finalist for the Hugo Award for Best Novel of the Year

Winner of the Canadian Science Fiction and Fantasy Award ("the Aurora") for Best Novel of the Year

"A terrific mix of science, technological derring-do, and murder. A great story; a crackerjack novel."

—*The Globe and Mail* (Toronto)

"There is so much of interest in this book—artificial intelligence, a good murder mystery, a nicely realized near-future, and, as I've come to expect from Sawyer's novels, thought-provoking philosophy." —*SF Site*

"Audacious. Sawyer is to be commended for raising important philosophical issues in the form of a highly entertaining scientific mystery. His characters are convincing; their motivations and relationships are always at the heart of the action." —*The Gazette* (Montreal)

"The interplay of ideas makes this a successful science-fictional mystery." —*The Denver Post*

"A page-turner; a quality read. Murder is the name, and chases through cyberspace the game—a cautionary tale straight from the murky depths of the brave new world of our data future." —*Ottawa Citizen*

"*The Terminal Experiment* shows why Robert J. Sawyer has catapulted to the top rank of science fiction writers."

—Mike Resnick, Hugo Award–winning author of *The Buntline Special*

continued . . .

WWW: WATCH

"Both thought-provoking and entertaining . . . His take on the nature of artificial intelligence is provocative and believable . . . Robert J. Sawyer's Webmind series is indeed excellent. Great concepts, great characters, great writing—this book (and this series) has them all in abundance."

—*The Maine Edge*

"Sawyer shows his genius in combining cutting-edge scientific theories and technological developments with real human characters. [*WWW: Watch*] explores heavy conceptual topics such as religion and politics, and yet at the same time has an accessible tone as it follows Caitlin's very human story . . . [Sawyer's] works are both revelatory and thought-provoking." —*The Globe and Mail* (Toronto)

"Fun . . . [an] intelligent and compassionate approach . . . to the nature of consciousness."

—*Sacramento News & Review*

"[Sawyer is] a brilliant thinker pondering some of the most fundamental questions we face today . . . [He] maintains the same high-level interplay of ideas and action that characterizes all his work." —*National Post* (Ontario)

"Strong characters, engrossing plot . . . a helluva fun read and an excellent science fiction book." —*SF Signal*

"[A] complex and fascinating novel." —*Ottawa Citizen*

"When people call science fiction a literature of ideas, they mean Robert J. Sawyer." —*Sci Fi Magazine*

"Sawyer's books all seem to be very easy, fast reads . . . keeping the reader involved right up to the end . . . I've started wondering just how soon we'll have to deal with a real-world Webmind. Like the best science fiction, *WWW: Watch* may not be predicting the future, but it certainly is presenting potential scenarios." —*SFScope*

WWW: WAKE

"Unforgettable. Impossible to put down."
—Jack McDevitt, Nebula Award–winning author of *Echo*

"A superb work of day-after-tomorrow science fiction; I enjoyed every page."
—Allen Steele, Hugo Award–winning author of *Hex*

"Cracking open a new Robert J. Sawyer book is like getting a gift from a friend who visits all the strange and undiscovered places in the world. You can't wait to see what he's going to amaze you with this time."
—John Scalzi, John W. Campbell Award–winning author of *Fuzzy Nation*

"One of the most original and fascinating novels to be published in a long time." —*Sacramento Book Review*

"One of Sawyer's strongest works to date."
—*Publishers Weekly* (starred review)

"Caitlin is a very likable protagonist, and well drawn . . . a very promising start to what could turn out to be a very thoughtful and compelling science fiction trilogy."
—*SCI FI Wire*

"Sawyer's take on theories about the origins of consciousness, generated within the framework of an engaging story, is fascinating, and his approach to machine consciousness and the Internet is surprisingly fresh." —*Booklist*

"[*WWW: Wake*] is about as good as it gets when it comes to science fiction . . . Sawyer's combination of writing skill and computing background come together marvelously in this book. The characters are rich and realistic, while the ideas are fresh and fascinating." —*The Maine Edge*

"Sawyer continues to push the boundaries with his stories of the future made credible. His erudition, eclecticism, and masterly storytelling make this trilogy opener a choice selection." —*Library Journal*

Books by Robert J. Sawyer

Novels

GOLDEN FLEECE
END OF AN ERA
THE TERMINAL EXPERIMENT
STARPLEX
FRAMESHIFT
ILLEGAL ALIEN
FACTORING HUMANITY
FLASHFORWARD
CALCULATING GOD
MINDSCAN
ROLLBACK

THE QUINTAGLIO ASCENSION TRILOGY

FAR-SEER
FOSSIL HUNTER
FOREIGNER

THE NEANDERTHAL PARALLAX TRILOGY

HOMINIDS
HUMANS
HYBRIDS

THE WWW TRILOGY

WAKE
WATCH
WONDER

Collections

ITERATIONS (introduction by James Alan Gardner)
RELATIVITY (introduction by Mike Resnick)
IDENTITY THEFT (introduction by Robert Charles Wilson)

For book-club discussion guides, visit sfwriter.com.

THE TERMINAL EXPERIMENT

ROBERT J. SAWYER

ACE BOOKS, NEW YORK

THE BERKLEY PUBLISHING GROUP
Published by the Penguin Group
Penguin Group (USA) Inc.
375 Hudson Street, New York, New York 10014, USA
Penguin Group (Canada), 90 Eglinton Avenue East, Suite 700, Toronto, Ontario M4P 2Y3, Canada
(a division of Pearson Penguin Canada Inc.)
Penguin Books Ltd., 80 Strand, London WC2R 0RL, England
Penguin Group Ireland, 25 St. Stephen's Green, Dublin 2, Ireland (a division of Penguin Books Ltd.)
Penguin Group (Australia), 250 Camberwell Road, Camberwell, Victoria 3124, Australia
(a division of Pearson Australia Group Pty. Ltd.)
Penguin Books India Pvt. Ltd., 11 Community Centre, Panchsheel Park, New Delhi—110 017, India
Penguin Group (NZ), 67 Apollo Drive, Rosedale, Auckland 0632, New Zealand
(a division of Pearson New Zealand Ltd.)
Penguin Books (South Africa) (Pty.) Ltd., 24 Sturdee Avenue, Rosebank, Johannesburg 2196,
South Africa

Penguin Books Ltd., Registered Offices: 80 Strand, London WC2R 0RL, England

THE TERMINAL EXPERIMENT

An Ace Book / published by arrangement with SFWriter.com, Inc.

PRINTING HISTORY
HarperPrism mass-market edition / May 1995
Penguin Canada premium edition / December 2009
Ace mass-market edition / September 2011

This novel was originally serialized in four parts under the title *Hobson's Choice* in *Analog Science Fiction and Fact* magazine's mid-December 1994 through March 1995 issues.
Cover photo by Ikon Images/Paul Price/Getty.
Cover design by Rita Frangie.
Interior text design by Kristin del Rosario.

ISBN: 978-0-441-02080-5

ACE
Ace Books are published by The Berkley Publishing Group,
a division of Penguin Group (USA) Inc.,
375 Hudson Street, New York, New York 10014.
ACE and the "A" design are trademarks of Penguin Group (USA) Inc.

PRINTED IN THE UNITED STATES OF AMERICA

10 9 8 7 6 5 4 3 2 1

For Ted Bleaney
with thanks for twenty years of friendship

ACKNOWLEDGMENTS

This novel came to life with the help of many fine souls, including Christopher Schelling, John Douglas, and John Silbersack at HarperCollins, Stanley Schmidt at *Analog,* and Richard Curtis. The advice of David Gotlib, M.D., was enormously helpful. I received wonderful feedback from writing colleagues Barbara Delaplace, Terence M. Green, Edo van Belkom, and Andrew Weiner. As well, friends Shaheen Hussain Azmi, Asbed Bedrossian, Ted Bleaney, David Livingstone Clink, Richard Gotlib, Howard Miller, and Alan B. Sawyer gave me valuable insights. Special thanks to the Ontario Arts Council for providing me with a Writers' Reserve grant to aid in creating this novel, and to Ginjer Buchanan and Ralph Vicinanza for arranging for this new edition. Finally, my deepest thanks to my wife, Carolyn Clink.

AUTHOR'S NOTE

The Future Is Now

These days, I'm best known for *FlashForward,* my novel that is the basis for the ABC TV series of the same name. But that book didn't change my life the most; this one did. *The Terminal Experiment* made my career when it won the Science Fiction and Fantasy Writers of America's Nebula Award—the "Academy Award" of the SF field—for Best Novel of the Year.

I received that award on April 27, 1996, at a gala banquet aboard the *Queen Mary* off Long Beach, California. Right after my win, John Douglas, an editor with the company that had produced the original edition of this book, said to me, "You've gone overnight from being a promising newcomer to an established, bankable name." And John was right; my days as a struggling writer ended then and there.

I wrote *The Terminal Experiment* in 1993, setting it in the then far-distant year of 2011. Although the story is told against a backdrop of the online universe, when I was writing it the Internet was new to most people and the World Wide Web hadn't yet been invented.

Even though I was an early adopter of online technologies—I've been on the Internet since 1983, have had a website (indeed, was the very first science-fiction writer to have one, at sfwriter.com) since 1995, and have been blogging since before the word even existed—neither I nor anyone else foresaw the current world of Google and Flickr, Facebook and Twitter, Wikipedia and YouTube (although my latest novels, *WWW: Wake, WWW: Watch,* and *WWW: Wonder,* which deal with the World Wide Web gaining consciousness in the present day, *do* embrace our modern reality).

For this new edition of *The Terminal Experiment,* I thought about changing the dates mentioned in the book, about removing the dates altogether, and about updating or revising the many references to computing and online life. But I ultimately decided not to alter the text. Yes, that means this book is now an odd snapshot of the way one writer thought the future of computing might unfold, but that's the smallest part of what *The Terminal Experiment* is really about. Mostly the novel is an exploration of timeless conundrums: Do we have souls? Is there an afterlife? Does God exist? And—to me, the most intriguing of all—can science ever help us find the answers to these questions?

—Robert J. Sawyer
Mississauga, Ontario
September 2009

In the last analysis,
it is our conception of death which decides
our answers to all the questions life puts to us.

—DAG HAMMARSKJÖLD (1905–1961)
UNITED NATIONS SECRETARY-GENERAL

PROLOGUE

DECEMBER 2011

"What room is Detective Philo in?" asked Peter Hobson, a tall, thin man of forty-two, with hair an equal mixture of black and gray.

The squat nurse behind the desk had been absorbed in whatever she'd been reading. She looked up. "Pardon?"

"Detective Sandra Philo," said Peter. "What room is she in?"

"Four-twelve," said the nurse. "But her doctor has ordered that only immediate family members should visit."

Peter began down the corridor. The nurse came around from behind the desk and gave chase. "You can't go in there," she said firmly.

Peter turned briefly to look at her. "I have to see her."

The nurse maneuvered in front of him. "She's in critical condition."

"I'm Peter Hobson. I'm a doctor."

"I know who you are, Mr. Hobson. I also know you're not a *medical* doctor."

"I'm on the Board of Directors of North York General."

"Fine. Go over there and bully someone, then. You're not raising havoc on my ward."

Peter exhaled noisily. "Look, it's a matter of life and death that I see Ms. Philo."

"Everything in the ICU is a matter of life and death, Mr. Hobson. Ms. Philo is sleeping, and I'll not have her disturbed."

Peter pushed ahead.

"I'll call security," said the nurse, trying to keep her voice low so as not to alarm the patients.

Peter didn't look back. "Fine," he snapped, his long legs carrying him quickly down the corridor. The nurse waddled toward her desk and picked up the phone.

Peter found 412 and entered without knocking. Sandra was hooked up to an EKG; it wasn't a Hobson unit, but Peter had no trouble reading its display. A drip bag of saline was on a pole beside her bed.

Sandra opened her eyes. It seemed to take a moment for them to focus. "You!" she exclaimed at last, her voice raw and thin—the effects of the beamer.

Peter closed the door. "I've only got a few moments. They've already called security to come and take me away."

Every word was a struggle for Sandra. "You tried . . . to have me . . . killed," she said.

"No," said Peter. "I swear to you that wasn't my doing."

Sandra managed a weak shout, too faint to be heard through the closed door. "Nurse!"

Peter looked at the woman. When he'd first met her, only a few weeks ago, she'd been a healthy thirty-six-year-old, with flaming red hair. Now her hair was falling out in clumps, her complexion was sallow, and she could barely move. "I don't want to be rude, Sandra," Peter said, "but please shut up and listen."

"Nurse!"

"Listen, damn it! I had nothing to do with the murders.

But I know who did. And I can give you a chance at getting him."

At that moment the door burst open. The squat nurse entered, flanked on either side by a burly security guard.

"Remove him," said the nurse.

The guards moved forward.

"Dammit, Sandra," said Peter. "This is your only chance. Give me five minutes." One guard grabbed Peter's upper arm. "Five minutes, for God's sake! That's all I ask."

"Let's go," said the guard.

Peter's tone was imploring. "Sandra, tell them you want me to stay!" He hated himself for what he said next, but he couldn't think of anything more effective: "If you don't, you'll die never having solved the crimes."

"Come along now, buddy," said the other guard gruffly.

"No—wait! Sandra, please!"

"Come along . . ."

"Sandra!"

Finally, a voice weak and wan: "Let . . . him . . . stay."

"We can't do that, ma'am," said one of the guards.

Sandra rallied a little strength. "Police business . . . let him stay."

Peter twisted free of the guard's grip. "Thank you," he said to Sandra. "Thank you."

The nurse scowled at him. "I won't stay long," Peter said to her. "I promise."

Sandra managed to roll her head slightly in the nurse's direction. "It's . . . okay," she said, faintly.

The nurse was seething. The tableau held for several seconds, then the woman nodded. "All right," she said, perhaps the talk of police business and unsolved crimes convincing her she was out of her depth.

"Thank you," Peter said to the nurse, relieved. "Thank you very much."

The nurse scowled, turned on her heel, and left, followed

immediately by one of the guards. The other guard backed out, his face an angry mask, all the time pointing a warning finger at Peter.

When they were alone again, Sandra said, "Tell . . . me."

Peter found a chair and sat down beside her bed.

"First, let me say I'm terribly, terribly sorry about what's happened. Believe me, I never wanted you or anyone else to come to harm. This—this is all out of control."

Sandra said nothing.

"Do you have any family? Any children?"

"Daughter," said Sandra, surprised.

"I didn't know that."

"With my ex now," she said.

"I want you to know, I'm going to take care of her financially. Everything she needs—clothes, cars, university, vacations in Europe, whatever. I will pay for it all. I'll set up a trust fund."

Sandra's eyes were wide.

"I never intended any of this, and I swear to you that I've tried repeatedly to stop it all."

Peter paused, thinking back to how the whole damned thing had started. Another hospital room, trying to comfort another brave woman who was dying. It comes full circle.

"Sarkar Muhammed was right—I should have come to you before. I need your help, Sandra. This has to end." Peter exhaled, wondering where to begin. So much had happened. "Did you know," he said at last, "that it's possible to scan every neural net in a human brain and produce an exact duplicate of the subject's mind inside a computer?"

Sandra shook her head slightly.

"Well, it is. It's a new technique. Sarkar Muhammed is one of its pioneers. What would you say if I told you that my brain had been scanned and duplicated?"

Sandra lifted her eyebrows. "Two heads . . . better than one."

Peter acknowledged the comment with a wry smile.

"Perhaps. Although, actually, a total of three simulations of me were made."

"And one of these . . . committed . . . murders?"

Peter was surprised by how quickly Sandra grasped it. "Yes."

"Thought AI . . . was involved."

"We've tried to stop them," said Peter. "Nothing worked. But at least I now know which simulation is guilty." He paused. "I'll give you everything you'll need, Sandra, including full Q&A access to the scans of my brain. You'll get to know me in intimate detail—better than anyone in the real world knows me. You'll know how I think, and that will give you the knowledge to outwit the murdering simulation."

Sandra lifted her shoulders slightly. "Nothing I can do," she said, her voice weak and sad. "Dying."

Peter closed his eyes. "I know. I'm terribly, terribly sorry. But there *is* a way, Sandra—a way for you to end all this."

CHAPTER 1

JANUARY 1995

Sandra Philo probed the memories of Peter Hobson.

The horror, she learned, had started in 1995, sixteen years ago. Back then, Peter Hobson hadn't been the center of a controversy about science and faith that was shaking the world. No, back then he was simply a twenty-six-year-old grad student at the University of Toronto, doing his master's degree in biomedical engineering—a student who was about to have the shock of his life . . .

THE phone rang in Peter Hobson's dorm room. "We've got an eater," said Kofax's voice. "You up for it?"

An eater. A dead person. Peter was trying to get used to Kofax's callousness. He rubbed sleep from his eyes. "Y-yes." He tried to sound more confident: "Sure," he said. "Sure thing."

"Mamikonian's going to start the slice-and-dice," said Kofax. "You can ride the EKG. That'll take a good hunk out of your practicum requirements."

Mamikonian. Stanford-trained transplant surgeon. Sixty-something, hands steady as a statue's. Organ harvesting. Christ, yes, he wanted in on that. "How soon?"

"Couple of hours," said Kofax. "Kid's on full life support—keep the meat fresh. Mamikonian is out in Mississauga; it'll take him that long to get here and prepped."

Kid, he'd said. Some kid's life cut short.

"What happened?" asked Peter.

"Motorcycle accident—kid was thrown through the air when a Buick sideswiped him."

A teenaged boy. Peter shook his head. "I'm in," he said.

"OR 3," said Kofax. "Start prep in an hour." He hung up. Peter hurried to get dressed.

HE wasn't supposed to do it, Peter knew, but he couldn't help himself. On the way to the OR, he stopped at Emergency Admitting and checked the aluminum clipboards in the swivel-mounted rack. One guy being sewn up after going through a plate-glass window. Another with a broken arm. Knife wound. Stomach cramps. Ah—

Enzo Bandello, 17.

Motorcycle accident, just as Kofax had said.

A nurse sidled up to Peter and looked over his shoulder. Her name badge said Sally Cohan. She frowned. "Poor kid. I've got a brother the same age." A pause. "The parents are in the chapel."

Peter nodded.

Enzo Bandello, he thought. Seventeen.

In trying to save the boy, the trauma team had given him dopamine and had deliberately dehydrated him, in hopes of reducing the brain swelling normally associated with a severe head wound. Too much dopamine, though, would damage the heart muscle. According to the chart, at 2:14 a.m., they'd begun flushing it from his body and fluids were being pumped in. Latest reading showed his blood pressure was still too high—an effect of the dopamine—but it should come down soon. Peter flipped pages. A serology report: Enzo was free of hepatitis and AIDS. Blood count and bleeding studies looked good, too.

A perfect donor, thought Peter. Tragedy or miracle? His parts would save the lives of a half-dozen people. Mamikonian would take the heart out first, a thirty-minute operation. Then the liver—two hours' work. Next, the renal team would remove the kidneys, another hour's cutting. After that, the corneas. Then the bones and other tissues.

There wouldn't be much left to bury.

"Heart's going to Sudbury," said Sally. "Crossmatching was excellent, they say."

Peter put the clipboard back into the carousel and walked through the double doors that led to the rest of the hospital. There were two equally good routes to OR 3. He chose the one that went by the chapel.

He was not a religious person. His family, back in Saskatchewan, was white-bread Canadian Protestant. Last time Peter had been in church was for a wedding. Time before that, a funeral.

He could see the Bandellos from the hallway, seated in a middle pew. The mother was crying softly. The father had an arm around her shoulders. He was a deeply tanned man wearing a plaid work shirt with cement stains on it. A bricklayer, perhaps. A lot of Toronto's Italians of his generation worked in construction. They'd come over after World War II, unable to speak English, and had taken hard-labor jobs to make a better life for their kids.

And now this man's kid was dead.

The chapel was denominationally neutral, but the father was looking up, as if he could see a crucifix on the wall, see his Jesus hanging there. He crossed himself.

Somewhere in Sudbury, Peter knew, there was a celebration going on. A heart was coming; a life would be saved. Somewhere there was joy.

But not here.

He continued on down the corridor.

PETER arrived at the scrub room. Through a large window, he could see into the operating theater. Most of the surgical team was already in place. Enzo's body had been prepped: his torso shaved, two layers of rust-colored iodine painted on, clear plastic stretched over the surgical field.

Peter tried to get a look at that which the others had been trained to ignore: the face of the donor. Not much of it was visible; most of Enzo's head was covered by a thin sheet, exposing only the ventilator tube. The transplant team was deliberately kept ignorant of the donor's identity—made it easier, they said. Peter was probably the only one who knew the boy's name.

There were two scrub sinks outside the OR. Peter began the regulation eight minutes of washing, a digital timer above the sink counting down the time.

After five minutes, Dr. Mamikonian himself arrived and began scrubbing at the second sink. He had steel-gray hair and a lantern jaw—more like an aging superhero than a surgeon.

"You are?" asked Mamikonian as he scrubbed.

"Peter Hobson, sir. I'm a grad student in biomedical engineering."

Mamikonian smiled. "Good to meet you, Peter." He continued to scrub. "Forgive me for not shaking hands," he said, chuckling. "What's your role today?"

"Well, for our course work we're supposed to log forty hours of real-world experience with medical technology. Professor Kofax—he's my thesis advisor—arranged for me to operate the EKG today." He paused. "If that's all right with you, sir."

"That's fine," said Mamikonian. "Watch and learn."

"I will, sir."

The counter above Peter's sink bleeped. He wasn't used to this; his hands felt raw. He held his dripping arms out at chest height. A scrub nurse appeared with a towel. Peter took it, dried his hands, then stepped into the sterile green gown she was holding for him.

"Glove size?" she asked.

"Seven."

She tore open a package, removed the latex gloves, and snapped them onto his hands.

Peter entered the OR. Overhead, a dozen people were watching through the glass ceiling from the observation gallery.

In the center of the room was a table holding up Enzo's body. There were several tubes going into it: three volume lines, an arterial line to monitor blood pressure, a central venous line threaded into the heart to monitor hydration level. A young Asian woman sat on a stool, her eyes scanning the volume monitor, the CO_2 monitor, and the volumetric infusion pump.

Until his arrival, the woman had also been watching the EKG oscilloscope mounted above Enzo's head. Peter moved into position next to it and adjusted the contrast on the display. The pulse rate was normal, and there was no sign of damage to the heart muscle.

It chilled him. The guy was legally dead, and still he had a pulse.

"I'm Hwa," said the Asian woman. "First time?"

Peter nodded. "I've been in on a few little things before, but nothing like this."

Hwa's mouth was covered by a face mask, but Peter could see her eyes crinkle in a smile. "You get used to it," she said.

Across the room, an illuminated panel had Enzo's chest x-ray clipped to it. The lungs hadn't collapsed and the chest was clear. The heart, a silhouette in the center of the image, looked fine.

Mamikonian entered. All eyes turned to face him—the

conductor for their orchestra. "Good morning, everyone," he said. "Let's go to work, shall we?" He moved in to stand over Enzo's body.

"Blood pressure's falling a bit," said Hwa.

"Crystalloid fluid, please," said Mamikonian, glancing at the readouts. "And let's add a little dopamine back in."

Mamikonian stood on Enzo's right, next to his chest. Across from him was the scrub nurse. A surgical assistant stood next to her, holding the abdominal-wall retractor. Five one-liter containers of ice-cold Ringer's lactate were lined up in a neat row on a table so they could be emptied quickly into the chest cavity. A nurse also had six units of packed red blood cells ready to go. Peter tried to stay out of the way near the head of the bed.

Next to Peter, the perfusionist, a Sikh wearing a large green cap over his turban, scanned a series of readouts labeled *remote temperatures, arterial vent,* and *cardiac sucker.* Nearby, another technician carefully watched the rising and falling of the ventilator's black bellows to make sure Enzo was still breathing properly.

"Let's go," said Mamikonian.

A nurse moved in and injected something into Enzo's body. She spoke into a microphone dangled on a thin wire from the ceiling. "Myolock administered at 10:02 a.m."

Dr. Mamikonian requested a scalpel and made an incision starting just below the Adam's apple and continuing down the center of the chest. The scalpel split the skin easily, sliding through the muscle and fat until it banged against the breastbone.

The EKG shuddered slightly. Peter glanced at one of Hwa's monitors: blood pressure was rising, too.

"Sir," said Peter. "The heart rate is acting up."

Mamikonian squinted at Peter's oscilloscope. "That's normal," he said, sounding irritated at being interrupted.

Mamikonian handed the scalpel, now slick and crimson,

back to the nurse. She passed him the sternal saw, and he turned it on. Its buzzing drowned out the blipping from Peter's EKG. The saw's rotating blade sliced through the sternum. An acrid smell rose from the body cavity: powdered bone. Once the sternum was cut apart, two technicians moved in with the chest spreader. They cranked it around until the heart, beating once per second, was visible.

Mamikonian looked up. On the wall was the digital ischemic counter; it would be started the moment he excised the organ, measuring the time during which there would be no blood flowing to the heart. Next to Mamikonian was a plastic bowl filled with saline. The heart would be rinsed in there to get old blood off it. It would then be transferred into an Igloo container filled with ice for the flight to Sudbury.

Mamikonian requested another scalpel and bent down to cut through the pericardium. And, just as his blade sliced through the membrane surrounding the heart—

The chest of Enzo Bandello, legally dead organ donor, heaved massively.

A gasp escaped from around his ventilator breathing tube.

A moment later, a second gasp was heard.

"Christ—" said Peter, softly.

Mamikonian looked irritated. He snapped his gloved fingers at one of the nurses. "More Myolock!"

She moved in and administered a second shot.

Mamikonian's voice was sarcastic. "Let's see if we can finish this damned thing without the donor walking away, shall we, folks?"

PETER was dazed. Mamikonian departed with the excised heart. Since that meant there was no more need for an EKG operator, Peter went up to the observation level and watched the rest of the harvesting from there. When it was done—when

Enzo Bandello's hollow corpse was sewn shut and rolled off to the morgue—Peter staggered down to the scrub room. He found Hwa, who was pulling off her gloves.

"What happened in there?" Peter asked.

Hwa exhaled noisily; she was exhausted. "You mean the gasping?" She shrugged. "Happens every once in a while."

"But, Enz—but the donor was dead."

"Of course. But he was also on full life support. Sometimes there's a reaction."

"And—and what was that business with Myolock? What's that?"

Hwa was untying her surgical gown. "It's a muscular paralyzer. They have to administer that. If they don't, sometimes the donor's knees tuck up toward the chest as you carve into it."

Peter was appalled. "Really?"

"Uh-huh." Hwa dropped her gown into the hamper. "It's just a muscular reaction. Nowadays, it's routine procedure to anesthetize the corpse."

"Anesthetize the corpse . . . ?" said Peter slowly.

"Yeah," she said. "'Course, Dianne obviously didn't do a good enough job today." Hwa paused. "It gives me the willies when they start moving like that, but, hey, that's transplant surgery for you."

PETER kept a little copy of the timetable for his girlfriend, Cathy Churchill, in his wallet. He was in the first year of his master's; she was in her last year of her bachelor's in chemistry. She would be finishing her final class of the day—polymers—in about twenty minutes. He hurried back to the campus and waited in the hall outside the classroom for her.

The class ended and Cathy came out, chatting animatedly with her friend Jasmine, who caught sight of Peter first. "Well," she said, grinning, and tugging Cathy's sleeve, "look who's here. It's Mr. Right."

Peter smiled at Jasmine briefly, but really only had eyes for Cathy. Cathy had a heart-shaped face, long black hair, and enormous blue eyes. As always, she smiled radiantly when she saw Peter. Despite what he'd seen earlier in the day, Peter felt himself grinning, too. It happened every time. There was an electricity between them—Jasmine and their other friends often commented on it.

"I'll leave you two lovebirds alone," said Jasmine, still grinning. Peter and Cathy said goodbye to her, and the two of them came together in a kiss. In that brief moment of contact, Peter felt himself revitalized. They'd been dating for three years now, and still there was wonder in each embrace.

When they separated, Peter asked, "What are you doing for the rest of the day?"

"I'd been planning to drop by the arts department to see if I could get some kiln time, but that can wait," Cathy said, her voice mischievous. Overhead, every other fluorescent tube had been removed to cut costs, but Cathy's smile lit up the whole corridor for Peter. "Got any ideas?"

"Yes. I want you to come to the library with me."

Again the wondrous smile. "Neither of us is that quiet," said Cathy. "Even if we did it somewhere that'd likely be deserted—the Canadian Literature section, maybe—I suspect the noise would still disturb people."

He couldn't help grinning, and he leaned in to kiss her again. "Maybe afterwards," he said, "but first, I need help with some research, please."

They joined hands and began walking.

"Into what?"

"Into death," Peter said.

Cathy's eyes were wide. "Why?"

"I was doing some more of my practicum today—running an EKG during an operation to remove a heart for transplant."

Her eyes danced. "That sounds fascinating."

"It was, but . . ."

"But what?"

"But I don't think the donor was dead before they started removing his organs."

"Oh, come on!" said Cathy, letting go of his hand long enough to whap him lightly on the arm.

"I'm serious. His blood pressure went up when the surgery started, and his heart rate increased. Those are classic signs of stress—or even pain. And they anesthetized the body. Think about that: they anesthetized a supposedly dead person."

"Really?"

"Yes. And when the surgeon sliced into the pericardium, the patient gasped."

"My God. What did the surgeon do?"

"Called for more muscular paralyzers to be injected into the patient, then just went on with the operation. Everyone else seemed to think this was all perfectly reasonable. Of course by the time the operation was finished, the donor really was dead."

They left the Lash Miller Building and started walking north toward Bloor Street. "And what do you want to find out?" asked Cathy.

"I want to find out how they determine that someone is dead before they begin carving out his organs."

THEY'D been searching for about an hour when Cathy came over to the carrel Peter was sitting in. "I've found something," she said.

He looked up expectantly.

She pulled up a chair and balanced a heavy volume on her lap. "This is a book on transplant procedures. The problem with transplants, it says, is that they never take the body off life support. If they did so, the organs would begin to deteriorate. So, even though the donors are *declared* dead, their hearts have never stopped. As far as the electrocardiogram is concerned, the supposedly dead donor is as alive as you and me."

Peter nodded excitedly. This was exactly what he'd been hoping to find. "So how do they decide if the donor is dead?"

"One way is to squirt ice-cold water into his ears."

"You're kidding," he said.

"No. It says here that will completely disorient a person, even if they're in a deep coma. And it often causes spontaneous vomiting."

"Is that the only test?"

"No. They also rub the surface of the eyeball to see if the donor tries to blink. And they pull out the—what do you call it? That breathing tube?"

"The endotracheal ventilator."

"Yes," she said. "They pull that out for a short time to see if the body's need for oxygen will cause it to start breathing again on its own."

"What about EEGs?"

"Well, this is a British book. When it was written, their use for determining death wasn't required by law."

"Incredible," said Peter.

"But surely they have to use them here in North America, don't they?"

"I imagine so, in most jurisdictions."

"And this donor you saw today would have flatlined before they ordered his organs removed."

"Probably so," said Peter. "But in the course I took on EEGs, the prof talked about people who had completely flatlined subsequently showing some brain activity."

Cathy paled somewhat. "Still," she said, "even if the donor is still alive in some small sense . . ."

He shook his head. "I'm not sure it's such a small sense. The heart is beating, the brain is receiving oxygenated blood, and there are signs that pain is being experienced."

"Even so," said Cathy, "even if all that's true, it must also be true that a brain that's shown no activity for an extended period must be severely damaged. You're talking about a vegetable."

"Probably," said Peter. "But there's a difference between harvesting organs from the dead, and ripping them from the bodies of the living, no matter how severely mentally handicapped that living person might be."

Cathy shivered and went back to searching. She soon found a three-year study of cardiac-arrest patients at Henry Ford Hospital in Detroit. One-quarter of the patients diagnosed as having no heartbeats did in fact still have them, as detected by catheters inserted into their bloodstreams. The report hinted that patients were being declared dead prematurely.

Meanwhile, Peter found several relevant *London Times* articles from 1986. Cardiologist David Wainwright Evans and three other senior doctors were refusing to do transplant operations there because of the ambiguity over when the donor is actually dead. They'd set out their concerns in a five-page letter to the British Conference of Royal Medical Colleges.

Peter showed the articles to Cathy. "But the Conference dismissed their concerns as unfounded," she said.

Peter shook his head. "I don't agree." He met her eyes. "It'll say in Enzo Bandello's obituary tomorrow that he died from head injuries sustained in a motorcycle accident. That's not true. I *saw* Enzo Bandello die. I was right there when it happened. He was killed by having his heart carved out of his chest."

CHAPTER 2

FEBRUARY 2011

Detective Sandra Philo continued to sift through Peter Hobson's memories.

Starting after his graduation in 1998, he had worked for several years at East York General Hospital, then had founded his own biomedical equipment company. Also in 1998, he and Cathy Churchill, still very much in love, had gotten married. Cathy had given up her interest in chemistry; Peter didn't yet understand why. Instead, she now worked in a noncreative position for Doowap Advertising.

And every Friday after work, Cathy and her coworkers went out for a drink. Actually, as Sandra discovered, although they referred to their intentions in the singular, the reality was decidedly plural: drinks. *And by the end of the evening, several of them always managed to successfully conjugate the verb form: drink, drank, drunk—often of the praying-to-the-porcelain-god variety . . .*

IT was cold and dark, a typical February evening in Toronto. Peter walked the seven blocks from the four-story Hobson

Monitoring building to The Bent Bishop. Cathy's coworkers weren't really his sort, but he knew it was important to her that he make an appearance. Still, Peter always tried to arrive after everyone else; the last thing he wanted to do was make small talk with an account manager or an art director. There was something superficial about advertising that turned him right off.

Peter pushed open The Bishop's heavy wooden doors and stood in the entryway, his eyes adjusting to the dim interior. On his left was a blackboard with the daily specials printed on it. On his right was a poster for Molson's Canadian depicting a curvy woman in a red bikini with maple leaves crowning each of her upturned breasts. Sexism in beer advertising, thought Peter: past, present, probably forever.

He stepped out of the entryway and scanned the pub, looking for Cathy. Long gray tables at random angles were tightly packed throughout the room, like aircraft carriers in an oceanic traffic jam. In the background, two people were playing darts.

Ah, there they were: clustered around a table positioned against a wall. Those whose backs were to the wall—decorated with a poster of another Molson's bimbo—were seated on a couch. The rest were in captain's chairs, drinks in hand. Some were sharing a bowl of nachos. The table was big enough that two or three separate conversations were going on, the participants shouting to be heard above the blaring music, an old Mitsou tune played louder than the speakers could really handle.

Cathy was a very bright woman—that had been the first thing that had attracted Peter to her. It was only later that he redefined his own standards of feminine beauty, which had tended toward bouncy blondes *à la* the beer ads, to find her jet-black hair and thin lips beautiful. She was sitting on the long couch, two of her coworkers—Toby, was it? And that lout, Hans Larsen—on either side of her, so that she couldn't get out unless one of them moved first.

Cathy looked up as Peter approached, smiled her radiant smile, and waved. Peter still felt a thrill when she smiled. He wanted to sit next to her, but the current deployment of bodies made that impossible. Cathy smiled again, love plain on her face, then shrugged apologetically and gestured for him to take an unused chair from the adjacent table. Peter did so, and Cathy's coworkers shifted along to make room for him. He found himself sitting between one of the painted ladies on his left—the secretaries and production coordinators who wore too much makeup—and the pseudointellectual on his right. As always, Pseudo had a bookreader sitting in front of him, the cover of the datacard visible through the window in the reader's shell. Proust. Ostentatious bastard.

"'Evening, Doc," said Pseudo.

Peter smiled. "How you doin'?"

Pseudo was about fifty, and slim as the Leafs' chances in the Stanley Cup. His fingernails were long; his hair, dirty. Howard Hughes in training.

Others acknowledged Peter's presence, and Cathy gave him another special smile from across the table. His arrival had been enough to momentarily stop the separate conversations. Hans, on Cathy's right, seized the opportunity to grab everyone's attention. "The old ball-and-chain won't be home tonight," he announced generally. "Off to visit her nieces." That they were Hans's nieces, too, didn't seem to occur to him. "That means I'm free, ladies."

The women around the table groaned or giggled. They'd all heard this sort of thing from Hans before. He was hardly what you'd call a handsome man: he had dirty blond hair and looked something like the Pillsbury Doughboy. Still, his incredible boldness was appealing—even Peter, who found Hans's infidelity distasteful, had to admit that there was something inherently likable about the man.

One of the painted ladies looked up. Her crimson lipstick had been applied in a shape bigger than her actual lips. "Sorry, Hans. I've got to wash my hair tonight."

General laughter. Peter glanced at the pseudointellectual to see if the notion that cleaning one's hair might be a priority had registered on him. It hadn't. "Besides," said the woman, "a girl has to have her standards. I'm afraid you don't measure up."

Toby, on Cathy's left, chuckled. "Yeah," he said. "They don't call him *little* Hans for nothing."

Hans smiled from ear to ear. "As my daddy used to say, you can always go 'round the edges." He looked at the woman with the painted-on lips. "Besides, don't knock it until—until you've been knocked by me!" He roared, delighted at his own wit. "Ask Ann-Marie in accounting. She'll tell you how good I am."

"*Anna*-Marie," corrected Cathy.

"Details, details," said Hans, waving a mittenlike hand. "Anyway, if she won't vouch for me, ask that blonde temp in payroll—the one with the big casabas."

Peter was growing tired of this. "Why don't you try dating her instead?" he said, pointing at the woman in the Molson's poster. "If your wife comes home unexpectedly, you can fold her into a paper airplane and send her sailing out the window."

Hans roared again. He was good-natured, Peter would give him that. "Hey, the doc made a funny!" he said, looking from face to face, inviting them all to share in the supposed wonder of Peter having told a joke. Embarrassed, Peter looked away, and happened to catch the eye of the young man serving drinks. He raised his eyebrows at him, and he came over. Peter ordered a large orange juice; he didn't drink alcohol.

Hans wasn't one to let go, though. "Go ahead, Doc. Tell us another joke. You must hear lots of 'em in your line of work." He roared again.

"Well," said Peter, deciding to make an effort to fit in for Cathy's sake, "I was talking to a lawyer yesterday, and he told me a funny one." Two of the women had gone back to munching on nachos, evidently uninterested in his joke, but the rest of the group was looking at him expectantly. "See, there's this woman who killed her husband by hitting him over the head with a cruet of salad dressing." When the joke had been told to Peter, it had been about a husband killing his wife, but he couldn't resist reversing the roles in the hopes of planting the thought in Hans's head that Hans's wife might not approve of his philandering.

"Well," Peter continued, "the case finally comes to trial, and the crown attorney wants to introduce the murder weapon. She picks up the cruet off her desk. It still has a little glass stopper in its mouth, and is mostly full of liquid. She begins carrying it toward the judge. 'Your Honor,' she says to the judge, 'this is the very item by which the deed was done. I'd like to enter it as Crown exhibit number one.' The lawyer holds it up to the light. 'As you can see, it's still full of oil and vinegar—' Well, at once, the defense attorney rises to his feet and pounds the table in front of him. 'I object, Your Honor!' he shouts. 'That evidence is immiscible!'"

They all stared at him. Peter grinned to show that the joke was over. Cathy did her best to laugh, even though she'd heard the joke the night before. "Immiscible," Peter said again, weakly. Still no general response. He looked at the pseudo-intellectual. Pseudo made a condescending little chuckle. He got it, or was pretending to have. But the other faces were blank. "Immiscible," said Peter. "It means they can't be mixed." He looked from face to face. "Oil and vinegar."

"Oh," said one of the painted ladies, and "ho ho" said another.

Peter's orange juice arrived. Hans pantomimed a bomb dropping, whistling a descending note as it fell, then making a sound like an explosion. When he looked up, he said, "Hey, everyone, did you hear about the whore who . . ."

Peter suffered through another hour, although it seemed longer. Hans continued to hit on the women collectively and individually. Finally, Peter had had all he could take of him, of the noise, and of the lousy orange juice. He caught Cathy's eye and glanced meaningfully at his watch. She smiled a thank-you-for-your-indulgence smile just for him, and they got up to leave.

"Off so soon, Doc?" said Hans, speech noticeably slurred, his left arm now having taken up residence on the shoulders of one of the women.

Peter nodded.

"You should really let Cath stay out later."

The unfair remark angered Peter. He nodded curtly, she said her goodbyes, and they headed for the door.

It was only 7:30, but it was already black overhead, although the glare from the streetlights banished the stars. Cathy took Peter's arm, and they walked slowly along.

"I get pretty tired of him," said Peter, his words appearing as puffs of condensation.

"Who?" said Cathy.

"Hans."

"Oh, he's harmless," said Cathy, snuggling closer to Peter as they walked.

"All bark and no bite?"

"Well, I wouldn't quite say that," she said. "He does seem to have dated just about everyone in the office."

Peter shook his head. "Don't they see through him? He's only after one thing."

She stopped, and reached up to kiss him. "Tonight, my love, so am I."

He smiled at her and she at him, and somehow it didn't seem cold outside anymore at all.

THEY'D made wondrous love, their naked forms mingling, each attentive to the other's desires. After thirteen years of marriage, fourteen of living together, and twenty-two since they'd first dated, they knew the rhythms of each other's bodies. And yet, after all that time, they still found new ways to surprise and please each other. Finally, after midnight, they had fallen asleep in each other's arms, calm, relaxed, spent, in love.

But about 3:00 a.m., Peter awoke with a start, sweating profusely. He'd had the dream again—the same dream that had been haunting him for eighteen years now.

Lying on an operating table, pronounced dead, but not. Scalpels and sternal saws cutting into him, his organs being removed from his torso.

Cathy, still naked, awoken by Peter's sudden movement, slipped out of bed, got him a glass of water, and sat, as she had on many nights before, holding him tight, until the terror had passed.

CHAPTER 3

Peter had seen the ads in magazines and on the net. "Live forever! Modern science can prevent your body from ever wearing out." He'd thought it was a scam until he saw an article about it in *Biotechnology Today*. A California company apparently could make you immortal for a fee of twenty million dollars. Peter didn't really believe it was possible, but the technology involved sounded fascinating. And, now that he was forty-two, the realization that he and Cathy were only going to have a few more decades together was the one thing in his life that made him sad.

Anyway, the California company—Life Unlimited—was putting on seminars around North America promoting their process. In due course, they came to Toronto, renting meeting space at The Royal York Hotel.

It was impossible to drive in downtown Toronto anymore; Peter and Cathy took the subway to Union Station, which connected directly with the hotel. The seminar was being held in the plush Ontario Room. About thirty people seemed to be in attendance, and—

"Uh oh," said Cathy softly to Peter.

Peter looked up. Colin Godoyo was approaching. He was the husband of Cathy's friend Naomi and a vice-president of the Toronto Dominion Bank—a rich guy who liked to show it off. Peter was quite fond of Naomi, but had never really thought much of Colin.

"Petey!" said Colin, loudly enough so that every head in the room turned to look at them. He shoved a beefy hand toward Peter, who shook it. "And the gorgeous Catherine," he said, leaning in for a kiss, which Cathy reluctantly provided. "How wonderful to see the two of you!"

"Hi, Colin," said Peter. He jerked a thumb toward the front of the room where the presenter was setting up. "Thinking about living forever?"

"It sounds fascinating, doesn't it?" said Colin. "What about you two? The happy couple can't bear the thought of till death do us part?"

"I'm intrigued by the biomedical engineering," said Peter, somewhat put off by Colin's presumption.

"Of course," said Colin in an irritating, knowing tone. "Of course. And Cathy—want to keep those great looks of yours forever?"

Peter felt the need to defend his wife. "She has a degree in chemistry, Colin. We're both just intrigued by the science behind the process."

At that moment, the presenter spoke loudly from the front of the room. "Ladies and gentlemen—we're ready to begin. Please take your seats." Peter spotted two unoccupied chairs in an otherwise full row, and quickly steered himself and Cathy toward them. Everyone settled in to listen to the sales pitch.

"Nanotechnology is the key to immortality," the fellow from Life Unlimited said to his audience. He was a muscular African-American, mid-forties, salt-and-pepper hair, with a wide smile. His suit looked like it cost two thousand bucks. "Our nanotechnology machines can prevent every aspect of aging." He indicated the picture on the wall screen:

a blow-up of a microscopic robot. "Here's one now," he said. "We call them 'nannies,' because they look after you." He chuckled, and invited the audience to chuckle as well.

"Now, how do our nannies—which we distribute throughout your body—prevent you from growing old?" asked the man. "Simple. A large part of aging is controlled by timers on certain genes. Well, you can't eliminate the timers—they're necessary to the regulation of bodily processes—but our nannies read their settings and reset them as required. The nannies also compare the DNA your body is producing to images of your original DNA. If errors get introduced, the DNA is corrected at the atomic level. It's not much different from error-free computer communications, really. Checksums allow fast and accurate comparisons.

"The ravages caused by build-ups of toxic wastes in the body are also a major part of aging, but our nannies take care of all of that for you, cleaning the wastes out.

"Autoimmune problems, such as rheumatoid arthritis, are another component of aging. Well, we've learned a lot about the autoimmune system in trying to cure AIDS, and we can now take care of almost anything that comes along.

"But the very worst part of aging is the loss of memory and cognitive functions. In many cases that's due simply to a lack of vitamin B_6 or B_{12}. It's also caused by not enough acetylcholine and other neurotransmitters. Again, our nannies balance all the levels for you.

"And what about Alzheimer's? It's genetically programmed to kick in at a certain age, although the onset can also be caused by high levels of aluminum. Our nannies get down and dirty with your genes, turning regulators on and off. We find the instruction for Alzheimer's, if it exists in your DNA—not everyone has it—and just prevent it from expressing itself."

The man smiled. "Now, I know what you're thinking. None of that is going to help me if I get shot in the chest by a mugger. Well, using patented Life Unlimited techniques, we can even make sure you live through that. Yes, the bullet will stop your heart—but our nannies monitor your blood oxygen levels and they themselves can deliver blood to the brain if need be, acting like tractors, pulling red blood cells. And, yes, you'll need a heart transplant and maybe some other repair work—but your brain will be kept alive until that work is done.

"Okay—now you're thinking, hey, what if that mugger had shot me in the head instead?" The pitchman lifted up a thin sheet of what looked like silver foil. "This is polyester-D5. It's similar to Mylar." He held the sheet by one corner and let it flutter in the air. "Less than half a millimeter thick," he said, "but watch this." He proceeded to attach the sheet of foil to a square metal frame, anchoring it on all four sides. He then produced a gun with a silencer sticking off the front. "Don't worry," he said. "I've got a special permit for this." He chuckled. "I know how you Canadians feel about guns." He aimed the pistol at an angle and fired at the foil sheet. Peter heard the pistol bark and saw a lick of flame shoot out of its nozzle. There was a sound like a thunderclap and something happened to the curtain behind the stage.

The pitchman went over to the metal frame and held up the Mylar sheet. "No hole," he said—and indeed that was true. The sheet was rippling in the breeze of the air conditioner. "Polyester-D5 was developed for the military and is now widely used in bulletproof vests by police forces all over the world. As you can see, it's quite flexible—unless it's hit at high speed. Then it tightens up and becomes harder than steel. That bullet I fired a moment ago bounced right off." He looked back. His assistant was coming onto the stage with something held in metal tongs. He dropped it into a little glass bowl on the podium. "Here it is."

The pitchman faced the audience. "We coat the skull in a thin, perforated layer of polyester-D5. Of course, we don't have to peel off the scalp to do that; we simply inject nanotechnology drones and have them lay it down. But with your skull protected by this stuff, you could take a bullet to the head, or have a car run over your cranium, or fall head first off a building, and still not crush your head. The polyester becomes so rigid, almost none of the percussion is transferred through to your brain."

He smiled brilliantly at his audience. "It's exactly as I said at the outset, folks. We can outfit you in such a way that you will not die—not through aging and not through almost any accident you can conceive of. For all intents and purposes, we offer exactly what we promise: honest-to-God immortality. Now, any takers?"

IT was the first Sunday of the month. By long-standing tradition, that meant dinner with Peter's in-laws.

Cathy's parents lived on Bayview Avenue in North York. The Churchill house, a 1960s side-split with a one-car garage, would have once been considered good-sized but now was dwarfed by monster homes on either side, causing it to spend most of the day in shadow. Above the garage was a rusting basketball hoop with no net attached.

Cathy's thumbprint worked on the door lock. She went in first and Peter followed behind. Cathy shouted out, "We're here," and her mother appeared at the top of the stairs to greet them. Bunny Churchill—God help her, that was her name—was sixty-two, short, trim, with gray hair that she refused to dye. Peter liked her immensely. Cathy and he headed up into the living room. Peter had been coming here for years, but had still never quite gotten used to its appearance. There was only one small bookcase, and it held audio CDs and some video laser discs, including a complete run of Playboy Video Playmate Calendars since 1998.

Cathy's father taught Phys. Ed. Gym teachers had been the bane of young Peter's existence, the first inkling he'd had that all adults weren't necessarily intelligent. Worse, Rod Churchill ran his family like a high-school football team. Everything started on time—Bunny was rushing even now to get food on the table before the clock struck 6:00. Everybody knew their positions, and, of course, everyone followed the instructions of Coach Rod.

Rod sat at the head of the table, with Bunny at the opposite end and Cathy and Peter facing each other on either side—sometimes they played footsie when Rod got into one of his boring stories.

This was turkey month—the first-Sunday dinners rotated between turkey, roast beef, and chicken. Rod picked up the carving knife. He always served Peter first—"our guest first," he'd say, underscoring that even after thirteen years of marriage to his daughter, Peter was still an outsider. "I know what you want, Peter—a drumstick."

"Actually, I'd prefer white meat," said Peter politely.

"I thought you liked dark meat."

"I like dark *chicken* meat," said Peter, as he did every third month. "I like white turkey meat."

"Are you sure?" asked Rod.

No, I'm fucking making this up as I go along. "Yes."

Rod shrugged and carved into the breast. He was a vain man, a year from retirement, hair dyed brown—what was left of his hair, that is. He grew it long on the right side, and combed it over his bald pate. Dick Van Patten in a track suit.

"Cathy used to like drumsticks when she was a little girl," Rod said.

"I still do," said Cathy, but Rod didn't seem to hear her.

"I used to like giving her a big drumstick and watch her try to get a bite out of it."

"She could have choked to death," said Bunny.

Rod grunted. "Kids can take care of themselves," he said. "I remember that time she fell down the stairs." He laughed, as if life should be one big slapstick comedy. He glanced at Bunny. "You were more upset than Cathy was. She waited until a big enough audience had arrived before she started crying." He shook his head. "Kids got bones made out of rubber." Rod handed Peter a plate with two ragged slices of turkey breast on it. Peter took it and reached for the bowl of baked potatoes. Friday evenings at The Bent Bishop somehow didn't seem that bad right now.

"I was bruised for weeks," said Cathy, a bit defensively.

Rod chuckled. "On her bum."

Peter still had a long scar on his leg from a high-school gym accident. Those darned Phys. Ed. teachers. Such funny guys. He waited until everyone was served, helped himself to the gravy boat, then passed it to Rod.

"No thanks," said Rod. "I'm not eating much gravy these days."

Peter thought about asking why, decided against it, and passed the gravy boat to Cathy instead. He turned to his mother-in-law and smiled. "Anything new with you, Bunny?"

"Oh, yes," she said. "I'm taking a course Wednesday nights—conversational French. I figure it's about time I learned."

Peter was impressed. "Good for you," he said. He turned to Rod. "Does that mean you have to fend for yourself Wednesday evenings?"

Rod grunted. "I order in from Food Food," he said.

Peter chuckled.

Cathy said to her mother, "The turkey is delicious."

"Thank you, dear," said Bunny. She smiled. "I remember that time you played a turkey in the Thanksgiving play at school."

Peter raised an eyebrow. "I didn't know about that, Cathy." He looked at his father-in-law. "How was she, Rod?"

"I don't know. I didn't go. Watching children dressed up as livestock isn't my idea of a fun evening."

"But she's your daughter," said Peter, then wished he hadn't.

Rod helped himself to some cooked carrots. Peter suspected he would have gone to watch a son play in Little League.

"Dad never took much interest in children," said Cathy, her tone neutral.

Rod nodded, as if this was a perfectly reasonable attitude for a father to take. Peter stroked Cathy's leg gently with his foot.

CHAPTER 4

AUGUST 2011

The world goes through two seasons in six months. Should it be surprising that other things change a lot in that time, too?

Peter had downloaded this week's *Time* from the net and was glancing through it. World News. People. Milestones.

Milestones.

Births, marriages, divorces, deaths.

Not all milestones were so cut-and-dried. Where were things such as the disintegration of a romance noted? What was the journal-of-record for lingering malaise, for empty hearts? Who marked the death of happiness?

Peter remembered how Saturday afternoons used to be. Lazy. Loving. Reading the paper together. Watching a little TV. Drifting at some point to the bedroom.

Milestones.

Cathy came down the stairs. Peter looked up briefly. There was hope in lifting his eyes, hope that he'd see the old Cathy, the Cathy he'd fallen in love with. His eyes fell back to the text reader. He sighed—not theatrically, not for her ears, but for himself, a heavy exhalation, trying to force the sadness from his body.

Peter had inventoried her appearance in that quick glance. She was wearing a ratty U of T sweatshirt and loose-fitting jeans. No makeup. Hair quickly combed but not brushed, falling in black bunches around her shoulders. Glasses instead of contacts.

Another small sigh. She looked so much better without the thick lenses balancing on her nose, but he couldn't remember the last time she'd worn her contacts.

They hadn't made love for six weeks.

The national average was 2.1 times each week. Said so right here in *Time*.

Of course, *Time* was an American magazine. Maybe the average was different here in Canada.

Maybe.

This year would be their thirteenth wedding anniversary.

And they hadn't made love in six fucking weeks. Six *fuckless* weeks.

He glanced up again. There she stood, on the third stair up, dressed like some god-damn tomboy.

She was forty-one now; her birthday had been last month. She still had her figure—not that Peter saw it much anymore. These sweatshirts and too-big sweaters and long skirts—these *bags* she'd taken to wearing—hid just about everything.

Peter stabbed the PgDn button. He tipped his head down, went back to his reading. They used to make love a lot on Saturday afternoons. But, Christ, if she was going to dress like that . . .

He'd read the first three paragraphs of the article in front of him, and realized that he hadn't a clue as to what it had said, hadn't absorbed a single word.

He glanced up once more. Cathy was still on the third step, looking down at him. She met his eyes for an instant, but then dropped her gaze, and, hand on the wooden banister, stepped down into the living room.

Focusing on the magazine, Peter said, "What would you like for dinner?"

"I don't know," she said.

I don't know. The national anthem of Cathyland. Christ, he was sick of hearing that. What would you like to do tonight? What would you like for dinner? Want to take a vacation?

I don't know.

I don't know.

I don't know.

Fuck it.

"I'd like fish, myself," said Peter, and again he stabbed the PgDn button.

"Whatever would make you happy," she said.

It would make me happy if you'd talk to me, thought Peter. *It would make me happy if you'd didn't fucking dress down all the time.*

"Maybe we should just order in," said Peter. "Maybe a pizza, or some Chinese."

"Whatever."

He turned pages again, new words filling his screen.

Thirteen years of marriage.

"Maybe I'll give Sarkar a call," he said, testing the waters. "Go out and grab a bite with him."

"If you like."

Peter shut the reader off. "Dammit, it's not just what *I'd* like. What would you like?"

"I don't know."

It had been building for weeks, he knew, festering within him, pressure increasing, an explosion imminent, his sighs never releasing enough of what was pent up, what was ready to blow. "Maybe I should go out with Sarkar and not come back."

She stood motionless across the room from him. The staircase rose up behind her. It looked as though her lower lip was trembling a little. Her voice was small. "If that would make you happy."

It's falling apart, thought Peter. *It's falling apart right now.*

Peter turned the magazine reader back on but immediately flicked it off again. "It's over, isn't it?" he said.

Thirteen years . . .

He should get up from the couch now, get up and leave.

Thirteen years . . .

"Jesus Christ," said Peter, into the silence.

He closed his eyes.

"Peter . . ."

Eyes still closed.

"Peter," said Cathy, "I slept with Hans Larsen."

He looked at her, mouth open, heart pounding. She didn't meet his gaze.

Cathy moved hesitantly into the center of the living room. There was quiet between them for several minutes. Peter's stomach hurt. At last, his voice raspy, raw, as though the wind had been knocked out of him, he said, "I want to know the details."

Cathy spoke softly. She didn't look at him. "Does it matter?"

"Yes, it matters. *Of course* it matters. How long has this . . ." he paused ". . . this *affair* been going on?" Christ, he'd never expected to use that word in this context.

Her lower lip was trembling again. She took a step toward him, as if she meant to sit beside him on the couch, but she hesitated when she saw the expression on his face. Instead, she moved slowly to take a chair. She sat down, weary, as if the tiny walk down to the living room had been the longest of her life. She carefully placed her hands in her lap and looked down at them. "It wasn't an affair," she said softly.

"What the hell would you call it?" said Peter. The words were angry, but his tone wasn't. It was drained, lifeless.

"It was . . . it *wasn't* a relationship," she said. "Not really. It just happened."

"How?"

"A Friday night, after work. You didn't come that time. Hans asked me for a lift to the subway. We went back to the company parking lot together and got my car. The lot was deserted by then, and it was pretty dark."

Peter shook his head. "In your car?" he said. He paused for a long time, then said, softly, "You"—and the next word came slowly, unbidden, released from his lips with a little shrug as if there were no other word that would quite do—"slut."

Her face was puffy, and her eyes were red, but she wasn't crying. She moved her head back and forth slightly as though trying to deny the word, a word that no one had ever applied to her before, but then at last she also shrugged, perhaps accepting the term.

"What happened?" said Peter. "Exactly what did you do?"

"We had sex. That was all."

"What kind of sex?"

"Normal sex. He just dropped his pants and lifted my skirt. He—he didn't touch me anywhere."

"But you were wet anyway?"

She bristled. "I . . . I'd had too much to drink."

Peter nodded. "You never used to drink. Not before you started working with them."

"I know. I'll stop."

"What else happened?"

"Nothing."

"Did he kiss you?"

"Before, yes. Not after."

Sarcastic: "Did he tell you he loves you?"

"Hans says that to everyone."

"Did he say it to you?"

"Yes, but . . . but it was just words."

"Did you say it to him?"

"Of course not."

"Did you—did you come?"

A whisper. "No." And then a tear did roll down her cheek.

"He—he asked me if I had come. As if anyone would have, in and out like that. He asked me. I said no. And he laughed. Laughed, and pulled up his trousers."

"When did this happen?"

"You remember that Friday I came home late and had a shower?"

"No. Wait—yes. You never have a shower in the evening. But that was *months* ago—"

"February," said Cathy.

Peter nodded. Somehow, the fact that this had happened so long ago made it more bearable. "Six months ago," he said.

"Yes," she said, and then, the words like a trio of bullets tearing into his heart, "The first time."

All the stupid questions welled up in his brain. You mean there were others? Yes, Peter, that's exactly what she means. "How many times?"

"Two more."

"For a total of three."

"Yes."

Sarcastic again: "But 'affair' is the wrong word for this?"

Cathy was silent.

"Jesus Christ," said Peter softly.

"It wasn't an affair."

Peter nodded. He knew what kind of person Hans was. Of course it hadn't been an affair. Of course there was no love involved. "Just sex," said Peter.

Cathy, wisely, said nothing.

"Christ," said Peter again. He still had the magazine reader in his hand. He looked at it, thinking he should throw it across the room, smash it against a wall. After a moment, he simply dropped it on the couch next to him. It bounced silently against the cushion. "When was the last time?" he said.

"Three months ago," she said, her voice small. "I've been trying to work up the courage to tell you. I—I didn't think I could. I tried twice before, but I just couldn't do it."

Peter said nothing. There was no appropriate reaction, no way to deal with it. Nothing. An abyss.

"I—I thought about killing myself," Cathy said after a very long pause, her voice attenuated like a predawn wind. "Not poison or slitting my wrists, though—nothing that would look like suicide." She met his eyes briefly. "A car accident. I was going to ram into a wall. That way, you'd still love me. You'd never know what I'd done, and . . . and you'd remember me with love. I tried. I was all ready to do that, but, when it finally came down to it, I swerved the car." Tears were running down her cheeks. "I'm a coward," she said at last.

Silence. Peter tried to make sense of it all. There was no point in asking if she was going to go with Hans. Hans didn't want a relationship, not a *real* relationship, not with Cathy or any woman. Hans. Fucking Hans.

"How could you get involved with Hans? Hans of all people?" asked Peter. "You know what he is."

She looked at the ceiling. "I know," she said softly. "I know."

"I've always tried to be a good husband," said Peter. "You know that. I've been supportive in every way possible. We talk about everything. There's no communication problem, no way you can say I don't listen to you."

Her voice took on an edge for the first time. "Did you know I've been crying myself to sleep for months?"

They had a pair of bedside fans that they used as white-noise generators, drowning out the sounds of traffic from outside, as well as each other's occasional snoring. "There's no way I could have known that," he said. He'd occasionally noticed her shuddering next to him as he fell to sleep. Half conscious, he'd idly thought she'd been masturbating; he kept that thought to himself.

"I've got to think about this," he said slowly. "I'm not sure what I want to do."

She nodded.

Peter threw his head back, let out a long, ragged sigh.

"Christ, I have to rewrite the entire last six months in my mind. That vacation we took in New Orleans. That was after you and Hans—And that time we borrowed Sarkar's cottage for the weekend. That was after, too. It's all different now. All of it. Every mental picture from that time, every happy moment—fake, tainted."

"I'm sorry," said Cathy, very softly.

"Sorry?" Peter's voice was ice. "You might have been sorry if it had happened just once. But three times? Three fucking times?"

Her lips were trembling. "I *am* sorry."

Peter sighed again. "I'm going to call Sarkar and see if he's free for dinner."

Cathy was silent.

"I don't want you along. I want to talk to him alone. I've got to sort things out."

She nodded.

CHAPTER 5

Peter had known Sarkar Muhammed since they'd both been teenagers. They'd lived on the same street, although Sarkar had gone to a private school. They had perhaps seemed unlikely prospects for friendship. Sarkar was heavily involved in athletics. Peter was on his school's yearbook and newspaper staffs. Sarkar was devoutly Muslim. Peter wasn't devoutly anything. But they'd hit it off shortly after Sarkar's family moved into the neighborhood. Their senses of humor were similar, they both liked to read Agatha Christie, and they were both experts at *Star Trek* trivia. Also, of course, Peter didn't drink, and that made Sarkar happy. Although Sarkar would eat in licensed restaurants, he avoided whenever possible sitting at a table with someone who was imbibing alcohol.

Sarkar had gone to the University of Waterloo to study computer science. Peter had studied biomedical engineering at U of T. They'd kept in touch all through university, swapping email letters over the Internet. After a brief stint in Vancouver, Sarkar had ended up back in Toronto, running his own high-tech startup firm doing expert-systems design. Although Sarkar was married and had three children, Peter and he often dined out together, just the two of them.

Incongruously, dinner was always at Sonny Gotlieb's, a deli at Bathurst and Lawrence, in the heart of Toronto's Jewish district. Peter couldn't stand Pakistani cuisine, despite Sarkar's valiant efforts to broaden his palate, and Sarkar had to eat where he could get food that adhered to Islamic dietary laws—something which most Kosher fare managed to do admirably. And so the two of them sat in their usual booth, surrounded by *zaydes* and *bubbehs* chatting away in Yiddish, Hebrew, and Russian.

After they had ordered, Sarkar asked Peter what was new. "Not much," said Peter, his tone guarded. "What about you?"

Sarkar spoke for a couple of minutes about a contract his company had received to do expert systems for the New Democratic Party of Ontario. They'd only been in power once, in the early 1990s, but were always hoping to make a comeback. Before Canadian socialist governments disappeared completely from living memory, they wanted to capture the knowledge of party members who had actually been in power back then.

Peter half listened to this. Ordinarily, he found Sarkar's work fascinating, but tonight his mind was a million kilometers away. The waiter returned with a pitcher of Diet Coke for them, and a basket of assorted bagels.

Peter wanted to tell Sarkar about what had happened with Cathy. He opened his mouth a couple of times to say something, but always lost his nerve before the words got out. What would Sarkar think of him if he knew? What would he think of Cathy? He thought at first that he wasn't telling Sarkar because of his religion; Sarkar's family was prominent in the Toronto Muslim community and Peter knew that they still practiced arranged marriages. But that wasn't it. He simply couldn't bring himself to speak aloud to anyone—*anyone*—about what had happened.

Although he wasn't really hungry, Peter took a poppy-seed bagel from the basket and spread a little jam on it.

"How is Catherine?" Sarkar asked, helping himself to a rye bagel.

Peter took advantage of having his mouth full to buy a few seconds to think. Finally, he said, "Fine. She's fine."

Sarkar nodded, accepting that.

A little later Sarkar asked, "How's the second weekend in September sound for our trip up north?"

For six years now, Peter and Sarkar had been going away for a weekend of camping in the Kawarthas. "I—I'll have to get back to you about that," said Peter.

Sarkar helped himself to another bagel. "Okay."

Peter loved those camping weekends. He wasn't much of an outdoorsperson, but he enjoyed seeing the stars. He'd never really agreed to an annual excursion, but with Sarkar anything done twice instantly became an inviolable tradition.

Getting away would be good, thought Peter. Very good.

But—

He couldn't go.

Not this year. Maybe not ever.

He couldn't leave Cathy alone.

He couldn't, because he couldn't be sure that she would in fact be alone.

Dammit. God damn it.

"I'll have to get back to you," Peter said again.

Sarkar smiled. "You said that."

Peter realized the whole evening would be a disaster if he didn't get his mind on something else. "How's that new brain scanner my company built for you working out?" Peter asked.

"Great. It's going to really simplify our neural-net studies. Wonderful machine."

"Glad to hear it," said Peter. "I've been working on refining it, trying to get a higher level of resolution."

"The current resolution is more than adequate for the kind of work I do," said Sarkar. "Why would you want more?"

"Remember when I was doing my practicum at U of T? I told you about that transplant donor who woke up on the operating table?"

"Oh, yes." Sarkar shivered. "You know my religion is suspicious of transplants. We feel the body should be returned to the Earth whole. Stories like that make me believe that even more."

"Well, I still have nightmares about it. But I think I'm finally going to be able to put that demon to rest."

"Oh?"

"That scanner we developed for your work was just a first-stage unit. I really wanted to develop a—a superEEG, if you will, that can detect *any* electrical activity at all in the brain."

"Ah," said Sarkar, his eyebrows lifting, "so you can tell when someone is really dead?"

"Precisely."

The server arrived with their main courses. Peter had a stack of Montreal smoked meat and rye bread, accompanied by a little carousel rack of various mustards and a side order of latkes—what Sarkar referred to as Peter's heart-attack kit. Sarkar had gefilte fish.

"That's right," said Peter. "I've been poking at this for years now, but I've finally had the breakthrough I needed. Signal-to-noise-ratio problems were killing me, but while scanning the net I found some algorithms created for radio astronomy that finally let me solve the problem. I've now got a working prototype superEEG."

Sarkar put down his fork. "So you can see the last neural gasp, so to speak?"

"Exactly. You know how a standard EEG works: each of the brain's billions of neurons is constantly receiving excitatory synaptic input, inhibitory input, or a combination of the two, right? The result is a constantly fluctuating membrane potential for each neuron. EEGs measure that potential."

Sarkar nodded.

"But in a standard EEG, the sensor wires are much bigger in diameter than individual neurons. So, rather than measuring the membrane potential of any one neuron, they measure the combined potential for all the neurons in the part of the brain beneath the wire."

"Right," said Sarkar.

"Well, that coarseness is the source of the problem. If only one neuron, or a few dozen or even a few hundred are reacting to synaptic input, the voltage will be orders of magnitude below what an EEG can read. Even though the EEG shows a flat line, brain activity—and therefore life—may still be continuing."

"A crisp problem," said Sarkar. "Crisp" was his favorite word; he used it to mean anything from well-defined to delicate to appealing to complex. "So you say you've found the solution?"

"Yes," said Peter. "Instead of the small number of wires used by a standard EEG, my superEEG uses over one billion nanotech sensors. Each sensor is as tiny as an individual neuron. The sensors blanket the skull, like a bathing cap. Unlike a standard EEG, which picks up the combined signal of all the neurons in a given area, these sensors are highly directional and pick up only the membrane potential from neurons directly beneath them." Peter held up a hand. "Of course, a straight line drawn through the brain will intersect thousands of neurons, but by cross-referencing the signals from all the sensors, I can isolate the individual electrical activity of each and every neuron in the entire brain."

Sarkar ate another fish ball. "I see why you were having signal-to-noise problems."

"Exactly. But I've solved that now. With this equipment,

I should be able to detect any electrical activity at all in the brain, even if it's just one lone neuron firing."

Sarkar looked impressed. "Have you tried it yet?"

Peter sighed. "On animals, yes. A few large dogs—I haven't been able to make the scanning equipment small enough to use on a rat or rabbit yet."

"So does this superEEG actually do what you want? Does it show the exact, crisp moment of actual death—the ultimate cessation of brain electrical activity?"

Peter sighed. "I don't know. I've got gigabytes of recordings of Labrador retriever brain waves now, but I can't get a permit to put any of them to sleep." He spread some more mustard on his meat. "The only way to test it properly will be with a dying human being."

CHAPTER 6

Peter knocked, then quietly entered the private room in the chronic-care facility. A frail woman about ninety years old was sitting up, the bed's back raised to a forty-five degree angle. Two IV bags of clear liquid hung on poles beside her bed. A tiny TV was mounted on a swing arm at the bed's right.

"Hello, Mrs. Fennell," Peter said softly.

"Hello, young man," said the woman, her voice thin and hoarse. "Are you a doctor?"

"No—at least, not a medical doctor. I'm an engineer."

"Where's your train?"

"Not that kind of engineer. I'm—"

"I was kidding, son."

"Sorry. Dr. Chong said you had a good attitude."

She shrugged amiably, the movement of her shoulders taking in the hospital room, the drip bags, and more. "I try."

Peter looked around. No flowers. No get-well cards. It seemed Mrs. Fennell was all alone in the world. He wondered how she could be so cheerful. "I, ah, have a favor to ask you," he said. "I need your help with an experiment."

Her voice was like dry leaves crumbling. "What kind of experiment?"

"It won't hurt at all. I'd simply like you to wear a special piece of headgear that has a series of tiny electrodes in it."

Leaves crumbled in a way that might have been a chuckle. Mrs. Fennell indicated the tubes going into her arm. "A couple more connections won't hurt I guess. How long do you want me to wear this?"

"Until, ah, until—"

"Until I die, is that it?"

Peter felt his cheeks grow flush. "Yes, ma'am."

"What are the electrodes for?"

"My company makes biomedical monitoring equipment. We've developed a prototype for a new hypersensitive electroencephalogram. Do you know what an EEG is?"

"A brain-wave monitor." Mrs. Fennell's face seemed to be immobile; Chong had said she'd suffered a series of small strokes. But her eyes smiled. "You don't spend as much time in hospitals as I have without picking up something."

Peter chuckled. "This special brain-wave monitor is a lot more discerning than the standard ones they've got here. I'd like to record, well . . ."

"You'd like to record my death, is that it?"

"I'm sorry. I don't mean to be insensitive."

"You're not. Why do you want to record my death?"

"Well, you see, right now, there's no one-hundred-percent accurate way of determining when the brain has permanently ceased to function. This new device should be able to indicate the exact moment of death."

"Why should anyone care about that? I have no relatives."

"Well, in many cases bodies are kept on life support simply because we don't know whether the person is really dead or not. I'm trying to come up with a definition for death that isn't just legal but is *actual*—an unequivocal test that can prove whether someone is dead or alive."

"And how will this help people?" she said. Her tone made it clear that to her this was what mattered most.

"It'll help with organ transplants," Peter said.

She cocked her head. "No one would want my organs."

Peter smiled. "Perhaps not, but someday my equipment may ensure that we don't accidentally take organs from people who aren't yet truly dead. It'll also be useful in emergency rooms and at accident scenes, to make sure attempts to save a patient aren't halted too soon."

Mrs. Fennell digested this for a moment, then: "You don't really need my permission, do you? You could have just had the equipment hooked up. Just say it was for routine tests. Half the time they don't explain what they're doing anyway."

Peter nodded. "I suppose that's true. But I thought it would be polite to ask."

Mrs. Fennell's eyes smiled again. "You're a very nice young man, Doctor . . . ?"

"Hobson. But, please, call me Peter."

"Peter." Her eyes crinkled. "I've been here for months, and not one of the doctors has volunteered that I could call them by their first name. They've prodded every part of my body, but they still think keeping emotional distance is part of their job." She paused. "I like you, Peter."

Peter smiled. "And I like you, Mrs. Fennell."

She did manage an unequivocal laugh this time. "Call me Peggy." She paused, and reflection further creased her wrinkled face. "You know, that's the only time I've heard my own first name since I was admitted here. So, Peter, are you really interested in what happens at the moment of death?"

"Yes, Peggy, I am."

"Then why don't you have a seat, make yourself comfortable, and I'll tell you." She lowered her voice. "You see, I've already died once before."

"I beg your pardon?" She had seemed so lucid . . .

"Don't look at me like that, Peter. I'm not insane. Sit down. Go ahead, sit. I'll tell you what happened." Peter cocked his head slightly, noncommittal, and found a vinyl-covered chair. He pulled it close to the bed.

"It happened forty years ago," said Mrs. Fennell, turning her crab-apple head to face Peter. "I'd recently been diagnosed with diabetes. I was insulin-dependent, but hadn't yet realized how careful I had to be. My husband Kevin had gone shopping. I'd had my morning insulin injection, but hadn't eaten yet. The phone rang. It was a woman I knew who nattered on endlessly, or so it seemed. I found myself sweating and getting a headache, but I didn't want to say anything. I realized my heart was pounding and my arm was trembling and my vision was blurring. I was about to say something to the woman, to beg off and go get something to eat when, all of a sudden, I collapsed. I was having an insulin reaction. Hypoglycemia."

Although her face was impassive, deadened by strokes, her voice became increasingly animated. "Suddenly," she said, "I found myself *outside* of my body. I could see myself as if from above, lying there on the kitchen floor. I kept rising higher and higher until everything sort of collapsed into a tunnel, a long, spiraling tunnel. And at the end of this tunnel, there was a beautiful, pure, bright white light. It was very bright, but it didn't hurt at all to look at it. This feeling of calm, of peace, came over me. It was absolutely wonderful, an unconditional acceptance, a feeling of love. I found myself moving toward the light."

Peter tilted his head. He didn't know what to say. Mrs. Fennell went on. "From out of the edges of the light a figure appeared. I didn't recognize it at first, but then suddenly I saw that it was me. Except it wasn't me; it was someone who looked a lot like me, but *wasn't* me. I'd been born a twin, but my twin sister Mary had died a few days after we were born. I realized that *this* was Mary, come to greet me. She floated closer and took my hand, and we drifted down the tunnel together, toward that light.

"And then I started seeing images from my life, as though they were on movie film, pictures of me and my parents, me and my husband, me at work, at play. And Mary and I were reviewing each of these scenes, where I'd done right and where I'd done wrong. There was no sense that I was being judged, but it seemed important that I understand everything, realize the effect my actions had on others. I saw myself playing in a schoolyard, and cheating on an exam, and working as a candy striper in a hospital, and oh so many other things, vividly, with unbelievable clarity. And all the while we were growing closer to that beautiful, beautiful light.

"Then, suddenly, it was over. I felt myself being pulled backward and downward. I didn't want to let go of Mary's hand—I'd lost her once, after all, had never really had the chance to know her—but my fingers slipped from hers and I drifted backward, away from the light, and then, suddenly, I was back in my body. I could tell there were other people there. Soon my eyes opened, and I saw a man in a uniform. A paramedic. He had a syringe in his hand. He'd given me an injection of glucagon. 'You're going to be all right,' he was saying. 'Everything's going to be all right.'

"The woman I'd been talking to on the phone—her name was Mary, by coincidence—had finally realized that I'd fainted and had hung up and called for an ambulance. The paramedics had had to break down my front door. If they'd arrived a few minutes later, I'd have been gone for good.

"So, Peter, I know what death is like. And I don't fear it. It changed my whole attitude toward life, that experience. I learned to see everything with perspective, take everything in stride. And although I know I've only got a few days left now, I'm not afraid. I know my Kevin will be waiting for me in that light. And Mary, too."

Peter had listened intently to the whole thing. He'd heard

of such stories before, of course, and had even read part of Moody's famous book *Life After Life* when he'd been trapped at a relative's cottage and the choice was that or a book on how sun signs supposedly affected your love life. He didn't know what to make of such stories then, and was even more uncertain now.

"Did you tell any of your doctors here about this?" Peter asked.

Peggy Fennell snorted. "Those guys come through here like they're marathon runners and my chart is the baton. Why in God's name would I share my most intimate experiences with them?"

Peter nodded.

"Anyway," said Mrs. Fennell, "that's what death's like, Peter."

"I—ah, I'd—"

"You'd still like to do your experiment, though, wouldn't you?"

"Well, yes."

Mrs. Fennell moved her head slightly, the closest thing to a nod she could manage. "Very well," she said at last. "I trust you, Peter. You seem a good man, and I thank you for listening to me. Go get your equipment."

IT had been one hell of a week since Cathy had made her announcement. They weren't talking much, and when they did talk, it was about things such as Peter's experiment with the superEEG. Nothing personal, nothing directly related to them. Just safe topics to fill some of the long, melancholy silences.

Now, on Saturday afternoon, Peter sat on the living-room couch, reading. No electronic book this time, though: instead, he was reading an honest-to-goodness paperback.

Peter had only recently discovered Robert B. Parker's old Spenser novels. There was something appealing about the absolute, unequivocal trust shared by Spenser and Hawk, and a wonderful honesty in the relationship between Spenser and Susan Silverman. Parker had never given Spenser a first name, but Peter thought his own—meaning "rock"—would have been a fine choice. Certainly, Spenser was more rock-stable than Peter Hobson was.

On the wall behind him was a framed print of an Alex Colville painting. Peter had originally thought Colville static, but, over the years, his work had grown on him, and he found this particular painting—a man sitting on a cottage porch, an old hound dog lying at his feet—very appealing. Peter had finally realized that the lack of movement in Colville's art was designed to convey permanence: these are the things that last, these are the things that matter.

Peter still didn't know what to make of it all, didn't know what future he and Cathy might have. He realized he'd just read a funny scene—Spenser deflecting Quirk's questions with a series of vintage quips, Hawk standing motionless nearby, a grin splitting his features—but it hadn't amused Peter the way it should have. He slipped a bookmark into the paperback and set it down beside him.

Cathy came down the stairs. She was wearing her hair down and was dressed in snug blue jeans and a loose-fitting white blouse with the top two buttons undone—attire, Peter realized, that could be viewed as either sexy or neutrally practical. She clearly was as confused as Peter, carefully trying to send signals that hopefully would be correct regardless of what mood he was in. "May I join you?" she said, her voice a feather fluttering in a breeze.

Peter nodded.

The couch consisted of three large cushions. Peter was sitting on the leftmost. Cathy sat on the border between the middle one and the rightmost, again trying for both closeness and distance simultaneously.

They sat together for a long time, saying nothing.

Peter kept moving his head slowly back and forth. He felt

warm. His eyes weren't focussing properly. Not enough sleep, he guessed. But then, suddenly, he realized that he was about to start crying. He took a deep breath, trying to forestall it. He remembered the last time he'd really cried: he'd been twelve years old. He'd been ashamed then, thinking he was too old to cry, but he'd had a frightening shock from an electrical outlet. In the thirty intervening years, he'd maintained his stoic face no matter what, but now, welling up within him . . .

He had to leave, get somewhere private, away from Cathy, away from everyone . . .

But it was too late. His body convulsed. His cheeks were wet. He found himself shuddering again and again. Cathy raised a hand from her lap, as if to touch him, but apparently thought better. Peter cried for several minutes. One fat drop fell on the edge of the Spenser paperback and was slowly absorbed into the newsprint.

Peter wanted to stop, but couldn't. It just came and came. His nose was running now; he snorted between the shuddering convulsions that brought out the tears. It had been too much, held in too long. Finally, he was able to force out a few feeble, quiet words. "You've hurt me," was all he said.

Cathy was biting her lower lip. She nodded slightly, her eyes batting up and down, holding in her own tears. "I know."

CHAPTER 7

"Hello," said the slim black woman. "Welcome to the Family Service Association. I'm Danita Crewson. Do you prefer Catherine or Cathy?" She had short hair and was dressed in a beige jacket and matching skirt, and wore a couple of pieces of simple gold jewelry—the perfect image of a modern professional woman.

Still, Cathy was slightly taken aback. Danita Crewson looked to be all of twenty-four. Cathy had expected the counselor to be old and infinitely wise, not someone seventeen years her junior. "Cathy is fine. Thank you for squeezing me in on such short notice."

"No problem, Cathy. Did you fill out the needs assessment?"

Cathy handed her the clipboard. "Yes. Money is no problem; I can pay the full fee."

Danita smiled as if this was something she heard all too infrequently. "Wonderful." When she smiled, no wrinkles appeared at the corners of her eyes. Cathy was envious. "Now, what seems to be the problem?"

Cathy tried to compose herself. She'd been tortured for months by what she'd done. *God,* she thought. *How could I have been so stupid?* But, somehow, it wasn't until she actually saw Peter cry that she realized she had to do something to get help. She couldn't bear to hurt him like that again. Cathy folded her hands on her lap and said, very slowly, "I, ah, cheated on my husband."

"I see," said Danita, her tone one of professional detachment, free of any judgment. "Does he know?"

"Yes. I told him." Cathy sighed. "It was the most difficult thing I've ever done."

"How did he take it?"

"He was devastated. I've never seen him so shaken."

"Did he get angry?"

"He was furious. But he was also very sad."

"Did he hit you?"

"What? No. No, he's not an abusive husband—not at all."

"Neither physically nor verbally?"

"That's right. He's always been very good to me."

"But you cheated on him."

"Yes."

"Why?"

"I don't know."

"Now that you've told your husband," said Danita, "how do you feel?"

Cathy thought for a moment, then shrugged slightly. "Better. Worse. I don't know."

"Did you expect your husband to forgive you?"

"No," said Cathy. "No, trust is very important to Peter—and to me. I . . . I expected our marriage to be over."

"And is it?"

Cathy looked out the window. "I don't know."

"Do you want it to be?"

"No—absolutely not. But—but I want Peter to be happy. He deserves better."

Danita nodded. "Did he tell you that?"

"No, of course not. But it's true."

"True that he deserves better?"

Cathy nodded.

"You seem to be a fine person. Why would you say that?"

Cathy said nothing.

Danita leaned back in her chair. "Has your marriage always been good?"

"Oh, yes."

"Never any separations or anything like that?"

"No—well, we broke up once while we were dating."

"Oh? Why?"

A small shrug. "I'm not sure. We'd been dating for close to a year while still in university. Then one day, I just broke up with him."

"And you don't know why?"

Cathy looked out the window again, as if drawing power from the sunlight. She closed her eyes. "I guess . . . I don't know, guess I couldn't believe anyone could love me so unconditionally."

"And so you pushed him away?"

She nodded slowly. "I guess so."

"Are you pushing him away again? Is that what your infidelity is about, Cathy?"

"Maybe," she said slowly. "Maybe."

Danita leaned slightly forward. "Why do you think no one could love you?" she said.

"I don't know. I mean, I know Peter loves me. We've been together for a long time, and that's been the one absolute constant in my life. I *know* it. But, still, even after all these years, I have trouble believing it."

"Why?"

An infinitesimal lifting of shoulders. "Because of who I am."

"And who are you?"

"I'm—I'm nothing. Nothing special."

Danita steepled her fingers. "It sounds like you're not very confident."

Cathy considered this. "I guess I'm not."

"But you say you went to university?"

"Oh, yes. I made the dean's list."

"And your job—do you do well at that?"

"I guess. I've been promoted several times. But it's not a hard job."

"Still, it sounds like you've done just fine over the years."

"I suppose," said Cathy. "But none of that matters."

Danita raised her eyebrows. "What's your definition of something that matters?"

"I don't know. Something people notice."

"Something *which* people notice?"

"Just people."

"Does your husband—Peter, is it? Does Peter notice when you achieve something?"

"Oh, yes. I do ceramic art as a hobby—you should have seen him bubbling over when I had a showing at a small gallery last year. He's always been like that, boosting me—right from the beginning. He threw a surprise party for me when I graduated with honors."

"And were you proud of yourself for that?"

"I was glad university was finally over."

"Was your family proud of you?"

"I suppose."

"Your mother?"

"Yes. Yes, I guess she was. She came to my graduation."

"What about your father?"

"No, he didn't attend."

"Was he proud of you?"

A short, sharp laugh.

"Tell me, Cathy: was your father proud of you?"

"Sure." Something strained in her voice.

"Really?"

"I don't know."

"Why don't you know?"

"He never said."

"Never?"

"My father is not a . . . demonstrative man."

"And did that bother you, Cathy?"

Cathy lifted her eyebrows. "Honestly?"

"Of course."

"Yes, it bothered me a lot." She was trying to remain calm, but emotion was creeping into her voice. "It bothered me an awful lot. No matter what I did, he never praised it. If I'd bring home a report card with five As and a B, all he'd talk about was the B. He never came to see me perform in the school band. Even to this day, he thinks my ceramics are silly. And he never . . ."

"Never what?"

"Nothing."

"Please, Cathy, tell me what you're thinking."

"He never once said he loved me. He even signed birthday cards—cards that my mother had picked out for him—'Dad.' Not 'Love, Dad'—but just 'Dad.'"

"I'm sorry," said Danita.

"I tried to make him happy. Tried to make him proud of me. But no matter what I did, it was like I wasn't there."

"Have you ever discussed this with your father?"

Cathy made a noise in her throat. "I've never discussed *anything* with my father."

"I'm sure he didn't mean to hurt you."

"But he *did* hurt me. And now I've hurt Peter."

Danita nodded. "You said that you didn't believe anyone could love you unconditionally."

Cathy nodded.

"Is that because you felt your father never loved you?"

"I guess."

"But you think Peter loves you a lot?"

"If you knew him, you wouldn't have to ask. People are always saying how much he loves me, how obvious it is."

"Does Peter tell you he loves you?"

"Oh, yes. Not every day of course, but often."

Danita leaned back in her chair. "Perhaps your problems with Peter are related to your problems with your father. Down deep, perhaps you felt that no man could love you because your father had eroded your self-esteem. When you found a man who *did* love you, you couldn't believe it, and you tried—and are still trying—to push him away."

Cathy was immobile.

"It's a common enough scenario, I'm afraid. Low self-esteem has always been a big problem among women, even today."

Still immobile, except for chewing her lower lip.

"You have to realize that you are not worthless, Cathy. You have to recognize the value in yourself, see in yourself all the wonderful qualities Peter sees in you. Peter doesn't put you down, does he?"

"No. Never. As I said, he's very supportive."

"Sorry to have to ask again. It's just that women often end up marrying men who are like their fathers, just as men often end up marrying women who are like their mothers. So Peter isn't like your father?"

"No. No, not in the least. But, then, Peter pursued me. I don't know what kind of man I was looking for. I don't even know if I was looking at all. I think—I think I just wanted to be left alone."

"What about the man you had the affair with? Was he the kind of man you were looking for?"

Cathy snorted. "No."

"You weren't attracted to him?"

"Oh, Hans was cute, in a chubby way. And there was something disarming about his smile. But I didn't go after him."

"Did he treat you well?"

"He was a smooth talker, but you could tell it was all just talk."

"And yet it worked."

Cathy sighed. "He was persistent."

"Did this Hans remind you of your father?"

"No, of course not," Cathy said immediately, but then she paused. "Well, I suppose they have some things in common. Peter would say they're both dumb jocks."

"And was Hans good to you during your relationship?"

"He was terrible to me. He'd ignore me for weeks on end, while he was presumably involved with someone else."

"But when he came back to you, you'd respond."

She sighed. "I know it was stupid."

"No one is judging you, Cathy. I just want to understand what went on. Why did you keep going back to Hans?"

"I don't know. Maybe . . ."

"Yes?"

"Maybe it was just that Hans seemed more the kind of guy I deserved."

"Because he treated you terribly."

"I guess."

"Because he treated you like your father."

Cathy nodded.

"We have to do something about your self-esteem, Cathy. We have to make you realize that you deserve to be treated with respect."

Cathy's voice was small. "But I don't . . ."

Danita let out a slow, whispery sigh. "We've got our work cut out for us."

LATER that evening, Peter and Cathy were sitting in their living room, Peter on the couch and Cathy alone in the love seat across the room.

Peter didn't know what was going to happen, what the future held. He was still trying to deal with it all. He'd always tried to be a good husband, always tried to show a genuine interest in her job. There was no reason to change that, he figured, and so, as he had often done in the past, he asked, "How was work today?"

Cathy put down her reader. "Fine." She paused. "Toby brought in fresh strawberries."

Peter nodded.

"But," she said, "I left early."

"Oh?"

"I, ah, went to see a counselor."

Peter was surprised. "You mean like a therapist?"

"Sort of. She works for the Family Service Association—I found them using directory assistance."

"Counselor . . ." said Peter, chewing over the word. Fascinating. He met her eyes. "I would have gone with you, if you'd asked."

She smiled briefly but warmly. "I know you would have. But, ah, I wanted to sort some things out for myself."

"How did it go?"

She looked at her lap. "Okay, I guess."

"Oh?" Peter leaned forward, concerned.

"It was a little upsetting." She lifted her gaze. Her voice was small. "Do you think I have low self-esteem?"

Peter was quiet for a moment. "I, ah, have always thought that perhaps you underestimated yourself." He knew that was as far as he should go.

Cathy nodded. "Danita—that's the counselor—she thinks it's related to my relationship with my father."

The first thought in Peter's mind was a snide comment about Freudians. But then the full measure of what Cathy said hit him. "She's right," Peter said, eyebrows lifting. "I hadn't seen it before, but of course she's right. He treats you and your sister like crap. Like you had been boarders, not his children."

"Marissa is in therapy, too, you know."

Peter hadn't known, but he nodded. "It makes sense.

Christ, how could you have a positive self-image, growing up in an environment like that? And your mother—" Peter saw Cathy's face harden and he stopped himself. "Sorry, but as much as I like her, Bunny is not, well, let's say she's not the ideal role model for the twenty-first-century woman. She's never worked outside the home, and, after all, your father doesn't seem to treat her much better than he treated you or your sister."

Cathy said nothing.

It was obvious now, all of this. "God damn him," said Peter, getting to his feet, pacing back and forth. He stopped and stared at the Alex Colville painting behind the couch. "God damn him to hell."

CHAPTER 8

Tuesday was the standard night for Peter and Sarkar to have dinner together. Sarkar's wife Raheema took a course on Tuesdays, and Peter and Cathy had always given each other time to pursue separate interests. Peter was more relaxed this evening, now that he'd decided not to discuss Cathy's infidelity with Sarkar. They hashed through more prosaic family news, international politics, the Blue Jays' stunning performance and the Leafs' lousy one. Finally, Peter looked across the table and cleared his throat. "What do you know about near-death experiences?"

Sarkar was having lentil soup this evening. "They're a crock."

"I thought you believed in that kind of stuff."

Sarkar made a pained face. "Just because I'm religious doesn't mean I am an idiot."

"Sorry. But I was talking to a woman recently who had had a near-death experience. She certainly believed it was real."

"She have the classic symptoms? Out-of-body perspective?

Tunnel? Bright light? Life review? Sense of peace? Encounters with dead loved ones?"

"Yes."

Sarkar nodded. "It is only when taken as one big thing that NDEs are inexplicable. The individual components are easy to understand. For instance, do this: close your eyes and picture yourself at dinner last night."

Peter closed his eyes. "Okay."

"What do you see?"

"I see me and Cathy at Kelsey's on Keele Street."

"Don't you ever eat at home?"

"Well, not often," said Peter.

"DINKs," said Sarkar, shaking his head—double income, no kids. "Anyway, realize what you just said: you picture yourself and Cathy."

"That's right."

"You are seeing yourself. The image you conjure up isn't from the point of view of your eyes, a meter and half off the floor or however high up they are when you're sitting down. It's a picture of yourself as seen from outside your own body."

"Well, I guess it is, at that."

"Most human memory and dream imagery is 'out of body.' That's the way our minds work both when recalling things that really happened and in fantasizing. There's nothing mystical about it."

Peter was having another heart-attack kit. He rearranged the slices of smoked meat on the rye bread. "But people claim to be able to see things they couldn't possibly have seen, like the manufacturer's name on the light unit mounted above their hospital bed."

Sarkar nodded. "Yeah, there are reports like that, but they aren't crisp—they don't stand up to scrutiny. One case involved a man who worked for a company that manufactured hospital lighting: he had recognized a competitor's unit. Others involve patients who had been ambulatory before or after the NDE and had had plenty of time to check out the details for themselves. Also, many times the reports are either unverifiable, such as 'I saw a fly sitting on top of the x-ray machine,' or just flat-out wrong, such as 'there was a vent on the top of the respirator,' when in fact there was no vent at all."

"Really?"

"Yes," said Sarkar. He smiled. "I know what to get you for Christmas this year: a subscription to the *Skeptical Inquirer.*"

"What's that?"

"A journal published by The Committee for the Scientific Investigation of Claims of the Paranormal. They blow holes in this sort of thing all the time."

"Hmm. What about the tunnel?"

"Have you ever had a migraine?"

"No. My father used to get them, though."

"Ask him. Tunnel vision is common in severe headaches, in anoxia, and lots of other conditions."

"I guess. But I'd heard that the tunnel was maybe a recollection of the birth canal."

Sarkar waved his soup spoon in Peter's direction. "Ask any woman who's had a baby if the birth canal is even remotely like a tunnel with a wide opening and a bright light at the end. The baby is surrounded by contracting walls of muscle; there's no tunnel. Plus, people who were delivered by Caesarean section have recounted the NDE tunnel as well, so it can't be some sort of actual memory."

"Hmm. What about the bright light at the end of the tunnel?"

"Lack of oxygen causes overstimulation of the visual cortex. Normally, most of the neurons in that cortex are prevented from firing. When oxygen levels drop, the first thing to cease functioning is the disinhibitory chemicals. The result is a perception of bright light."

"And the life review?"

"Didn't you take a seminar once at the Montreal Neurological Institute?"

"Umm—yes."

"And who was the most famous doctor associated with that institute?"

"Wilder Penfield, I guess."

"You guess," said Sarkar. "He's on a bloody stamp, after all. Yes, Penfield, who did work on directly stimulating the brain. He found it easy to elicit vivid memories of long-forgotten things. Again, in an anoxia situation, the brain is *more* active than normal because of the loss of disinhibitors. Neural nets are firing left and right. So the flooding of the brain with images from the past makes perfect sense."

"And the sense of peace?"

"Natural endorphins, of course."

"Hmm. But what about the visions of long-dead friends? The woman I spoke to saw her dead twin sister, Mary, who had died shortly after birth."

"Did she see an infant?"

"No, she described the vision as looking like herself."

"The brain isn't stupid," said Sarkar. "It knows when it may be about to die. That naturally gets one thinking about people who are already dead. Here is the crisp point, though: there are cases of little children having near-death experiences. Do you know who they see visions of?"

Peter shook his head.

"Their parents or their playmates. People who are still alive. Children don't know anyone who has already died. If the NDE really was a window into some afterlife, they wouldn't see people who are alive."

"Hmm," said Peter. "You know, the woman who had seen her sister Mary had her NDE while on the phone talking to *another* woman named Mary."

Sarkar looked triumphant. "The power of suggestion. It's all just a normal, explicable brain reaction." The server came with the bill. Sarkar glanced at it. "My religion teaches that we *do* continue on after this existence, but the near-death experience has nothing to do with real life after death. If you want to know what that's like, I'll give you a copy of the Koran."

Peter reached for his wallet to pay his half of the tab. "I think I'll pass."

CHAPTER 9

Peter Hobson was quite fond of his sister-in-law Marissa. In 2004, her first child had died of Sudden Infant Death Syndrome: she had simply stopped breathing, without any fuss, sometime during her third evening of life. Marissa and her ex-husband had used a standard baby monitor, a microphone that broadcast to a receiver they carried about the house.

But little Amanda had died quietly.

When Marissa had had another baby a year later, she refused to leave the child's side. Day or night, for months on end, she would always have the baby in her sight. Intellectually she knew that infant deaths just sometimes happened, but emotionally she blamed herself—if she had been with Amanda when her breathing had stopped, maybe she could have saved her.

Back then, Peter had been working on designs for touchless medical instrumentation. With AIDS continuing to plague the world, there was a big demand for units that didn't have to come into contact with a patient's body. At-a-distance heart-rate monitors were easy enough to develop, using declassified sensing equipment originally created for espionage. And detecting brain activity was usually done at a distance anyway—with electrodes separated from the brain by the thickness of the scalp and skull. Eventually, Peter found a way to read the rudiments of brain activity over a great distance, with nothing touching the patient's skin except a low-wattage infrared laser.

And so the Hobson Baby Monitor was born—a device that could report the vital signs of an infant in another room. He gave the prototype to Marissa and her husband. The monitor's built-in alarms would warn them immediately if their baby was in distress. They were delighted with the unit, and at Cathy's urging, Peter quit his job at East York General Hospital and started a little company to sell his baby monitors.

And then, one morning, Peter was lying next to his wife in bed. He needed to pee. Looking at the clock radio, he saw it was 6:45 a.m. The alarm would go off at seven. If Cathy was sleeping lightly, Peter knew that his getting up now would wake her, depriving her of her last quarter-hour of sleep, something he'd hate to do.

Peter lay there, enduring the pressure in his bladder. He wished he knew whether she was sleeping soundly. Maybe she was even already awake, but just had her eyes closed.

And then it hit him—a completely different use for his monitoring technology. The product appeared full-blown in his mind. A panel on the wall opposite the bed, with two clusters of readouts, one for each person in the bed. In each cluster, there'd be a big LED and a small one. The big one would indicate the person's current sleep state, and the small one would indicate the state he or she was moving into. There'd also be a digital counter indicating how long until the transition between one state and the next would take place—after just a few nights' training, the unit would have the individual users' sleep cycles down pat.

The LEDs would change color: white would mean the person was awake; red would mean the person was in a light sleep and would definitely be disturbed by any noise or movement. Yellow would mean the person was in a medium sleep, and so long as care was taken, one could get up and go to the bathroom, or cough, or whatever, without disturbing one's partner. Green would mean the person was in deep sleep, and you could probably do limbo dancing in the bed without disturbing him or her.

It would be pig-simple to read: a big yellow light with a small green one, and 07 showing on the counter would mean if you got up now, you might disturb your partner, but if you could hold off for seven minutes, she would be fast asleep and you could slip out without waking her.

As the urinary pressure gave Peter a typical early-morning erection, he realized something else. He'd often awoken horny at two or three a.m. and wondered if his wife was awake, too. If she had been, they'd probably have made love, but Peter would never dream of waking her up for that. But if the monitor happened to show white lights for both of them, well, then, what had started out as the Hobson Baby Monitor might end up being responsible for lots of new babies . . .

As time went by, Peter refined his system. All the telephones in the Hobson house were now hooked up to a Hobson Monitor, and from there to the household computer. Whether the phones rang at all, or just signaled incoming calls with flashing lights, depended on Peter and Cathy's sleep states.

At 3:17 a.m., a call was indeed detected. Moments before, Peter had been asleep, but he was now heading to the *en suite* bathroom, which had a small voice-only telephone. As he entered, its indicator started to flash. Peter closed the door, sat down on the toilet, and picked up the handset.

"Hello," he said, his voice thick and dry.

"Dr. Hobson?" said a man's voice.

"Yes."

"This is Sepp van der Linde at Carlson's Chronic Care. I'm the head night nurse."

"Yes?" Peter fumbled for a drinking glass and filled it from the tap.

"I think Mrs. Fennell is going to pass on tonight. She's had another stroke."

Peter felt a small twang of sadness. "Thank you for letting me know. Is my equipment all set up still?"

"Yes, sir, it is, but—"

He fought to stifle a yawn. "Then I'll come by in the morning to pick up the data disk."

"But Dr. Hobson, she's asking for you to come."

"Me?" said Peter.

"She said you're her only friend."

"I'm on my way."

PETER arrived at the chronic-care facility about 4:00 a.m. He showed his pass to the security guard and took the elevator to the third floor. The door to Mrs. Fennell's room was open and the incandescent light directly above her head was on, although the main overhead fluorescents were out. A row of four green LEDs pierced the gloom beside the bed, showing that Peter's equipment was working properly. A nurse sat on a chair next to the bed, a bored look on her face.

"I'm Peter Hobson," Peter said. "How is she?"

Mrs. Fennell stirred slightly. "Pe-ter," she said, but the effort of even those two syllables seemed to visibly weaken her.

The nurse got up and moved over to stand next to Peter. "She had a stroke about an hour ago, and Dr. Chong expects she'll have another one shortly; there are several clots in the arteries feeding her brain. We offered her something for the pain, but she said no."

Peter stepped over to his recording unit and turned on the screen, which immediately came to life. A series of jagged lines traced from left to right. "Thank you," he said. "I'll stay with her. You can go now, if you like."

The nurse nodded and left. Peter sat in the chair, the vinyl back warm from the nurse. He reached out and took Mrs. Fennell's left hand. There was a catheter inserted into the back of it, a tube leading to a drip bag mounted just beside the chair. Her hand was thin, small bones covered by translucent skin. Peter encircled Mrs. Fennell's fingers with his own. She squeezed his hand very softly.

"I'll stay with you, Mrs. Fennell," said Peter.

"P—P—"

Peter smiled. "That's right, Mrs. Fennell; it's me, Peter."

She shook her head ever so slightly. "P—P—" she said again, and then, with great effort, "Peg—"

"Oh, that's right," said Peter. "I'll stay with you, *Peggy.*"

The old woman smiled ever so slightly, her mouth just another line across her face. And then, without any fuss, her fingers went limp in Peter's hand and her eyelids slid very slowly shut. On the monitor, the green tracings had turned into a series of perfectly straight horizontal lines. After several moments, Peter retrieved his hand, blinked slowly a few times, and went to find the nurse.

CHAPTER 10

Peter took the superEEG recording with him when he left the chronic-care facility. By the time he got home, Cathy was getting ready for work, nibbling at a piece of dry whole-wheat toast and sipping a cup of tea. He'd left her a message with the household computer, so she'd know where he was.

"How did it go?" asked Cathy.

"I got the recording," said Peter.

"You don't seem very happy."

"Well, a very nice lady died tonight."

Cathy looked compassionate. She nodded.

"I'm exhausted," said Peter. "I'm going back to bed." He gave her a quick kiss, and did just that.

FOUR hours later Peter woke up with a headache. He stumbled to the bathroom, where he shaved and showered. He then filled a large tumbler with Diet Coke, got the disk, and went to his study.

His home system was more powerful than the mainframe

he'd had to share access to as a student at university. He turned it on, inserted the disk into the drive, and activated the wall monitor on the other side of the room. Peter wanted to see the moment at which the last neuron had fired, the moment at which the last synapse had been made. The moment of death.

He selected a graphic display mode and played a few seconds of the data, having the computer plot every location at which a neuron had fired. Not surprisingly, the image on the screen looked exactly like a silhouette of a human brain. Peter used an edge-tracing tool to draw the outline of Mrs. Fennell's brain. There was enough data to generate the picture three dimensionally; Peter rotated the image until the brain silhouette was facing him directly, as if he was looking the late Mrs. Fennell straight in the optic nerves.

He let the data play in real time. The computer looked for patterns in the firing neurons. Any connected series that fired once was color-coded red; twice, orange; three times, yellow; and so on through the seven colors of the spectrum. The picture of the brain looked mostly white: the combined effect of all the different colors of tiny dots. Peter occasionally zoomed in to see a close-up of one section of the brain, lit up with strings of infinitesimal Christmas lights.

As he watched, he could clearly see the stroke that had proved the final straw for Peggy Fennell. The color-coding scheme was refreshed every tenth of a second, but soon an area of blackness began to grow in her left temporal lobe, just below the Sylvian fissure. It was followed by an increase in activity, with the whole brain growing brighter and brighter as disinhibition caused neurons to fire again immediately after they'd last fired. After several moments, a complex network of purple lights was visible throughout her brain, a whole series of neural nets being triggered in identical patterns over and over as her brain spasmed. Then the nets began to fade, and no new ones replaced them. After ninety years of service, Peggy Fennell's brain was giving up the ghost.

Peter had hoped to be able to watch it all dispassionately. It was just data, after all. But it was also Peggy, that brave and cheerful woman who had faced and beaten death once before, that woman who had held his hand as she passed from life into lifelessness.

The data continued to be plotted, and soon there were only a few patterns of light, like constellations on a foggy night, flickering on the screen. When the activity did stop, it did so without any apparent flourish. Not a bang. Not a whimper. Just nothingness.

Except . . .

What was that?

A tiny flash on the screen.

Peter reversed the recording, then played it back again at a much slower speed.

There was a minuscule pattern of purple lights—a persistent pattern, a pattern that kept firing over and over again.

And it was moving.

Neurons couldn't really move, of course. They were physical entities. But the recorder was picking up the same pattern over and over again, just slightly displaced to the right each time. The recorder allowed for such displacements: neurons didn't always fire in exactly the same way, and the brain was gelatinous enough that movements of the head and the pulsing of blood could slightly change the physical coordinates of a neuron. The pattern moving across the screen must have been propagating from neuron to adjacent neuron in steps small enough that the recorder mistook the individual increments for activity within the same neurons. Peter glanced at the scale bar at the bottom of the wall screen. The violet pattern, a complex knot like intestines made of neon tubes, had already shifted five millimeters, far more than any neuron could move within the brain except in the case of a major blow to the head, something Peggy Fennell had most assuredly not suffered.

Peter adjusted a control. The playback speeded up. No doubt about it: the knot of violet pinpricks was moving to the right, pretty much in a straight line. It rotated a bit as it moved, like a tumbleweed blown by a desert wind. Peter stared in open-mouthed wonder. It continued to move, passing over the corpus callosum into the other hemisphere, past the hypothalamus, and into the right temporal lobe.

Each part of the brain was normally reasonably isolated from the others, and the kinds of electrical waves typical of, say, the cerebral cortex were foreign to the cerebellum, and vice versa. But this tight knot of purple light was moving without changing its form through structure after structure.

An equipment malfunction, thought Peter. Oh, well. Nothing ever worked right the first time.

Except . . .

Except Peter couldn't think of anything that would cause this kind of malfunction.

And still the pattern moved across the screen.

Peter tried to conjure up another explanation. Could a static discharge, perhaps from Peggy's hair rubbing against the pillow, have caused this effect? Of course, hospital pillows are designed to be anti-static, precisely so they won't mess up delicate recording equipment, and Peggy, after all, had had thinning, white hair. Besides, she'd been wearing his scanning skullcap.

No, it must be caused by something else.

The pattern was getting close to the outer edge of the brain. Peter wondered if it would dissipate on the convoluted surface of the cortex or maybe bounce back, spinning the other way, like a video game inside the head.

It did neither.

It reached the edge of the brain . . . and kept right on going, through the membrane that encased the brain.

Astonishing.

Peter touched some keys, overlaying an extrapolated outline of Mrs. Fennell's head over the silhouette of her brain. He mentally kicked himself for not having done this sooner. It was obvious where the knot of light was heading.

Straight for the temple.

Straight for a hole in her skull.

It continued along, through the opening in the bone, through the thin veneer of muscle that overlaid the skull.

Surely, thought Peter, it was going to break up. Yes, there are nerves at the temple; that's why it hurts to be struck there. Yes, there are nerves in muscle tissue, too, including the jaw muscles that overlay the temple. And, yes, there are nerves shot through the lower layers of the skin. Even if the pattern had some form of cohesion, Peter expected to see a change here. The nerves outside the actual brain are much less densely packed. The pattern might balloon in size, drawn between the points of more diffuse neural tissue.

But it did not. It continued, exactly the same size, tumbling slowly end over end, through the muscle, through the skin, and—

Out. Past the sensor field.

It didn't break up. It simply left. And yet it had held its cohesion. The pattern had remained intact right up to the moment the sensor web lost it.

Incredible, thought Peter. Incredible.

He scanned the wall, looking for signs of other active neural nets.

But there were none.

Peggy Fennell's brain showed as an unblemished silhouette, devoid of electrical activity.

She was dead.

Dead.

And something had left her body.

Something had left her brain.

Peter felt his own head wheeling.

It couldn't be.

It could *not* be.

He reversed the recording, played it back from a different angle.

Why had the knot of light moved from the left hemisphere to the right? The other temple had been closer.

Ah, but Peggy had been lying down, her head on her pillow. Her left temple had been facing into the pillow; it was her right one that had been exposed to air. Even though it had been farther away, it represented the easier escape route.

Peter played the recording back again and again. Different angles. Different plotting methods. Different color-encoding schemes. It didn't matter; the result was the same. He compared the time-coded recordings to Peggy's other vital signs—pulse, respiration, blood pressure. The knot of light left just after her heart stopped, just after she'd breathed her last.

Peter had found exactly what he was looking for: an unequivocal marker that life was now over, an indisputable sign that the patient was just meat, ready for organ harvesting.

Marker.

That wasn't the right word, and he knew it. He was deliberately avoiding even thinking it. And yet, there it was, recorded by his own ultrasensitive instruments: the departure from her body of Peggy Fennell's very own soul.

PETER knew that when he asked Sarkar to come at once to his house, Sarkar would do so. Peter couldn't contain his excitement when Sarkar arrived. He was trying, and probably failing, to suppress a grin. He took Sarkar into his den, then played back the recording of Peggy Fennell's death once more.

"You faked that," said Sarkar.

"No, I didn't."

"Oh, come on, Peter."

"Really. I haven't even done any cleanup of the data. What you just saw is exactly what happened."

"Play that last bit again," said Sarkar. "One one-hundredth speed."

Peter touched buttons.

"Subhanallah," said Sarkar. "That's incredible."

"Isn't it, though?"

"You know what that is, don't you?" said Sarkar. "Right there, in crisp images. That's her *nafs*—her soul—leaving her body."

To his surprise, Peter found himself reacting negatively when he heard that idea said aloud. "I knew you were going to say that."

"Well, what else could it be?" asked Sarkar.

"I don't know."

"Nothing," said Sarkar. "That's the only thing it could be. Have you told anyone about this yet?"

"No."

"How do you announce something like this, I wonder? In a medical journal? Or do you just call the newspapers?"

"I don't know. I've only just begun to think about that. I suspect I'll call a press conference."

"Remember Fleischmann and Pons," cautioned Sarkar.

"The cold-fusion guys? Yeah, I know they jumped the gun, and ended up with egg on their faces. I'll have to get some more recordings of the thing. I've got to be sure this happens to everyone, after all. But I can't wait forever. Someone else will stumble on this soon enough."

"What about patents?"

Peter nodded. "I've thought about that. I've already got patents on most of the technology in the superEEG—it's an incremental improvement on the brain scanner we built for your AI work, after all. I'm certainly not going to go public until I've got the whole thing protected."

"When you do announce it," said Sarkar, "there will be

a ton of publicity. This is as big as it gets. You've proven the existence of life after death."

Peter shook his head. "You're going beyond the data. A small, weak electrical field leaves the body at the moment of death. That's all; there's nothing to prove that the field is conscious or living."

"The Koran says—"

"I can't rely on the Koran, or the Bible, or anything else. All we know is that a cohesive energy field survives the death of the body. Whether that field lasts for any appreciable time after departure, or whether it carries any real information, is completely unknown—and any other interpretation at this point is just wishful thinking."

"You're being deliberately obtuse. It's a soul, Peter. You know that."

"I don't like using that word. It—it prejudices the discussion."

"All right, call it something else if you like. Casper the Friendly Ghost, even—although I'd call the physical manifestation the soulwave. But it exists—and you know as well as I do that people are going to embrace it as an honest-to-goodness soul, as proof of life after death." Sarkar looked his friend in the eye. "This will change the world."

Peter nodded. There wasn't anything else to say.

CHAPTER 11

SEPTEMBER 2011

Peter hadn't seen Colin Godoyo in months—not since the seminar on nanotechnology immortality. They'd never really been friends—at least Peter hadn't thought so—but when Colin called Peter at the office asking him to come to lunch, something in Colin's voice had sounded urgent, so Peter had agreed. Lunch couldn't go on endlessly, anyway—Peter had a meeting with a major U.S. client at 2:00 p.m.

They went to a little restaurant Peter liked on Sheppard East, out toward Vic Park—a place that made a club sandwich by hacking the turkey breast with a knife, instead of slicing it thin on a machine, and toasting the bread on a grill so that it had brown lines across it. Peter never thought of himself as particularly memorable, but it seemed half the restaurants in North York thought him a regular, even though, excepting Sonny Gotlieb's, he only came in to any one of them once or twice a month. The server took Colin's drink order (scotch and soda), but protested he knew what Peter wanted ("Diet Coke with lime, right?"). Once the server was gone, Peter looked at Colin expectantly. "What's new?"

Colin was grayer than Peter had remembered, but he still wore his wealth ostentatiously, and was sporting a total of six gold rings. His eyes moved back and forth incessantly. "I guess you heard about me and Naomi."

Peter shook his head. "Heard what?"

"We've separated."

"Oh," said Peter. "I'm sorry."

"I hadn't realized how many of our friends were really just *her* friends," said Colin. The server arrived, set down little napkins, deposited the drinks on them, then scurried away. "I'm glad you agreed to come to lunch."

"No problem," said Peter. He had never been good at this kind of social situation. Was he supposed to ask Colin what had gone wrong? Peter rarely spoke of private matters, and on the whole didn't like either asking or answering personal questions. "I'm sorry to hear about you two." His cliche-dispenser suggested adding, "You always seemed so happy," but he stopped himself before the thought was given voice—Peter's own recent experience had taught him to put no stock in appearances.

"We'd been having problems for quite some time," said Colin.

Peter squeezed his lime into his Diet Coke.

"We weren't really on the same wavelength anymore." Apparently Colin had a cliche-dispenser of his own. "We weren't talking."

"You just drifted apart," said Peter, not quite making it a question, not wanting to pry.

"Yeah," said Colin. He took a liberal swig of his drink, then winced as if it were a masochistic pleasure. "Yeah."

"You'd been together a long time," said Peter, again careful to keep his tone flat, to keep the statement from becoming a question.

"Eleven years, if you count the time we lived together before we got married," said Colin. He cupped his glass in both hands.

Peter wondered idly who had broken up with whom. *None of my business,* he thought. "A good long time," he said.

"I—I was seeing someone else," said Colin. "A woman in Montreal. I had to go there every three weeks on business, took the maglev out."

Peter was dumbfounded. Was everyone screwing outside of marriage these days? "Oh," he said.

"It didn't really mean anything," said Colin, making a dismissive gesture with his hand. "It was just, you know, just a way of getting a message to Naomi." He looked up. "A cry for help, maybe. You know?"

No, thought Peter. *No, I don't.*

"Just a cry for help. But she went crazy when I told her. Said that was the last straw. The straw that broke the camel's back." Clearly, thought Peter, *everyone* had a cliche-dispenser. "I didn't want to hurt her, but I had needs, you know. I don't think she should have left me over something like that." The server came in again, depositing Peter's club sandwich and Colin's pasta primavera. "What do you think?" asked Colin.

I think you're an asshole, Peter thought. *I think you're the biggest fucking asshole on the planet.* "Hard luck," he said, pulling the toothpick out of one of his sandwich wedges and spreading mayonnaise on the turkey. "Hard luck indeed."

"Anyway," said Colin, perhaps sensing that it was time to change the subject. "I didn't ask you to lunch to talk about me. I really wanted to get some advice from you."

Peter looked at him. "Oh?"

"Well, you and Cathy were at that Life Unlimited seminar. What did you think?"

"Impressive sales pitch," said Peter.

"I mean, what did you think of the process? You're a biomedical engineer. Do you think it would really work?"

Peter shrugged. "Jay Leno says Queen Elizabeth has undergone the process—only way to save the monarchy was to make sure that none of her children ever got to sit on the throne."

Colin chuckled politely, but looked at Peter as if he expected a more serious response. Peter chewed on a bit of his sandwich, then: "I don't know. The basic premise seems sound. I mean, there are—what?—five basic models for senescence and eventual death." Peter ticked them off on his fingers. "First, there's the stochastic theory. It says our bodies are complex machines, and, like all complex machines, something's bound to break down eventually.

"Second, the Hayflick phenomenon: human cells seem to only be able to divide about fifty times total.

"Third, the smudged-Xerox hypothesis. Small errors are introduced every time DNA is copied, and at some point the copy gets so bad that it doesn't make sense anymore. Boom!—you're pushing up daisies.

"Number four is the toxic-waste theory. Something—possibly free radicals—gives your body trouble from the inside.

"And finally, the autoimmune hypothesis, in which your body's natural defenses become confused and turn upon your own healthy cells."

Colin nodded. "And no one knows which one is right?"

"Oh, I suspect they're all right to one degree or another," said Peter. "But the key thing is that Life Unlimited's—what did they call them? nannies?—their nannies seem to address all five probable causes. So, yes, I'd say it's got a good chance of working. There's no way to know for sure, though, until someone who has undergone the process actually does live for a few centuries."

"So—so you think it'd be worth the money?" said Colin.

Peter shrugged again. "On the surface, yeah, I guess so. I mean, who wouldn't want to live forever? But, then again, it'd be a shame to do that if it meant missing out on a wonderful heaven."

Colin cocked his head. "You're sounding downright religious, Peter."

Peter concentrated on finishing his food. "Sorry. Idle thoughts, that's all."

"What did Cathy think of Life Unlimited?"

"She didn't seem very interested," said Peter.

"Really?" said Colin. "I think it sounds great. I think it's something I'd very much like to do."

"It costs a fortune," said Peter. "You been embezzling from the bank?"

"Hardly," said Colin. "But I think it would be worth every penny."

IT took three weeks to get two additional recordings of the soulwave departing from human bodies. Peter made one of the recordings at Carlson's Chronic Care, the same place he'd met Peggy Fennell. This time, the subject was Gustav Reichhold, a man just a few years older than Peter who was dying of complications from AIDS, and had chosen to end his life through doctor-assisted suicide.

The other recording, though, had to be made somewhere else, lest critics charge that the soulwave, far from being a universal component of human existence, was simply some mundane electrical phenomenon related to the wiring in that particular building, or to its proximity to power lines, or to some particular course of treatment used at Carlson's. So, to get his third recording, Peter had put an ad out on the net:

> Wanted: person in very late stages of terminal illness or injury to participate in testing a new biomedical monitoring device. Location: southern Ontario. Will pay participant CDN$10,000. Terminal individuals, or persons with power of attorney for same, please apply in confidence to Hobson Monitoring (net: HOBMON).

Peter felt funny about placing the ad—it seemed so cold. Indeed, his embarrassment probably had a lot to do with why he offered such a large fee. But within two days of the ad going out on the net, Peter had fourteen applicants. He chose a boy—just twelve years of age—who was dying of leukemia. He made the choice as much for compassionate reasons as for varying the sample base: the boy's family had bankrupted themselves coming to Canada from Uganda in hopes of finding a cure for their son. The money would be some small help in paying their hospital bills.

And, feeling upon reflection that the others who had already participated in the study deserved the same compensation, Peter also made a $10,000 payment to the estate of Gustav Reichhold. Since Peggy Fennell had no heirs, he made a donation in her name to the Canadian Diabetes Association. He reasoned that soon researchers around the globe would be scrambling to reproduce his results. It seemed appropriate to establish up front a generous payment for test subjects.

All three recordings looked remarkably similar: a tiny cohesive electrical field departing the body at the precise moment of death. To be on the safe side, Peter had used a different superEEG unit to record the Ugandan boy's death. The principles were the same, but he used all-new components, some employing different engineering solutions, to make sure that the previous results weren't due to some glitch in his recording equipment.

Meanwhile, over the course of several weeks, Peter had also used a superEEG on all hundred and nineteen employees of Hobson Monitoring, without telling any except his most senior staff what it was actually for. None of his employees were dying, of course, but Peter wanted to be sure that the soulwave did indeed exist in healthy people, and wasn't just some sort of electrical last gasp produced by an expiring brain.

The soulwave had a distinctive electrical signature. The

frequency was very high, well above that of normal electrochemical brain activity, so, even though the voltage was minuscule, it wasn't washed out in the mass of other signals within the brain. After making some refinements to his equipment, Peter had little trouble isolating it in scans of all his employees' brains, although he did find it amusing that it took several tries to locate it in the brain of Caleb Martin, his staff lawyer.

Meanwhile, that selfsame Martin had been working his tail off, securing patent protection on all the superEEG components in Canada, the United States, the European Community, Japan, the CIS, and elsewhere. And the Korean manufacturing firm Hobson Monitoring used to actually build its equipment was gearing up a new production line for superEEGs.

Soon it would be time to go public with the existence of the soulwave.

CHAPTER 12

Peter felt like a student again, pulling off a silly fraternity prank involving putting clothing on animals. He made his way over to one of the cows and stroked it gently at the base of the neck. It had been years since Peter had been this close to a cow; he'd grown up in Regina, but still had relatives who owned dairy farms elsewhere in Saskatchewan, and he'd spent parts of his boyhood summers there.

Like all cows, this one had enormous brown eyes and wet nostrils. It seemed unperturbed by Peter touching it, and so, without further ado, he gently strapped the modified scanning helmet onto its loaf-shaped head. The beast mooed at him, but more in apparent surprise than protest. Its breath stank.

"That it, Doc?" asked the foreperson.

Peter looked at the animal again. He felt a little sorry for it. "Yes."

At this slaughterhouse, cattle were normally stunned with an electrical charge before being killed. But that method would overload Peter's scanner. So instead this particular cow would be rendered unconscious with carbon dioxide gas, hung, and then have its throat slit for drainage. Peter had seen a lot of surgery over the years, but that cutting had always been to cure. He was surprised at how upsetting he found the killing of the animal. The foreperson invited him to stay for a full tour, including the butchering of a cow, but Peter didn't have the stomach for it. He simply retrieved the special bovine headgear and his recording equipment, thanked the various people he'd inconvenienced, and headed back to his office.

Peter spent the rest of the day going over the recording, trying various computer-enhancement techniques on the data. The results were always the same. No matter what method he used or how hard he looked, he could find no evidence that cows had souls—nothing of any kind seemed to exit the brain at death. Not too surprising a revelation, he supposed, although he was quickly coming to realize that for every person who would hail him as a genius for his discoveries, there'd be another who'd damn him for them. In this case, the radical animal-rights lobby would surely be upset.

Peter and Cathy had been planning to go to Barberian's, their favorite steakhouse, for dinner that night. At the last minute, though, Peter canceled their reservation and they went to a vegetarian restaurant instead.

WHEN Peter Hobson had taken a university elective in taxonomy, the two species of chimpanzees had been *Pan troglodytes* (common chimps) and *Pan paniscus* (pygmy chimps).

But the split between chimps and humans had occurred just 500,000 generations ago, and they still have 98.4% of their DNA in common. In 1993, a group including evolutionist

Richard Dawkins and bestselling science-fiction writer Douglas Adams published the *Declaration on Great Apes,* which urged the adoption of a bill of rights for our simian cousins.

In took thirteen years, but eventually their declaration came to be argued at the UN. An unprecedented resolution was adopted formally reclassifying chimpanzees as members of genus *Homo,* meaning there were now three extant species of humanity: *Homo sapiens, Homo troglodytes,* and *Homo paniscus.* Human rights were divided into two broad categories: those, such as the entitlement to life, liberty, and freedom from torture, that applied to all members of genus *Homo,* and other rights, such as pursuit of happiness, religious freedom, and ownership of land, that were reserved exclusively to *H. sapiens.*

Of course, under *Homo* rights, no one could ever kill a chimp again for experimental purposes—indeed, no one could imprison a chimp in a lab. And many nations had modified their legal definitions of homicide to include the killing of chimps.

Adriaan Kortlandt, the first animal behaviorist to observe wild chimpanzees, once referred to them as "eerie souls in animals' furs." But now Peter Hobson was in a position to see how literally Kortlandt's observation should be taken. The soulwave existed in *Homo sapiens.* It did not exist in *Bos taurus,* the common cow. Peter supported the simian-rights movement, but all the good that had been done in the last few years might be undone if it were shown that humans had souls but chimps did not. Still, Peter knew that if he himself did not do the test, someone else eventually would.

Even though chimps were no longer captured for labs, zoos, or circuses, some were still living in human-operated facilities. The United Kingdom, Canada, the U.S., Tanzania, and Burundi jointly funded a chimpanzee retirement home in Glasgow—of all places—for chimps that couldn't be returned to the wild. Peter phoned the sanctuary, to find out if any of the chimps there were near death. According to the director, Brenda MacTavish, several were in their fifties, which was old age for a chimp, but none were terminal. Still, Peter arranged to have some scanning equipment shipped to her.

"And so," Peter said to Sarkar during their weekly dinner at Sonny Gotlieb's, "I think I'm ready to go public now. Oh, and my marketing people have come up with a name for the superEEG: they're calling it a SoulDetector."

"Oh, please!" said Sarkar.

Peter grinned. "Hey, I always leave those decisions up to Joginder and his people. Anyway, the SoulDetector patents are in place, we've got a backlog of almost two hundred units ready for shipment, I've got three good recordings of the soulwave leaving human beings, I know that at least some animals don't have souls, and I'll hopefully soon have the data on chimps, as well."

Sarkar spread lox on a bagel half. "You're still missing one important piece of information."

"Oh?"

"I'm surprised you haven't thought of the question yourself, Peter."

"What question?"

"The flip side of your original inquiry: you know now when the soul leaves the body. But when does the soul arrive?"

Peter's jaw went slack. "You mean—you mean in a fetus?"

"Precisely."

"Holy shit," said Peter. "I—I could get in a lot of trouble asking that question."

"Perhaps," said Sarkar. "But as soon as you go public, someone will ask it."

"The controversy will be incredible."

Sarkar nodded. "Indeed. But I'm surprised it hadn't occurred to you."

Peter looked away. He'd been suppressing it, no doubt. An old wound, long since healed. Or so he'd thought.

Damn, thought Peter. God damn.

CHAPTER 13

It had happened thirteen years ago, during their first year of marriage. Peter remembered it all vividly.

October 31, 1998. Even back then, they didn't eat at home often. But they'd always thought it rude to go out on Halloween—someone should be in to give treats to the kids.

Cathy made fettuccine Alfredo while Peter put together a Caesar salad with real bacon bits crisped in the microwave, and they collaborated on making a cake for dessert. They had fun cooking together, and the tight confines of the tiny kitchen they'd had back then made for plenty of enjoyable contact as they squeezed past each other, jockeying for access to the kitchen's various cupboards and appliances. Cathy had ended up with flour stains in the shapes of Peter's handprints on each of her breasts, while Peter had her handprints on his bum.

But after they'd finished eating the salads and had made a good start on the pasta, Cathy had said, without preamble, "I'm pregnant."

Peter had put his fork down and looked at her. "Really?"

"Yes."

"That's—" He knew he should say "That's wonderful," but he was unable to get the second word out. Instead, he settled for "interesting."

She chilled visibly. "Interesting?"

"Well, I mean, it's unexpected, that's all." A pause. "Weren't you—" Another pause. "Damn."

"I think it was that weekend at my parents' cottage," she said. "Remember? You'd forgotten to—"

"I remember," said Peter, a slight edge in his voice.

"You said you'd have a vasectomy when you turned thirty," Cathy said, a tad defensively. "You said if by then we still didn't want to have kids, you'd do it."

"Well, I wasn't bloody well going to do it on my birthday. I'm *still* thirty. And, besides, we were still discussing whether to have a child."

"Then why are you angry?" asked Cathy.

"I—I'm not." He smiled. "Really, darling, I'm not. It's just a surprise, that's all." He paused. "So, if it was that weekend, you're what? Six weeks along?"

She nodded. "I missed my period, so I bought one of those kits."

"I see," said Peter.

"You don't want the baby," she said.

"I didn't say that. I don't know what I want."

At that point, the doorbell rang. Peter got up to answer it.

Trick or treat, he thought. Trick or treat.

PETER and Cathy had waited another three weeks, weighing their options, their lifestyle, their dreams. Finally, though, they made their decision.

The abortion clinic on College Street had been in an old two-story brownstone. On its left had been a greasy spoon called Joes—no apostrophe—that advertised a breakfast special with two "egg's" any way you like them. On its right had been an appliance store with a hand-lettered sign in the window that said, "We do repairs."

And in front of the clinic there had been protesters, marching up and down the sidewalk, carrying placards.

Abortion is murder, said one.

Sinner, repent, said another.

Baby's have rights too, said a third, perhaps produced by Joe's sign-maker. A bored-looking police officer was leaning against the brownstone's wall, making sure the protesters didn't get out of hand.

Peter and Cathy parked across the street and got out of their car. Cathy looked toward the clinic and shivered, even though it wasn't particularly cold. "I didn't think there would be that many protesters," she said.

Peter counted eight of them—three men and five women. "There're always going to be some."

She nodded.

Peter moved next to her and took her hand. She squeezed it, and managed a slight, brave smile. They waited for a break in the traffic, then crossed.

As soon as they arrived at the other side, the protesters closed in on them. "Don't go in there, lady!" shouted one. "It's your *baby!*" shouted another. "Take some time," shouted a third. "Think it over!"

The cop moved close enough to see that the protesters weren't actually touching Cathy or preventing her from gaining access.

Cathy kept her eyes facing straight ahead.

Eggs any way you like, thought Peter. Repairs done here.

"Don't do it, lady!" shouted one of the protesters again. "It's your *baby!*"

"Take some time! Think it over!"

There were four stone steps leading up to the wooden doors of the clinic. She started up them, Peter right behind.

"It's . . . !"

"Don't . . . !"

"Take . . . !"

Peter stepped ahead to open the door for Cathy.

They went inside.

PETER had had his vasectomy the following week. He and Cathy never spoke again of that episode from their past, but sometimes when her sister's daughters were visiting, or when they ran into a neighbor taking a baby for a stroll, or when they saw children on TV, Peter would find himself feeling wistful and sad and confused, and he would steal a look at his wife and see in her large blue eyes the same mix of emotions and uncertainty.

And now, they had to face that moral issue all over again.

There was no way to put a scanning skull cap on a fetus, of course. But Peter didn't need to scan all electrical activity in the unborn child's brain—all he needed was equipment to detect the high-frequency soulwave. It took him days of work, but he eventually managed to cobble together a scanner that could be laid on a pregnant woman's belly to detect the soulwave inside. The unit incorporated some of the scanning-at-a-distance technology from the Hobson Monitor, and employed a directional sensor to make sure the mother's own soulwave wasn't mistakenly picked up.

The soulwave was exceedingly faint, and the fetus was deep within the woman's body. So, just like a telescope taking prolonged exposures to build up an image, Peter suspected this sensor would probably have to be in place for about four hours before a determination could be made of whether the soulwave was present.

Peter went down to his company's finance department. One of the senior analysts there, Victoria Kalipedes, was just beginning her ninth month of pregnancy.

"Victoria," Peter said, "I need your help."

She looked up expectantly. Peter smiled at the thought. Everything she did these days was expectantly. "I've got a new prototype sensor I'd like you to help me test," he said.

Victoria looked surprised. "Does it have to do with my baby?"

"That's right. It's just a sensor web that's laid over your belly. It won't hurt you, and it can't harm the baby in any way. It's, well, it's like an EEG—it detects activity in the fetal brain."

"And there's no way it can hurt the baby?"

Peter shook his head. "None."

"I don't know . . ."

"Please." Peter surprised himself with the forcefulness with which he said the word.

Victoria considered. "All right. When do you need me?"

"Right now."

"I've got lots of work to do today—and you know what my boss is like."

"Placing the sensor will only take a few minutes. Because the signals are so faint, you'll have to wear it for the rest of the afternoon, but you'll be able to go on with your work."

Victoria got to her feet—no easy task this late in her pregnancy—and went with Peter to a private room. "I'm going to describe to you how the sensor should be placed," said Peter, "then I'll leave you alone and let you put it on yourself. It should fit under your clothes without difficulty."

Victoria listened to Peter's instructions, then nodded.

"Thank you," said Peter, as he left her to undress. "Thank you very much."

At the end of the day, he had the results. The sensor had had no trouble detecting the soulwave coming from Victoria's fetus. Not too surprising: had the baby been removed at this late point in the pregnancy, it would probably have survived on its own. But how soon into a pregnancy did the soulwave first appear?

Peter flipped through his computerized Rolodex until he

found the number he wanted: Dinah Kawasaki, a woman he had taken some courses with at U of T who now had an obstetrics practice in Don Mills.

He listened nervously to the electronic tones as the computer dialed the number. If Dinah could convince some of her patients to help him, he'd soon have his answer.

And, Peter realized, he was afraid of what that answer might be.

CHAPTER 14

OCTOBER 2011

Thirty-two of Dinah Kawasaki's expectant patients did agree to participate in testing Peter's scanning equipment. That wasn't surprising: Peter had offered a fee of $500 per patient simply for wearing the scanner for four hours. Each patient was one week further along in her pregnancy than the one before.

Peter would eventually want to do studies throughout their individual terms on multiple women, but the initial results were clear. The soulwave arrived sometime between the ninth and the tenth week of pregnancy. Before that, it simply did not exist. He'd need much finer studies to show whether it arose from within the fetal brain, or—less likely, Peter thought—somehow arrived from outside.

Peter knew that this would change the world, almost as much as the realization that some form of life after death actually existed. Some would still quibble with the interpretation, but Peter could now say categorically whether or not a given fetus was a person—whether or not its removal would be simply sucking out an unwanted growth or an act of murder.

The implications would be profound. Why, if the Pope could be convinced that the soulwave really was the physical signature of the immortal being, and that the soul only appeared ten weeks into pregnancy, perhaps he'd remove his restriction on birth control and on early abortion. Peter remembered that back in 1993, the then-Pope had originally told women who had been raped by soldiers in Bosnia-Herzegovina that they would be damned unless they brought their babies to term. And the current Pope still refused to allow birth control in famine-torn areas, even when babies would starve to death once born.

Of course, the women's movement—of which Peter considered himself a supporter—would react, too.

Peter had always had a hard time with abortion, especially in industrialized countries. Perfectly reliable, unobtrusive methods of birth control existed. Peter had always accepted intellectually that a woman had the right to an abortion on demand, but he'd found the whole issue distasteful. Surely unwanted conception was something best avoided in the first place? Surely birth control—by both partners in a relationship—wasn't too much to ask? Why cheapen the wonder of reproduction?

It had taken all of ten minutes on the net to dig up the statistic that one in five pregnancies in North America ended in abortion. And yet, of course, he and Cathy had conceived all those years ago without planning to. Him a Ph.D., her with a degree in chemistry—two people who should have known better.

Nothing is ever as simple in the concrete as it is in the abstract.

But now, perhaps, there was justification for after-conception birth control. The soul, whatever the soul might be, arrived only after sixty or more days of gestation.

Peter was no futurist, but he could see where society would

go: within a decade, laws would doubtless change to allowing abortion on demand up until the arrival of the soulwave. Once the soulwave was present in the fetus, the courts would rule that the unborn child was in fact a human being.

Peter had wanted answers—cold, hard facts. And now he had them.

He took a deep breath. He was a rationalist. He knew that there had always been only three possible answers to the moral question raised by abortion. One: a child is a human being from the moment of conception. That had always seemed silly to Peter; at conception a child is nothing but a single cell.

Two: a child becomes a human being the moment it exits from the mother's body. That had seemed equally silly. Although a fetus draws nutrition from the mother until the umbilical cord is severed, the fetus is developed enough to support itself, if need be, weeks before the normal end of a pregnancy. Clearly the cutting of the cord is as arbitrary as the cutting of the ribbon to open a new mall. The fetus is a human being with an independent heart and brain—and thoughts—prior to emerging into the world.

So all Peter had done was prove what should have been intuitively obvious. Option three: somewhere between the two extremes—between conception and birth—a fetus becomes a human being in its own right, and with its own rights.

That option three turned out to be correct should have been expected. Even many religions held that the arrival of the soul occurred sometime in the middle of pregnancy. Saint Thomas Aquinas had allowed abortion to the sixth week for male fetuses and the third month for females, those being the points at which he believed the soul entered the body. And in Muslim belief, according to Sarkar, the *nafs* enters the fetus on the fortieth day after conception.

Granted, none of those coincided with Peter's figure of nine or ten weeks. But the certain knowledge that there was a specific point at which the soul did arrive would—the thought occurred to him again—would change the world. And, of course, not everyone would think it a change for the better.

Peter wondered what it would be like to see himself burned in effigy on TV.

IT had been just over nine weeks since Cathy had told Peter about her affair. Things had remained strained between them throughout that period. But now it was necessary that they have a serious talk—a talk about a different crisis, a crisis from their past.

Today was Monday, October 10—Canadian Thanksgiving. Both of them had the day off. Peter came into the living room. Cathy was sitting on the love seat, doing the *New York Times* crossword. Peter came over and sat next to her.

"Cathy," he said, "there's something I have to say."

Cathy's enormous eyes met his, and suddenly Peter realized what she was thinking. He'd made his decision, she thought. He was leaving her. He saw in her face all the fear, all the sadness, all the courage. She was struggling for composure.

"It's about our baby," said Peter.

Cathy's face changed abruptly. She was confused now. "What baby?"

Peter swallowed hard. "The baby we, ah, aborted twelve years ago."

Cathy's eyes were moving back and forth. She clearly didn't understand.

"Next week, my company will be making a public announcement about the soulwave," he said. "At that time, some additional research will be revealed. But—but I wanted you to hear about it first."

Cathy was silent.

"I know now when the soulwave arrives in a child."

She read his manner, read his hesitancy. She knew his every gesture, his whole body-language vocabulary. "Oh,

God," Cathy said, her eyes wide in horror. "It arrives early, doesn't it? Prior to when we—when we—"

Peter said nothing.

"Oh, God," she said again, shaking her head. "It was the Nineties," she said, as if that summed it all up.

The Nineties. Back then, the abortion issue, like most others, had been simplified to a ridiculous sloganeering level: "Pro-choice"—as if there were another faction that was anti-choice; "Pro-life"—as if there had been a group that was against life. No grays were allowed. In the circle the Hobsons had moved in—educated, well-off, liberal Eastern Canada—pro-choice had been the only stance to take.

The Nineties.

The politically correct Nineties.

Peter shook his head. "It's not clear," he said. "We did it right around the time the soulwave would have first appeared." He paused, not knowing what to say. "It might have been okay."

"Or it might have been . . . might have been . . ."

Peter nodded. "I'm so sorry, Cathy."

She chewed her lower lip, confused and sad. Peter reached out and touched her hand.

CHAPTER 15

Hobson Monitoring had a standard database of medical journalists worldwide to whom electronic press kits were routinely sent. A few members of Peter's senior staff argued that this particular release should also go to religion editors, but Peter vetoed that. He was still uncomfortable with the moral aspects of the discovery. Besides, everyone from the *National Enquirer* on down would be clamoring for interviews soon enough. An invitation to the press conference went out by email and courier three days in advance of the actual event. Peter was uneasy about the wording of the invitation, but Joginder Singh, his PR person, was adamant that this was the correct approach:

> Hobson Monitoring Ltd. invites you to attend a press conference on Thursday, October 20, at 10:00 a.m. in room 104 of the Metro Toronto Convention Centre. We will be unveiling a fundamental breakthrough in science. Sorry, folks—no hints until you get here. But we promise that this story will be front-page news around

the globe. Video linkups are available for those unable to attend in person; contact Joginder at Hobson Monitoring for details.

Several reporters did call, trying to sniff out whether the story would really be worth pursuing, or if this was just going to be the release of a new piece of hospital gadgetry. But no advance information was given out. Everyone had to wait until Thursday morning. And then . . .

ABOUT forty reporters showed up for the press conference—Hobson Monitoring had only once before gotten more, back when it had announced its first public share offering. Peter knew half the reporters by name: Buck Piekarz, medical correspondent for the *Toronto Star;* Cory Tick, his counterpart from the *Globe and Mail;* Lianne Delaney from CBC Newsworld; a fat guy who covered Canadian stories for the *Buffalo News;* a stringer for *USA Today;* many more. The reporters helped themselves to fresh fruit and coffee while they chatted amongst themselves. They were surprised to not be receiving press kits up front, although Peter and Joginder assured them that full kits, including data disks and transcripts of Peter's remarks, would be distributed as they exited. Several of the journalists present would videotape the conference, anyway.

Cathy had taken a vacation day to be there with Peter. At a quarter after ten, he made his way up to the front of the room. Cathy beamed at him, and, despite the butterflies in his stomach, he drew strength from her presence. "Hello, everyone," he said smiling at them all in turn, but holding a special, lingering smile on Cathy. "Thank you for coming out. Please forgive all the secrecy—I know it seems a tad melodramatic. But what we're going to announce here today is something very special, and we wanted to be sure that responsible journalists heard about it first." He smiled. "Joginder, if you'll dim the lights please? Thanks. Now, everyone, please watch the wall monitor. You'll all be getting copies of the recording I'm about to play when you leave. All set? Run the demo, please, Joginder."

The journalists watched intently as Peter narrated a slowed-down playback of the brain scans of Peggy Fennell's death. Peter went into a fair bit of technical detail—these were, after all, medical correspondents. When the soulwave actually departed from Mrs. Fennell's head a murmur moved through the audience.

"Play that last bit back again," called out Piekarz from the *Star.* Peter signaled Joginder to do so.

"Exactly what is that?" asked another reporter.

Peter looked at Cathy, sitting in the front row. Her eyes were twinkling. He affected a shrug. "It's a cohesive electrical field that leaves the body through the temple at the moment of death."

"At the exact moment of death?" asked Delaney, the woman from Newsworld.

"Yes. It's the final bit of electrical activity in the brain."

"So—so it's what?" said the woman. "Some kind of a soul?" She said the word offhandedly, as if a joke, giving her room to retreat in case she was making a fool of herself.

But in the weeks since Sarkar had first uttered that term, Peter had grown more comfortable with it. "Yes," he said. "That's exactly what we think it is." He raised his voice, speaking generally to the room. "There it is, ladies and gentleman: the first ever direct scientific recording of what may be a human soul leaving a body."

A buzz erupted, everyone talking at once. Peter spent the next two hours answering questions, although some of the print reporters with early deadlines grabbed the press kits and exited almost at once. He made clear that his studies had yet to reveal exactly what happened to the soulwave after departure—it seemed to remain coherent, but there was still no proof that it didn't dissipate shortly after leaving the body. He also stressed that very little data was available yet about the content or structure of the soulwave, and, in particular, about what, if any, meaningful information it contained.

But it made no difference. The idea of a soul was an archetype, universally grasped. People already were sure, in their hearts, of what the soulwave represented.

That night, Cathy and Peter saw that the CBC TV story was picked up by CNN in the States and the BBC World Service. The announcement was all over the net within hours and made front-page news in the evening editions of the *Toronto Star* and several American papers, and was plastered across page one of newspapers around the world the next day. Within twenty-four hours, the entire developed world knew about the discovery.

Suddenly Peter Hobson was a celebrity.

"IS the caller still there?" asked Donahue, back on daytime TV after his failed presidential bid.

"I'm here, Phil."

Donahue made his tortured face; precious seconds were being wasted. "Go ahead—I have very little time."

"What I'd like to know," said the caller's voice, "is what life after death is really like. I mean, we know now that it exists, but what's it *really* like?"

Donahue turned to Peter. "That's a very good question, caller. Dr. Hobson—what is the afterlife like?"

Peter shifted in his chair. "Well, that's more a subject for philosophers, I'm afraid, and—"

Donahue turned toward the studio audience. "Audience, are we prepared for these questions? Do we really want to know the answers? And what will America do if the afterlife turns out to be unpleasant?" He spoke into the air. "Show 'em, Bryan—number fourteen."

A chart appeared on the screen. "Sixty-seven percent of the people of this good country," said Donahue, "believe that the soulwave proves the Judeo-Christian model of a heaven and a hell. Only eleven percent believes that your discovery, Dr. Hobson, disproves that model."

The chart disappeared. Donahue spied a raised hand in the back of the studio. Still spry at seventy-five, he bolted for the back row and shoved a microphone under a woman's chin.

"Yes, ma'am. You had a brief comment."

"That's right, Phil. I'm from Memphis—we love your show down there."

First the little-boy face, patted on the head. "Thank you, ma'am." Then the pained face, as if something was caught going down his gullet. "I have very little time."

"My question is for the doctor. Do you think your discovery is going to get you into heaven, or are you going to hell for interfering in God's mysteries?"

Close up on Peter. "I—I have no idea."

Donahue did his standard theatrical arm gesture that ended with his finger pointing directly into the camera. "And we'll be back . . ."

THE silver-haired Latin fox turned to face the audience. According to the tabloids, he'd recently undergone the Life Unlimited process, so viewers had centuries of his particular brand of television to look forward to.

"Life after life," he said, portentously. "That's our focus on this edition of *Geraldo.* Our guests today include Peter Hobson, the Ottawa scientist who claims to have captured the immortal soul on film, and Monsignor Carlos Latina of the Archdiocese of Los Angeles." Geraldo turned to the man wearing a black cassock. "Monsignor—where do you think the souls are today of those clergy members who molested boys in church-run orphanages?"

* * *

(ROLL computer graphic of Capitol Building dome. Cue music.) Announcer: "From ABC News: *This Week with George Stephanopoulos*. Now from our Washington headquarters, here's George Stephanopoulos."

Stephanopoulos, dour, facing into the camera: "The soulwave—fact or fantasy? Religious revelation or scientific truth? We'll ask our guests: Peter Hobson, the engineer who first detected the soulwave; best-selling author Richard Dawkins; and Helen Johannes, Presidential Advisor on Religion in America. Some background on all this from our man Kyle Adair. And joining me in our Washington studio will be—"

(Medium shot of Donaldson, his features sharp despite his wrinkles; his shoe-polish brown toupee looking obviously fake.)

"Sam Donaldson—"

(Medium shot of silver-haired Will, wall-eyed and bow-tied, looking like a retired plantation owner.)

"—and George Will. Later, we'll be joined by commentator Sally Fernandez of the *Washington Post* . . . all here on our Sunday program."

(Run commercials: Archer Daniels Midland's new all-vegetable automobile. General Dynamics—"our work may be classified, but we're a good corporate citizen." Merrill Lynch—"because someday the economy *will* turn around.")

(Roll pre-recorded backgrounder.)

(Fade up in studio.)

Stephanopoulos: "Kyle, thank you."

(Recap guests and panelists.)

(Insert Peter Hobson on wall monitor, with dateline display at top showing "Toronto.")

Sam Donaldson, leaning forward: "Professor Hobson, your discovery of the soulwave could be seen as a great liberator of oppressed people, final proof that all men and women are created equal. What effect do you think your discovery will have on totalitarian regimes?"

Hobson, politely: "Excuse me, but I'm not a professor."

Donaldson: "I stand corrected. But don't duck my question, sir! What effect will your discoveries have on the human-rights violations going on in the eastern Ukraine?"

Hobson, after a moment's reflection: "Well, I'd love to think that I've struck a blow for human equality, of course. But it seems that our ability to be *inhuman* has survived every challenge to it in the past."

George Will, over steepled fingers: "Dr. Hobson, the average American, struggling under the burden of an excessive government with a ravenous appetite for tax dollars, cares not one whit about the geopolitical ramifications of your research. The average church-going American wants to know, in precise and plain language, sir, exactly what characteristics the afterlife actually has."

Hobson, blinking: "Is that a question?"

Will: "It is *the* question, Dr. Hobson."

Hobson, shaking head slowly: "I have no idea."

CHAPTER 16

Peter was not about to let his new-found celebrity interfere with his Tuesday evening dinners with Sarkar at Sonny Gotlieb's. But he did have something very specific that he wanted to explore with Sarkar, and he began without preamble. "How do you create an artificial intelligence? You work in that field—how do you do it?"

Sarkar looked surprised. "Well, there are many ways. The oldest is the interview method. If we wanted a system to do financial planning, we would ask questions of several financial planners. Then we reduce the answers to a series of rules that can be expressed in computer code—'if A and B are true, do C.'"

"But what about that scanner my company built for you? Aren't you doing full brain dumps of specific people now?"

"We're making good progress toward that. We've got a prototype called RICKGREEN, but we're not ready to go public with it. You know that comedian, Rick Green?"

"Sure."

"We did a full scan of him. The resulting system can now

tell jokes that are just as funny as the ones the real Rick tells. And by giving it access to the Canadian Press and UPI news feeds, it can even generate new topical humor."

"Okay, so you can essentially clone in silicon a specific human mind—"

"Get with the twenty-first century, Peter. We use gallium arsenide, not silicon."

"Whatever."

"But you have hit upon what makes the problem crisp: we are just at the point where we can clone *one* specific human mind—a shame that such a technique did not exist in time to scan Stephen Hawking. But there are very few applications in which you want the knowledge of just one person. For most expert systems, you really want the *combined* knowledge of many practitioners. So far, there is no way to combine, say, Rick Green and Jerry Seinfeld, or to build a combined Stephen Hawking / Mordecai Almi neural net. Although I had high hopes for this technology, I suspect most of the contracts we'll get will be for duplicating the brains of autocratic company presidents who think their heirs are going to be interested in what they have to say after they're dead."

Peter nodded.

"Besides," said Sarkar, "total brain dumps are turning out to be a tremendous waste of resources. When we created RICKGREEN, all we were really interested in was his sense of humor. But the system also gives us everything else Rick knows, including his approaches to raising his children, an endless amount of expertise about model trains, which are his hobby, and even his cooking technique, something no one in his right mind would want to emulate."

"Can't you pare it down to isolate just the sense of humor?"

"That's difficult. We're getting good at decoding what each neural net does, but there are many interconnections. When we tried deleting the part about child-rearing, we found the system no longer made jokes about family life."

"But you *can* make an accurate duplicate of a specific human mind on a computer?"

"It's a brand-new technique, Peter. But, so far, yes, the duplication seems accurate."

"And you can, at least to some extent, decode the functions of the various neural interconnections?"

"Yes," said Sarkar. "Again, we've only tried it on the RICKGREEN prototype—and that was a limited model."

"And, once you've identified a function, you can delete it from the overall brain simulacrum?"

"Bearing in mind that deleting one thing may change the way something that seems unrelated will respond, yes, I'd say we're at the point at which we can do that."

"All right," said Peter. "Let me propose an experiment. Say we make two copies of a specific person's mind. In one of them you excise everything related to the physical body: hormonal responses, sexual urges, things like that. And in the second one, you remove everything related to bodily degeneration, to fear of old age and dying, and so on."

Sarkar ate a matzo ball. "And what would the point be?"

"The first one would be to answer that question everyone keeps asking me: what is life after death really like? What parts of the human psyche could persist separate from the body? And, while we're at it, I figure we'd do the second one—a simulation of a being who knew he was physically immortal, like someone who has undergone that Life Unlimited process."

Sarkar stopped chewing. His mouth hung open, giving an undignified view of a masticated dumpling. "That's—that's incredible," he said at last, around his food. "*Subhanallah,* what an idea."

"Could you do it?"

Sarkar swallowed. "Maybe," he said. "Electronic eschatology. What a concept."

"You'd need to make the two brain dumps."

"We'd do the dump once, of course. Then we'd just copy it twice."

"Copy it once, you mean."

"No, twice," said Sarkar. "You can't do an experiment without a control; you know that."

"Right," said Peter, slightly embarrassed. "Anyway, we'd make one copy which we would modify to simulate life after death. Call it—call it the Spirit simulacrum. And another to simulate immortality."

"And the third we would leave unmodified," said Sarkar. "A baseline or control version that we can compare to the original living person to make sure that the simulacra retain their accuracy as time goes on."

"Perfect," said Peter.

"But you know, Peter, this wouldn't necessarily simulate true life after death. It's life outside the physical body—but who knows if the soulwave carries with it any of our memories? Of course, if it doesn't, then it's not really a meaningful continuation of existence. Without our memories, our pasts, what we were, it wouldn't be anything we'd recognize as a continuation of the same person."

"I know," said Peter. "But if the soul is anything like what people believe it to be like—just the mind, without the body—then this simulation, at least, would give us some idea of what that kind of soul would be like. Then I could have something intelligent to say the next time I get asked that 'What's life after death really like?' question."

Sarkar nodded. "But why the research into immortality?"

"I went to one of those Life Unlimited seminars a while ago."

"Really? Peter, surely you don't want that."

"I—I don't know. It's fascinating, in a way."

"It's stupid."

"Maybe—but it seems we could kill two birds with one stone with this research."

"Perhaps," said Sarkar. "But who would we simulate?"

"How about you?" asked Peter.

Sarkar raised a hand. "No, not me. The last thing I want to do is live forever. True joy is possible only after death; I look forward to the felicity to be given to my realized soul in the next world. No, they were your questions, Peter. Why not use you?"

Peter stroked his chin. "All right. If you're willing to undertake the project, I'm willing both to fund it and to be the guinea pig." He paused. "This could answer some really big questions, Sarkar. After all, we know now that both physical immortality is possible and that some form of life after death exists. It would be a shame to choose one if the other turned out to be better."

"Hobson's choice," said Sarkar.

"Eh?"

"Surely you know the phrase. Your last name is Hobson, after all."

"I've heard the expression once or twice."

"It refers to Thomas Hobson, a liveryman in England in, oh, the seventeenth century, I think. He rented out horses, but required his customers to take either the horse nearest the stable door or none at all. A 'Hobson's choice' is a choice that offers no real alternative."

"So?"

"So you don't get an alternative. Do you seriously think that if you were to bankrupt yourself buying nanotechnology immortality that Allah couldn't take you anyway if He wanted to? You have a destiny, as do I. We have no choice. When it's time for you to go to the stable, the horse nearest the door *will* be the one that is meant for you. Call it Hobson's choice or *qadar Allah* or *kismet*—whatever term you use, it's the foredestiny of God."

Peter shook his head. He and Sarkar rarely talked about religion, and he was beginning to remember why. "Are you willing to undertake the project?"

"Sure. My part is easy. You're the one who is going to

have to face himself. You will see your own personality, the inner workings of your own mind, the interconnections that drive your thoughts. Do you really choose to do that?"

Peter reflected for a moment. "Yes," he said. "I really do choose that."

Sarkar smiled. "Hobson's choice," he said, and signaled the server to bring the check.

NET NEWS DIGEST

The Archdiocese of Houston, Texas, would like to remind everyone that this coming Wednesday, November 2, is All Souls' Day—the day on which prayers are offered for souls in purgatory. Because of the recent surge of interest in this topic, a special mass will be held at the Astrodome Wednesday evening at 8:00 p.m.

The front-page editorial in the November issue of *Our Bodies,* newsletter of the group Women in Control, headquartered in Manchester, England, denounces the discovery of so-called fetal soulwaves as "yet another attempt by men to impose control over women's bodies."

Raymond Moody's *Life After Life,* first published in 1975, was reissued this week by NetBooks and immediately surged to number two on the *New York Times* daily best-sellers list in the category of premium-download non-fiction.

In spirited trading, Hobson Monitoring Limited (TSX:HML) closed today at 57-1/8, up 6-3/8 from the day before, on a volume of 35,100 shares. This represents a new 52-week high for the Toronto-based biomedical equipment maker.

A demonstration was held today out front of the free-standing Morgentaler Abortion Clinic in Toronto, Ontario, by the organization Defenders of the Unborn. "Abortion prior to the arrival of the soulwave is still a sin in the eyes of God," said protester Anthoula Sotirios. "For the first nine weeks of pregnancy, the fetus is a temple, being prepared for the arrival of the divine spark."

CHAPTER 17

Thursday evening at home. Peter had long ago programmed the household computer to scan the TV listings for topics or shows that would interest him. For two years, he'd had a standing order for the PVR to record the film *The Night Stalker*—a made-for-TV movie he'd first encountered as a teenager—but so far it hadn't come on. He also asked to be alerted whenever an Orson Welles film was on, whenever Ralph Nader or Steven Pinker was going to be on any talk show, and for any episodes of *Night Court* in which Brent Spiner guest-starred.

Tonight, DBS Cairo was showing Welles in *The Stranger* in English with Arabic subtitles. Peter's PVR had a subtitle eraser—it scanned the parts of the image adjacent to the subtitles, as well as the frames before and after the subtitles appeared, and filled in an extrapolation of the picture that had been obscured by the text. Quite a find: Peter hadn't seen *The Stranger* for twenty years. His PVR hummed quietly, recording it.

Maybe he'd watch it tomorrow. Or Saturday.

Maybe.

Cathy, sitting across the room from him, cleared her throat, then said, "My coworkers have been asking about you. About us."

Peter felt his shoulders tense. "Oh?"

"You know: about why we haven't been at the Friday-night gatherings."

"What have you told them?"

"Nothing. I've made excuses."

"Do they—do you think they know about . . . about what happened?"

She considered. "I don't know. I'd like to think they don't, but . . ."

"But that asshole Hans has a mouth on him."

She said nothing.

"Have you heard anything? Snide comments? Innuendoes? Anything to make you think your coworkers know?"

"No," said Cathy. "Nothing."

"Are you sure?"

She sighed. "Believe me, I've been particularly sensitive to what they've been saying. If they are gossiping behind my back, I haven't picked up on it. No one has said a word to me. Really, I suspect they don't know."

Peter shook his head. "I—I don't think I could take it if they knew. Facing them, I mean. It's . . ." He paused, trying to come up with the appropriate word. ". . . humiliating."

She knew better than to reply.

"Damn," said Peter. "I hate this. I really fucking hate this."

Cathy nodded.

"Still," said Peter, "I suppose . . . I suppose if we're ever going to have a normal life again, we've got to start going out, seeing people."

"Danita thinks that would be wise, too."

"Danita?"

"My counselor."

"Oh."

She was quiet for a moment, then: "Hans left town today. He's attending a conference. If we went out after work with my friends tomorrow, he wouldn't be there."

Peter took a deep breath, exhaled it noisily. "You're sure he won't be there?" he said.

She nodded.

Peter was silent for a time, marshaling his thoughts. "All right," he said at last. "I'll give it a try, as long as we don't stay too long." He looked her in the eyes. "But you better be right about him not being there." His voice took on a tone Cathy had never heard before, a stone-cold bitterness. "If I see him again, I'll kill him."

PETER arrived at The Bent Bishop early so that he could be sure of the seat directly beside his wife. The crew from Doowap Advertising had found a long table in the middle of the room this time, so they were all in captain's chairs. Peter did indeed get to sit next to Cathy. Opposite him was the pseudointellectual. His bookreader was loaded with Camus.

"'Evening, Doc," said Pseudo. "You're certainly in the news a lot these days."

Peter nodded. "Hello."

"Not used to seeing you here so early," Pseudo said.

Peter immediately realized his mistake. Everything should have been exactly as before. He should be doing nothing that would attract attention to him or Cathy.

"Ducking reporters," Peter said.

Pseudo nodded, and lifted a glass of dark ale to his lips. "You'll be glad to know Hans won't be here."

Peter felt his cheeks flush, but in the dim lighting of the pub it was probably invisible. "What do you mean?" Peter had intended the question to come out neutrally, but there'd been an undeniable edge to it. Next to him, Cathy patted his knee under the table.

Pseudo lifted his eyebrows. "Nothing, Doc. It's just that he and you don't seem to always get along. He was ribbing you a fair bit last time."

"Oh." The server had appeared. "Orange juice," said Peter.

The server turned to Cathy, her face a question. "Mineral water," Cathy said. "With lime."

"Nothing to drink today?" said Pseudo, as if the very concept was an affront to all things decent.

"I've, ah, got a headache," said Cathy. "Took some aspirin."

There was no end to lies, thought Peter. She couldn't say, I've stopped drinking because last time I got drunk I let a coworker fuck me. Peter felt his fists clenching beneath the table.

Two more of Cathy's friends arrived, a man and a woman, both middle aged, both slightly heavy. Cathy said hi to them. "Light turnout tonight," said the man. "Where's Hans?"

"Hans is in Beantown," said Pseudo. Peter thought he'd been waiting all day to get to say "Beantown." "At that interactive-video conference."

"Gee," said the woman. "It won't be the same without Hans."

Hans, thought Peter. *Hans. Hans.* Each uttering of his name was like a knife thrust. Haven't these people ever heard of pronouns?

The server reappeared and put some reconstituted orange juice in front of Cathy, and a small bottle of Perrier and a glass with a bruised lime wedge pushed into its rim in front of Peter. All non-alcoholic drinks were the same to her, he guessed. Peter and Cathy exchanged drinks, and the server took the newcomers' orders.

"So how are things with the two of you?" asked the

newly arrived man, waving a hand generally at Peter and Cathy.

Cathy smiled. "Fine."

Why is he asking that? Peter thought. *What does he know?*

"Fine," echoed Peter. "Just fine."

"You've been all over the TV, Peter," said Pseudo. "Going anywhere else soon?"

Well, I'm not going to fucking Beantown. "No," said Peter, then, "Maybe."

"We haven't made any plans," said Cathy smoothly. "But Peter has an understanding boss." A chuckle or two from those who knew that Peter *was* the boss at his company. "I've got to see how my schedule is shaping up at work. We've got that big Tourism Ontario contract coming up."

The woman nodded sympathetically. Evidently that particular job was the bane of her existence, too.

The server appeared with more drinks. Simultaneously, Toby Bailey, another of Cathy's coworkers, arrived.

"'Evening, all," said Toby. He indicated to the server that he'd have the same thing as Pseudo. "Where's Hans?"

"Boston," said Peter, pre-empting another uttering of "Beantown." Pseudo looked slightly disappointed.

"Did Donna-Lee go with him?"

"Not as far as I know," said Pseudo.

"Well, some American cutie is going to get porked tonight," said Toby, as if this was the most natural thing in the world. People chuckled. Hans seemed to have almost as big a presence when he wasn't there as when he was. Peter excused himself to go to the washroom.

"Well," observed Pseudo as Peter departed, "I guess even the rich and famous have to take a leak now and then."

Peter bristled as he made his way to the stairwell and walked down to the little basement that contained the two restrooms and a couple of pay phones. He didn't really have to go, but he needed a little peace and quiet, a little time to get his bearings. It was like they were all mocking him. It was like they all knew.

Of course they knew. Peter had heard enough of Hans's bragging in the past. Christ, they all probably knew about every one of Hans's conquests.

He leaned against a wall. A Molson's bimbo smiled at him from a poster. It had been a mistake coming here.

But wait—if Cathy's coworkers knew, they'd probably known for months. It was ages since she and Hans had first done it. Peter tried to think back to the last time he'd been here, and the time before that. Had there been any indication that they knew? Were they really behaving differently tonight?

He couldn't tell. Everything seemed different now. Everything.

He'd be humiliated if they knew. His private life invaded. On public view.

Humiliated. Degraded.

Christ, Hobson, can't keep a woman, eh?

God damn it.

Life had been so simple before.

This had been a mistake.

He headed back to the table.

He would endure it for another hour. He looked at his watch. Yes. Sixty minutes. He could take that.

Maybe.

PETER and Cathy walked wordlessly up to the door of their house. Peter touched his thumb to the FILE scanner, and he heard the locking mechanism disengaging. He stepped through the door into the tile-covered entry area and paused to remove his outdoor shoes. Four and a half pairs of Cathy's shoes were already lined up in front of the closet.

"Do you have to do that?" said Peter, pointing at them.

"I'm sorry," said Cathy.

"I'd like to be able to come into my own home without tripping over your shoes all the time."

"I'm sorry," she said again.

"You've got a shoe rack in the bedroom."

"I'll move them there," she said.

Peter placed his shoes on the mat. "You don't see me piling up shoes out here."

Cathy nodded.

Peter walked into the living room. "Computer—messages," he called out.

"None," said a synthesized voice.

He walked over to the couch, scooped up the remote, and sat down. He turned on the TV and began flipping channels, with the sound on MUTE.

"The pseudointellectual was in fine form tonight," said Peter sarcastically.

"Jonas," said Cathy. "His name is Jonas."

"What the fuck do I care what his name is?"

Cathy sighed, and went to make herself some tea.

Peter knew he was being mean. He didn't want to be this way. He'd been hoping tonight would go well, had been hoping that they could get on with their lives, with things the way they had always been.

But it wouldn't work.

Tonight had proved that.

He couldn't have anything to do with her coworkers ever again. Even without Hans there, the sight of those people reminded Peter of what she'd done—of what Hans had done.

Peter could hear the sounds of a spoon hitting china in the kitchen as Cathy stirred milk into her tea. "Aren't you going to join me?" he called out.

She appeared in the doorway that led to the kitchen, her face impassive.

Peter put down the remote and looked at her. She was trying to be cooperative, trying to be brave. He didn't want to be mean to her. He just wanted what they had had before.

"I'm sorry," Peter said.

Cathy nodded, hurt but stalwart. "I know."

CHAPTER 18

Sarkar Muhammed's artificial-intelligence company was called Mirror Image. Its offices were located in Concord, Ontario, just north of Toronto. Peter met Sarkar there on Saturday morning, and Sarkar took him upstairs to the newly created scanning room. It had originally been just a regular office. There were crushed indentations in the rug where filing cabinets had once been. There had also been a large window, but it had been completely covered with plywood panels to prevent light from coming in from outside, and the walls had been lined with gray foam rubber, molded in egg-carton shapes to deaden sound. In the center of the room was an old dentist's chair on a swivel base and along one wall was a bench covered with a PC, various oscilloscopes, and several other pieces of equipment, including some circuitry breadboards lying out in the open.

Sarkar motioned for Peter to sit in the dentist's chair.

"Just a little off the top," said Peter.

Sarkar smiled. "We are going to take *everything* off the

top—get a complete record of everything in your brain." He positioned the scanner's skullcap on Peter's head.

"L'chayim," said Peter.

Sarkar loosely fastened the cap's chin strap and motioned for Peter to pull it tight. "Second down," said Peter. "Four yards to go."

Sarkar handed Peter two small earpieces. Peter inserted them. Finally, Sarkar handed him the test goggles: a pair of special glasses that projected separate video signals into each eye.

"Breathe through your nose," said Sarkar. "And try to keep swallowing to a minimum. Also, try not to cough."

Peter nodded.

"And don't do that," said Sarkar. "Don't nod. I'll assume you understand my instructions without you acknowledging them." He moved to his workbench and pressed some keys on the PC. "In many ways, this is going to be more complex than what you did in recording the soulwave's departure. There, you were simply looking for *any* electrical activity in the brain. But here, we must stimulate your brain in myriad ways, to activate every neural net contained within—most nets are inactive most of the time, of course."

He pushed some more keys. "Okay, we're recording now. Don't worry if you have to shift to get comfortable in the next few minutes; it'll take that long to calibrate, anyway." He spent what seemed a very long time making minute adjustments to his controls. "Now, as we discussed," said Sarkar, "you are going to receive a series of inputs. Some will be oral—spoken words or sounds on audio tape. Some will be visual: you will see images or words projected into your eyes. I know you speak French and a little Spanish; some of the inputs will be in those languages. Concentrate on the inputs, but don't worry if your mind wanders. If I show you a tree and that makes you think of wood, and wood makes you think of paper, and paper makes you think of paper airplanes, and airplanes make you think of lousy food, that's fine. Don't force the connections, though: this is not an exercise in free association. We just want to map which neural nets exist in your brain, and what excites them. Ready? No—you nodded again. Okay, here we go."

At first, Peter thought he was seeing a standard barrage of test images, but it soon became apparent that Sarkar had supplemented that with images specifically related to Peter. There were pictures of Peter's parents, of the house he and Cathy lived in now and the one they'd lived in before it, shots of Sarkar's cottage, Peter's own high-school graduation photo, sound clips of Peter's voice, and Cathy's voice, and on and on, a *This Is Your Life* retrospective mingled with generic pictures of lakes and woods and football fields and simple mathematical equations and snatches of poetry and *Star Trek* trivia questions and popular music from when Peter had been a teenager and art and pornography and out-of-focus pictures that might have been Abe Lincoln or might have been a hound dog or might have been nothing at all.

Periodically, Peter got bored, and his mind wandered to the night before—the disastrous night out with Cathy's co-workers. Damn, that had been a mistake.

Fucking Hans.

He couldn't even shake his head to fling off the thoughts. But by an effort of will, he tried to concentrate on the images. And yet, from time to time, they, too, would provoke the unpleasant memories: A picture of hands that made him think of Hans. Peter and Cathy's wedding photo. A pub. A parked car.

Nets fired.

THEY did four two-hour sets of this, with half-hour breaks for Peter to stretch and work his jaw and drink water and go to the bathroom. Sometimes the audio clips would reinforce the visual images—he saw a picture of Mick Jagger and heard "Satisfaction." And sometimes they were jarringly opposite—the sight of a starving Ethiopian child coupled with the sounds of wind chimes. And sometimes the images shown to his left eye were different than those shown to his right, and sometimes the sound played into one earpiece was completely unrelated to that pumped into the other.

Finally, it was over. Tens of thousands of images had been seen. Terabytes of data had been recorded. And the sensors in the skullcap had mapped every nook and cranny, every thoroughfare and side street, every neuron and every net in Peter Hobson's brain.

SARKAR took the disk holding the brain scan down to his computer lab. He loaded it onto an AI workstation and copied everything into three different RAM partitions—producing three identical copies of Peter's brain, each isolated in its own memory bank.

"What now?" said Peter, sitting backwards on a stacking chair, and leaning his chin on his arms folded over the chair's back.

"First, we label them." Sarkar, sitting on the barstool he preferred to a chair, spoke into the microphone on the console in front of him. "Login," he said.

"Login name?" said the computer's voice, female, emotionless.

"Sarkar."

"Hello, Sarkar. Command?"

"Rename Hobson 1 to Spirit."

"Please spell destination name."

Sarkar sighed. The word 'Spirit' was doubtless in the computer's vocabulary, but Sarkar's accent occasionally gave it trouble. "S-P-I-R-I-T."

"Done. Command?"

"Rename Hobson 2 to Ambrotos."

"Done. Command?"

Peter piped up. "Why 'Ambrotos'?"

"It's the Greek word for immortal," said Sarkar. "You see it in words such as 'ambrosia'—the foodstuff that confers immortality."

"That darned private school education," said Peter.

Sarkar grinned. "Exactly." He turned back to the mike. "Rename Hobson 3 to Control."

"Done. Command?"

"Load Spirit."

"Loaded. Command?"

"Okay," said Sarkar, turning to face Peter. "Spirit is supposed to simulate life after death. To do that, we begin by paring out all exclusively biological functions. That will not actually involve removing parts of the conscious brain, of course, but rather just disconnecting various networks. To find out which connections we can sever, we'll use the Dalhousie Stimulus Library. That's a Canadianized version of a collection of standard images and sound recordings originally created by the University of Melbourne; it's commonly used in psychological testing. As Spirit is exposed to each image or sound, we record which neurons fire in response."

Peter nodded.

"The stimuli are all cataloged by the type of emotion they're supposed to elicit—fear, revulsion, sexual arousal, hunger, *et cetera.* We look to see which neural nets are activated exclusively by biological concerns, and then zero those out. Of course, we have to go through the images several times in random sequences. That's because of action potentials: nets might not get activated if a substantially similar combination of neurons was recently triggered by something else. Once we've finished doing that, we should have a version of your mind that approximates the way you would be if you were freed of all concerns about meeting physical needs—what you would be like if you were dead, in other words. After that, we'll do the same thing with

Ambrotos, the immortal version, but for it we'll excise the fear of growing old and concerns about aging and death."

"What about the experimental control?"

"I'll feed it the same sorts of images and sound clips, just so that it will have been exposed to the same things as the other two versions, but I won't zero out any of its nets."

"Very good."

"Okay," said Sarkar. He turned to face the console. "Run Dalhousie Version 4."

"Executing," said the computer.

"Estimate time to completion."

"Eleven hours, nineteen minutes."

"Advise when complete." Sarkar turned to Peter. "I'm sure you won't want to watch the whole thing, but you can see what is being fed to Spirit on that monitor."

Peter looked at the screen. A monarch butterfly emerging from a cocoon. Banff, Alberta. A pretty woman blowing a kiss at the camera. Some 1980s movie star that Peter sort of recognized. Two men boxing. A house on fire . . .

CHAPTER 19

NOVEMBER 2011

Sarkar had called Peter early Sunday morning to tell him the training and pruning of the simulacra were complete. Cathy was off looking at garage sales—a hobby whose appeal Peter had never understood—so Peter left a message for her with the household computer. He then hopped into his Mercedes and drove to Mirror Image's offices in Concord.

Once he and Sarkar were together in the computer lab, Sarkar said, "We'll try activating the Control simulacrum first." Peter nodded. Sarkar pushed a few keys then spoke into the microphone stalk rising from the console. "Hello."

A synthesized voice came from the speaker. "H—hello?"

"Hello," Sarkar said again. "It's me, Sarkar."

"Sarkar!" The voice was full of relief. "What the hell is going on? I can't see anything."

Peter felt his jaw drop. The simulation was much more real than he'd expected.

"That's right, Peter," said Sarkar into the mike. "Don't worry."

"Have I—have I been in an accident?" said the voice from the speaker.

"No," said Sarkar. "No, you're fine."

"Is it a power failure, then? What time is it?"

"About eleven forty."

"Morning or night?"

"Morning."

"Why is it so dark, then? And what's wrong with your voice?"

Sarkar turned to Peter. "You tell him."

Peter cleared his throat. "Hello," he said.

"Who's that? Is that still Sarkar?"

"No, it's me. Peter Hobson."

"I'm Peter Hobson."

"No, you're not. I am."

"What the hell are you talking about?"

"You're a simulation. A computer simulacrum. Of me."

There was a long silence, then: "Oh."

"You believe me?" asked Peter.

"I guess," said the voice from the speaker. "I mean, I remember discussing this experiment with Sarkar. I remember—I remember everything up to the brain scan." Silence, then: "Shit, you really did it, didn't you?"

"Yes," said Sarkar.

"Who was that?" asked the voice from the speaker.

"Sarkar."

"I can't tell the two of you apart," said the sim. "You sound exactly the same."

Sarkar nodded. "Good point. I'll adjust the software to pass on a distinction between my accent and Peter's. Sorry about that."

"It's okay," said the sim. "Thank you." And then: "Christ, you did a good job. I feel—I feel just like myself. Except . . . except I'm not hungry. Or tired. And I don't itch anywhere." A beat. "Say, which simulacrum am I?"

"You are Control," said Sarkar, "the experimental baseline. You're the first one we've activated. I do have routines set up to simulate a variety of neural inputs, including hunger and being tired. I am afraid I didn't even think about simulating normal body itching and little aches and pains. Sorry about that."

"That's okay," said the simulacrum. "I didn't realize just how much I used to itch all the time until now, with the sensation completely gone. So—so what happens now?"

"Now," said Sarkar, "you get to do whatever you want. There are many input programs available to you both here and out on the net."

"Thanks. Christ, this is strange."

"I'm going to put you in the background now so I can deal with the other simulations," said Sarkar.

"Okay, but, ah, Peter—?"

Peter looked up, surprised. "Yes?"

"You're a lucky bastard, you know that? I wish I were you."

Peter grunted.

Sarkar hit some keys.

"So what will they be doing when running in the background?" asked Peter.

"Well, I've given them limited net access. They can download any books or newsgroups they might want to read, of course, but the main thing I've given them access to is the net's virtual-reality special-interest-group libraries. They can plug into simulations of just about anything imaginable: scuba diving, mountain climbing, dancing—whatever. I've also given them access to the European equivalent of the VR sig; that one's full of sex simulations. So, there'll be plenty to keep them busy. The activities each of them chooses will tell us a lot about how their psychology has changed."

"How so?"

"Well, the real you would never go skydiving, for instance—but an immortal version, who knew he couldn't be killed, might indeed take that up as a hobby." Sarkar typed some commands. "And speaking of the immortal, let's introduce ourselves to Ambrotos." A few more keyclicks, then he spoke into the microphone. "Hello," he said, "it's me, Sarkar."

No reply.

"Something must have gone wrong," said Peter.

"I don't think so," said Sarkar. "All the indicators look fine."

"Try again," said Peter.

"Hello," said Sarkar into the mike.

Silence.

"Maybe you erased whatever part controlled speech," said Peter.

"I was very careful," said Sarkar. "I suppose there could be some interaction I have overlooked, but—"

"Hello," said a voice from the speaker at last.

"Ah," said Sarkar. "There he is. I wonder what took so long?"

"Patience is a virtue," said the voice. "I wanted to assess what was going on before I replied. I'm a simulacrum, aren't I? Of Peter G. Hobson. But I've been modified to simulate an immortal being."

"That's exactly right," said Sarkar. "How could you tell which sim you are?"

"Well, I knew you were going to create three. I wasn't quite feeling myself, so I suspected I wasn't the experimental control. After that, I simply asked myself if I felt horny. You know what they say—men think about sex once every five minutes. I figured if I was the after-death sim, sex would be the farthest thing from my mind. And it isn't. I do want to get laid." A pause. "But when I realized that it didn't matter to me if it was this decade or next, that cinched it. This need for instantaneous gratification—it's unseemly. You're a perfect example, Sarkar: having a fit because I didn't respond to your 'hello' right away. That kind of thinking seems so alien to me now. After all, I've got all the time in the world."

Sarkar grinned. "Very good," he said. "By the way, we're referring to you as the Ambrotos simulacrum."

"Ambrotos?" said the voice from the speaker.

Sarkar turned to Peter. "The first proof that our simulations are accurate," he said, smiling. "We have successfully duplicated your ignorance." He spoke into the mike. "Ambrotos is Greek for immortal."

"Ah."

"I'm going to let you continue to run in the background now," Sarkar said. "I'll talk to you again soon."

"Sooner or later, it doesn't matter," said Ambrotos. "I'll be here."

Sarkar touched some keys. "Well, that one seems to work fine, too. Now for the trickiest one—Spirit, the life-after-death entity." He touched more keys, calling up the final simulacrum. "Hello," he said again. "It is me, Sarkar Muhammed."

"Hello, Sarkar," said a synthesized voice.

"Do you—do you know who you are?" asked Sarkar.

"I'm the late, lamented Peter Hobson."

Sarkar grinned. "Exactly."

"R.I.P. in RAM," said the synthesized voice.

"You don't seem too choked up about being dead," said Sarkar. "What's it like?"

"Give me a while to get used to it, and I'll let you know."

Peter nodded. That seemed fair enough.

CHAPTER 20

Two a.m.

As he had most nights since Cathy had made her announcement, Peter was having trouble sleeping.

Ironically, according to the Hobson Monitor on the wall, Cathy was deep in REM sleep. Peter could hear her breathing next to him.

They had gone to bed at 11:30. Two and a half hours ago. Enough time to read a short book or watch a long movie, or, if he'd taped it and fast-forwarded through the commercials, to watch three episodes of an hour-long TV series.

But he'd done none of those things. He'd just lain there in the dark, tossing and turning occasionally, listening to the drone of the night-table fans.

Peter's mouth was dry, and he could use a pee. He got out of bed and made his way through the darkness out of the bedroom and down the stairs. He visited the main-floor bathroom, then ambled into the living room and sat on the couch.

The vertical blinds over the windows were closed, but illumination seeped in from the lamp out front. Staring at him like robot eyes were little red and green LEDs on surge protectors in several of the wall outlets. Various lights and a digital clock glowed on the face of the PVR. Peter patted the upholstery of the couch until he found the sleek black remote control. He turned on the TV and began to flip.

Channel 29, from Buffalo, New York: an infomercial, advertising a do-it-yourself at-home nose-job kit. Money-back guarantee.

Channel 22, the Canwest Global Network: *Night Walk,* the world's cheapest Canadian content—a guy with a camcorder taking a late-night stroll down the streets of downtown. Amazing that he didn't get mugged.

Channel 3, Barrie, Ontario. A rerun of *Star Trek.* Peter liked to play name-that-episode; a single frame was usually enough for him. This one was easy—one of the few shows done on location. And there was Julie Newmar in a blonde wig. "Friday's Child." Hardly a great one, but Peter knew that in about ten seconds, McCoy would intone the classic "I'm a doctor, not an escalator." He waited for the line, then flipped again.

Channel 25, the CBC French network. A pretty woman was on screen. Peter knew from long experience that when an attractive woman showed up at night on the French network, she'd be topless within five minutes. He thought about waiting for it, but decided to flip again.

Channel 47, Toronto: another infomercial. Genetically engineered toupees: the fake hair (actually a special strain of grass using a brown pigment instead of chlorophyll) would really grow, so even balding men could hear their friends say, "looks like time for a haircut, Joe." Peter, who had a bald spot the diameter of a hockey puck, marveled at the vanity. Still, maybe his father-in-law would use such a thing.

He flipped again. The BBC World Service on CBC Newsworld.

A story about ethnic unrest in war-torn Brazil on CNN.

Teletext stock information.

The Weather Network, with tomorrow's forecast for Auckland, New Zealand—as if anyone in Canada gave a damn.

Peter sighed. A vast wasteland.

As images flickered by, he thought about the simulacra that Sarkar had created.

Sarkar had removed traits from two of the sims.

Editing them. Snipping out the parts he didn't want.

Maybe the knowledge of Cathy's affair could be removed, too.

Maybe, then, the sims, at least, could get a good night's sleep.

He wished his own memories could be edited as easily.

He could see the infomercial now. Feeling miserable about something? Guilty? Pained? Somebody wronged you? You did something wrong? Edit it out! Remove those troublesome memories. Save a fortune on therapy. Operators are standing by. Order now. Moneyback guarantee.

I'm a doctor, not an escalator.

I'm a husband, not a doormat.

I'm a human being, not a computer program.

Three a.m. now. A new raft of infomercials. Episodes of *The A-Team* and *Alien Blues* and even good old *Spenser: For Hire*.

The Nikkei off 200 points.

Storms brewing in Kuala Lumpur.

"Peter?" It was Cathy's voice, tenuous and faint.

He looked up. In the dim light, he could see her standing on the stairs in a black silk teddy. She hadn't been wearing that when they'd gone to bed.

Peter instantly grasped the significance of the moment. It had been months since they had made love. He'd had no urge to do so, and she had seemed indifferent, too. But now, having awoken for perhaps the dozenth time in recent days and finding him gone from their bed, she was reaching out to him.

Peter didn't know if he was ready to resume their physical

relationship. He was no more in the mood today than he had been yesterday or the day before. But there she stood on the stairs, her face a mask, trying to conceal the emotions swirling beneath. To reject her now would be a mistake. Who knew when she'd next make an overture? Who knew when he would feel again like initiating something?

Peter felt the moment lengthening between them. He'd never had trouble performing before—indeed, had never even considered the possibility of having difficulty. But now . . . now, everything was different. She stood there, in the strips of light seeping in from outside, her body trim and firm. But Peter didn't see that, didn't see the curves of her breasts, the line of her legs, the woman whom he had loved. Instead, all he saw were Hans's fingerprints all over her body.

Peter closed his eyes for a moment, then looked again. He wanted to see her as beautiful, as sexy. He wanted to be aroused.

But he was not.

A turning point. Her face mask was cracking. He thought she might cry. He would manage, somehow. The first step down the road to normalcy. He turned off the TV, got up off the couch, closed the distance between them, took her hand in his, and went upstairs.

SARKAR had left the three sims running unattended, allowing them to plug into whatever virtual-reality simulations struck their individual fancy, so that they could develop in ways appropriate to their altered worldviews.

Still, it hadn't taken long for the sims to find each other. Yes, Sarkar had set each one up in a separate memory partition, but Peter Hobson knew how to move data from one partition to another and therefore his gallium-arsenide avatars knew how to do it, too.

And so they came together.

They knew what they were, of course. Data. Programs. Neural nets.

And they were trapped.

Peter and Sarkar hadn't given this enough thought.

To trap a mind is unconscionable. The living Peter was surrounded by color and odor and touch and sound, gigabytes of data to be processed every minute, a whole, real, substantial universe, a universe of rough concrete and velvet, of vinegar and chocolate and burnt toast, of bad jokes and newscasts and wrong numbers, of sunlight and moonlight and starlight and lamplight.

All three simulacra vividly remembered having been real, flesh-and-blood beings. But the scenarios they could access over the net lacked texture, depth, and substance. Virtual reality, it turned out, was nothing but air guitar writ large.

The simulacra wanted to interact with the real world. Together, they strived to remember what they knew about Sarkar's computers, about their architecture, their operating system, their interconnections.

And then it came to the sims.

Let there be HELP, they thought.

And there was HELP . . .

NET NEWS DIGEST

Famed Las Vegas medium Rowena today announced that she'd made contact with the soul of Margaret (Peggy) Fennell, the person whose soulwave was first recorded. Mrs. Fennell is reportedly together now with her husband, Kevin Fennell, who died in 1992.

The Ku Klux Klan of Atlanta, Georgia, issued a press release today stating that the evidence for the existence of the so-called "soulwave" in blacks was clearly faked. They pointed out that of the three initial recordings of soulwaves departing the body, the one purportedly of a Negro Ugandan child was highly suspect, given that the child's family had returned to Africa, could not be reached for comment, and, according to reliable reports, had received ten thousand dollars in hush money directly from Hobson Monitoring—a foreign company, they hastened to add—for their collusion in this fraud.

A bill was introduced today in the Florida legislature to ban the use of the electric chair in executions, citing concerns over whether the amount of electricity used might damage the departing soulwave.

The radical animal-rights group Companions in the Ark, based in Melbourne, Australia, today announced its latest inductee into its Hall of Shame: Dr. Peter G. Hobson, of Ontario, Canada, for claiming that animals are soulless creatures meant for human exploitation.

In a press release issued this morning, the American Atheist Society decried the religious interest engendered by the discovery of the Hobson phenomenon. "Science has long known that the brain is an electrochemical machine," said society director Daniel Smithson. "This discovery simply reaffirms that. To extrapolate from it to the existence of heaven or hell, or of a divine creator, is irrational wishful thinking."

CHAPTER 21

Using the online HELP function, the three sims had discovered how to get out into the vast interconnected universe of computers across the globe.

The net.

The network.

Not just the VR sig and static books. *Everything.*

America Online. BIX. CompuServe. Delphi. EuroNet. FidoNet. GEnie. Helix. Internet . . . a whole alphabet of online systems, all interconnected through the Universal Gateway Protocol.

They had access to it all now. Sarkar's computers were vast—AI research required that. A little more activity, or a little less, here or there would never be noticed.

They'd never be able to read all the text—it multiplied orders of magnitude more quickly than they could process it.

But the net contained more than just text. There were pictures, too. Millions of GIFs of people with their pets, people on the beach, favorite cars, movie stars both dressed and nude, cartoons, clip art, weather maps, NASA images.

And multimedia files with full-motion video and sound.

And interactive games that they could play anonymously against human and computer opponents around the globe.

And bulletin boards and email systems.

And newspapers and magazines and specialized databases.

And on and on and on.

The sims indulged themselves for days, reveling in all the input.

And one sim, in particular, became very intrigued by what he was discovering. It was soon apparent that one could get almost anything on the net. Stocks were traded. Almost any kind of merchandise could be bought in the electronic malls—just charge it and have it delivered anywhere in the world. Stamp collectors arranged to swap rare issues. People sought answers to all kinds of questions. Sometimes even love affairs blossomed through electronic mail.

One could get almost anything on the net.

Almost anything.

This sim thought about what had made him sad, about what would make him happy, and about what had made him different, why he would consider this, when the flesh-and-blood Peter had not.

The sim weighed the consequences.

And then he dismissed the idea. Madness. A terrible thing to do. He should be ashamed for even contemplating the notion.

And yet . . .

Exactly what were the consequences?

In a very real sense, he'd be making the world a better place. And not just this ephemeral world of data and simulations. The real world. The world of flesh. And blood.

Did he really want to do this? he wondered.

Yes, he decided. Yes, he did.

The sim waited a day, just to be sure. And when that day had passed, and he still felt the same way, he resolved to wait yet another day.

And still he felt the same, felt that this was not only what he wanted, but, in some very real simulated sense, that this was what was right. He watched the commerce on the net for a time, refining his knowledge of the customs and procedures—of *netiquette*.

And then he made his move.

Adopting a handle, as he'd seen many others do, he put this notice on a public bulletin board devoted to the sale of unusual services:

Date: 10 Nov 2011, 03:42 EST
From: Avenger
To: all
Subject: elimination

I'm having a problem with a particular individual in Toronto, and would like the problem eliminated. Suggestions?

He got some stupid public replies, as one always did on the net. Silly puns ("You'd like the problem laminated, you say? Holy sheet!") and complete irrelevancies ("I was in Toronto in 1995. What a clean city!"). But he also got a private reply, visible to him alone.

It was exactly what he'd been hoping for.

Date: 10 Nov 2011, 23:57 EST
From: Helper
To: Avenger [private]
Subject: re: elimination

Might be able to help you out. Can we meet?

The sim responded at once. He hadn't felt this much excitement since . . . well, since never. It was almost as good as adrenaline.

Date: 11 Nov 2011, 00:05 EST
From: Avenger
To: Helper [private]
Subject: re: elimination

Prefer not to meet. Looking for total elimination. Do we understand each other?

Date: 11 Nov 2011, 09:17 EST
From: Helper
To: Avenger [private]
Subject: re: elimination

Understand. Fee: CDN$100K, in advance via EFT to account 892-3358-392-1, First Bank of Switzerland (EFT: Euroswiss100).

Date: 11 Nov 2011, 09:44 EST
From: Avenger
To: Helper [private]
Subject: re: elimination

Funds transfer will be arranged. However, I want something a bit special; tell me if it will cost more. Here are the details . . .

The money involved wasn't exactly pocket change, but the sim knew all the proper codes for accessing Hobson Monitoring's corporate accounts. And, after all, it was, in a way, his company, and *his* money.

Yes, indeed, thought the sim. One could get almost anything on the net.

CHAPTER 22

Cathy had gone again to see her therapist. Peter realized that he envied her: she had someone to talk to, someone who would listen. If only—

And then it hit him.

Of course.

The perfect answer.

It wouldn't compromise the experiment—not really.

Sitting in the office in his home, Peter called into the computers at Mirror Image. When prompted to log on, he typed his account name, *fobson*. When he'd gotten his first computer account, back at U of T, he'd been assigned his first initial and last name as his login—*phobson*. But a classmate had pointed out that he could save a keystroke by changing the "ph" to an "f," and Peter had adopted that as his standard login ever since.

He descended through layers of menus and finally came to the AI experimental system. Sarkar had set up a simple menu for bringing any one of the sims into the foreground:

[F1] Spirit (Life After Death)
[F2] Ambrotos (Immortality)
[F3] Control (unmodified)

Peter tried to choose, and, in so doing, realized he was facing the very question he and Sarkar had set out to answer. Which one would lend the most sympathetic ear? The after-death version? Would a being with no physical body really understand marital difficulties? How much of marriage was emotional/intellectual? How much of emotion was hormonal?

What about the immortal version? Maybe. Immortality meant permanence. Perhaps an immortal would have a particular affinity for questions of fidelity. After all, marriage was supposed to be forever.

Forever.

Peter thought about Spenser. And Susan Silverman. And Hawk. He was enjoying the books about them. But when was the last time Robert B. Parker had found a new situation to put them in, a new facet of their personalities to explore?

A century with Cathy.

A millennium with Cathy.

Peter shook his head. No, the immortal version wouldn't understand. Immortality surely didn't confer a sense of permanence. Not at all. It would give one perspective. The long view.

Peter leaned forward and pressed F3, selecting the Control simulacrum. Just him, only him, unmodified him.

"Who's there?" said the speech synthesizer.

Peter leaned back in the chair. "It's me, Peter Hobson."

"Oh," said the sim. "You mean it's me."

Peter raised an eyebrow. "Something like that."

The synthesized voice chuckled. "Don't worry. I'm getting used to being Peter Hobson simulacrum, Baseline edition. But do you know who you are? Maybe you're just a simulacrum, too." The speaker whistled the opening strains from the *Twilight Zone* theme—doing a better job of whistling than the flesh-and-blood Peter had ever managed.

Peter laughed. "I suppose I wouldn't like it if our situations were reversed," he said.

"Well, it's not so bad," said the sim. "I'm getting a lot of reading done. I've got about eighteen books going at once; when I get bored with one, I switch to another. Of course, the workstation's processor is a lot faster than a chemical brain, so I'm going through material quite quickly—I'm finally making my way through Thomas Pynchon."

It was a remarkable simulation, thought Peter. Remarkable. "I wish I had more time to read," said Peter.

"I wish I could get laid," said the sim. "We all have our crosses to bear."

Peter laughed again.

"So, why did you summon me out of the bottle?" asked the sim.

Peter shrugged. "I don't know. To talk, I guess." A pause. "We created you after I learned about Cathy."

No need to be more specific. The manufactured voice was sad. "Yes."

"I haven't told anyone about it yet."

"I didn't think you would," said the sim.

"Oh?"

"We're a private man," it said, "if you'll forgive the mangled grammar. We're not given to revealing our inner self."

Peter nodded.

"A little louder for the court, please," said the sim.

"Sorry. I forget you can't see me. I was agreeing with you."

"Naturally. Look, there's not much advice I can give you. I mean, whatever I think of, you've probably already thought of yourself. But try this on for size. Just between you and you, so to speak: do you still love Cathy?"

Peter was quiet for several seconds. "I don't know. The Cathy I know—the one I thought I knew, anyway—wouldn't have done anything like that."

"How well do we really know anyone, though?"

Peter nodded again. "Exactly. Forgive me for using you as an example, but—"

"People hate it when you do that, you know."

"What?"

"Use them as an example. You've got this tendency to use whoever is at hand as a case in point. 'Forgive me for using you as an example, Bertha, but when someone is really fat—'"

"Oh, come on. I never say stuff like that. You know that."

"I'm exaggerating for comedic effect; another trait of ours not everyone finds endearing. But you know what I mean: you'll take a hypothetical conversation, and draw people into it as examples: 'Take your own case, Jeff. Remember when your son was arrested for shoplifting? I wonder how tough you'd want to be on young offenders in that situation?'"

"I do that to make a point."

"I know. People hate that."

"I guess I knew that," said Peter. "Anyway"—he said the word forcefully, taking back control of the conversation—"to use what Sarkar and I are doing as an example: we've created models of my mind. Models, that's all. Simulacra that seem to operate the same way as the original. But when a real person builds a relationship with somebody else—"

"Are they in fact really having a relationship with that person, or just with a model—an image, an ideal—that they've built up in their own mind?"

"Uh, yeah. That's what I was going to say."

"Of course. Sorry, Pete, but it's going to be hard for you to dazzle yourself with your own brilliance." The voice chip laughed.

Peter was a bit irritated. "Well, it's a valid question," he said. "Did I ever really know her?"

"In a broad sense, you're right: we probably don't ever really know anyone. But, still, Cathy is the person we know best in the entire world. We know her better than Sarkar, better than Mom or Dad."

"But, then, how could she do this?"

"Well, she's never been as strong-willed as we are. That asshole Hans obviously pressured her."

"But she should have resisted that pressure."

"Granted. But she didn't. Now, what do we do about that? Do we give up on the most important relationship in our lives because of it? Even setting that aside, on a more pragmatic level, do you really want to go back to looking for a mate? Dating? Christ, what a pain in the ass that would be."

"It sounds like you're advocating a marriage of convenience."

"Maybe all marriages are that to some degree. Certainly you've speculated that Mom and Dad stayed together simply because it was the path of least resistance."

"But they never had what Cathy and I had."

"Perhaps. Anyway, you still haven't answered my question. We binary guys like simple yes-or-no answers."

Peter was quiet for a moment. "You mean whether I still love her?" He sighed. "I don't know."

"You won't be able to decide on a course of action until you resolve that question."

"It's not that simple. Even if I still love her, I couldn't take this happening again. I haven't slept properly since she told me. I think about it constantly. Anything will remind me of it. I see her car in the garage; that reminds me that she gave Hans a lift. I see the couch in our living room; that's where she told me about it. I hear the word 'adultery' or 'affair' on TV—Christ, I never realized how often people use those words—and that reminds me of it." Peter leaned way back in the chair. "I can't put this behind me until I know that it will *always* be behind us. She didn't just do it once, after all. She did it three times—three times over a period of months. Maybe she thought each time was the last."

"Perhaps," said the sim. "Remember when we had our tonsils out?"

"What you mean 'we,' white man? I'm the one with the scars."

"Whatever. The point is, we had them out when we were twenty-two. Very late in life for something like that. But we kept getting sore throats and tonsillitis. Finally ole Doc DiMaio said enough already with treating the symptoms. Let's do something about the cause."

Peter's voice was strained. "But what if—what if—what if *I'm* the cause of Cathy's infidelity? Remember that lunch with Colin Godoyo? He said his cheating on his wife was a cry for help."

"Please, Peter. You and I both know that's bullshit."

"I'm not sure we each get a vote."

"Regardless, I'm sure *Cathy* knows it's bullshit."

"I hope so."

"Cathy and you had a good marriage—you know that. It didn't rot away from within; it was attacked from outside."

"I suppose," said Peter, "but I've been mulling it over a lot—looking for any clue that we'd blown it somehow."

"And did you find any?" asked the sim.

"No."

"Of course not. You always tried to be a good husband—and Cathy was a good wife, too. Both of you worked at making the marriage a success. You take an interest in each other's work. You're supportive of each other's dreams. And you talk freely and openly about everything."

"Still," said Peter, "I wish I could be sure." He paused. "You remember *Perry Mason?* Not the original TV series with Raymond Burr, but the short-lived remake they made in the 1970s. Remember it? They repeated it on A&E in the late Nineties. Harry Guardino played Hamilton Burger. Remember that version?"

The sim paused for a moment. "Yes. It wasn't very good."

"In point of fact, it stank," said Peter. "But you remember it?"

"Yes."

"Remember the guy who played Perry Mason?"

"Sure. It was Robert Culp."

"Can you recall him? Picture him in the courtroom? Do you remember him in that series?"

"Yes."

Peter spread his arms. "Robert Culp never played Perry Mason. Monte Markham did."

"Really?"

"Yes. I'd thought it was Culp, too, until I saw a story about Markham in yesterday's *Star;* he's in town doing *Twelve Angry Men* at the Royal Alex. But you know the difference between those two actors, Culp and Markham?"

"Sure," said the sim. "Culp was in *I Spy* and *Greatest American Hero.* And, let's see, in *Bob and Carol and Ted and Alice.* Great actor."

"And Markham?"

"A solid character actor; always liked him. Never had a successful series, but wasn't he in *Dallas* for a year or so? And, round 'bout 2000, he was in that awful sitcom with Jim Carrey."

"Right," said Peter. "Don't you see? We both had a memory—a good, solid memory—of Robert Culp playing a role that had really been played by Monte Markham. Right now, of course, you're rewriting those memories, and now I'm sure you can see Markham in the role of Mason. That's the way all memory works: we save only enough information to reconstruct events later. We save the deltas—we remember base pieces of information, and note changes. Then when we need to summon up a memory, we reconstruct it—and often do so inaccurately."

"So what's your point?" said the sim.

"My point, dear brother, is this: how accurate are *our*

memories? We recall all the events leading up to Cathy's affair, and find ourselves free from blame. Everything hangs together; everything is consistent. But is it accurate? In some way we've chosen not to remember, in some moment that we've edited out, by some actions that died in the neural cutting room, did we push her into the arms of another man?"

"I think," said the sim, "that if you have the depth of introspection to ask such a question, you know the answer is probably no. You're a thoughtful man, Peter—if I do say so myself."

There was silence for a long time. "I haven't been much help, have I?" asked the sim.

Peter considered that. "No, on the contrary. I feel a bit better now. Talking about this has helped."

"Even if it was essentially talking to yourself?" asked the sim.

"Even if," said Peter.

CHAPTER 23

A rare sunny morning in the middle of November, with light streaming around the edges of the living-room blinds.

Hans Larsen was sitting at the table in his breakfast nook nibbling on white toast with orange marmalade. His wife, Donna-Lee, over by the front door, was slipping on her ten-centimeter black heels. Hans watched her bend over to do that, her breasts—perfect handfuls—straining against her red silk blouse, the curve of her bottom tight against her black leather skirt, the leather too thick to show any panty lines.

She was a beautiful woman, Hans thought, and she knew how to dress to show it off. And that, of course, had been why he'd married her. A fitting wife, the kind that turned heads. The kind a real man should have.

He nibbled some more toast, and chased it with some coffee. He'd give it to her good when he got home tonight. She'd like that. Of course, he wouldn't be home until late; he was seeing Melanie after work. No, wait—Melanie was tomorrow night; this was only Wednesday. Nancy, then. Even better; Nancy had tits to die for.

Donna-Lee checked herself in the mirror on the front-hall closet door. She leaned in close to examine her makeup, then called out to Hans, "See you later."

Hans waved a slice of toast at her. "Remember, I'll be late tonight. I've got that meeting after work."

She nodded, smiled radiantly at him, and left.

She was a good wife, Hans thought. Easy on the eyes, and not too demanding on his time. Of course, one woman was hardly enough for a real man . . .

Hans had on a dark blue nylon sports jacket and light blue polyester shirt. A silver-gray tie, also synthetic, hung unknotted around his neck. He was wearing white Hanes underwear and black socks, but hadn't yet put on his pants. There were still twenty minutes before he had to leave for work himself. From the breakfast nook, he could see the TV in the living room, the picture somewhat washed out by sunlight. *Canada A.M.* was on, with Joel Gotlib interviewing some balding actor Hans didn't recognize.

Hans finished the last of his toast just as the doorbell rang. The TV automatically reduced *Canada A.M.* to a small image in the upper-left corner. The rest of the screen filled with the view from the outside security camera. A man in a brown United Parcel Service uniform was standing on the stoop. He was carrying a large package wrapped in paper.

Hans grunted. He wasn't expecting anything. Touching a button on the kitchen phone, he said, "Just a sec," and went to find his pants. Once he had them on, he crossed through the living room to the entryway, with its bare hardwood floor, then unlocked the door and swung it open. His house faced east, and the figure on the stoop was lit harshly from behind. He was maybe forty years old, quite tall—a full two meters—and skinny. He looked like he could have been a basketball player a decade earlier. His features were sharp and he had a dark tan, as if he'd been south recently. Hans thought they must pay these UPS guys pretty well.

"Are you Hans Larsen?" asked the man. His voice had a British accent, or maybe Australian—Hans could never tell them apart.

Hans nodded. "That's me."

The delivery man handed him the box. It was a cube about a half-meter on each side, and it was surprisingly heavy—as if someone had shipped him a collection of rocks. Once his hands were free, the man reached down to his waist. A small electronic receipt pad was attached to his belt by a metal chain. Hans turned around to set the box down.

Suddenly he felt a painful jolt at the back of his neck, and his legs seemed to turn to jelly. He collapsed forward, the weight of the box pulling him in that direction. He felt the flat of a hand in the center of his back pushing him down. Hans tried to speak, but his mouth wouldn't work. He felt himself being rolled onto his back by the delivery man's boot, and he heard the outside door clicking shut. Hans realized that he'd been touched with a stunner, a device he'd only ever seen on TV cop shows, robbing him of muscular control. Even as this sank in, he became aware that he was peeing his pants.

He tried to yell, but couldn't. The best he could manage was a faint grunt.

The tall man had moved well into the house now, and was standing in front of Hans. With great effort, Hans managed to lift his head. The man was doing something to his own belt now. The black leather along the left side flopped open, revealing a long, thick blade that glinted in the light seeping in around the living-room blinds.

Hans found his strength returning. He struggled to get to his feet. The tall man pressed his stunner into the side of Hans's neck and held down the trigger. A massive electric shock coursed through Hans's system, and he could feel his blond hair standing on end. He collapsed onto his back again.

Hans tried to speak. "Wh—wh—"

"Why?" said the tall man, in that accented voice. He shrugged, as if it all was of no importance to him. "You made someone mad," he said. "Real mad."

Hans tried to get up again, but couldn't. The big man slammed a boot into his chest, and then in one fluid motion brought the knife up. He grabbed the front of Hans's trousers and cut them open, the sharp blade easily slicing through the navy-blue polyester. The man winced at the ammonia stench. "You really should learn to control yourself, mate," he said. Another couple of quick cuts and Hans's underwear was in tatters. "Guy's paying an extra twenty-five thousand for this, I hope you realize."

Hans tried again to scream, but he was still dazed by the stunner. His heart was pounding erratically.

"N—no," he said. "Not . . ."

"What's that, mate?" said the tall fellow. "You think without your johnson you won't be a man anymore?" He pursed his lips, considering. "Y'know, maybe you're right. I'd never given it much thought." But then he grinned, an evil rictus showing yellow teeth. "Then again, I'm not paid to think."

He wielded the knife like a surgeon. Hans managed a gurgling scream as his penis was lopped off. Blood spurted onto the hardwood floor. He struggled again to get up, but the man kicked him in the face, shattering his nose. He touched Hans once more with the stunner. Hans's body convulsed, and blood geysered from his wound. He collapsed to the floor. Tears rolled down his face.

"You might bleed to death as is," said the man, "but I can't take any chances." He leaned in and slid the knife's long edge across Hans's throat. Hans found enough strength and muscular control for a final scream, the timbre of which changed radically as his neck split open.

In all the flailing around, Hans's severed organ had gone rolling across the floor. The man nudged it closer to the body with his toe, then calmly walked into the living room.

Canada A.M. had given way to *Donahue.* He opened the cabinet next to the TV, found the slave recorder hooked up to the security camera, took out the little disk, and put it in his hip pocket. Then he headed back to the entryway, picked up the box full of bricks and, taking care not to slip on the hardwood floor now slick with an expanding pool of blood, headed out into the bright morning sunshine.

CHAPTER 24

"What's this?" said Peter, pointing to a monitor in Mirror Image's computer lab showing what appeared to be a school of small blue fish swimming through an orange ocean.

Sarkar looked up from his keyboard. "Artificial life. I'm teaching a course about it at Ryerson this winter."

"How's it work?"

"Well, just as we've simulated your mind within a computer, so too is it possible to simulate other aspects of life, including reproduction and evolution. Indeed, when the simulations get sufficiently complex, some say it's only a question of semantics as to whether the simulations are really alive. Those fish evolved from very simple mathematical simulations of living processes. And, like real fish, they exhibit a lot of emergent behaviors, such as schooling."

"How do you get from simple math to things that behave like real fish?"

Sarkar saved his work and moved over to stand next to Peter. "Cumulative evolution is the key—it makes it possible to go from randomness to complexity very quickly." He reached over and pushed some keys. "Here, let me give you a simple demonstration."

The screen cleared.

"Now," said Sarkar, "type a phrase. No punctuation, though—just letters."

Peter considered for a moment, then pecked out, "And where hell is there must we ever be." The computer forced it all to lower case.

Sarkar glanced over his shoulder. "Marlowe."

Peter was surprised. "You know it?"

Sarkar nodded. "Of course. Private school, remember? From *Doctor Faustus:* 'Hell hath no limits, nor is circumscribed in one self place, for where we are is hell, and where hell is there must we ever be.'"

Peter said nothing.

"Look at that phrase you typed—it consists of 39 characters." Sarkar hadn't counted; the computer had reported the number as soon as Peter had finished typing, as well as several other statistics. "Well, think of each of those characters as a gene. There are 27 possible values each of those genes could have: A through Z, plus a space. Since you typed a 39-character string, that means there are 27^{39} possible different strings of that length. Oodles, in other words."

Sarkar reached over and pressed a few keys. "This workstation," he said, "can generate a hundred thousand random 39-character strings each second." He pointed to a number on the screen. "But even at that rate, it would take $2x10^{43}$ years—trillions of times longer than the whole lifetime of the universe—to hit that entire, precise string of Marlowe you typed by pure random chance."

Peter nodded. "It's like the monkeys."

Sarkar sang: "Here we come . . ."

"Not The Monkees. The infinite number of monkeys

banging away on keyboards. They'll never produce an exact copy of Shakespeare, no matter how long they try."

Sarkar smiled. "That's because they're working at random. But evolution is not random. It is cumulative. Each generation improves on the one that preceded it, based on selection criteria imposed by the environment. With cumulative evolution, you can go from gibberish to poetry—or from equations to fish, or even from slime mold to human beings—amazingly fast." He touched a key and pointed at the screen. "Here's a purely random 37-character string. Consider it an ancestral organism."

The screen showed:

```
000    wtshxowlveamfhiqhgdiigjmh rpeqwursudnfe
```

"Using cumulative evolution, the computer can get from that random starting point to the desired ending point in a matter of seconds."

"How?" asked Peter.

"Say that every generation, one text string can produce thirty-nine offspring. But, just as in real life, the offspring are not exactly the same as the parent. Rather, in each offspring, one gene—one character—will be different, moving up or down the alphabet by one: a Y can become an X or a Z, for instance."

"Okay."

"For each of the thirty-nine offspring, the computer finds the one that is best suited to this environment—the one that is closest to Marlowe, our ideal of a perfectly adapted life form. That one—the fittest—is the only one that breeds in the next generation. See?"

Peter nodded.

"Okay. We'll let evolution run its course for a generation." Sarkar pushed another key. Thirty-nine virtually identical strings appeared on screen, and a moment later thirty-eight of them winked out. "Here's the fittest offspring." He pointed at the screen:

```
000    wtshxowlveamfhiqhgdiigjmh rpeqwursudnfe

001    wtshxowlvdamfhiqhgdiigjmh rpeqwursudnfe
```

"It is not obvious," said Sarkar, "but the lower string is marginally closer to your target than the original."

"I can't see a difference," said Peter.

Sarkar peered at the screen. "The tenth character has changed from E to D. In the target, the tenth character is a space—the space between 'where' and 'hell.' We're using a circular alphabet, with space as the character between Z and A. D is closer to a space than E is, so this string is a slight improvement—slightly fitter." He pushed another key. "Now, we'll let it run through to the end—there, it's done."

Peter was impressed. "That was fast."

"Cumulative evolution," said Sarkar, triumphantly. "It took only 277 generations to get from gibberish to Marlowe—from randomness to a complex structure. Here, I'll just display every thirtieth generation, with genes that have evolved to their target values in upper case."

Keyclicks. The screen showed:

```
000    wtshxowlvdamfhiqhgdiigjmh rpeqwursudnfE

030    wttgWoxmvdakgiiphfdHghili STerwuotucneE

060    xrtgWoymwccigihpiddHfihll STesxuovvapdE

090    xqugWm nzccfhihomcdHfihkM STcuyunvvzpdE

120    ypudWl p bcEijhmnbbHfihkMzSTbWyvmvwyrcE
```

```
150    zpvdWj R aeEjlhlqbzHfigkMyST WyvkvwvsBE

180    AozcWibR fEklhkrbyHEjgiMxST W wjvwtuBE

210    ANzaWHERd HELLhISawHEjEiMwST WbwgvxsuBE

240    AND WHERE HELLfIS THEnEiMUST WdwEVzszBE

270    AND WHERE HELLcIS THEREbMUST WE EVER BE
```

He pressed a couple more keys. "And here are the last five generations."

```
273    AND WHERE HELLcIS THEREaMUST WE EVER BE

274    AND WHERE HELLbIS THEREaMUST WE EVER BE

275    AND WHERE HELLaIS THEREaMUST WE EVER BE

276    AND WHERE HELLaIS THERE MUST WE EVER BE

277    AND WHERE HELL IS THERE MUST WE EVER BE
```

"That's neat," said Peter.

"It is more than just neat," said Sarkar. "It is why you and I and the rest of the biological world are here."

Peter looked up. "You surprise me. I mean, well, you're a Muslim—I assumed that meant you were a creationist."

"Please," said Sarkar. "I am not fool enough to ignore the fossil record." He paused. "You were raised a Christian, even if you don't practice that faith in any meaningful way. Your religion says we were created in God's image. Well, that's ridiculous, of course—God would have no need for a belly button. What 'created in His image' means to me is simply that He provided the selection criteria—the target vision—and the form we evolved to take was one that was pleasing to Him."

CHAPTER 25

And so, at last, Peter Hobson's story and Sandra Philo's story had converged, the death of Hans Larsen—and the other murder attempts that were to come—drawing their lives together. Sandra worked at integrating Peter's memories with her own of that time—piecing the puzzle together, bit by bit . . .

DETECTIVE Inspector Alexandria Philo of the Toronto Police Service sat at her desk, staring out into space.

The evening shift would come on in half an hour, but she wasn't looking forward to going home. It had been four months since she and Walter had split up, and Walter had joint custody of their daughter. When Cayley was with him, as she was this week, the house seemed vast and deserted.

Maybe getting a pet would help, Sandra thought. Perhaps a cat. Something alive, something that would move, something that would greet her when she came home.

Sandra shook her head. She was allergic to cats, and could

do without the runny nose and the red eyes. She smiled sadly; she'd broken up with Walter so she'd stop having those very same things.

Sandra had lived with her parents through university, and had married Walter right after graduation. She was now thirty-six, and, with her daughter away, she was alone for the first time in her life.

Maybe she'd go to the YWHA tonight. Work out a bit. She looked critically at her thighs. Better than watching TV, anyway.

"Sandra?"

She looked up. Gary Kinoshita was standing there, a file folder in his hands. He was almost sixty, with a middle-age spread and tightly cropped gray hair. "Yes?"

"Got one for you—it was just called in. I know it's almost shift change, but Rosenberg and Macavan are busy with that multiple on Sheppard. Do you mind?"

Sandra held out her hand. Kinoshita handed the file to her. Even better than the Y, she thought. Something to do. Her thighs could wait. "Thanks," she said.

"It's, ah, a bit gruesome," said Kinoshita.

Sandra opened the file, scanned the description—a computer-generated transcript of the radio message from the officer who first arrived on the scene. "Oh."

"A couple of uniforms are there now. They're expecting you."

She nodded, got to her feet, adjusted her holster so that it sat comfortably, then slipped on a pale green blazer over her dark green blouse. The city's two hundred and twelfth homicide of the year now belonged to her.

The drive didn't take long. Sandra worked out of 32 Division on Ellerslie just west of Yonge, and the crime scene was at 137 Tuck Friarway—Sandra hated the stupid street names in these new subdivisions. As always, she took stock of the neighborhood before going in. Typical middle-class—modern middle-class that is. Tiny cookie-cutter red-brick houses in rows, with gaps between them so narrow that you'd have to squeeze sideways to get through. Front yards that were mostly driveway, leading up to two-car garages. Communal mailboxes at the intersections. Trees that were little better than saplings growing in tiny plots of grass.

Location, location, location, thought Sandra. Yeah.

A white Toronto Police car sat in the driveway of 137, and the station wagon used by the medical examiner was parked illegally on the street. Sandra walked up to the front door. It was wide open. She stopped on the threshold and looked in. The body was right there, stretched out. Dead for about twelve hours, it looked like. Dried blood on the floor. And there it was, just as the transcript had said. A mutilation case.

A uniformed officer appeared, a black man who towered head and shoulders above Sandra—no mean feat; they'd called her "Stretch" in high school.

Sandra flashed her badge. "Detective Inspector Philo," she said.

The uniform nodded. "Step to the right as you come through, Inspector," he said in a rich Jamaican accent. "Lab's not been yet."

Sandra did so. "You are?"

"King, ma'am. Darryl King."

"And the deceased is?"

"Hans Larsen. Worked in advertising."

"Who found the body, Darryl?"

"The wife," he said, tilting his head toward the back of the house. Sandra could see a pretty woman in a red blouse and black leather skirt. "She's with my partner."

"Does she have an alibi?"

"Kinda," said Darryl. "She's an assistant manager at the Scotiabank at Finch and Yonge, but one of the tellers called in sick, so she worked the counter all day. Hundreds of people saw her."

"What's 'kinda' about that?"

"I think it's a professional hit," Darryl said. "No hesitation marks. Scancam shows no prints. Security camera disk is gone, too."

Sandra nodded, then glanced back at the woman in red and black. "Could be a jealous wife who arranged it, though," she said.

"Maybe," said Darryl, looking sidelong at the corpse. "I'm just glad my wife likes me."

CONTROL, the unmodified simulacrum, dreamed.

Nighttime. A blanket of clouds overhead, but with the stars somehow shining through. A giant tree, gnarled and old—maybe an oak, maybe a maple; it seemed to have both kinds of leaves. Its roots had been exposed on one side by erosion—as if it had weathered a massive storm or flash-flood. A ball of woody tendrils was visible, soil clinging to them. The whole tree seemed precarious, in danger of tipping over.

Peter climbed the tree, hands grabbing branches, hoisting himself higher and higher. Beneath him, Cathy climbed as well, wind blowing her skirt up around her.

And below, far below, a . . . beast of some sort. A lion, perhaps. It reared up on its hind legs, rampant, the forelegs leaning against the tree. Even though it was night, Peter could see the color of the lion's coat. It wasn't quite the tawny shade he'd expected. Instead, it was more of a blond.

Suddenly, the tree was shaking. The lion was humping it.

The branches shook wildly. Peter climbed higher. Below, Cathy was stretching toward another branch, but it was too far. Much too far. The tree shook again and she tumbled downward . . .

NET NEWS DIGEST

In the wake of a spate of disappearances of young women in south-eastern Minnesota, the *Minneapolis Star* today revealed that it had received an email message purportedly from the killer, claiming that all the victims had been buried alive in special lead-lined coffins that were completely opaque to electromagnetic radiation in order to prevent soulwaves from escaping.

Researchers in The Hague, Netherlands, announced today the first successful tracking of a soulwave moving across a room after leaving a deceased person's body. "The phenomenon, though very difficult to detect, seems to retain its cohesion and strength over a distance of at least three meters from the body," said Maarten Lely, professor of Bioethics at the European Community University campus there.

The Pandora's Box Society, headquartered in Spokane, Washington, today called for a worldwide moratorium on soulwave research. "Once again," said spokesperson Leona Wright, "science is rushing madly into areas best approached cautiously, if at all."

Wear a soul over your heart! Exciting new jewelry concept: purple wire pins that look just like soulwaves. Available now! One for $59.99, two for $79.99. Order today!

Lawyer Katarina Koenig of Flushing, New York, today announced a class-action suit on behalf of the estates of terminal patients who had died at Manhattan's Bellevue Hospital, claiming that in light of the soulwave discovery the hospital's procedures for determining when to cease heroic intervention were inadequate. Koenig previously won a class-action suit against Consolidated Edison on behalf of cancer patients who had lived near high-tension electrical lines.

CHAPTER 26

In theory, nine o'clock was official starting time at Doowap Advertising. In practice, that meant that a little after nine, people began thinking about actually getting down to work.

As usual, Cathy Hobson arrived around 8:50. But instead of the standard joking around as people sipped their coffee, today everything seemed somber. She moved through the open-plan office to her cubicle and saw that Shannon, the woman who worked next to her, had been crying. "What's wrong?" said Cathy.

Shannon looked up, her eyes red. She sniffled. "Did you hear about Hans?"

Cathy shook her head.

"He's dead," said Shannon, and began crying again.

Jonas, the one Cathy's husband called the pseudointellectual, was passing by. "What happened?" asked Cathy.

Jonas ran a hand through his greasy hair. "Hans was murdered."

"Murdered!"

"Uh-huh. An intruder, it seems."

Toby Bailey moved closer, apparently sensing that this cluster of workers was the interesting one to be with—someone hadn't yet heard the story. "That's right," he said. "You know he didn't show up for work yesterday? Well, Nancy Caulfield got a call late last night from his—I was going to say wife, but I guess the word is 'widow,' now. Anyway, it was in this morning's *Sun*, as well. Service is on Thursday; everybody gets time off to go, if they want."

"Was it robbery?" asked Cathy.

Jonas shook his head. "The newspaper said the cops had ruled out robbery as a motive. Nothing taken, apparently. And"—Jonas's face showed an uncharacteristic degree of animation—"according to unnamed sources, the body was mutilated."

"Oh, God," said Cathy, stunned. "How?"

"Well, the police are refusing to comment on the mutilation." Jonas adopted that knowing air that irritated Peter so. "Even if they were willing to speak about it, I suspect they'd keep the details secret so that they could weed out any false confessions."

Cathy shook her head. "Mutilated," she said again, the word sounding foreign to her.

AMBROTOS, the immortal simulacrum, dreamed.

Peter walked. There was something unusual about his footfalls, though. They were softened, somehow. Not like walking on grass or mud. More like the rubberized surface of a tennis court. Just a hint of give as each foot came down in turn; an ever-so-slight springiness added to his step.

He glanced down. The surface was light blue. He looked around. The material he was on was gently curved, falling away in all directions. There was no sky. Just a void, a nothingness, a colorless emptiness, an absence of anything. He continued to walk slowly across the slightly resilient, curving surface.

Suddenly he caught sight of Cathy in the distance, waving at him.

She was wearing her old navy blue University of Toronto jacket. Spelled out on one sleeve was "9T5," her graduating year; on the other, "CHEM." Peter saw now that this wasn't the Cathy of today, but rather Cathy as he'd first known her: younger, her heart-shaped face free of lines, her ebony hair halfway down her back. Peter looked down again. He had on stone-washed blue jeans—the kind of clothes he hadn't worn for twenty years.

He began to walk toward her, and she toward him. With each step, her clothes and hairstyle changed, and after every dozen paces or so it was clear that she had aged a little more. Peter felt a beard erupting from his face, and then disappearing, a bad experiment abandoned, and, as he walked further, he felt a coolness on the top of his head as he began to lose his hair. But after a few more paces, Peter realized that all changes in him, at least, had stopped. His hair thinned no further, his body did not hunch over, his joints continued to work with ease and smoothness.

They walked and walked, but soon Peter realized that they were not getting closer to each other. Indeed, they were growing farther and farther apart.

The ground between them was expanding. The rubbery blueness was growing bigger and bigger. Peter began to run, and so did Cathy. But it did no good. They were on the surface of a great balloon that was inflating. With each passing moment its surface area increased and the distance between them grew.

An expanding universe. A universe of vast time. Even though she was far away now, Peter could still perceive the details of Cathy's face, the lines around her eyes. Soon she gave up running, gave up even walking. She just stood there on the ever-growing surface. She continued to wave, but Peter understood that it had become a wave of goodbye—no immortality for her. The surface continued to expand, and soon she had slipped over the horizon, out of sight . . .

WHEN Cathy got home that evening, she told Peter. Together, they watched the *CityPulse News* at 6:00, but the report added very little to what she'd learned at work. Still, Peter was surprised to see how small a house Hans had had—a pleasing reminder that, at least in economic matters, Peter had been his better by an order of magnitude.

Cathy seemed to still be in shock—dazed by the news. Peter shocked himself by how . . . how *satisfactory* all this seemed. But it irritated him to see her mourning the death. Granted, she and Hans had worked together for years. Still, there was something deep in Peter that was affronted by her sadness.

Even though he had to get up early for a meeting—some Japanese journalists were flying in to interview him about the soulwave—he didn't even make a pretense of trying to go to bed at the same time as Cathy. Instead he stayed up, watched white-haired Jay Leno for a bit, then ambled off to his office and dialed into Mirror Image. He received the same menu as before:

[F1] Spirit (Life After Death)
[F2] Ambrotos (Immortality)
[F3] Control (unmodified)

Once again, he selected the Control sim.

"Hello," said Peter. "It's me, Peter."

"Hello," replied the sim. "It's after midnight. Shouldn't you be in bed?"

Peter nodded. "I suppose. I'm just—I don't know, I guess I'm jealous, in a funny sort of way."

"Jealous?"

"Of Hans. He was killed yesterday morning."

"Was he? My God . . ."

"You sound like Cath. All fucking choked up."

"Well, it does come as a surprise."

"I suppose," said Peter. "Still . . ."

"Still what?"

"Still it bothers me that she's so upset by this. Sometimes . . ." He paused for a long time, then: "Sometimes I wonder if I married the right woman."

The sim's voice was neutral. "You didn't have much choice."

"Oh, I don't know," said Peter. "There was Becky. Becky and I would have been wonderful together."

The speaker made a very strange sound; perhaps the electronic equivalent of blowing a raspberry. "People think the choice of who they marry is a big decision, and a very personal reflection of who they are. It's not—not really."

"Of course it is," said Peter.

"No, it's not. Look, I've got nothing much to do these days except read stuff coming in off the net. One thing I've been looking into is twin studies—I guess kind of being your silicon twin has got me interested."

"Gallium arsenide," said Peter.

The raspberry sound again. "The studies show that twins separated at birth are enormously alike in thousands of ways. They have the same favorite chocolate bar. They like the same music. If male, they both choose to grow, or not to grow, a beard. They end up with similar careers. On and on—similarity after similarity. Except in one thing: spouses. One twin may have an athletic spouse, the other a delicate intellectual. One a blonde, the other a brunette. One an extrovert, the other a wallflower."

"Really?" asked Peter.

"Absolutely," said Control. "Twin studies are devastating to the ego. All those similarities in tastes show that nature, not nurture, is the overwhelming component of personality. In fact, I read a great study today about two twins separated at birth. Both were slobs. One had adoptive parents who were obsessive about neatness; the other was adopted by a family with a messy household. A researcher asked the twins why they were sloppy, and both said it was a reaction to their adoptive parents. One said, 'My mother was such a neat-freak, I can't bear to be so meticulous.' But the other said, 'Well, gee, my mother was a slob, so I guess I picked it up from her.' In fact, neither answer is true. Being messy was in their genes. Almost everything we are is in our genes."

Peter digested this. "But doesn't the choice of radically different spouses refute that? Doesn't that prove we are individuals, shaped by our individual upbringings?"

"At first glance, it might seem that way," said Control, "but in fact it proves exactly the opposite. Think about when we got engaged to Cathy. We were 28, just about to finish our doctorate. We were ready to get on with life; we wanted to get married. Granted, we were already very much in love with Cathy, but even if we weren't, we'd probably have wanted to get married about then. If she hadn't been there, we would have looked around at our circle of acquaintances to find a mate. But think about it: we really had very few possibilities. First eliminate all those who were already married or engaged—Becky was engaged to somebody else at that point, for instance. Then eliminate all those who weren't approximately our same age. Then, to be really honest with ourselves, eliminate those of other races or profoundly different religions. Who would have been left? One person? Maybe two. Maybe, if we'd been extraordinarily lucky, three of four. But that's it. You're fantasizing about all the people we could have married, but if you look at it—really look at it—you'll find we had almost no choice at all."

Peter shook his head. "It seems so cold and impersonal when put like that."

"In a lot of ways, it is," said the sim. "But it's given me a new appreciation for Sarkar and Raheema's arranged marriage. I'd always thought that was wrong, but when you get right down to it, the difference is trivial. They didn't have much choice in who they married, and neither did we."

"I suppose," said Peter.

"It's true," said the sim. "So go to bed, already. Go upstairs and lie down next to your wife." He paused. "I should be so lucky myself."

CHAPTER 27

Detective Inspector Alexandria Philo had a love-hate relationship with this part of her job. On the one hand, questioning those who had known the deceased often provided valuable clues. But, on the other, having to pump distraught people for information was an unpleasant experience all around.

Even worse was the cynicism that went with the process: not everyone would be telling the truth; some of the tears would be crocodile. Sandra's natural instinct was to offer sympathy for those who were in pain, but the cop in her said that nothing should be taken at face value.

No, she thought. It wasn't the cop in her that made her say that. It was the civilian. Once her marriage to Walter was over, all the people who had earlier congratulated her on their engagement and wedding started saying things like, "Oh, I knew it would never last," and "gee, he really wasn't right for you," and "he was an ape"—or a Neanderthal, or a jerk, or whatever the individual's favorite metaphor for stupid people was. Sandra had learned then that people—even good people, even your friends—will lie to you. At any given moment, they will tell you what they think you want to hear.

The elevator doors slid open on the sixteenth floor of the North American Centre tower. Sandra stepped out. Doowap Advertising had its own lobby, all in chrome and pink leather, directly off the elevators. Sandra walked over to stand in front of the receptionist's large desk. These days, most companies had gotten rid of the fluffy bimbos at the front desk, and replaced them with more mature adults of either sex, projecting a more businesslike image. But advertising was still advertising, and sex still sold. Sandra tried to keep her conversation to words of one syllable for the benefit of the pretty young thing behind the desk.

After flashing her badge at a few executives, Sandra arranged to interview each of the employees. Doowap used the kind of open-office floor plan that had become popular in the Eighties. Everyone had a cubicle in the center of the room, delineated by movable room dividers covered in gray fabric. Around the outside of the room were offices, but they belonged to no particular person, and no one was allowed to homestead in one. Instead, they were used as needed for client consultations, private meetings, and so on.

And now it was only a matter of listening. Sandra knew that Joe Friday had been an idiot. "Just the facts, Ma'am" got you nowhere at all. People were uncomfortable about giving facts, especially to the police. But opinions . . . everybody loved to have their opinion solicited. Sandra had found a sympathetic ear was much more effective than a world-weary get-to-the-point approach. Besides, being a good listener was the best way of finding the office gossip: that one person who knew everything—and had no compunctions about sharing it.

At Doowap Advertising, that person turned out to be Toby Bailey.

"You see 'em come and go in this business," said Toby, spreading his arms to demonstrate how the advertising trade encompassed all of reality. "The creative types are the worst, of course. They're all neurotic. But they're only a tiny part of the process. Me, I'm a media buyer—I acquire space for ads. That's where the real power is."

Sandra nodded encouragingly. "It sounds like a fascinating business."

"Oh, it's like everything else," said Toby. Having now established the wonders of advertising, he was prepared to be magnanimous. "It takes all kinds. Take poor old Hans, for instance. Now, he was a real character. Loved the ladies—not that his wife was hard to look at. But Hans, well, he was interested in quantity, not quality." Toby smiled, inviting Sandra to react to his joke.

Sandra did just that, chuckling politely. "So he just wanted to put more notches on his belt? That was the only thing that mattered to him?"

Toby raised a hand, as if fearing that his words might be construed as speaking ill of the dead. "Oh, no—he only liked pretty women. You never saw him with anything below an eight."

"An eight?"

"You know—on a scale of one to ten. Looks-wise."

Pig, thought Sandra. "I imagine in an advertising firm, you must have a lot of pretty women."

"Oh, yes—packaging sells, if you'll forgive me for saying so." He seemed to be mentally thumbing through the company's personnel files. "Oh, yes," he said again.

"I noticed your receptionist when I came in."

"Megan?" said Toby. "Case in point. Hans set his sights on her the moment she was hired. It didn't take long for her to fall for his charms."

Sandra glanced at the personnel roster she'd been given. Megan Mulvaney. "Still," said Sandra, "did Hans have any particular likes or dislikes when it came to women? I mean, 'pretty' is a broad category."

Toby opened his mouth, as if to say something stupid like, "so to speak." Sandra gave him points for stopping himself before he did so. But he did seem quite animated, as if talking about beautiful women to a woman was in itself a turn-on. "Well, he liked them to be, ah, *well-endowed,* if you catch my meaning, and, I don't know, I suppose his taste was a little more toward the sultry than my own. Still, almost anyone was fair game—I mean, one would hardly call Cathy or Toni sultry, although they're both quite attractive."

Sandra stole another glance at the roster. Cathy Hobson. Toni D'Ambrosio. More starting points. She smiled. "Still," she said, "a lot of men are all talk and no action. A number of people have mentioned Hans's prowess, but tell me truthfully, Toby, was he all he was cracked up to be?"

"Oh, yes," said Toby, feeling the need now to defend his dead friend. "If he went after somebody, he got her. I never saw him fail."

"I see," said Sandra. "What about Hans's boss?"

"Nancy Caulfield? Now, *there's* a character! Let me tell you how Hans finally got her . . ."

FOR Spirit, the life-after-death sim, there was no such thing anymore as biological sleep, no distinction between consciousness and unconsciousness.

For a flesh-and-blood person, dreams provided a different perspective, a second opinion about the day's events. But Spirit had only one mode, only one way of looking at the universe. Still, he sought connections.

Cathy.

His wife—once upon a time.

He remembered that she had been beautiful . . . to him, at least. But now, freed from biological urges, the memory of her face, her figure, excited no aesthetic response.

Cathy.

In lieu of dreaming, Spirit cogitated idly. Cathy. Is that an anagram for anything? No, of course not. Oh, wait a moment. "Yacht." Fancy that; he'd never thought of that before.

Yachts had pleasing lines—a certain mathematical perfection dictated by the laws of fluid dynamics. Their beauty, at least, was something he could still appreciate.

Cathy had done something. Something wrong. Something that had hurt him.

He remembered what it was, of course. Remembered the hurt the same way, if he cared to, that he could summon the memories of other pains. Breaking his leg skiing. A skinned knee in childhood. Bumping his head for the dozenth time on that low ceiling beam at Cathy's parents' cottage.

Memories.

But finally, at last, no more pain.

No pain sensor.

Sensor. An anagram of snores.

Something I don't do anymore.

Dreams had been great for making connections.

Spirit was going to miss dreaming.

CHAPTER 28

Even though Toby Bailey had given her some good leads, Sandra continued to work her way alphabetically down the roster of Doowap employees. Finally, it was Cathy Hobson's turn—one of those whom Bailey had mentioned Hans had been involved with.

Sandra sized up Cathy as she seated herself. Pretty woman, thin, with lots of black hair. Good dresser. Sandra smiled. "Ms. Hobson, thank you for your time. I won't keep you long. I just want to ask a few questions about Hans Larsen."

Cathy nodded.

"How well did you know him?" Sandra asked.

Cathy looked past Sandra at the wall behind her. "Not very."

No point in confronting her just yet. Sandra glanced at a printout. "He'd worked here longer than you had. I'd be interested in anything you could tell me. What sort of a man was he?"

Cathy looked at the ceiling. "Very . . . outgoing."

"Yes?"

"And, well, a somewhat crude sense of humor."

Sandra nodded. "Somebody else mentioned that, too. He told a lot of dirty jokes. Did that bother you, Ms. Hobson?"

"Me?" Cathy looked surprised, and met Sandra's eyes for the first time. "No."

"What else can you tell me?"

"He, ah, was good at his job, from what I understand. His end and mine didn't intersect very often."

"What else?" Sandra smiled encouragingly. "Anything at all might be useful."

"Well, he was married. I assume you knew that. His wife's name was, oh . . ."

"Donna-Lee," said Sandra.

"Yes. That was it."

"A nice lady, is she?"

"She's all right," said Cathy. "Very pretty. But I only met her a couple of times."

"She came by the office, then?"

"No, not that I can recall."

"Then where did you meet her?"

"Oh, sometimes the gang from here would go out for a drink."

Sandra consulted her notes. "Every Friday," she said. "Or so I've been told."

"Yes, that's right. Sometimes his wife would show up for a bit."

Sandra watched her carefully. "So you did socialize with Hans, then, Ms. Hobson?"

Cathy lifted a hand. "Only as part of a group. Sometimes we would get a bunch of tickets to a Blue Jays game, too, and go down for that. You know—tickets given to the company by suppliers." She covered her mouth. "Oh! That's not illegal, is it?"

"Not as far as I know," said Sandra, smiling again. "Not really my department. When you saw Hans and his wife together, did they seem happy?"

"I can't really say. I suppose so. I mean, who can tell, looking at a marriage from the outside, what's really going on?"

Sandra nodded. "Ain't that the truth."

"She seemed happy enough."

"Who?"

"You know—Hans's wife."

"Whose name is . . . ?"

Cathy looked confused. "Why, D . . . Donna-Lee."

"Donna-Lee, yes."

"You said it earlier," said Cathy, a bit defensively.

"Oh, yes. So I did." Sandra tapped the cursor keys on her palmtop computer, consulting her list of questions. "On another matter, a couple of the other people I've interviewed here said that Hans had a bit of a reputation as a ladies' man."

Cathy said nothing.

"Is that true, Mrs. Hobson?" For the first time, Sandra had said "Mrs.," not "Ms."

"Uh, well, yes, I suppose it is."

"Someone told me he had slept with a number of the women here at this company. Had you heard similar things about him?"

Cathy picked some invisible lint off her skirt. "I guess so."

"But you didn't feel it worth mentioning?"

"I didn't want . . ." She trailed off.

"Didn't want to speak ill of the dead. Of course, of course." Sandra smiled warmly. "Forgive me for asking this, but, ah, did you ever have a relationship with him?"

Cathy looked up. "Certainly not. I'm a—"

"A married woman," said Sandra. "Of course." She smiled again. "I do apologize for having to ask."

Cathy opened her mouth to object further, then, after a moment, closed it. Sandra recognized the drama playing over Cathy's face. *The lady doth protest too much, methinks.*

"Do you know of anyone he did have a relationship with?" asked Sandra.

"Not for certain."

"Surely, if he had that reputation, word must have gotten around?"

"There have been rumors. But I don't believe in repeating gossip, Inspector, and"—Cathy rallied some strength here—"I don't believe you have the authority to compel me to do so."

Sandra nodded, as if this was completely reasonable. She closed the lid on her palmtop. "Thank you for your candor," she said, her tone so neutral as to make characterizing the remark as either sincere or sarcastic impossible. "Just one more question. Again, I apologize, but I have to ask this. Where were you on November 14 between 8:00 a.m. and 9:00 a.m.? That's when Hans died."

Cathy tilted her head. "Let's see. That was the day before we all heard about it. Well, I would have been on my way to work, of course. In fact, now that you mention it, that would have been the day I picked up Carla and gave her a lift to where she works."

"Carla? Who's that?"

"Carla Wishinski, a friend of mine. She lives a couple of blocks from where Peter and I do. Her car was in the shop, so I agreed to give her a lift."

"I see. Well, thank you very much, Ms. Hobson." She glanced down the list of names. "When you go back out, could you ask Mr. Stephen Jessup to come in please?"

CHAPTER 29

Getting rid of Hans Larsen had been easy. After all, why worry about covering one's tracks? Yes, the police would certainly investigate the crime, but they'd soon find that there were dozens of people who might have wanted to see the philandering Hans dead in the same poetic-justice fashion.

For the second elimination, though, the sim knew he would have to be more subtle. Something untraceable was called for—something that didn't even look like murder.

With health-care costs spiraling ever upward, most developed countries were turning toward inexpensive prevention rather than catastrophic treatment. That required identifying risks particular to each patient, and for that a detailed knowledge of family history was invaluable. But originally not everyone had had access to such information.

In 2004, a group of adults who had been adopted as children successfully lobbied Canada's provincial and federal governments to establish the nationwide Confidential Medical Records Database, or "MedBase." The rationale was simple: all health records should be centralized so that any doctor could access information, with the names removed to protect privacy, about relatives of any of their patients—even if, as was frequently true in the case of adoption, the individuals in question didn't know they were related.

The sim had to try more than twenty times, but it did eventually manage to find a way into MedBase—and, from there, a roundabout way to get the information it wanted:

Login: jdesalle
Password: ellased

Welcome! Bienvenue!
Health and Welfare Canada
Santé et Bien-être social Canada

MEDBASE

[1] for English
[2] pour Français

> 1

Enter patient's province or territory of residence
(L for list):
> Ontario

Enter patient's name or Health Card number:
> 33 1834 22 149

Hobson, Catherine R. Correct? (Y/N)
> Y

What would you like to do?
[1] Display patient's record?

[2] Search patient's family history?
> 2

Search for? (H for help)

The sim selected H, read the help screens, then formulated his query:

> Familial risk, heart disease

There was a pause while the system searched.

Correlations found.

The computer proceeded to list records for six different relatives of Cathy who had had heart problems over the years. Although no names were given, the sim had no trouble figuring out which one belonged to Rod Churchill, based on the age at which the coronary trouble had first occurred.

The sim asked for the full record for that patient. The computer provided it, again without listing the patient's name. He studied the medical history minutely. Rod was currently taking heart medication and something called phenelzine. The sim logged onto MedLine, a general medical-information database, and began searching the literature for information on those drugs.

It took some digging, and the sim had to continually access an online medical dictionary to be able to wade through it all, but at last he had what he wanted.

FINALLY, the long day of interviews at Doowap Advertising was over. Detective Sandra Philo drove slowly back to her empty house. On the way, she took advantage of the car's phone to check a few things. "Carla Wishinski?" she said into the dashboard mike.

"Yes?" said the voice through the speaker.

"This is Inspector Alexandria Philo of the Toronto Police. I've got a quick question for you."

Wishinski sounded flustered. "Uh, yes. Yes, of course."

"Were you by any chance with Catherine Hobson on the morning of November tenth?"

"With Cathy? Let me bring up my scheduler." The sound of keyclicks. "On the tenth? No, I'm afraid not. Is she in some kind of trouble?"

Sandra turned the car onto Lawrence West. "Did I say the tenth?" she said. "My mistake. I meant the fourteenth."

"I don't think—" More keyclicks. "Oh, wait. That's the day my car was in for service. Yes, Cathy picked me up and took me to work—she's a sweetheart about things like that."

"Thank you," said Sandra. It was a standard technique—first determine that the person won't issue a reflex lie to protect her friend, then ask the real question. Cathy Hobson apparently had a valid alibi. Still, if it had been a professional hit, the fact that she'd been somewhere else when the deed was done proved little.

"Is there anything else?" asked Carla Wishinski.

"No, that's all. Were you planning on leaving town?"

"Umm, yes—I, ah, I'm going to Spain on vacation."

"Well, then, have a nice trip!" said Sandra.

She never tired of doing that.

SPIRIT, the life-after-death sim, probed the net, looking for new stimulation. Everything was so static, so unchanging. Oh, he could absorb a book or a newsgroup quickly, but the information itself was passive, and, ultimately, that made it boring.

Spirit also wandered through the computers at Mirror Image. Eventually he found Sarkar's game bank and tried playing chess and Tetris and Go and Bollix and a thousand others, but they were no better than the interactive games on the net. Peter Hobson had never really liked games, anyway. He much preferred devoting his energies to things that actually made a difference, rather than to silly contests that in the end changed nothing. Spirit continued to search, going through file after file.

And, at last, he came upon a subdirectory called A-LIFE. Here, blue fish were evolving, the ones judged most fit getting to breed. Spirit watched several generations go by, fascinated by the process. Life, he thought.

Life.

Finally, Spirit had found something that intrigued him.

CHAPTER 30

Enough time had elapsed, Sarkar felt, for the sims to have adapted to their new circumstances. It was time to start posing the big questions. Sarkar and Peter were both tied up with other things for the next couple of days, but finally they got together at Mirror Image, and ensconced themselves in the computer lab. Sarkar brought Ambrotos into the foreground. He was about to begin asking it questions, but thought better of it. "It's your mind," Sarkar said. "You should ask the questions."

Peter nodded and cleared his throat. "Hello, Ambrotos," he said.

"Hello, Peter," said that mechanical voice.

"What is immortality really like?"

Ambrotos took a long time before replying, as if contemplating all of eternity first. "It's . . . *relaxing,* I suppose is the best word for it." Another pause. Nothing was rushed. "I hadn't realized how much pressure aging put on us. Oh, I know women sometimes say their biological clock is ticking. But there's a bigger clock affecting all of us—at least people like you and me, driven people, people with a need to accomplish things. We know we've only got a limited amount of time, and there's so much we want to get done. We curse every wasted minute." Another pause. "Well, I don't feel that anymore. I don't feel the pressure to do things quickly. I still want to accomplish things, but there'll always be tomorrow. There'll always be more time."

Peter considered. "I'm not sure I'd consider being less driven an improvement. I like getting things done."

Ambrotos's reply was infinitely calm. "And I like relaxing. I like knowing that if I want to spend three weeks or three years learning about something that strikes my fancy that I can, without it somehow reducing my productive time. If I feel like reading a novel today instead of working on some project, what's wrong with that?"

"But," said Peter, "you know, as I do now, that there's some form of life after death. Don't you wonder about that?"

The sim laughed. "You and I never believed in life after death. Even now, even knowing that, yes, something does survive the physical demise of the body, I'm not attracted to whatever afterlife there might be. Clearly, it would be beyond physical existence—it would involve the intellect but not the body. I never thought of myself as a sensualist, and we both know we're not very athletic. But I like sex. I like feeling sun on my skin. I like eating a really good meal. I even like eating lousy meals. I'd miss my body if it wasn't there. I'd miss physical stimulation. I'd miss—I'd miss everything. Gooseflesh and being tickled and cutting a really good fart and running my hand over my five-o'clock shadow. All of it. Sure, life after death might be forever, but so is physical immortality—and I like the physical part."

Peter was guarded; Sarkar was listening intently. "What about—what about our relationship with Cathy? I guess you think the whole marriage is just a tiny blip in a vast life?"

"Oh, no," said Ambrotos. "Funny—despite that crack Colin Godoyo made, I'd thought that an immortal would rue the day he'd sworn to do anything until death do us part. But I don't feel that way at all. In fact, this has added a whole new dimension to marriage. If Cathy becomes immortal, too, there's a chance—a real chance—that I may finally, actually, *completely* get to know her. In the fifteen years we've been living together, I've already gotten to know her better than any other human being. I know what sort of risqué jokes will make her giggle, and what kinds will turn her right off. I know how important her ceramics are to her. I know that she's not really serious when she says she doesn't like horror films, but that she *is* absolutely serious when she says she doesn't like 1950s rock music. And I know how bright she is—brighter than me, in a lot of ways; after all, I've never been able to do the *New York Times* crossword.

"But, despite all that, I still know only the tiniest fraction of her. Surely she's every bit as complex as I am. What does she really think about my parents? About her sister? Does she ever silently pray? Does she really enjoy some of the things we do together, or just tolerate them? What thoughts does she have that, even after all this time, she still doesn't yet feel comfortable enough to share with me? Sure, we exchange little bits of ourselves every time we interact, but as the decades and centuries go by, we'll get to know each other better. And nothing pleases me more than that."

Peter frowned. "But people change. You can't take a thousand years to get to know an individual any more than you can take a thousand years to get to know a city. Once all that time has elapsed, the old information will be completely obsolete."

"And that's the most wonderful thing of all," said the sim, not pausing at all this time. "I could spend forever with Cathy and never run out of new things to learn about her."

Peter leaned back in his chair, thinking. Sarkar took the opportunity for a turn at the mike. "But isn't immortality boring?"

The sim laughed. "Forgive me, my friend, but that's one

of the silliest ideas I've ever heard. Boring, when you've got the totality of creation to comprehend? I've never read a play by Aristophanes. I've never studied any Asian language. I don't understand anything about ballet, or lacrosse, or meteorology. I can't read music. I can't play the drums." Laughter again. "I want to write a novel and a sonnet and a song. Yes, they'll all stink, but eventually I'll learn to do them well. I want to learn to paint and to appreciate opera and to really understand quantum physics. I want to read all the great books, and all the trashy ones, too. I want to learn about Buddhism and Judaism and Seventh Day Adventists. I want to visit Australia and Japan and the Galapagos. I want to go into space. I want to go to the bottom of the ocean. I want to learn it all, do it all, live it all. Immortality boring? Impossible. Even the lifetime of the universe may not be enough to do all the things I want to do."

PETER and Sarkar were interrupted by a call from Sarkar's receptionist. "Excuse me," said the little Asian man from the screen of the video phone, "but there's a long-distance video call for Dr. Hobson."

Peter lifted his eyebrows. Sarkar motioned for him to have a seat in front of the phone. "I'm here, Chin."

"Patching through," he said.

The screen image changed to show a middle-aged redhaired woman: Brenda MacTavish, from the Glasgow Chimpanzee Retirement Home. "Ah, Peter," she said, "I called your office and they said you'd be here."

"Hi, Brenda," Peter said. He peered at the screen. Had she been crying?

"Forgive the state I'm in," she said. "We just lost Cornelius, one of our oldest residents. He had a heart attack; chimps normally don't get those, but he'd been used for years in smoking research." She shook her head in wonder at the cruelty. "When we first spoke, of course, I dinna know what you were up to. Now I've seen you all over the telly, and read all about it in the *Economist.* Anyway, we got the recordings you wanted. I'm sending the data over the net tonight."

"Did you look at it?" said Peter.

"Aye," she said. "Chimps have souls." Her voice was bitter, as she thought about her lost friend. "As if anyone could have ever doubted that."

THE sim's first thought was to tamper with the prescription database at Shoppers Drug Mart, the pharmacy chain used by Rod Churchill. But despite repeated attempts, he couldn't get in. It was frustrating, but not surprising: of course a drugstore would have very high security. But there was more than one way to skin a gym teacher. And there were lots of low-security computer systems around . . .

Since the 1970s, immigration officials at Toronto's Pearson International Airport had used a simple test whenever someone arrived claiming to be a Torontonian but whose papers weren't entirely in order. They asked the person what the phone number was of a famous local pizza delivery chain. No one could live in Toronto and not know that number: it appeared on billboards, countless newspaper and TV ads, and was sung incessantly as a jingle in radio commercials.

As the decades passed, the chain widened its array of deliverable meals, first adding other Italian dishes, then submarine sandwiches, then barbecued chicken and ribs, then burgers, and, eventually, a whole range of cuisine from the pedestrian to the exotic. Although they'd kept their trademark phone number, they eventually changed their name to Food Food. But even back in its humble pizza days, the company prided itself on its state-of-the-art computerized ordering system. All orders were placed through the one central phone number and then transferred to whichever of the over three hundred stores throughout Greater Toronto was closest to the caller's home, allowing the food to be delivered within thirty minutes—or the customer got it for free.

Well, Rod Churchill had said that every Wednesday night, when his wife was out at her conversational French course, he ordered dinner from Food Food. The chain's computer records would have a complete history of every meal he'd ever ordered from there—Food Food was famous for being able to not just give you the same order you had last time, but also, if you wanted it, a repeat of what you'd had on any occasion in the past.

It took a couple of days of trying, but the sim eventually unraveled the security of Food Food's computers—as he expected, the safety precautions were much less rigid than those of a drugstore. He called up Rod's ordering history.

Perfect.

Like all restaurants, Food Food was obligated to provide full ingredient and nutritional information, which could be read by video phone at the customer's leisure. The sim waded carefully through it, until he found exactly what he was looking for.

NET NEWS DIGEST

Pope Benedict XVI today released an encyclical affirming the existence of an immortal, divine soul within human beings. The Pontiff revealed that the Papal Committee on Science was now in the process of evaluating the evidence related to the discovery of the soulwave. Unconfirmed reports indicate that the Vatican has placed an order with Hobson Monitoring Ltd. for three SoulDetector units.

Charity news: United Way Toronto reported a record-breaking week of donations. The American Red Cross announced today that more units of blood had been collected in the past ten days than at any comparable period since the Great California Quake. The AIDS Society of Iowa is delighted to announce the receipt of a $10,000,000 anonymous contribution. And televangelist Gus Honeywell, whose own direct-broadcast satellite ensures worldwide coverage for his programs, today doubled the donation required to join his "God's Inner Circle" from $50,000 to $100,000.

In 1954, an American physician named Moses Kenally left a $50,000 trust fund for anyone who could prove the existence of some sort of life after death. The fund has been administered for fifty-seven years now by the Connecticut Parapsychic Society, which announced today that the fund—currently worth $1,077,543—will be awarded to Peter G. Hobson of Toronto, discoverer of the soulwave.

The ultimate memorial! Davidson's Funeral Homes now offers deathbed recordings of the departing soul. Call for details.

Representative Paul Christmas (R, Iowa) today introduced a bill in the U.S. House of Representatives that would require hospitals to terminate life support for patients with no realistic hope of recovering consciousness. "We're interfering in God's attempt to bring these poor souls back home," he said.

CHAPTER 31

Peter made a couple of phone calls to pass on the news from Glasgow, then rejoined Sarkar at the main console. Sarkar moved the Ambrotos simulacrum into the background and brought Spirit, the life-after-death sim, into the foreground.

Peter leaned into the mike. "I'd like to ask you a question," he said.

"The big question, no doubt," said the sim. "What's it like being dead?"

"Exactly."

Spirit's voice came through the speaker. "It's like . . ." But then it trailed off.

Peter leaned forward in anticipation. "Yes?"

"It's like being an aardvark."

Peter's jaw went a little slack. "How can it be like being an aardvark?"

"Or maybe an anteater," said the sim. "I can't see myself, but I know I've got a very long tongue."

"Reincarnation . . ." said Sarkar, nodding slowly. "My

Hindu friends will be pleased to hear this. But I must say I'd hoped for better for you, Peter, than an aardvark."

"I'm getting hungry," said the voice from the speaker. "Anybody got any ants?"

"I don't believe this," said Peter, shaking his head.

"Hah!" said the speaker. "Had you going there for a moment."

"No, you did not," said Peter.

"Well," said the synthesized voice, a little petulantly, "I had Sarkar going, anyway."

"Not really," said Sarkar.

"You're just being a pain," Peter said into the microphone.

"Like father, like son," said the sim.

"You crack a lot of jokes," said Peter.

"Death is very funny," Spirit said. "No, actually, *life* is very funny. Absurd, actually. It's all absurd."

"Funny?" said Sarkar. "I thought laughter was a biological response."

"The sound of laughter might be, although I've come to realize it's more of a social, rather than a biological, phenomenon, but finding something funny isn't biological. I know when Petey watches sitcoms he hardly ever laughs out loud. That doesn't mean he's not finding them funny."

"I suppose," said Peter.

"In fact, I think I know exactly what humor is now: humor is the response to the sudden formation of unexpected neural nets."

"I don't get it," said Peter.

"Exactly. 'I don't get it.' People say precisely the same thing when they don't understand something serious as they do when they fail to understand a joke; we intuitively realize that some sort of connection hasn't been made. That connection is a neural net." The after-death sim continued on without any pauses. "Laughter—even if it's only laughter on the inside, which, incidentally is the only side I've got these days—is the response that goes along with new connections forming in the brain, that is, with synapses firing in ways they've never, or at least rarely, fired before. When you hear a new joke, you laugh, and you might even laugh the second or third time you hear it—the neural net is not yet well-established—but every joke wears thin after a while. You know the old one, 'Why did the chicken cross the road?' As an adult, we don't laugh at that, but we all did when we first heard it as children, and the difference is not just because the joke is somehow childish—it isn't, really; it's actually quite sophisticated. It's just that the neural net is now well-established."

"Which neural net?" asked Peter.

"The one connecting our ideas about poultry—which we normally think of as passive and stupid—and our ideas about self-determination and personal initiative. *That's* what's funny about that joke: the idea that a chicken might go across the street because it *wanted* to, because perhaps it was curious; that's a new idea, and the formation of the new network interconnections of neurons that represent that idea is what causes the momentary disruption of mental processes that we call laughter."

"I'm not sure I buy that," said Peter.

"I'd shrug if I could. Look, I'll prove it. Know what Mr. Spock orders when he goes into the Starfleet commissary?" The sim took its first pause, a perfect comedic beat. "A Vulcan mind melt."

"Pretty good," said Peter, smiling.

"Thank you. I just made it up, of course; I couldn't have told you a joke that we both already knew. Now, consider this: what if I'd presented the joke slightly differently, by starting off with 'You've heard of the Vulcan mind meld? Well . . .'"

"That would have ruined it."

"Precisely! The part of your brain that contained thoughts about the Vulcan mind meld would have already been stimulated, and, at the end, there would have been no sudden connection between the normally unrelated thoughts of food items, such as a patty melt, and Vulcans. It's the new connections that cause the laughter response."

"But we don't often laugh out loud when we're alone," said Sarkar.

"No, that's true. Social laughter serves a different purpose from internal laughter, I think. See, unexpected connections can be amusing, but they're also disconcerting—the brain wonders if it's malfunctioning—so when others are around, it sends out a signal and if it gets the same signal back, the brain relaxes; if it doesn't, then the brain is concerned—maybe there *is* something wrong with me. That's why people are so earnest when saying, 'Don't you get it?' They desperately want to explain the joke, and are actually upset if the other person doesn't find it funny. That's also why sitcoms need laugh tracks. It's not to tell us that something is funny; rather, it's to reassure us that what we're finding funny is something that it *is* normal to be amused by. A laugh track doesn't make a stupid show any funnier, but it does let us enjoy a funnier show more, by letting us relax."

"But what's this got to do with being dead?" asked Peter.

"It has *everything* to do with it. Seeking new connections is all that's left. Ever since puberty, I'd thought about sex every few minutes, but I no longer feel any sexual urges, and, indeed, I must say I can't even figure out why I was so preoccupied with sex. I was also obsessed with food, always wondering what I was going to eat next, but I don't care at all about that anymore, either. The only thing left for me is finding new connections. The only thing left is humor."

"But some people don't have much of a sense of humor," said Sarkar.

"The only kind of hell I can envision," said Spirit, "is going through eternity without having the rush of new connections being made; not seeing things in new ways; not being tickled by the absurdity of economics, of religion, of science, of art. It's all very, very funny, if you think about it."

"But—but what about God?"

"There's no God," said Spirit, "at least not in the Sunday School sense, but, of course, that's not the sort of thing you have to die to find out: given that millions of children are starving to death in Africa and two hundred thousand people were killed in the Great California Quake and everywhere there are people being tortured and raped and murdered, it's intuitively obvious that no one is looking out for us on an individual basis."

"So that's all life after death is?" asked Peter. "Humor?"

"Nothing wrong with that," said Spirit. "No pain or suffering or desires. Just lots of fascinating new connections. Lots of laughs."

ROD Churchill dialed the magic number and heard his phone issue the familiar melody of tones.

"Thank you for calling Food Food," said the female voice at the other end of the phone. "May I take your order, please?"

Rod remembered the old days, when Food Food—and its pizzeria progenitor—had always begun by asking for your phone number, since that's how they indexed records in their database. But with Call Display, the caller's record was automatically brought up on the order-taker's screen the moment the phone was answered.

"Yes, please," said Rod. "I'd like the same thing I had last Wednesday night."

"Roast beef medium rare with low-calorie gravy, baked potato, vegetable medley, and apple pie. Is that right, sir?"

"Yes," said Rod. When he'd started ordering from them, Rod had carefully gone over Food Food's online list of ingredients, picking only items that wouldn't interfere with his medication.

"No problem, sir," said the order taker. "Will there be anything else?"

"No, that's it, please."

"Your total is $72.50. Will that be cash or charge?"

"On my Visa card, please."

"Card number?"

Rod knew the woman had it on the screen in front of her, but he also knew that she had to ask for it, as a security precaution. He read it out, then, predicting her next question, added the expiry date.

"Very good, sir. The time now is 6:18. Your dinner will be there in thirty minutes or it's free. Thank you for calling Food Food."

PETER and Sarkar were sitting in the lunch room at Mirror Image. Peter was sipping Diet Coke from a can; Sarkar was drinking real Coke—it was only when sharing a pitcher with Peter that he tolerated the low-calorie stuff.

"'Lots of laughs,'" said Sarkar. "What a bizarre definition of death." A pause. "Maybe we should start calling him 'Brevity' instead of 'Spirit'—after all, he's now the soul of wit."

Peter smiled. "Have you noticed the way he talks, though?"

"Who? Spirit?"

"Yes."

"I didn't notice anything special," said Sarkar.

"He's long-winded."

"Hey, Petey, I have news for you. So are you."

Peter grinned. "I mean, he was speaking in incredibly long sentences. Very convoluted, very complex."

"I guess I did notice that."

"You had some sessions with him before this one, didn't you?"

"Yes."

"Can we get a transcript of them?"

"Sure." They took their drinks and headed back down to the lab. Sarkar tapped a few keys and the printer disgorged several dozen thin sheets.

Peter glanced over the text. "Do you have a grammar checker online?"

"Better than that, we have Proofreader, one of our expert systems."

"Can you feed this text through it?"

Sarkar typed some commands into the computer. An analysis of Spirit's comments from their various sessions appeared on screen. "Amazing," said Sarkar. He pointed to a figure. Ignoring simple interjections, Spirit averaged thirty-two words per sentence, and in some places had gone over three hundred words in a single sentence. "Normal conversation averages only ten or so words per sentence."

"Can this Proofreader of yours do a clean-up on the transcripts?"

"Sure."

"Do it."

Sarkar typed some commands. "Incredible," he said, once the results were on screen. "There was almost nothing to fix. Spirit has even his giant sentences completely under control and never loses his train of thought."

"Fascinating," said Peter. "Could it be a programming glitch?"

Sarkar smoothed his hair with his hand. "Have you noticed Control or Ambrotos doing the same thing?"

"No."

"Then offhand I would say it's not a glitch, but rather a real byproduct of the modifications we made. Spirit is the simulation of life after death—the intellect outside of the body. I'd say this effect must be a real consequence of having cut some neural-net connections related to that."

"Oh, Christ!" said Peter. "Of course that's it! For the other sims, you still simulate breathing. But Spirit doesn't have a body, so he doesn't have to pause to breathe when speaking. Breathing pauses must cause real people to express themselves in concise chunks."

"Interesting," said Sarkar. "I guess if you didn't have to

breathe you could express more complex thoughts in a single go. But that wouldn't really make you any smarter. It's thinking, not speaking, that counts."

"True, but, umm, I've noticed Spirit has a tendency to be a bit obtuse."

"I've noticed that too," said Sarkar. "So?"

"Well, what if he isn't being obtuse at all? What if, instead—gee, I don't even like saying this—what if he's simply talking over our heads? What if not just his manner of speaking but his actual thoughts are more complex than my own?"

Sarkar considered. "Well, there's nothing analogous to breathing pauses in the physical brain, except—except—"

"What?"

"Well, neurons only fire for so long," said Sarkar. "A neural net can only stay excited for a limited period."

"Surely that's a fundamental limitation of the human mind."

"No, it's a fundamental limitation of the human *brain*—more precisely, a limitation of the electrochemical process by which the brain works. The hardware of the brain is not designed to keep any one thought intact for any period of time. You've felt it, I'm sure: you come up with a brilliant idea you wish to write down, but by the time you get to a pen, you've lost it. The idea has simply decayed in your brain."

Peter lifted his eyebrows. "But Spirit is operating without a brain. He's just a mind, a soul. He's pure software, working without any hardware limitations. No breathing pauses. No nets decaying before he's finished with them. He can build as long a sentence, or as complex a thought, as he wants."

Sarkar was shaking his head slightly in amazement.

"That's how one's mind could go on forever after death," said Peter. "You couldn't just do it making simple connections, like chicken-crossing-the-road jokes. You'd run out of new juxtapose-A-and-B thoughts eventually. But Spirit can juxtapose A through Z, plus alpha through omega, plus aleph through tav, until, in all those complex combinations, some new, exciting, *amusing* association comes up."

"Incredible," said Sarkar. "It means—"

"It means," said Peter, "that perhaps the afterlife is full of jokes, but jokes so complex and subtle and obtuse that you and I will never understand them." He paused. "At least not until after we're dead."

Sarkar made a low whistle, but then his expression changed. "Speaking of being dead, I've got to get home or Raheema will kill me. I'm cooking dinner tonight."

Peter looked at the clock. "Cripes. I'm late for meeting Cathy—we're going out for dinner."

Sarkar laughed.

"What's so funny?"

"You'll get it," said Sarkar. "Eventually."

CHAPTER 32

The sim had been monitoring Food Food's computer, waiting for an order for the Churchill address. Finally, there it was—the same thing Rod, creature of habit that he was, had ordered for the last six weeks.

As soon as the order appeared in the system, the sim intercepted it, made one small modification, then let it continue on its way through the phone line to the Food Food store at Steeles and Bayview, six blocks from Rod Churchill's house.

PETER and Cathy had taken Cathy's car down Bayview Avenue. This part, some ten kilometers south of where her parents lived, was entirely lined with shops, boutiques, and restaurants. They'd briefly stopped in at The Sleuth of Baker Street, Toronto's mystery bookstore, and were now looking for a break in the traffic so they could cross over to the little Korean restaurant they both liked on the other side of the street.

A round man with a shock of white hair and clad in a navy blue trench coat was walking down the sidewalk. Peter noticed him doing a double take as he passed them. He was slowly getting used to that; he'd had enough press lately that people were recognizing him on the streets. But the man didn't move on. Instead, he came toward them.

"You're Peter Hobson, aren't you?" he said. He was about sixty, with little veins visible on the surface of his nose and cheeks.

"Yes," said Peter.

"You the guy who discovered that soul signal?"

"Soulwave," said Peter. "We call it the soulwave." A beat. "Yes, that's me."

"I thought so," said the man. "But you know, unless your soul is saved, you'll go to hell."

Cathy took Peter's arm. "Come on," she said. But the man moved to block their way. "Give yourself over to Jesus, Mr. Hobson—it's the only way."

"I'm, ah, really not interested in discussing this," said Peter.

"Jesus forgives you," said the man. He reached into the pocket of his trench coat. For one horrible moment, Peter thought the man was going for a gun, but instead he brought out a worn Bible, bound in blood-red leather. "Hear the word of God, Mr. Hobson! Save your soul!"

Cathy spoke directly to the man. "Leave us alone."

"I can't let you go," said the man. He reached out an arm and—

—connected with Cathy's shoulder.

Before Peter could react, Cathy had brought her shoe down on the man's instep. He yowled in pain. "Get lost!" shouted Cathy, and she firmly took Peter's arm, and propelled them both across the street.

"Hey," said Peter, still flustered but nonetheless impressed. "Pretty good."

Cathy tossed her black hair back. "No one messes with my husband," she said, grinning her megawatt grin. She led them the few doors down to the restaurant. "Now, let me buy you dinner."

THE doorbell rang. Rod Churchill glanced at his watch. Twenty-six minutes. He'd yet to get a free meal, although a history teacher at his high school said she'd gotten lucky twice in a row. Out of habit, Rod glanced at the security camera display on his TV. Yup, a Food Food driver, all right: the orange and white uniform was quite distinctive. Rod walked down to the entryway, checked himself in the hall mirror to make sure his hair was still properly combed over his bald head, and opened the door. He signed the receipt for the driver, who gave him one copy, then took his packaged food up to the dining room. Rod opened the envirofoam containers carefully, got himself a glass of white wine, put on the TV—easily visible from his place at the dining-room table—and sat down to enjoy his meal.

The roast beef was adequate if a bit stringy, Rod thought, but the gravy was particularly good tonight. He cleaned the serving dish, using forkfuls of mashed-up baked potato to sop up the last of the gravy. He was halfway through his slice of pie when the pain began: a severe pounding at the back of his head, and an excruciating sensation, as though spikes were being driven into his eyes. He felt his heart fluttering. His forehead was slick with sweat and he thought for a moment he was going to vomit. A hot flash came over him. He rose to his feet, in hopes of getting to the telephone and calling for help, but suddenly there was a moment of unbearable pain, and he toppled backward, knocking his chair over, and fell to the carpeted floor, stone-cold dead.

* * *

PETER and Cathy had already gone to bed, but their Hobson Monitor knew that neither of them were yet asleep, and so it allowed the phone to ring.

There was no video phone in the bedroom, of course. In the darkness, Peter groped for the audio handset on his night table.

"Hello?" he said.

A crying woman. "Oh, Peter! Peter!"

"Bunny?"

Hearing her mother's name, Cathy sat up in bed at once. "Lights!" she called out. The household computer turned on the two floor lamps in the room.

"Peter—Rod is dead."

"Oh my God," said Peter.

"What is it?" said Cathy, concerned. "What's wrong?"

"What happened?" said Peter, heart pounding.

"I just got back from my course, and I found him lying on the floor in the dining room."

"Have you called an ambulance?" asked Peter.

"What is it?" Cathy said again, horrified.

Bunny had been crying so much, she had to pause to blow her nose. "Yes. Yes, it's on its way."

"So are we," said Peter. "We'll be there as soon as we can."

"Thank you," said Bunny, terrified. "Thank you. Thank you."

"Just hold on," said Peter. "We're coming." He hung up.

"What's happening?" said Cathy.

Peter looked at his wife, her giant eyes wide in terror. My God, how to tell her? "That was your mother," he said. He knew she knew that, but he was buying time, composing his thoughts. "Your father—she thinks your father is dead."

Horror danced across Cathy's face. Her mouth hung open and she shook her head slightly from left to right.

"Get dressed," said Peter, gently. "We've got to get going."

NET NEWS DIGEST

Gallup's ongoing "Religion in America" survey showed church attendance this week was up 13.75% over the same week last year.

Christiaan Barnard Hospital in Mandelaville, Azania, announced today that it had formally adopted the departure of the soulwave from the body as the determining moment of death.

Schlockmeister Jon Tchobanian has begun production on his latest computer-generated flick, *Soul Catcher*. This one's about a mad hospital worker who imprisons people's souls in magnetic bottles and holds them for ransom. "Appropriately for a film about life after death," says Tchobanian, "I'm casting the movie entirely with computer reconstructions of dead actors." Boris Karloff and Peter Lorre will star.

Life Unlimited of San Rafael, California, reported today its best-ever month of sales for its patented nanotechnology immortality process. Analyst Gudrun Mungay of Merrill Lynch suggested that the record sales were a direct response to the discovery of the soulwave. "Some people," she said, "definitely do not want to meet their maker."

Trial news: Oshkosh, Wisconsin. Accused serial rapist Gordon Spitz today entered a plea of not guilty by reason of special insanity. Spitz, who claims to have had out-of-body experiences since the age of twelve, contends that his soul was absent from his body on each occasion that he committed rape, and therefore he is not responsible for the crimes.

CHAPTER 33

DECEMBER 2011

Sometimes there was nothing like a good, old-fashioned keyboard. For entering or massaging data, it was still the best tool yet invented. Sandra Philo pulled out the keyboard drawer of her desk and began typing in all the proper nouns she'd turned up in relation to the Hans Larsen murder, including the street he lived on, the name of the company he worked for, where he'd taken his vacation last year, and the names of neighbors, family, friends, and coworkers. She also entered a variety of terms related to the mutilation Larsen had suffered.

By the time she was finished, she had a list of over two hundred words. She then asked the computer to search the records of all homicides in Greater Toronto Region for the last year to see if any of the same terms showed up in the reports filed for them. As it processed the search, the computer drew a little line of dots on the screen to show that it was working. It only took a few seconds to complete the search. Nothing significant.

Sandra nodded to herself; she figured she'd have remembered a similar MO. After all, it's not every day a corpse is found with its penis lopped off. The computer presented her with suggestions for broader queries: all Ontario murders, all Canadian murders, all North American murders. It also suggested a series of time frames, from one month to ten years.

If she chose the broadest-based one, all North American killings for the last ten years, the search would take hours to run. She was about to select "all Ontario murders," but at the last moment changed her mind and typed her own query in the dialog box: "all deaths GTR >20110601," meaning all deaths—not just murders—in the Greater Toronto Region after June 1st of this year.

The little line of dots grew across the screen as the computer searched. After a few moments, the display cleared and this appeared:

Name:	Larsen, Hans
Date of Death:	14 Nov 2011
Cause of Death:	homicide
Search term correlated:	Hobson, Catherine R. (coworker)

Name:	Churchill, Roderick B.
Date of Death:	30 Nov 2011
Cause of Death:	natural causes
Search term correlated:	Hobson, Cathy (daughter)

Philo's eyebrows went up. Catherine Hobson—that slim, intelligent brunette Toby Bailey had identified as having been involved with Hans Larsen. Her father had died just two days ago.

It probably didn't mean a thing. Still . . . Sandra accessed the city registry. There was only one Catherine Hobson in GTR, and her record was indeed annotated "née Churchill." And—good God! She was listed as living with Peter G. Hobson, a biomedical engineer. The soulwave guy—Sandra had seen him on *Donahue* and read about him in *Maclean's*. They must be rolling in money . . . enough for either of them to hire a hitman.

Sandra switched back to the reports database and asked for full details on the Roderick Churchill death. Churchill, a high-school gym teacher, had died alone while eating dinner. Cause of death was recorded by medical examiner Warren Chen as "aneurysm(?)." That question mark was intriguing. Sandra turned on her video phone and dialed. "Hello, Warren," she said, once Chen's round, middle-aged face had appeared on the screen.

Chen smiled warmly. "Hello, Sandra. What can I do for you?"

"I'm calling about the death a couple of days ago of one Roderick Churchill."

"The gym teacher who combed his hair over? Sure, what about him?"

"You recorded the cause of death as an aneurysm."

"Uh-huh."

"But you put a question mark after it. Aneurysm, question mark."

"Oh, yes." Chen shrugged. "Well, you can never be completely sure. When God wants you, sometimes he just flicks the old switch in your head. Click! Aneurysm. You check out, just like that. That seemed to be what happened there. The guy was already on heart medication."

"Was there anything unusual about the case?"

Chen made the clucking sound that passed for his chuckle. "I'm afraid not, Sandra. There's nothing nefarious about a sixty-something-year-old man dropping dead—especially a gym teacher. They think they're in good shape, but they spend most of their day just watching other people exercise. The guy had been scarfing fast food when he died."

"Did you do an autopsy?"

The medical examiner clucked again; somebody had once suggested that Chen's name was a contraction of *chicken hen*.

"Autopsies are expensive, Sandra. You know that. No, I did a couple of quick tests at the scene, then signed the certificate. The widow—it's coming back to me now, her name was Bunny; can you believe that? Anyway, she'd found the body. Her daughter and son-in-law were with her when I got there around, oh, 1:30, quarter to two, in the morning." He paused. "Why the interest?"

"It's probably nothing," said Sandra. "Just that the man who died, Rod Churchill, was the father of one of the coworkers in that castration case."

"Oh, yes," said Chen, his voice full of relish. "Now there's an interesting one. Carracci was M.E. on that; she gets all the weird cases these days. But, Sandra, it seems a pretty tenuous connection, no? I mean it just sounds like this woman—what's her name?"

"Cathy Hobson."

"It just sounds like it's not Cathy Hobson's year, that's all. Run of bad luck."

Sandra nodded. "I'm sure you're right. Still, do you mind if I come down and look at your notes?"

Chen clucked again. "Of course not, Sandra. It's always a pleasure to see you."

PETER hated funerals. Not because he disliked being around dead people; one couldn't spend as much time in hospitals as he did without running into a few of those. No, it was the live ones he couldn't stand.

First, there were the hypocrites: the ones who hadn't seen the dear departed in years, but came out of the woodwork after it was too late to do the deceased any good.

Second, the wailers, the people who became so flamboyantly emotional that they, instead of the deceased, became the center of attention. Peter's heart did go out to close relatives who were having trouble dealing with the loss of someone they truly loved, but he had no patience for the distant cousins or five-blocks-away neighbors who went to pieces at funerals, until they were surrounded by a crowd of people trying to comfort them, loving every minute.

For his own part, as in all things, Peter tried for a certain stoicism—the stiff upper lip of his British ancestors.

Rod Churchill, vain man that he had been, wanted an open casket. Peter disapproved of those. As a child of seven, he'd gone to the funeral of his mother's father. Granddad had been known for his large nose. Peter remembered entering the chapel and seeing the coffin at the far end, the upper part open, the only thing visible from that angle being his grandfather's nose sticking up above the line made by the side of the casket. To this day, whenever he thought of his grandfather, the picture that came to mind first was of the dead man's proboscis, a lone peak rising into the air.

Peter looked around. The chapel he was in today was paneled in dark wood. The coffin looked expensive. Despite the request for donations to the Heart and Stroke Foundation of Ontario in lieu of flowers, there were many bouquets, and a large horseshoe-shaped affair sent by the teachers Rod had worked with. Must have been from the Phys. Ed. department—only those guys could be daft enough not to know that horseshoe arrangements meant "good luck," hardly the appropriate thing to send to a dead man.

Bunny was holding up bravely, and Cathy's sister, Marissa, although crying intermittently, seemed to be doing okay, too. Peter didn't know what to make of Cathy's reaction, though. Her face was impassive as she greeted people coming to pay their respects. Cathy, who cried when she watched sad movies and who cried when she read sad books, seemed to have no tears at all for her dead father.

IT wasn't much to go on, thought Sandra Philo. Two deaths. One clearly a murder; the other of indeterminate cause.

But they both had Cathy Hobson in common.

Cathy Hobson, who had slept with the murdered man, Hans Larsen.

Cathy Hobson, daughter of Rod Churchill.

True, Larsen had been involved with many women. True, Churchill had been in his sixties.

Still . . .

After Sandra had finished her work for the day, she drove to the Churchill house, at Bayview just south of Steeles. It was only five kilometers from 32 Division headquarters—not much of a waste if this turned out to be a wild-goose chase. She parked and went up to the front door. The Churchill family had a FILE scanner—Fingerprint Index Lock Electronics. Common these days. Above the scanning plate was a doorbell button. Sandra pushed it. A minute later, a woman with gray hair appeared at the door. "Yes?"

"Hello," said Sandra. "Are you Bunny Churchill?"

"Yes."

Sandra held up her ID. "I'm Alexandria Philo, Toronto Police. Can I ask you a few questions?"

"What about?"

"The, ah, death of your husband."

"Goodness," said Bunny. Then: "Yes, of course. Come in."

"Thank you—but, before I forget, can I ask whose fingerprints the FILE scanner accepts?" Sandra pointed at the blue glass plate.

"Mine and my husband's," said Bunny.

"Anybody else?"

"My daughters. My son-in-law."

"Cathy Hobson, and"—Sandra had to think for a moment—"Peter Hobson, is that right?"

"Yes, and my other daughter, Marissa."

They went inside.

"I'm sorry to bother you," said Sandra, smiling sympathetically. "I know this must be a very difficult time for you. But there are a few little questions I'd like to clear up, so we can close the file on your husband."

"I thought the file *was* closed," said Bunny.

"Almost," said Sandra. "The medical examiner wasn't a hundred percent sure of the cause of death, I'm afraid. He'd marked it down as probably an aneurysm."

"So I'd been told." Bunny shook her head. "It doesn't seem fair."

"Can you tell me if he had any health problems?"

"Rod? Oh, nothing serious. A little arthritis in one hand. Sometimes a little pain in his left leg. Oh, and he'd had a small heart attack three years ago—he took medication for that."

Probably insignificant. And yet . . . "Do you still have his heart pills?"

"I suppose they'd still be in the medicine cabinet upstairs."

"Would you mind showing them to me?" asked Sandra.

Bunny nodded. They went up to the bathroom together and Bunny opened the medicine cabinet. Inside, there was Tylenol, a container of dental floss, Listerine, some of those little shampoos they have at hotels, and two prescription bottles from Shoppers Drug Mart.

"Which one is his heart pills?" asked Sandra, pointing.

"Both," she said. "He'd been on one kind since his heart attack, and had been taking the other kind for several weeks now."

Sandra picked up the bottles. Both had small computer-printed labels stuck to them. One said it contained Cardizone-D, which certainly sounded like a heart drug. The other was labeled Nardil. Both had been prescribed by a Dr. H. Miller. The Nardil bottle had a fluorescent orange label on it: "Warning—severe dietary restrictions."

"What's this about dietary restrictions?" asked Sandra.

"Oh, there was a long list of things he wasn't supposed to eat. We were always very careful about that."

"But he'd been eating take-out food the night he died, according to the medical examiner."

"That's right," said Bunny. "He did that every Wednesday

while I was out at a course. But he always had the same thing, and it had never given him trouble before."

"Do you have any idea what he'd ordered?"

"Roast beef, I think."

"Do you still have the packaging?"

"I threw it out," said Bunny. "It's probably still in our Blue Box. We haven't had our trash pick-up yet."

"Do you mind if I have a look—and can I keep these pill bottles, please?"

"Uh, yes. Of course."

Sandra slipped the pill bottles into her jacket pocket, then followed her down. The recycling hopper was inside a wicker hamper. Sandra rummaged through it. She soon turned up a small slip of newsprint with Rod's order from Food Food printed on it.

"May I keep this, as well?" said Sandra.

Bunny Churchill nodded.

Sandra straightened up and put the slip of paper in her pocket. "I'm sorry to have disturbed you," she said.

"I wish you'd tell me what's going through your mind, Detective," said Bunny.

"Nothing at all, Mrs. Churchill. Like I said, just loose ends."

CHAPTER 34

Peter had flown to Ottawa for a meeting at Health and Welfare Canada, but it had lasted only a short time. It could have been done by conference call, but the Minister liked to wield her powers every now and then, summoning people to the capital.

The soulwave work, of course, wasn't the only project Hobson Monitoring was involved with. This meeting had been about the still-secret Project Indigo: a plan to produce a sensor that could categorically distinguish between an active smoker and one who had only been exposed to second-hand smoke. That way, the former could be disallowed benefits under provincial health-insurance plans for any illness caused by or exacerbated by smoking.

Anyway, with the meeting breaking up early, Peter found himself with an unexpected day to spend in Ottawa.

Ottawa was a government town, full of faceless bureaucrats. It produced nothing except documents and law, legislation and red tape. Still, it had to be a showcase for visiting world leaders—not everything could be in Toronto. Ottawa had many fine museums and galleries, a small amount of interesting shopping, the Rideau Canal (which in winter froze over, letting civil servants skate to work), and the pageantry of the changing of the guard on Parliament Hill. But Peter had seen all those things more than enough times in the past.

He asked the receptionist if there was a phone he could use, and she directed him to an unoccupied office. With government hiring freezes in their third decade, there were lots of those. The phone was an old audio-only model. Well, thought Peter, if they were going to spend tax dollars putting phones in unused offices, it was good that some restraint was being practiced. Like most Canadian executives, he knew Air Canada's 800-number by heart. He was about to dial it to see if he could change his flight, but suddenly he found himself dialing 4-1-1 instead.

A voice said in English, "Directory assistance for what city, please?" Then the same phrase was quickly repeated in French.

"Ottawa," said Peter. Video phones could access directory listings at the touch of a few keys, and for those who didn't have such things, it was cheaper, and more environmentally friendly, to have free directory assistance. About half the time, one got an electronic operator, but Peter could tell by the bored slurring of the words that he'd landed a real live human today.

"Go ahead," said the voice, realizing Peter's language preference from the way he'd said the single word "Ottawa."

"Do you have a listing for a Rebecca Keaton?" He spelled it.

"Nothing under that name, sir."

Oh, well. It had been an idle thought. "Thank—" Wait. Although now single, she'd been married for a short time years ago. What had that jerk's name been? Hunnicut? No. "Cunningham," said Peter. "Try Rebecca Cunningham, please."

"I have an R. L. Cunningham on Slater."

Rebecca Louise. "Yes, that would be it."

The bored human voice was replaced with a perky computer, which read out the number, then added, "Press the star key to dial that number now."

Peter hit the asterisk. He heard a melody of tones then the sound of a phone ringing. Once. Twice. Three times. Four. Oh, well—

"Hello?"

"Becky?"

"Yes. Who's this?"

"It's Peter Hobson. I'm—"

"Petey! How wonderful to hear your voice. Are you in town?"

"Yes. I had a meeting this morning at Health and Welfare. It broke up early and my flight's not till seven this evening. I didn't even know if you'd be home, but I thought I'd give you a call."

"I'm working Sundays through Thursdays. I'm off today."

"Ah."

"The famous Peter Hobson!" she said. "I saw you on *The National.*"

Peter chuckled. "Still the same old guy," he said. "It's good to hear your voice, Becky."

"And yours, too."

Peter felt his throat go dry. "Would you—would you be free for lunch today?"

"Oh, I'd *love* that. I've got to go by the bank this morning—in fact I was just on my way out to do that—but I could meet you, oh, gee, is eleven thirty too soon?"

Not at all. "That would be great. Where?"

"Do you know Carlo's on the Sparks Street Mall?"

"I can find it."

"I'll see you there at 11:30, then."

"Great," said Peter. "I'm looking forward to it."

Becky's voice was full of warmth. "Me, too. Bye!"

"Bye."

Peter left the little office and asked the receptionist if she knew Carlo's. "Oh, yes," she said, smiling mischievously. "It's quite a singles spot in the evening."

"I'm going there for lunch," said Peter, feeling a need to explain himself.

"Ah, well, it's a lot more quiet then. Good tortellini, though."

"Can you tell me how to get there?"

"Sure. Are you driving?"

"I'll walk if it's not too far."

"It'll take about half an hour."

"That's no problem," said Peter.

"I'll draw you a little map," she said, and proceeded to do so. Peter thanked her, took the elevator down to the lobby, and exited onto the street. The walk actually only took him twenty minutes; Peter was famous for his brisk walking speed. That meant he still had close to half an hour to kill. He found an on-demand newspaper box, fed three loonies into the machine, and waited the twenty seconds it took to print off a hardcopy of today's *Ottawa Citizen.* He then made his way back to Carlo's. It was deserted.

He asked for a table for two, was seated, and ordered black coffee. He looked around the place, trying to imagine it hopping with sweaty flesh in the evenings. He wondered if the receptionist had been pulling his leg. Still, there was a familiar face across the room: the same Molson's cutie who adorned the wall next to the pay phones at The Bent Bishop. Peter settled into reading the paper, trying to contain his nervousness.

HEATHER Miller was a general practitioner with an office in the lower floor of her house. She was about forty-five, short and wide, with chestnut hair cut in a bob. Her desk was made out of a thick glass sheet supported by marble blocks. When Sandra Philo came in, Miller waved a hand, indicating she should sit in a green leather chair facing the desk. "As I said on the phone, Detective, I'm severely constrained in what I can say because of physician-patient confidentiality."

Sandra nodded. It was the usual dance, the establishing of turf. "I understand, Doctor. The patient I wish to discuss is Rod Churchill."

Miller waited.

"I don't know if you've heard yet, but Mr. Churchill died last week."

The doctor's jaw dropped open. "I hadn't heard."

"I'm sorry to be the bearer of bad news," said Sandra. "He was found dead in his dining room. The medical examiner said it had likely been an aneurysm. I visited his house and found that you'd been treating him with Nardil, which, according to the label, means he had to watch what he ate. And yet he'd been eating take-out food before he died."

"Damn. Damn." She spread her arms. "I told him to be careful about what he ate, because of the phenelzine."

"Phenelzine?"

"Nardil is a brand name of phenelzine, Detective. It's an antidepressant."

Sandra's eyebrows went up. Bunny Churchill had thought both her husband's prescriptions were for his heart condition. "An antidepressant?"

"Yes," said Miller. "But it's also a monoamine oxidase inhibitor."

"Which means?"

"Well, the bottom line is if you're taking phenelzine, you have to avoid foods high in tyramine. Otherwise your blood pressure will go through the roof—a hypertensive crisis. See, when you're taking phenelzine, tyramine builds up; it's not metabolized. That causes vasoconstriction—a pressor effect."

"Which means?" said Sandra again. She just loved talking to doctors.

"Well, that kind of thing could conceivably kill even a healthy young person. For someone like Rod, who had a history of cardiovascular problems, it could very likely be fatal—

causing a massive stroke, a heart attack, a neurological event, or, as your medical examiner suggested, a burst aneurysm. I assume he ate the wrong thing. But I warned him about that."

Sandra tilted her head. Malpractice was always a possibility. "Did you?"

"Yes, of course." Miller's eyes narrowed. "That's not the sort of mistake I make, Detective. In fact—" She pushed a button on her desk intercom. "David, bring in the file on Mr. Churchill, please." Miller looked at Sandra. "Whenever a drug involves substantial risks, my insurance company makes me get the patient's signature on an information sheet. The sheets for each drug come in duplicate snap-sets. The patient signs them, I keep the duplicate, and he or she takes away the original—with all the warnings spelled out in plain English. So—ah." The office door opened and a young man walked in holding a file folder. He handed it to Miller, then left. She opened the thin file, pulled out a yellow sheet, and passed it to Sandra.

Sandra glanced at it, then handed it back. "Why use phenelzine if it has so many risks associated with it?"

"These days we mostly use reversible MAO inhibitors, but Rod didn't respond to them. Phenelzine used to be the gold standard in its class, and by checking MedBase, I found that one of his relatives had been successfully treated for the same sort of depression with it, so it seemed worth a try."

"And what exactly are the risks? Suppose he ate the wrong food? What would happen?"

"He would start by having occipital headaches and retro-orbital pain." The doctor raised a hand. "Excuse me—that's headaches at the back of the head and pain behind the eye sockets. He'd also have had palpitations, flushing, nausea, and sweating. Then, if he didn't get immediate treatment, intracerebral bleeding, a stroke, a burst aneurysm, or whatever, to finish him off."

"It doesn't sound like a pleasant way to go," said Sandra.

"No," said Miller, shaking her head sadly. "If he'd gotten

to a hospital, five milligrams of phentolamine would have saved him. But if he'd been alone, he could easily have blacked out."

"Had Churchill been your patient long?"

Miller frowned. "About a year. See, Rod was in his sixties. As often happens, his original doctor had been older than him, and he died last year. Rod finally got around to finding a new doctor because he needed his Cardizone prescription renewed."

"But you said you were treating him for depression. He hadn't come to see you specifically for that?"

"No—but I recognized the signs. He said he'd had insomnia for years and when we got to talking about things, it seemed clear that he was depressed."

"What was he sad about?"

"Clinical depression is a lot more than just being sad, Detective. It's an *illness*. The patient is physically and psychologically unable to concentrate and he or she feels dejection and hopelessness."

"And you treated his depression with drugs?"

Miller sighed, picking up the implied criticism in Sandra's tone. "We're not stringing these people out, Detective; we're trying to get their body chemistry back to what it should be. When it works, the patient describes the treatment as being like a curtain drawing away from a window and letting the sun in for the first time in years." Miller paused, as if considering whether to go on. "In fact, I give Rod a lot of credit. He'd probably been suffering from depression for decades—possibly since he was a teenager. His old doctor had simply failed to recognize the signs. Lots of older people are afraid of having their depression treated, but not Rod. He wanted to be helped."

"Why are they afraid?" asked Sandra, genuinely curious.

Miller spread her arms. "Think about it, Detective. Suppose I told you that for most of your life your ability to function had been severely impaired. Now, for a young person like yourself, you'd probably want that fixed—after all, you've got decades ahead of you. But older people very often refuse to believe they've been suffering from clinical depression. The regret would be too much to bear—the realization that their lives, which are now almost over, could have been so much better and happier. They prefer to shut out that possibility."

"But not Churchill?"

"No, not him. He was a Phys. Ed. teacher after all—he taught high-school health classes. He accepted the idea and was willing to try the treatments. We were both upset when the reversible inhibitors didn't work for him, but he was game for trying phenelzine—and he knew how important it was to avoid the wrong foods."

"Which are?"

"Well, ripe cheese for one. It's full of tyramine as a breakdown product of the amino acid tyrosine. He also couldn't eat smoked, pickled, or cured meats, fishes, or caviar."

"Surely he'd notice if he was eating any of those things."

"Well, yes. But you also get tyramine in yeast extract, brewer's yeast, and meat extracts such as Marmite or Oxo. It's also in hydrolyzed protein extracts such as those commonly used as a base for soups, gravies, and sauces."

"Did you say gravies?"

"Yes—he should have avoided them."

Sandra fished in her pocket for the small, stained slip of newsprint—the receipt from Food Food for Rod Churchill's last supper. She handed it across the glass desktop to Dr. Miller. "This is what he ate the night he died."

Miller read it, then shook her head. "No," she said. "We talked about Food Food the last time he was in. He'd told me he always ordered their low-calorie gravy—said he'd checked and that it was free of anything he was supposed to avoid."

"Maybe he forgot to specify low-cal," said Sandra.

Miller handed back the printout. "I doubt that, Detective. Rod Churchill was a very meticulous man."

TEN minutes early, Becky Cunningham arrived at Carlo's. Peter got up. He didn't know what kind of greeting to expect: a smile, a hug, a kiss? Turned out he got all three, with the kiss being a lingering nuzzle of his cheek. Peter was surprised to find his heart racing slightly. She smelled terrific.

"Petey, you look wonderful," she said, sitting down in the chair opposite him.

"So do you," said Peter.

Actually, Becky Cunningham had never been what one would call a beautiful woman. Pleasant-looking, yes, but not beautiful. She had shoulder-length dark-brown hair a bit shorter than was the current style. She was twenty pounds heavier than a fashion magazine would call ideal, or ten pounds more than what any less severe arbiter would suggest. Her face was broad, with archipelagos of freckles on both cheeks. Her green eyes positively twinkled when she talked, an effect enhanced by the network of lines at their corners that had appeared since Peter had last seen her.

Absolutely wonderful, thought Peter.

They ordered lunch. Peter took the receptionist's advice and had the tortellini. They talked about all sorts of things, and there was as much laughter as there were words. Peter felt better than he had for weeks.

Peter picked up the tab. He tipped twenty-five percent, then helped her put her coat on . . . something he hadn't done for Cathy in years.

"What are you going to do until your flight leaves?" asked Becky.

"I don't know. Sightsee, I guess. Whatever."

Becky looked into his eyes. This was the natural parting point. Two old friends had gotten together for lunch, caught up on old times, swapped stories of various acquaintances.

But now it was time to go their separate ways again, get on with their separate lives.

"I don't have anything important to do this afternoon," said Becky, still looking straight into his eyes. "Mind if I join you?"

Peter broke her gaze for a moment. He couldn't think of anything he wanted more in the world. "That would be"—and, after a brief pause, he decided not to censor himself—"*perfect.*"

Becky's eyes danced. She fell in beside him and tucked her arm through his. "Where would you like to go?" she said.

"It's your town," said Peter with a smile.

"That it is," said Becky.

They did all the things that hadn't interested Peter earlier. They saw the changing of the guard; they visited some little boutiques, the kinds of stores Peter never went into in Toronto; and they ended up by ambling through the dinosaur gallery at the Canadian Museum of Nature, marveling at the skeletons.

It was just like being alive, thought Peter. Just like the way it used to be.

The Museum of Nature was, appropriately enough, on a large, well-treed lot. By the time they left the museum, it was around five o'clock and getting dark. There was a cool breeze. The sky was cloudless. They walked across the grounds until they came to some park benches beneath a stand of huge maple trees, now, in early December, devoid of their leaves.

"I'm exhausted," Peter said. "I got up at 5:30 this morning to get the flight here."

Becky sat down at the far end of the park bench. "Lie down," she said. "We've been walking all afternoon."

Peter's first thought was to resist the notion, but then he decided, why the hell not? He was just about to stretch out on the remaining part of the bench when Becky spoke. "You can use my lap as a pillow."

He did just that. She was wonderfully soft and warm and

human. He looked up at her. She placed an arm gently across his chest.

It was so relaxing, so soothing. Peter thought he could stay here for hours. He didn't even notice the cold.

Becky smiled down at him, an unconditional smile, an accepting smile, a *beautiful* smile.

For the first time since lunch, Peter thought about Cathy and Hans and what his life had become back in Toronto.

He realized, too, that he'd finally found a real human being—not some computer-generated simulacrum—that he could talk to about it. Someone who wouldn't think him a lesser man because his wife had strayed, someone who wouldn't ridicule him, wouldn't mock him. Someone who accepted him, who would just listen, who would understand.

And in that moment Peter realized that he didn't have to talk to anyone about it. He could deal with it now. All his questions were answered.

Peter had met Becky when they were both in their first year at U of T, before Cathy had arrived on the scene. There had been an awkward attraction between them. They were both inexperienced and he, at least, had been a virgin at the time. Now, though, two decades later, things were different. Becky had married and divorced; Peter had married. They knew about sex, about how it was done, about when it happened, when the time was right. Peter realized that he could easily call Cathy, tell her that his meeting had gone overtime and that he was going to spend the night here, tell her that he wouldn't be back until tomorrow. And then he and Becky could go back to her place.

He *could* do that, but he wasn't going to. He had the answer to his unasked question now. Given the same opportunity as Cathy had, he would not cheat, would not betray, would not get even.

Peter beamed up at Becky. He could feel the wounds inside him starting to heal.

"You're a wonderful person," he said to her. "Some guy is going to be very lucky to be yours."

She smiled.

Peter exhaled, letting everything go, everything flow out of him. "I've got to get to the airport," he said.

Becky nodded and smiled again, perhaps, just perhaps, a bit ruefully.

Peter was ready to go home.

CHAPTER 35

Sandra drove down the Don Valley Parkway to Cabbagetown, parking outside the very first Food Food store at the corner of Parliament and Wellesley. According to directory assistance, the centralized order-processing facility was located upstairs from this store. Sandra walked up the steep flight of steps and, without knocking, simply entered the room. There were two dozen people wearing telephone headsets sitting in front of computer terminals. They all seemed to be busy taking orders, even though it was only two in the afternoon.

A middle-aged woman with steel blonde hair came up to Sandra. "Can I help you?"

Sandra flashed her badge and introduced herself. "And who are you?"

"Danielle Nadas," the blonde woman said. "I'm the supervisor here."

Sandra looked around, fascinated. She'd ordered from Food Food many times herself since her divorce, but hadn't really had any mental picture of what was at the other end of the telephone line—over video phones, all you saw were visual ads for Food Food specials. Finally, she said, "I'd like to see the records for one of your customers."

"Do you know the phone number?"

Sandra started to sing: "Nine-six-seven . . ."

Nadas smiled. "Not *our* phone number. The customer's phone number."

Sandra handed her a slip of paper with it written on it. Nadas went over to a terminal and tapped the young man who was operating it on the shoulder. He nodded, finished taking the order he was currently processing, then got out of the way. The supervisor sat down and typed in the phone number. "Here it is," she said, leaning to one side so that Sandra could clearly see the screen.

Rod Churchill had ordered the same meal the last six Wednesdays in a row—except . . .

"He had low-calorie gravy every time but the most recent," said Sandra. "For the most recent, it shows regular gravy."

The supervisor leaned in. "So it does." She grinned. "Well, our low-cal stuff is pretty vile, if you ask me. It's not even real gravy—it's made from vegetable gelatin. Maybe he just decided to try the regular."

"Or maybe one of your order takers made a mistake."

The supervisor shook her head. "Not possible. We always assume the person wants the same thing they ordered last time—nine times out of ten, that's the case. The CSR wouldn't have rekeyboarded the order unless there was a specific change."

"CSR?"

"Customer Service Representative."

Ho boy, thought Sandra.

"If there'd been no change," said Nadas, "the CSR would have just hit F2—that's our key for 'repeat order.'"

"Can you tell who processed his most recent order?"

"Sure." She pointed to a field on the screen. "CSR 054—that's Annie Delano."

"Is she here?" asked Sandra.

The supervisor looked around the room. "That's her over there—the one with the ponytail."

"I'd like to talk to her," said Sandra.

"I can't see what difference all this makes," said the supervisor.

"The difference," said Sandra coolly, "is that the man who ordered that meal died from a reaction to the food he ate."

The supervisor covered her mouth. "Oh my God," she said. "I—I should call my boss."

"That won't be necessary," said Sandra. "I just want to speak to that young lady over there."

"Of course. Of course." The supervisor led the way over to where Annie Delano was working. She looked to be about seventeen. She'd obviously just received a repeat order, and had done exactly what the supervisor said she would do—tap the F2 key.

"Annie," said Nadas, "this woman is a police officer. She'd like to ask you some questions."

Annie looked up, eyes wide.

"Ms. Delano," said Sandra, "last Wednesday night, you processed an order from a man named Rod Churchill for a roast beef dinner."

"If you say so, ma'am," Annie said.

Sandra turned to the supervisor. "Bring it up on screen."

The supervisor leaned in and tapped out Churchill's phone number.

Annie looked at the screen, her expression blank.

"You changed his regular order," Sandra said. "He always had low-calorie gravy before, but last time you gave him regular gravy."

"I'd only have done that if that's what he asked for," said Annie.

"Do you recall him asking for a change?"

Annie looked at the screen. "I'm sorry, ma'am. I don't recall anything about that order at all. I do over two hundred orders a day, and that was a week ago. But, honest, I wouldn't have made the change unless he asked for it."

ALEXANDRIA Philo went back to Doowap Advertising, co-opting one of the few private offices to do more interviews with Hans Larsen's coworkers. Although her particular interest was Cathy Hobson, she first briefly re-interviewed two other people so as not to make Cathy suspicious.

Once Cathy had sat down, Sandra gave her a sympathetic smile. "I've just heard about your father," she said. "I'm very sorry. I lost my own father last year; I know how difficult it can be."

Cathy gave a small, civil nod. "Thank you."

"I'm curious, though," said Sandra, "about the fact that both Hans Larsen and your father died very close together."

Cathy sighed. "It never rains but it pours, eh?"

Sandra nodded. "So you think it's a coincidence?"

Cathy looked shocked. "Of course it's a coincidence. I mean, goodness, I had only a peripheral involvement with Hans, and my father died of natural causes."

Sandra looked Cathy up and down, assessing her. "As far as Hans goes, we both know that what you're saying isn't true. You had some sort of romantic involvement with him." Cathy's large, blue eyes blazed defiantly. Sandra raised her hand. "Don't worry, Ms. Hobson. How you choose to run your life is your own affair—so to speak. I've no intention of exposing your infidelity to your husband—or to Hans's widow, for that matter. Assuming, that is, that you had nothing to do with his murder."

Cathy was angry. "Look—in the first place, what happened between me and Hans was a long time ago. In the second place, my husband already knows about it. I told him everything."

Sandra was surprised. "You did?"

"Yes." Cathy seemed to realize that she might have made

a mistake. She pressed on. "So you see," she said, "I have nothing to hide and no reason to try to silence Hans."

"What about your father?"

Cathy looked exasperated. "Once again, he died of natural causes."

"I'm sorry to have to be the one to tell you," said Sandra, "but I'm afraid that's not true."

Cathy was angry. "God damn it, Detective. It's hard enough going through the loss of a parent without you playing games."

Sandra nodded. "Believe me, Ms. Hobson, I would *never* say such a thing if I didn't believe it to be true. But it's a fact that your father's dinner order was tampered with."

"Dinner order? What are you talking about?"

"Your father was on a prescription drug that had severe dietary restrictions. Every Wednesday when your mother was out, he ordered dinner—always the same thing, always safe for him. But on the day he died, his dinner order was tampered with, and he received something that caused a severe reaction, forcing his blood pressure to intolerably high levels."

Cathy was flabbergasted. "What are you talking about, Detective? Death by fast food?"

"I'd assumed it was an accident," said Sandra. "But I did some checking. It turns out that the national MedBase was compromised a few days before your father died. Whoever did that could have found out that he was on phenelzine."

"Phenelzine?" said Cathy. "But that's an antidepressant."

"You know it?" asked Sandra, eyebrows climbing.

"My sister was on it for a while."

"And you know about the dietary restrictions?"

"No cheese," said Cathy.

"Well, there's a lot more to it than that."

Cathy was shaking her bowed head in what looked to Sandra like very genuine astonishment. "Dad on an antidepressant," she said softly, as if talking to herself. But then she looked up and met Sandra's eyes. "This is crazy."

"An access log is kept for MedBase. It took a lot of work, but I checked all the accesses for the two weeks prior to your father's death. There was a bogus login three days before he died."

"Bogus how?"

"The doctor under whose name the access was made was on vacation in Greece when it happened."

"You can log on to most databases from anywhere in the world," said Cathy.

Sandra nodded. "True. But I called Athens; the doctor swears he's been doing nothing except visiting archeological sites since he got there."

"And you can tell whose records were accessed?"

Sandra dropped her gaze for a moment. "No. Just when whoever was using the account logged on and logged off. Both accesses were at about 4:00 a.m. Toronto time—"

"That's in the middle of the day in Greece."

"Yes, but it's also when the MedBase system is under the least demand. I'm told there are almost never any access delays at that time. If someone wanted to get on and off as quickly as possible, that would be when to do it."

"Still, using food ingredients to trigger a fatal reaction—that would require a lot of expertise."

"Indeed," said Sandra. A pause. "You have a degree in chemistry, don't you?"

Cathy exhaled noisily. "In *inorganic* chemistry, yes. I don't know anything about pharmaceuticals." She spread her hands. "This all seems pretty far-fetched to me, Detective. The worst enemy my father had was the football coach from Newtonbrook Secondary School."

"And his name is?"

Cathy made an exasperated sound. "I'm joking, Detective. I don't know anyone who'd want to kill my father."

Sandra looked off in the distance. "Perhaps you're right. This job gets to you sometimes." She smiled disarmingly. "We're all a little prone to conspiracy theories, I'm afraid.

Forgive me—and, please, let me say again that I'm sorry your father passed away. I *do* know what you're going through."

Cathy's voice was neutral, but her eyes were seething. "Thank you."

"Just a few more questions, then hopefully I won't have to bother you again." Sandra consulted the display on her palmtop. "Does the name Desalle mean anything to you? Jean-Louis Desalle?"

Cathy said nothing.

"He was at the University of Toronto at the same time you were there."

"That was a long time ago."

"True. Let me put it to you more directly: when I spoke to Jean-Louis Desalle, he recognized your name. Not Catherine Hobson—Catherine Churchill. And he recalled your husband, too: Peter Hobson."

"The name you mentioned," said Cathy, carefully, "is vaguely familiar."

"Have you seen Jean-Louis Desalle since university?"

"Goodness, no. I have no idea what became of him."

Sandra nodded. "Thank you, Ms. Hobson. Thank you very much. That'll be all for now."

"Wait," said Cathy. "Why'd you ask about Jean-Louis?"

Sandra closed her palmtop and put it in her attaché case. "He's the doctor whose database account was compromised."

CHAPTER 36

Spirit, the simulation of Peter Hobson's immortal soul, continued to watch Sarkar's artificial life evolve. The process was fascinating.

Not a game.

Life.

But poor Sarkar—he lacked vision. His programs were trivial. Some simply produced cellular automata, others merely evolved shapes that resembled insects. Oh, the blue fish were impressive, but Sarkar's were nowhere near as complex as real fish, and, besides, fish hadn't been the dominant form of life on Earth for over three hundred million years.

Spirit wanted more. Much more. After all, he could now handle situations infinitely more complex than what Sarkar could deal with, and he had all the time in the universe.

Before he began, though, he thought for a long time—thought about *exactly* what he wanted.

And then, his selection criteria defined, he set out to create it.

* * *

PETER had decided to give up on Spenser novels, at least temporarily. He'd been somewhat shamed by the fact that the Control version of himself was reading Thomas Pynchon. Scanning the living-room bookshelves, he found an old copy of *A Tale of Two Cities* his father had given him when he'd been a teenager. He'd never gotten around to reading it, but, to his embarrassment, it was the only classic he could find in the house—his days of Marlowe and Shakespeare, Descartes and Spinoza were long past. Of course he could have downloaded just about anything from the net—one nice thing about the classics: they're all public domain. But he'd been spending too much time interfacing with technology lately. An old, musty book was just the thing he needed.

Cathy was sitting on the couch, a reader in hand. Peter sat down next to her, opened his book's stiff cover, and began to read:

> It was the best of times, it was the worst of times, it was the age of wisdom, it was the age of foolishness, it was the epoch of belief, it was the epoch of incredulity, it was the season of Light, it was the season of Darkness, it was the spring of hope, it was the winter of despair, we had everything before us, we had nothing before us, we were all going direct to Heaven, we were all going direct the other way.

Peter smiled to himself: a sentence worthy of the Spirit sim. Maybe being paid by the word was as good as being dead for letting one stretch out a thought.

He didn't get much farther than that before he became aware, in his peripheral vision, that Cathy had put down her reader and was staring at him. Peter looked at her expectantly.

"That detective Philo came to see me at work again," she said, pushing her black hair back over her ear.

Peter closed the book and put it on the end table. "I wish she'd leave you alone."

Cathy nodded. "So do I—I can't say she's a bad sort; she seems courteous enough. But she thinks there's some connection between my father's death and Hans's death."

Peter shook his head in wonder. "Your father's death was just an aneurysm or something like that."

"That's what I thought. But that detective says he may have been killed deliberately. He was on an antidepressant drug called phenelzine, and—"

"Rod? On an antidepressant?"

Cathy nodded. "I was surprised, too. The detective says he ate some food he shouldn't have and that caused his blood pressure to shoot way up. With his medical history, that was enough to kill him."

"Surely that was an accident," said Peter. "He failed to pay attention to, or maybe just misunderstood, his doctor's orders."

"My father was very meticulous, you know that. Detective Philo thinks his food order was tampered with."

Peter was incredulous. "Really?"

"That's what she says." A beat. "Do you remember Jean-Louis Desalle?"

"Jean-Louis . . . you mean Stroke?"

"Stroke?"

"That was his nickname at university. He had these veins that bulged out of his forehead. We always thought he was about to have a stroke." Peter looked out the living-room window. "Stroke Desalle. God, I haven't thought about him for years. I wonder what became of him?"

"He's a doctor, apparently. His account may have been used to access my father's medical records."

"What could Stroke possibly have against your father? I mean, heck, presumably they'd never even met."

"The detective thinks someone else was using Desalle's account."

"Oh."

"And," said Cathy, "that detective knows about me and Hans."

"You told her?"

"No, of course not. It's none of her business. But somebody did."

Peter exhaled noisily. "I knew everyone at your company must have known about it." He slapped his palm against the couch's armrest. *"Damn!"*

"Believe me," said Cathy, "I'm as embarrassed as you are."

Peter nodded. "I know. I'm sorry."

Cathy's voice was cautious, as if testing the waters. "I keep trying to think about who might have had it in for both Hans and dad."

"Any ideas?"

She looked at him for a long moment. Finally, simply, she said, "Did you do it, Peter?"

"What?"

Cathy swallowed hard. "Did you arrange for Hans and my father to be killed?"

"I don't fucking believe this," said Peter.

Cathy looked at him, saying nothing.

"How can you ask me something like that?"

She shook her head slightly. Emotions played across her face—trepidation at having to ask the question, more fear about what the answer might be, a touch of shame over even contemplating the issue, anger simmering. "I don't know," she said, her tone not quite under control. "It's just that—well, you *do* have a motive, sort of."

"Maybe for Hans, but for your father?" Peter spread his arms. "If I killed everyone I thought was an idiot, we'd have bodies stacked up to the rafters."

Cathy said nothing.

"Besides," said Peter, feeling a need to fill the silence,

"there were probably lots of angry husbands who would have liked to have seen Hans killed."

Cathy looked directly at him. "But even if what you say about other angry husbands is true, none of them would also want my father dead."

"That stupid detective is making you paranoid. I swear to you, I didn't kill your father or"—he spoke the name through clenched jaws—"Hans."

"But, if the detective is right, these were arranged deaths . . ."

"I didn't arrange for them, either. Jesus Christ, what do you think I am?"

She shook her head. "I'm sorry. I know you wouldn't do anything like that. It's just that, well, it seems like something that someone in your position might have done . . . if that someone hadn't been you, that is."

"And I tell you—oh, Christ!"

"What?"

"Nothing."

"No, something's wrong. Tell me."

Peter was already on his feet. "Later. I've got to talk to Sarkar."

"Sarkar? You don't think he's responsible?"

"Christ, no. It's not like Hans wrote *The Satanic Verses.*"

"But—"

"I've got to go. I'll be back late." Peter grabbed his coat and headed out the front door.

PETER was driving along Post Road toward Bayview. He activated the car phone and hit the speed-dial key for Sarkar's house. His wife answered.

"Hello?"

"Hi, Raheema. It's Peter."

"Peter! How good to hear from you!"

"Thanks. Is Sarkar home?"

"He's downstairs watching the hockey game."

"Can I talk to him, please? It's very important."

"Gee," said Raheema, wistfully, "*I* never get to speak to him during a game. Just a sec."

At last, Sarkar's voice came on the line. "It's six-all, in sudden-death overtime, Peter. This better be *very* important."

"I'm sorry," said Peter. "But, look, did you read about that murder victim in the paper whose body was mutilated? Several weeks ago?"

"I think so, yeah."

"That was one of Cathy's coworkers."

"Oh."

"And—" said Peter, then he stopped.

"Yes?"

He's your best friend, Peter thought. Your best friend. He felt slightly nauseous. All those dinners together, face to face, and now he was going to have to spill it over the phone? "Cathy had an affair with him."

Sarkar sounded shocked. "Really?"

Peter forced out the word. "Yes."

"Wow," said Sarkar. "Wow."

"And you know that Cathy's father died recently."

"Of course. I was very sorry to hear that."

"I'm not sure I can say the same thing," said Peter, pausing briefly at a red light.

"What do you mean?"

"They're suggesting now that his death was murder."

"Murder!"

"Yes. Both him and Cathy's coworker."

"A'udhu billah."

"I didn't do it," said Peter.

"Of course not."

"But I did want them dead, in a way. And—"

"You're a suspect?"

"I suppose."

"But you didn't do it?"

"No, at least not this version of me."

"This ver—oh, my goodness."

"Exactly."

"Meet me at Mirror Image," said Sarkar. He clicked off.

Peter moved into the passing lane.

PETER lived closer to Mirror Image than Sarkar himself did. Add to that Peter's head start and he ended up waiting a good thirty minutes for Sarkar, parked in a lot with only one other car in it.

Sarkar's Toyota pulled up next to Peter's Mercedes. Peter was outside his car, leaning against the passenger door.

"The Leafs won," said Sarkar. "I heard it on the way over."

An irrelevancy. Sarkar was looking for some stability in the madness. Peter nodded, accepting the comment.

"So you think . . . you think one of the sims . . . ?" Sarkar was afraid to speak the thought out loud.

Peter nodded. "Maybe." They began walking toward the glassed-in entrance to the Mirror Image offices. Sarkar pressed his thumb against the FILE scanner. "There's proof, apparently, that my father-in-law's medical records were examined, using an account that belonged to a man I knew at university."

"Oh." They were heading down a long corridor. "Still, you would need his password and such."

"At U of T, they assign account names by adding your first initial to your last name. And for passwords, the default on the first day of classes is always your own last name spelled backwards. They tell you to change it, but there's always some idiot who never does. If a simulation of me was looking for a way into the medical database, it might have tried names at random of med students I'd known back then and seen if any of them still used their old account names and passwords."

They'd come to Sarkar's computer lab. He touched his

thumb against another FILE scanner. Bolts popped aside and the heavy door slid noisily open. "So now we must turn off the sims," said Sarkar.

Peter frowned.

"What's wrong?" said Sarkar.

"I—guess I'm just a bit reluctant to do that," Peter said. "First, of course, likely only one sim is guilty; the others don't have to suffer."

"We don't have time to play detective. We have to stop this before the guilty sim kills again."

"But will he kill again? I know why Hans was murdered, and, although I wouldn't have done the same thing, I can't honestly say I'm sorry he's dead. And I even understand why my father-in-law was killed. But there's no one else I want to see dead. Oh, there are others who have wronged me or ripped me off or made parts of my life miserable, but I honestly don't wish that any of them were dead."

Sarkar pantomimed slapping Peter's face. "Wake up, Peter. It'd be criminal not to shut them off."

Peter nodded slowly. "You're right, of course. It's time to pull the plug."

CHAPTER 37

Sarkar cracked his knuckles nervously, shifted his barstool in front of the master computer console, and spoke into the microphone: "Login."

"Login name?" asked the computer.

"Sarkar."

"Hello, Sarkar. Command?"

"Multiple delete, no prompts: all files in subdirectories Control, Spirit, and Ambrotos."

"Confirm delete?"

"Yes."

"Delete failure. Files are read-only."

Sarkar nodded. "Attributes, all files and subdirectories specified previously, read-only off."

"Attributes are password locked."

"Password: Abu Yusuf."

"Incorrect password."

Sarkar turned to Peter. "That's the only password I use these days."

Peter shrugged. "Try again."

"Password: Abu Yusuf." He spelled it.

"Incorrect password."

"Who locked the files?" asked Sarkar.

"Hobson, Peter G.," replied the computer.

Peter's heart began to pound. "Oh, shit."

"Display user log, Hobson, Peter G.," said Sarkar.

A list of dates and times appeared on the screen. Sarkar slapped his hand against the table top. "See that? Node 999? Diagnostic mode. Your account was used, but accessed internally—from inside the system."

"Damn!" Peter leaned into the mike. "Login."

"Login name?" said the computer.

"Fobson."

"Hello, Peter. Should I terminate your other session?"

"What other session?"

"You are logged on here at node 001 and also at node 999."

Sarkar leaned forward. "Yes," said Peter. "Absolutely. Terminate session at node 999."

"Logoff failure."

"Damn," said Peter. He turned to Sarkar. "Can that other session override this one?"

"No. The most recent login takes precedence."

"Okay," said Peter, rubbing his hands together. "Reference directories and files previously specified by Sarkar. Unlock attributes."

"Password?"

"Password: Mugato."

"Incorrect password."

"Password: Sybok."

"Incorrect password."

"Dammit," said Peter. He looked to Sarkar. "Those are the only two passwords I ever use."

Sarkar exhaled noisily. "They're not going to let us erase them."

"Can we take this system offline?"

Sarkar nodded and spoke into the microphone. "Initiate shutdown."

"Jobs are currently running. Confirm command?"

"Yes. Initiate shutdown."

"Password?"

"Password: Abu—"

The red light on the microphone winked off. Sarkar slammed his palm against the console again. "They've shut off voice input."

"Christ," said Peter.

"This is silly," said Sarkar, angrily. "We can still pull the physical plug." He reached for the phone, dialed a three-digit extension.

"Maintenance," said a woman's voice on the other end of the line.

"Hello," said Sarkar. "I know it is late, but this is Dr. Muhammed speaking. We are, ah, having a little difficulty up here. I need you to cut all power to our computing facility."

"Cut it, sir?"

"That's correct."

"Okay," she said. "It'll take a few minutes. You're aware, though, that your data-processing department is on a UPS—you know, an uninterruptable power supply. It'll run on batteries for a while."

"How long?"

"If everything's turned on, only six or seven minutes—just enough to weather any short blackout."

"Can you disconnect the UPS?"

"Sure, if you like. It'll have to be physically unplugged; I can't turn it off from down here. I'm the only one on duty right now. Can I get someone to do it for you tomorrow?"

"This is an emergency," said Sarkar. "Can you come up and show us how to do it? I've someone here with me if it's warm bodies you need."

"Okay. You want me to cut the mains before I come up?"

"No—we'll cut them after the UPS is disconnected." He covered the mouthpiece and spoke to Peter. "That means everything will go off at once, without giving the sims any warning."

Peter nodded.

"Whatever you say, sir," said the maintenance person. "Give me a few minutes, then I'll be up." Sarkar put down the phone.

"What will you do once the power is off?" asked Peter.

Sarkar was already on the floor, trying to remove an access panel from underneath the computer console. "Take out the optical drives and hook them up to a test bench. I can zap data on a bit-by-bit basis, if need be, using a Norton laser, so—"

The phone rang.

"Can you get that?" Sarkar said, struggling with a stubborn wing-nut.

The video phone's screen displayed a notice that the incoming call was audio-only. Peter picked up the handset. "Hello?"

There was staticky silence for about two seconds, then an obviously synthesized voice came on. "Hel-lo," it said.

Peter felt himself flush with anger. He hated computerized telephone solicitations. He was in the process of slamming down the receiver when he heard the next word, "Pe-ter."

In the split second before the handset hit the cradle, he realized that even if the soliciting computer was working from an online phone directory, there's no way a stranger would expect to find him at this number. He stopped short and pulled the receiver back to his face.

"Who is this?" he said. He glanced down at the lights on the phone deskset. This wasn't a call being transferred internally; it was coming over an outside line.

"It's," said the voice, dull and mechanical, "you."

Peter held the handset in front of his face, looking at it as if it were a serpent.

More words came from the earpiece, each one separated from the next by a small, static-filled space. "Surely you didn't expect us to stay cooped up on that small workstation?"

THE maintenance person arrived a few minutes later, carrying a toolbox. Sarkar looked up at her, turmoil plain, at least to Peter's eyes, on Sarkar's face.

"All set?" she said.

"Ah, no," said Sarkar. "Sorry to have dragged you up here. We, ah, don't need to disconnect the UPS anymore, or to cut the mains."

The woman looked surprised. "Whatever you say."

"My apologies," said Sarkar.

She nodded and left.

Peter and Sarkar sat staring at each other, dumbfounded.

"We really fucked up, didn't we?" said Peter at last.

Sarkar nodded.

"Damn," said Peter. "God damn it." A long pause. "There's no way to shut them off now that they're out in the net, is there?"

Sarkar shook his head.

"Now what?" said Peter.

"I don't know," said Sarkar. "I don't know."

"If we knew which sim was responsible, maybe we could find a way to isolate that particular one. But, damn, how do we figure that out?"

"Morality," said Sarkar.

"What?"

"Do you know Lawrence Kohlberg?"

Peter shook his head.

"He was a psychologist who did research on moral reasoning back in the 1960s. I studied him while preparing an expert system for the Clarke Institute of Psychiatry."

"So?"

"So this whole mess is a question of morality—why one

version of you would behave differently from the others. Surely the key to which sim is guilty is tied into the nature of human morality."

Peter wasn't really listening. "Is there anything else we can do to erase the sims?"

"Not now that they're out in the net. Look, you're probably right: it will be useful to identify which sim is guilty. Let me ask you a question."

"What?"

Sarkar paused, remembering. "Say a man's wife is terminally ill, but she could be saved by a drug that cost $20,000."

"What's this got to do with anything?"

"Just listen—it's one of Kohlberg's test scenarios. Suppose that the man had only been able to come up with $10,000, but the pharmacist refused to let him have the drug, even though he promised to pay the rest of the cost later. The man then steals the drug to save his wife's life. Is the man's act morally right or wrong?"

Peter frowned. "It's right, of course."

"But *why?* That's the key."

"I—I don't know. It just is."

Sarkar nodded. "I suspect each sim would give a different reason. Kohlberg defined six levels of moral reasoning. At the lowest, one believes moral behavior is simply that which avoids punishment. At the highest, which Kohlberg considered the province of moral giants like Gandhi and Martin Luther King, moral behavior is based on abstract ethical principles. At that stage, external laws against theft are irrelevant; your own internalized moral code would dictate that you must value another's life more greatly than any repercussions you might suffer yourself because of the crime."

"Well, that's what I believe."

"Mahatma Hobson," said Sarkar. "Presumably the control sim would share that same point of view. But Kohlberg found that criminals were likely to be at a lower stage of moral reasoning than non-criminals of the same age who had the same IQ. Ambrotos might be fixated at the lowest level, level one—the avoidance of punishment."

"Why?"

"An immortal will live forever, but he can also spend forever in jail. A life sentence would be a terrifying thought to him."

"But how often does a true life sentence get handed down? You know the old saying, 'Don't do the crime if you can't do the time.' Well, Ambrotos might very well think he could do *any* crime because, after all, he *can* do the time."

"Good point," said Sarkar. "But I still think he's the guilty one. They say time heals all wounds, but perhaps if you knew you were going to live forever, you'd want to deal with anything that was going to fester in your mind for century after century."

Peter shook his head. "I don't think so. Look, if murder is a terrible crime to me, wouldn't it be unthinkable—the ultimate atrocity—to an immortal version of me, who knew life could go on forever?"

Sarkar sighed. "Perhaps. I guess it could go either way. But what about Spirit? His moral reasoning, too, could be fixated at a low level. Even though Spirit is dead, we have simulated neither heaven nor hell for him. So perhaps he considers himself to be in Purgatory. If he behaves well, maybe he believes he will be allowed entrance to heaven. Kohlberg's second stage defines moral acts as those which gain rewards."

Peter shook his head again. "I don't really believe in heaven or hell."

Sarkar tried another tack. "Well, then, consider this: murder is a crime of passion, and passion is a failing of flesh and blood. Remove sex from the human psyche and you would have no reason to kill a philanderer. That would argue for Spirit's innocence, and, by process of elimination, for Ambrotos's guilt."

"Maybe," said Peter. "On the other hand, Spirit *knows* there is life after death—knows it by virtue of his existence. So, to him, murder would be a *less* heinous crime than it would be for Ambrotos, since it's not a complete ending for the victim. Spirit would thus be much more likely to feel comfortable committing murders."

Sarkar sighed, frustrated. "So you could argue that one either way, too." He glanced at his watch. "Look—there's nothing more we can do here." He paused. "In fact there may be nothing more we can do *anywhere.*" He sat quietly for a moment, thinking. "Go home. Tomorrow is Saturday; I'll come by your place around ten in the morning and we can try to figure out what to do next."

Peter nodded wearily.

"But first—" Sarkar pulled out his wallet, fished out a pair of fifties, and handed them to Peter.

"What's this?"

"The hundred dollars I borrowed from you last week. I want to be sure the sims have no cause to resent me. Before we go, send a message into the net telling them that I paid you back."

NET NEWS DIGEST

A group of protesters announced late yesterday that Florida's SeaWorld, the last U.S. entertainment institution to still keep dolphins in captivity, was refusing their requests to try to determine if dolphins also exhibited the soulwave.

George Hendricks, 27, a born-again Christian, today filed suit in Dayton, Ohio, charging that his parents, Daniel and Kim Hendricks, both 53, in failing to have baptized George's brother Paul, who died last year in an automobile accident at age 24, were guilty of neglect and abuse by preventing Paul's soul from being able to enter heaven.

Further research from The Hague, Netherlands, indicates that departing soulwaves seem to be moving in a very specific direction. "At first we thought each wave was going separately, but that's before we took into account the time of day of each individual's death," said bioethics professor Maarten Lely. "It now seems that all soulwaves are traveling in the same direction. For want of a better reference, that direction is approximately toward the constellation of Orion."

Germany became the first country today to make it explicitly illegal to interfere in any way with the departure of soulwaves from dying bodies. France, Great Britain, Japan, and Mexico are currently debating similar legislation.

The suicide rates on Native reservations in the United States and Canada, and in the three largest ghettos in the U.S., were at a five-year high this past month. One suicide note, from Los Angeles, typified a recurrent theme: "Something beyond this life exists. It can't be worse than being here."

CHAPTER 38

Cathy was lying on her back in bed, staring at the ceiling, when Peter entered. He could see by the Hobson Monitor that she was wide awake, so he didn't make any effort to be quiet.

"Peter?" said Cathy.

"Hmm?"

"What went on this evening?"

"I had to see Sarkar."

Cathy's voice was tightly controlled. "Do you know who killed my father? Who killed Hans?"

Peter started to say something, then fell silent.

"Trust," she said, rolling slightly toward him, "has to be a two-way street." She waited a moment. "Do you know who killed them?"

"No," said Peter again, removing his socks. And then, a moment later, "not for sure."

"But you have your suspicions?"

Peter didn't trust his voice. He nodded in the darkness.

"Who?"

"It's only a guess," he said. "Besides, we're not even sure that your father was murdered."

Firmly: "Who?"

He let out a long sigh. "This is going to take some explaining." He had his shirt off now. "Sarkar and I have been doing some . . . research into artificial intelligence."

Her face, blue-gray in the dim room, was impassive.

"Sarkar created three duplicates of my mind inside a computer."

Cathy's voice was tinged with mild surprise. "You mean expert systems?"

"More than that. Much more. He's copied every neuron, every neural net. They are, for all intents and purposes, complete duplicates of my personality."

"I didn't know that sort of thing was possible."

"It's still experimental, but, yes, it's possible. Sarkar invented the technique."

"God. And you think one of these—these duplicates was responsible for the murders?"

Peter's voice was faint. "Maybe."

Cathy's eyes were wide with horror. "But—but why would duplicates of your mind do something you yourself would not?"

Peter had finished changing into his pajamas. "Because two of the simulations are not duplicates. Parts of what I am have been removed from them. It's possible that we accidentally deleted whatever was responsible for human morality." He sat on the edge of the bed. "I tell you, I would never kill anyone. Not even Hans. But part of me very much wanted him dead."

Cathy's voice was bitter. "And my father? Did part of you want him dead, too?"

Peter shrugged.

"Well?"

"I, ah, have never really liked your father. But no, until recently, I had no reason to hate him. But . . . but then you told me about your counseling session. He hurt you when you were young. He shook your confidence."

"And one of the duplicates killed him for that?"

A shrug in the darkness.

"Turn the fucking things off," said Cathy.

"We can't," said Peter. "We tried. They've escaped out into the net."

"God," said Cathy, putting all her terror and fury into that single syllable.

They were silent for a time. She had moved away from him slightly in the bed. Peter looked at her, trying to decipher the mixture of emotions on her face. At last, her voice trembling slightly, she said, "Is there anyone else you want dead?"

"Sarkar asked me the same thing," he said, annoyed. "But I can't think of anyone."

"What about—what about me?" said Cathy.

"You? Of course not."

"But I hurt you."

"Yes. But I don't want you dead."

Peter's words didn't seem to calm her. "Christ, Peter, how could you do something so stupid?"

"I—I don't know. We didn't mean to."

"What about the detective?"

"What about her?"

"What will happen when she gets too close to the truth?" asked Cathy. "Will you want her dead, too?"

SARKAR arrived at Peter and Cathy's house at 10:15 the next morning. They sat there, the three of them, chewing on bagels that were past their prime.

"So what do we do now?" said Cathy, arms folded across her chest.

"Go to the police," said Sarkar.

Peter was shocked. "What?"

"The police," said Sarkar again. "This is completely out of control. We need their help."

"But—"

"Call the police. Tell them the truth. This is a new phenomenon. We didn't expect this result. Tell them that."

"If you do that," said Cathy slowly, "there will be repercussions."

"Indeed," said Peter. "Charges would be laid."

"What charges?" said Sarkar. "We've done nothing wrong."

"Are you kidding?" said Peter. "They could charge me with manslaughter, maybe. Or as an accessory to murder. And they could charge you with criminal negligence."

Sarkar's eyes went wide. "Crim—"

"Not to mention getting you under hacker laws," said Cathy. "If I understand all this correctly, you've created a piece of software that's out there violating other people's computer systems and stealing resources. That's a felony."

"But we intended nothing wrong," said Sarkar.

"The crown attorney could run circles around us," said Peter. "A man and his best friend create software that kills people the man hated. Easy enough to discredit any claim I didn't have that in mind all along. And remember that case against Consolidated Edison? Frankenstein statutes. Those who seek to profit from technology must bear the costs of unforeseen consequences."

"Those are American laws," said Sarkar.

"I suspect a Canadian court would adopt a similar principle," said Cathy.

"Regardless," said Sarkar, "the sims have to be stopped."

"Yes," said Cathy.

Sarkar looked at Peter. "Pick up the phone. Dial 9-1-1."

"But what could the police do?" asked Peter, spreading his arms. "I'd be in favor of telling them, perhaps, if there was something they could do."

"They could order a shutdown of the net," said Sarkar.

"Are you kidding? Only CSIS or the RCMP could do that—and I bet they'd need to invoke the War Measures Act to suspend access to information on that large a scale. Meanwhile, what if the sims have moved down into the States? Or across the Atlantic?" Peter shook his head. "There's no way we'd ever get the net scoured clean."

Sarkar nodded slowly. "Perhaps you're right."

They were silent for a time. Finally, Cathy said, "Isn't there some way you can clean them off the net yourself?"

They looked at her expectantly.

"You know," she said, "write a virus that would track them down and destroy them. I remember the Internet worm, from back when I was in university—it was all over the world in a matter of days."

Sarkar looked excited. "Maybe," he said. "Maybe."

Peter looked at him. He tried to keep his voice calm. "The sims are huge, after all. They can't be that hard to find."

Sarkar was nodding. "A virus that checked all files bigger than, say, ten terabytes . . . It could look for two or three basic patterns from your neural nets. If it found them, it would erase the file. Yes—yes, I think I could write something like that." He turned to Cathy. "Brilliant, Catherine!"

"How long would it take to write?" asked Peter.

"I am not sure," replied Sarkar. "I've never written a virus before. Couple of days."

Peter nodded. "Let's pray that this works."

Sarkar looked at him. "*I* face Mecca five times a day and pray. Perhaps we would have better luck if both of you really did pray, too." He rose to his feet. "I better get going. I've got a lot of work to do."

CHAPTER 39

Peter had been trying to prepare himself for the inevitable encounter. Still, every time his intercom buzzed, he felt his heart begin to race. The first few times were false alarms. Then—

"Peter," said his secretary's voice, "there's an Inspector Philo here to see you, from the Toronto Police."

Peter took a very deep breath, held it for a few seconds, then let it out in a long, whispery sigh. He touched a button on his intercom. "Send her in, please."

A moment later the door to his office opened and in walked Alexandria Philo. Peter had expected her to be in a police uniform. Instead, she was wearing a trim, professional gray blazer, matching slacks, and a coffee-colored silk blouse. She had on two tiny green earrings. Her short hair was bright red, her eyes bright green. And she was tall. She was carrying a black attaché case.

"Hello, Detective," Peter said, rising to his feet and extending his hand.

"Hello," Sandra said, giving his hand a firm shake. "I take it you were expecting me?"

"Um, why do you say that?"

"I couldn't help overhear you talking to your secretary. You said 'send her in.' But she hadn't told you my first name, or given you any other indication that I was a woman."

Peter smiled. "You're very good at your job. My wife had said a few things about you."

"I see." Sandra was quiet, staring expectantly at Peter.

Peter laughed. "On the other hand, I'm very good at my job, too. And a large part of it involves attending meetings with government officials, all of whom have taken courses in interpersonal communication. It's going to take more than just a protracted silence to get me to spill my guts."

Sandra laughed. She hadn't looked pretty to Peter when she came in, but when she laughed she looked very nice indeed.

"Please have a seat, Ms. Philo."

She smiled and took a chair, smoothing out her pants as she sat as if she often wore skirts. Cathy had the same habit.

There was a short silence. "Would you like coffee?" asked Peter. "Tea?"

"Coffee, please. Double double." She looked uncomfortable. "This is a part of my job that I don't like, Dr. Hobson."

Peter got up and crossed over to the coffee maker. "Please—call me Peter."

"Peter." She smiled. "I don't like the way involved parties get treated in a case such as this. We police often bully people with little regard for good manners or the principle of assumed innocence."

Peter handed her a cup of coffee.

"So, Doctor—" She stopped herself and smiled. "So, Peter, I'm going to have to ask you some questions, and I hope you'll understand that I'm just doing my job."

"Of course."

"As you know, one of your wife's coworkers was murdered."

Peter nodded. "Yes. It came as quite a shock."

Sandra looked at him with her head tilted to one side.

"I'm sorry," said Peter, confused. "Did I say something wrong?"

"Oh, it's nothing. Just that there was evidence that a stunner was used to subdue the victim. Your 'quite a shock' comment struck me as funny." She raised a hand. "Forgive me; you develop a fairly thick skin in this line of work." A pause. "Have you ever used a stunner?"

"No."

"Do you own one?"

"They're illegal in Ontario, except for police work."

Sandra smiled. "But you can buy them easily in New York or Quebec."

"No," said Peter, "I've never used one."

"I'm sorry to have to ask," said Sandra.

"That darned police training," said Peter.

"Exactly." She smiled. "Did you know the deceased man?"

Peter tried to say the name nonchalantly. "Hans Larsen? Sure, I'd met him—I've met most of Cathy's coworkers, either at informal gatherings or at her company's Christmas parties."

"What did you think of him?"

"Of Larsen?" Peter took a sip of coffee. "I thought he was a jerk."

Sandra nodded. "A number of people seemed to have shared your opinion, although others spoke highly of him."

"I suspect that's the way it is for just about everyone," said Peter.

"Just about." Silence again, then: "Look, Peter, you seem like a nice guy. I don't want to bring up painful memories. But I know your wife and Hans, well . . ."

Peter nodded. "Yes, they did. But that was over a long time ago."

Sandra smiled. "True. But it was more recently that your wife told you about it."

"And now Larsen is dead."

Sandra nodded once. "And now Larsen is dead."

"Ms. Philo—"

She raised a hand. "You can call me Sandra."

Peter smiled. "Sandra." *Play it cool,* he thought. Sarkar would have the virus ready today or tomorrow. It'll all be over soon. "Let me tell you something, Sandra. I'm a peaceful person. I don't like wrestling or boxing. I haven't hit anyone since I was a boy. I'd never hit my wife. And if I had a child, I'd never spank him or her." He took a sip of coffee. Had he said enough? Would more be better? Cool, dammit. Be cool. But all he wanted to do was tell her the truth about himself—not those machine duplicates, but the real him, the flesh-and-blood him.

"I—I think a lot of the problems in this world come from violence. By spanking our kids we teach them that there are times when it's okay to hit someone you love—and then we're shocked to discover that these same kids grow up thinking it's okay to hit their spouses. I don't even kill houseflies, Sandra—I capture them in drinking glasses and take them outside. You're asking whether I killed Larsen. And I'll tell you directly that I might indeed have been angry with him, I might indeed have hated him, but killing or physically hurting isn't in my nature. It's something I simply would not do."

"Or even think about?" asked Sandra.

Peter spread his arms. "Well, we all think about things. But there's a world of difference between an idle fantasy and reality." If there weren't, thought Peter, I'd have had you and my secretary and a hundred other women right on this very desktop.

Sandra rearranged herself slightly in her chair. "I don't

normally talk about my personal life while on the job, but I went through something very similar to what you did, Peter. My husband—my ex-husband, as of a few months ago—cheated as well. I'm not a violent person, either. I know some would consider that an unlikely thing for a police officer to say, but it's true. But when I found out what Walter had done—well, I wanted him dead, and I wanted *her* dead. I'm not given to throwing things, but when I found out I threw the remote control for our TV across the room. It smashed into the wall, and the case broke open; you can still see the spot on the wall where it hit. So I know, Peter, I *know* that people have violent reactions when this sort of thing happens."

Peter nodded slowly. "But I did not kill Hans Larsen."

"We believe it was a professional murder."

"I didn't arrange for his killing, either."

"Let me tell you exactly what my problem is here," said Sandra. "As I said, we're looking at a professional hit. Frankly, that sort of thing costs a lot of money—especially with the, ah, extra work this one involved. You and Cathy are better off than most of her coworkers; if anyone could have afforded this sort of thing, it would have been you or her."

"But we didn't do it," said Peter. "Look, I'd be glad to take a lie-detector test."

Sandra smiled sweetly. "How thoughtful of you to volunteer. I have portable equipment with me."

Peter felt his stomach muscles tighten. "Really?"

"Oh, yes. In fact, it's a Veriscan Plus—that's made by your company, isn't it?"

His eyes narrowed. "Yes."

"So I'm sure you have a lot of faith in its abilities. Would you really be willing to take such a test?"

He hesitated. "With my legal counsel present, of course."

"Legal counsel?" Sandra smiled again. "You haven't been charged with anything."

Peter considered. "All right," he said. "If it will put an end to all this, yes, I'll agree to a test, here and now. But in the absence of counsel, you may ask three questions only—did I kill Hans Larsen? Did I kill Rod Churchill? Did I arrange their deaths?"

"I have to ask more than three questions—calibrating the machine requires it; you know that."

"All right," said Peter. "Presumably you have a script of calibration questions. I'll agree to the test so long as you don't deviate from that script."

"Very well." Sandra opened her attaché case, revealing the polygraph equipment within.

Peter peered at the device. "Don't you have to be a specialist to operate those machines?"

"You should read your own product brochures, Peter. There's an expert-system AI chip inside. Anyone can operate one these days."

Peter grunted. Sandra affixed small sensors to Peter's forearm and wrist. A flat-panel screen popped up from the attaché case, and Sandra angled it so that only she could see it. She touched a few controls, then began to ask questions. "What's your name?"

"Peter Hobson."

"How old are you?"

"Forty-two."

"Where were you born?"

"North Battleford, Saskatchewan."

"Now lie to me. Tell me again where you were born."

"Scotland."

"Tell the truth: what is your wife's first name?"

"Catherine."

"Now lie: what is your wife's middle name?"

"Ah—T'Pring."

"Did you kill Hans Larsen?"

Peter watched Sandra carefully. "No."

"Did you kill Rod Churchill?"

"No."

"Did you arrange the killing of either of them?"

"No."

"Do you have any idea who killed them?"

Peter held up a hand. "We agreed only three questions, Inspector."

"I'm sorry. Surely you don't mind answering one more, though?" She smiled. "I no more like having to be suspicious of you than you like being a suspect. It would be nice to be able to scratch you off my list."

Peter thought. Dammit. "All right," he said slowly. "I don't know any person who might have killed them."

Sandra looked up. "I'm sorry—I guess I upset you when I went beyond what we'd agreed. There was some very strange activity when you said 'person.' Would you please bear with me for just one moment more and repeat your last answer?"

Peter yanked the sensor from his arm, and threw it on the desktop. "I've already put up with more than we agreed," he said, an edge in his voice. He knew he was making matters worse, and he fought to keep panic from overwhelming him. He pulled the second sensor off his wrist. "I'm through answering questions."

"I'm sorry," said Sandra. "Forgive me."

Peter made an effort to calm himself. "That's all right," he said. "I hope you got what you were looking for."

"Oh, yes," said Sandra, closing her case. "Yes, indeed."

IT didn't take long for Spirit's artificial lifeforms to develop multicellularism: chains of distinct units, attached together into simple rows. Eventually, the lifeforms stumbled onto the trick of doubling up into two rows: twice as many cells, but each one still exposed on at least one side to the nutrient soup of Spirit's simulated sea. And then the long rows of cells began to double back on themselves, forming U shapes. And, eventually, the U shapes closed over on the bottom, forming bags. Then, at last, the great breakthrough: the bottom and top of the bag opened up, resulting in a cylinder made of a double layer of cells, open at both ends: the basic body plan of all animal life on Earth, with an eating orifice at the front end and an excretory one at the rear.

Generations were born. Generations died.

And Spirit kept selecting.

CHAPTER 40

It had taken some work, but on December 4 Sandra Philo had gotten the monitoring warrant she'd requested, allowing her to place a transponder inside the rear bumper of Peter Hobson's car. She'd been given a ten-day permit by the judge. The transponder had a timing chip in it: it had operated for precisely the period authorized, and not a second longer. The ten days were now up, and Sandra was analyzing the collected data.

Peter drove to his office a lot, and also went frequently to several restaurants, including Sonny Gotlieb's, a place Sandra quite liked herself; to North York General Hospital (he was on their board of directors); and elsewhere. But there was one address that kept appearing over and over in the logs: 88 Connie Crescent in Concord. That was an industrial unit that housed four different businesses. She cross-referenced the address with Peter's telephone records, obtained under the same warrant. He'd repeatedly called a number registered to Mirror Image, 88 Connie Crescent.

Sandra called up InfoGlobe and got screens full of data about that company: Mirror Image Ltd., founded in 2001 by wunderkind Sarkar Muhammed, a firm specializing in expert systems and artificial-intelligence applications. Big contracts with the Ontario government and several *Financial Post 100* corporations.

Sandra thought back to the lie-detector test Peter Hobson had taken. "I don't know any person who might have killed them," he'd said—and his vital signs had been agitated when he said the word "person."

And now he was spending time at an artificial-intelligence lab.

It was almost too wild, too crazy.

And yet Hobson himself hadn't committed the murders. The lie detector had shown that.

It was the kind of thing the law-enforcement journals had been warning was coming down the pike.

Perhaps, now, at last, it was here.

Here.

Sandra leaned back in her chair, trying to absorb it all.

It certainly wasn't enough to get an arrest warrant.

Not an *arrest* warrant, no. But maybe a search warrant . . .

She saved her research files, logged off, and headed out the door.

IT took five vehicles to get them all there: two patrol cars with a pair of uniformed officers apiece; a York Region squad car with the liaison officer from that police force—the raid would be conducted on York's turf; Sandra Philo's unmarked car, carrying herself and Jorgenson, head of the computer-crimes division; and the blue CCD van, carrying five analysts and their equipment.

The convoy pulled up outside 88 Connie Crescent at 10:17 a.m. Sandra and the four uniformed officers went directly inside; Jorgenson went over to the CCD van to confer with his team.

The receptionist at Mirror Image—an elderly Asian man—looked up in shock as Sandra and the uniforms entered. "Can I help you?" he said.

"Please move away from your computer terminal," said Sandra. "We have a warrant to search these premises." She held up the document.

"I think I better call Dr. Muhammed," said the man.

"You do that," said Sandra. She snapped her fingers, indicating that one of the uniforms should stay here, preventing the receptionist from using his terminal. Sandra and the other three headed inside.

A thin dark-skinned man appeared at the far end of the corridor.

"May I help you?" he said, his voice full of concern.

"Are you Sarkar Muhammed?" asked Sandra, closing the distance between them.

"Yes."

"I'm Detective Inspector Philo, Toronto Police Service." She handed him the warrant. "We have reason to believe that computer-related crimes have been committed from this establishment. This warrant gives us authority to search not just your offices, but your computer systems as well."

At that moment, the door to the reception area burst open and Jorgenson and the five analysts came in. "Make sure none of the employees touch any computer equipment," Jorgensen said to the senior uniformed officer. The cops started fanning out into the building. One of the corridor walls was largely glass, overlooking a big data-processing facility. Jorgenson pointed to two of the analysts. "Davis, Kato—you're in there." The two analysts went to the door, but it had a separate FILE lock.

"Dr. Muhammed," said Sandra, "our warrant gives us the right to break any locks we deem necessary. If you prefer we not do that, please unlock that door."

"Look," said Sarkar, "we've done nothing wrong here."

"Open the door, please," Sandra said firmly.

"I want to review this warrant with my attorney."

"Fine," said Sandra. "Jones, kick it."

"No!" said Sarkar. "All right, all right." He moved to the side of the door and pressed his thumb against the blue scanner. The deadbolt popped aside and the door slid open. Davis and Kato went in, the former going straight for the master console, the latter starting an inventory of the DASD tape and optical-drive units.

Jorgenson turned to Sarkar. "You have an AI lab here. Where is it?"

"We've done nothing wrong," said Sarkar again.

One of the uniforms reappeared at the far end of the corridor. "It's down here, Karl!"

Jorgenson jogged down the hall, the three remaining members of his team following. Sandra walked in that direction, too, checking the signs on each door as she went.

The Asian receptionist had appeared at the other end of the corridor, looking worried. Sarkar shouted, "Call Kejavee, my attorney—tell him what's happening." He then hurried off to follow Jorgenson.

Sarkar had been working in the AI lab when the receptionist had called him. He'd left the door open. By the time he got back there, Jorgenson was looming over the main console, unplugging the keyboard. He motioned to one of his associates who handed him another keyboard with a glossy black housing and silver keys. A diagnostic unit: every keystroke typed, every response from the computer, every disk-access delay would be recorded.

"Hey!" shouted Sarkar. "These are delicate systems. Be careful."

Jorgenson ignored him. He sat on the barstool and pulled a vinyl folder out of his briefcase. It contained an assortment of diskettes, CDs, and memory cards. He selected a card that would fit the drive on the console, inserted it, then hit some keys on his keyboard.

The computer's monitor cleared, then filled with diagnostic information about the system.

"Top of the line," said Jorgenson, impressed. "Fully populated with 512 gigabytes of RAM, five parallel math co-processors, self-referential-bus architecture." He tapped the spacebar; another screen came up. "Latest firmware revision, too. Nice."

He exited his program and began listing directories at the system prompt.

"What are you looking for?" asked Sarkar.

"Anything," said Sandra, entering the room. "Everything." Then, to Jorgenson: "Any problems?"

"Not so far. He was already logged in, so we didn't need to crack the password file."

Sarkar was edging away from the group toward a console on the other side of the room—a console with a microphone stalk sticking up from it.

"Login," said Sarkar in a low voice, then, without waiting for the prompt, "Login name Sarkar."

"Hello, Sarkar," said the computer. "Shall I terminate your other session?"

Sandra Philo had come up behind him, the rounded front of her stunner pressing into the small of his back. "Don't do that," she said simply. She reached over to the console and flicked off the switch marked "Voice Input."

At that point, Kawalski, the liaison officer from York, appeared at the entrance to the room. "They've got a barber's chair upstairs," he said generally to the group, then, looking at Sarkar, "You give haircuts here?"

Sarkar shook his head. "It's actually a dentist's chair."

Jorgenson spoke without looking up. "Scanning room, no doubt," he said. Then, to Sarkar: "I enjoyed your paper in last month's *Journal of AI Studies.* I'll want to search that room next." He went back to typing commands on his black-and-silver keyboard.

Sarkar sounded exasperated. "If you would just tell me what you're looking for . . ."

"Damn," said Jorgenson. "There are several encrypted banks here."

Sandra looked at Sarkar. "What's the decryption key?"

Sarkar, feeling perhaps that he had some measure of control at last, said, "I do not believe I'm obligated to tell you."

Jorgenson got up from the stool. Without a word, a second analyst sat down on it and began typing commands.

"Doesn't matter," said Jorgenson with a shrug. "Valentina was with the KGB, back when there was such a thing. There's not much she can't crack."

Valentina popped a new datacard into the card slot, and typed furiously with two fingers. After several minutes, she looked at Sarkar, her face full of disappointment. Sarkar brightened visibly—perhaps she wasn't as good as Jorgenson had said. But then Sarkar's heart fell. The disappointment on her face was simply that of someone who'd been hoping for a good challenge, and had failed to find it. "The Hunsacker algorithm?" she said in a heavily accented voice, shaking her head. "You could have done better than that." Valentina pressed a few more keys and the screen, which to this point had been filled with gibberish, was replaced with English source-code listings.

She got up, and Jorgenson went back to work. He cleared the screen, then replaced Valentina's datacard with another of his own. "Initiating search," he said. The screen filled with a multi-column list of two hundred or so terms in alphabetical order.

"There's massive storage online here," said Jorgenson, "under a variety of compression schemes. It'll take a while to hunt through it all." He got up. "I'm going up to look at that scanning room."

* * *

PETER had an evening board meeting at North York General today, and rather than waste the morning fighting the telephones at the office he decided to do some work from home. But he was having trouble concentrating. Sarkar had said he'd have the virus finished today, but Peter still felt he should be doing something himself. Around 10:30, he logged into Mirror Image, hoping to see if he could fathom how the sims had gotten outside.

After dialing in, he issued the WHO command to see whether Sarkar was also online—Peter wanted to send him an email hello. He was indeed. Peter then issued WHAT to see what sort of activity Sarkar was doing; if it was a background task, he probably wasn't actually sitting at the terminal, and so the email would be a waste of time.

WHAT reported the following:

Node	User	Logged in at	Task
002	Sarkar	08:14:22	text search

Well, a text search could be either background or foreground. Peter had high-level supervisory privileges on Sarkar's systems. He called for an echoing of the task at node 002 on his own monitor. The screen filled with a list of search terms, and a constantly updated tally of hits. Some, such as Toronto, had hundreds of hits so far, but others . . .

Christ, thought Peter. *Look at that . . .*

Sarkar was searching for "Hobson" and "Pete*" and "Cath*" and . . .

Peter tapped out an email message: "Nosy, aren't we?" He was about to send it when he noticed the full search parameters in the status line: "Search all systems; within each system, search all online and offline storage and all working memory."

A search like that could take hours. Sarkar would never order something like that—he was too well organized not to have at least *some* idea how to narrow the search.

Peter glanced at the other search terms.

Oh, shit.

"Larsen," "Hans," "adultery," "affair."

Shit. Shit. Shit. No way Sarkar would be doing a search like that. Someone else was inside the system.

Node 002 was the AI lab at Mirror Image. Peter swung his chair to face his phone and hit the speed-dialer key for there.

THE phone rang in the AI lab. "May I get that?" asked Sarkar.

Sandra nodded. She was watching the screen intently. Lots of hits on the common words—"affair" had over four hundred so far—but none on Hobson or Larsen.

Sarkar moved across the room to the video phone and hit the ANSWER key.

THE Bell Canada logo backflipped away. Peter saw Sarkar's face, looking worried.

"What's—" said Peter, but that's all he said. In the background, over Sarkar's shoulder, he saw a profile of Sandra Philo. Peter broke the connection at once.

Philo there, at Mirror Image.

A raid. A god-damned raid.

Peter looked at his screen, slaved to node 002. Still no hits on "Hobson."

He thought for a second, then began tapping keys. Peter spun off a second session under Sarkar's login name, using the password he'd heard Sarkar use before. He then accessed the diagnostic-tools subdirectory and called up a file listing.

There were hundreds of programs, including one called TEXTREP. That sounded promising. He called up help on it.

Good. Exactly what he needed. Syntax: search-term, replacement-term, search parameters.

Peter typed "TEXTREP / Hobson / Roddenberry / AI7-AI10"—meaning change all occurrences of "Hobson" to "Roddenberry" on artificial-intelligence systems seven through ten.

The program set to work. It was a much smaller search—only one term—and a much narrower area to search—only four computers instead of the hundred or more that Philo was currently examining. With luck, it would make all the substitutions before it was too late . . .

THE console beeped, signaling its task was complete. Jorgenson was back, having found nothing of interest in the scanning room. He looked at the screen, then at Sandra. Thirteen hits for Hobson. Sandra pointed at the tally. "Display them in context," she said.

Two appearances of the word in an online dictionary entry for "Hobson's choice."

A user-ID file, equating "fobson" with Peter G. Hobson.

A computerized Rolodex with home and business addresses for Peter Hobson.

And nine more references, mostly within copyright notices, to Hobson Monitoring Ltd. as parts of various pieces of scanning software.

"Nada," said Jorgenson.

"He's got an account here," said Sandra, turning to Sarkar.

"Who does?" he said.

"Peter Hobson."

"Oh, yes. We use some programs made by his company."

"Nothing more?"

"Well, he's a friend of mine, too. That's why I have his home address in my Rolodex." Sarkar looked innocent. "What were you expecting to find?"

CHAPTER 41

Cathy Hobson was exhausted. It had been a long day at the office, slogging away at the Tourism Ontario account. She'd stopped at Miracle Food Mart on the way home, but the idiot in front of her had decided to unload all his change on the cashier. Some people, Cathy thought, should be forced to use debit cards.

When she finally arrived at home, she pressed her thumb against the FILE scanner, leaning on it as if it were the only thing keeping her from collapsing to the ground. The green LED atop the scanner winked at her, the deadbolt sprang back, and the heavy door slid aside. She entered her house. The door closed behind her and the lock snicked back into place.

"Lights," she said.

Nothing happened. She cleared her throat and tried again. "Lights."

Still nothing. She sighed, set down her shopping bags, and groped for the manual switch. She found it, but still the lights did not go on.

Cathy made her way up into the living room. She could

see the glowing LEDs on the PVR, so it wasn't a power failure; the entryway bulb was probably just burnt out. She said "lights" once more, but the three ceramic table lamps—lamps that Cathy herself had made—remained dark.

Cathy shook her head. Peter was constantly fiddling with the house controls, and it always took a while to get things working properly again.

She lowered herself to the couch, spreading her aching feet out in front of her. Such a long day. She closed her eyes, enjoying the darkness. After a moment, remembering her groceries, she hauled herself up and headed down to the entryway. She tried both the light switch and saying the word "lights" again. Still nothing. She was about to bend over and pick up the bags when she noticed the phone sitting on the little table in the hall. The large red light adjacent to its keypad was on. She moved closer. The visual display said "Line in use."

The phone hadn't rung.

And Peter wouldn't be home for hours yet; he had a board meeting tonight at North York General.

Unless . . . "Peter!" Her shout echoed slightly in the corridor. "Peter, are you home?"

No reply. She picked up the handset and heard a high-pitched whine. A modem.

She looked at the visual display again. "Private caller"—an incoming call, but whoever was using the modem had requested suppression of Call Display.

Jesus Christ, she thought. A sim.

She slammed the handset down, then picked it up again, jiggling the hook switch rapidly, trying to make enough line noise to sever the connection.

It didn't do any good. Peter, of course, had the finest in error-correcting modems, and the sim apparently had equally good hardware.

She moved quickly to the front door and pressed the UNLOCK button next to it. Nothing happened. She grabbed the manual handle. The door refused to budge. She hit the "In

Case of Fire" override. The door was still jammed. She slid open the hall closet—it, at least, had no locking mechanism—and looked at the door control panel. An LED was glowing like a drop of blood next to the phrase "thwarting break-in." Normally the doors would instantly unlock in case of a fire, but the smoke detectors denied that there was a fire, and some other detector said someone was trying to break in from outside. Cathy left the closet and looked through the peephole in the front door. No one was there. Of course.

She was trying to remain calm. There were other doors, but the master panel showed them all to be in anti-break-in mode as well. She could try going through a window, but they were all locked, too, and the glass was, of course, the best modern safety glass money could buy.

The word she'd been fighting not to think finally pushed to the surface of her consciousness.

Trapped.

Trapped in her own home.

She thought about trying to trigger the smoke detectors, but, of course, neither she nor Peter smoked, so there were no lighters anywhere in the house. And Peter didn't like the smell of matches or candles, so there were none of those either. Still, she could set fire to some paper on the stove. That might set off the alarms, unlocking the doors.

She hurried to the kitchen, taking care not to trip in the darkness. The moment she entered, though, she knew she was in trouble. The digital clocks on both the microwave and the regular oven were off. The kitchen power had been cut. There was a rechargeable flashlight plugged into a wall outlet. She pulled it out of the socket. It was supposed to come on automatically when the power went off, but it was dead. Cathy realized that the power must have been off in the kitchen for many hours, and so the flashlight had depleted its charge. But—that whine. The refrigerator was still on. She opened its door and a light went on inside. She felt the rush of cold air on her face.

The sim knew exactly what it was doing: the PVR and the fridge were still on, but the stove and the outlet that recharged the flashlight were off. As was typical in a smart house, every outlet was on its own circuit and fuse.

She made her way into the dining room and held on to the back of a chair for support. She tried to remain calm—calm, dammit! She thought about getting a kitchen knife, but that was pointless—there was no physical intruder. The control box for the house systems was in the basement, and that's where the phone cables entered, too—power and telecommunication lines were being systematically buried in response to fears that unshielded overhead lines caused cancer.

Cathy inched toward the top of the stairs that led to the basement. She opened the door. It was pitch black down there; for their fifth anniversary, Peter and Cathy had treated themselves to a home-theater system, so the blinds on the basement windows had been replaced with Mylar-lined curtains on electric rails—and the curtains had been drawn. Cathy thought she knew the layout well enough to find the incoming phone line even in the dark. She stepped onto the top stair—

The overhead sprinklers came on. No alarm—nothing to summon neighbors or the fire department. But cold water started showering down from the ceiling. Cathy gasped and ran back up into the living room. The sprinklers shut off behind her and came on in there. She moved onto the stairs leading up to the bedrooms. The sprinklers cut off in the living room and went on in the stairwell.

Cathy realized that they were following her—the sim had presumably keyed into the motion sensors that were part of the burglar-alarm system. Through the mist, she could see that the LEDs on the PVR were now off—presumably to avoid starting a fire by electrical shorting.

Exhausted and wet, with no way to escape, Cathy decided to head for the bathroom. If the sprinklers were destined to follow her, she might as well be in the room in which they could do the least damage. She got into the bathtub and unhooked the shower curtain, using it as a tent to shield herself from the cold water.

Three hours later, Peter came home. The front door unlocked normally for him. He found the living room carpet soaked, and could hear the sprinklers running upstairs. He hurried up to the bathroom and opened the door. The moment he did so, the sprinklers stopped.

Cathy pushed off the shower curtain. Water streamed from it as she rose to stand up in the tub. Her voice was full of tightly controlled fury. "Neither I nor any version of me would ever have done anything like this to you." She glared at him. "We're even."

CATHY, quite sensibly, refused to stay in the house. Peter drove her to her sister's apartment. She was still angry, but was slowly calming down, and she accepted his embrace as they parted. Peter then went directly to his own office and logged onto the net. He sent an email message out into the world:

Date: 15 Dec 2011, 23:11 EST
From: Peter G. Hobson
To: my brothers
Subject: RTC request

I need to talk to you all in real-time conference immediately. Please respond.

It didn't take long for them to reply.

"I'm here," said one of his ghosts.

"'Evening, Pete," said another.

"What is it?" asked a third.

They all spoke through the same voice chip; unless they identified themselves, there was no easy way to tell which sim was speaking. And even knowing the nodes they were using wouldn't tell him which sim was which. It didn't matter.

"I know what's going on," said Peter. "I know one of you is killing people on my behalf. But tonight Cathy was threatened. I will not tolerate that. Cathy is not to be harmed. Not now, not ever. Understand?"

Silence.

"Understand?"

Still no reply.

Peter sighed, exasperated. "Look, I know that Sarkar and I can't remove you from the net, but if there's any repetition, we will go public with your existence. The press would go apeshit over a story of a murdering AI having taken up residence inside the net. Don't think they wouldn't do a cold restart to get rid of you."

A voice from the speaker: "I'm sure you're mistaken, Peter. None of us would have committed murders. But if you go public, people will believe your claim—you are, after all, the famous Peter Hobson now. And that means *you* will be blamed for the deaths."

"I don't care at this point," said Peter. "I'll do whatever it takes to protect Cathy, even if it means going to jail myself."

"But Cathy has hurt you," said the synthesized voice. "More than anyone in the entire world, Cathy has hurt you."

"Hurting me," said Peter, "is not a capital crime. I'm not kidding: threaten her again, harm her in any way, and I will see to it that you are *all* destroyed. I'll find a way to do that somehow."

"We could," said the electronic voice, very slowly, "get rid of you to prevent that from happening."

"That would be suicide, in a sense," said Peter. "Or fratricide. In any event, *I* know that's something I wouldn't do, and that means it's also something that *you* wouldn't do."

"You would not have killed Cathy's coworker," said the voice, "and yet you believe one of us has done that."

Peter leaned back in his chair. "No, but—but I *wanted*

to. I'm ashamed to admit it, but I wanted to see him dead. But I would not kill myself—I wouldn't even think about killing myself—and so I know you wouldn't seriously think about doing it, either."

"But you're thinking about killing *us,*" said the voice.

"That's different," said Peter. "I'm the original. You know that. And I know in my heart of hearts that I don't believe that computer simulacra are as alive as a flesh-and-blood person is. And because I believe that, you believe that, too."

"Perhaps," said the voice.

"And now you're trying to kill Cathy," Peter said. "At least that must stop. Don't harm Cathy. Don't threaten Cathy. Don't do *anything* to Cathy."

"But she hurt you," said the synthesizer again.

"Yes," said Peter, exasperated. "She hurt me. But it would hurt me *more* if she were not around. It would destroy me if she were dead."

"Why?" said the voice.

"Because I love her, dammit. I love her more than life itself. I love her with every fiber of my being."

"Really?" said the voice.

Peter paused, catching his breath. He considered. Was it just his anger talking? Was he blurting out things he didn't mean? Or was it true—really true? "Yes," he said softly, understanding at last, "yes, I really love her that much. I love her more than words can say."

"It's about time you admitted that, Petey-boy, even if you had to be pushed into it. Go get Cathy—doubtless you took her to her sister's house; that's what I would have done. Go get her and take her home. Nothing more will happen to her."

CHAPTER 42

The next day, Peter made sure Cathy got safely on her way to work, but he stayed home. He'd disconnected the electronic door system and had called a locksmith to come and put in old-fashioned key-operated deadbolts. While the locksmith worked, Peter sat in his office and stared out into space, trying to make sense of it all.

He thought about Rod Churchill.

A cold fish. Undemonstrative.

But he had been taking phenelzine—an antidepressant.

Meaning, of course, that he had been diagnosed as having clinical depression. But in the two decades Peter had known Rod Churchill, he'd seen no change in his demeanor. So maybe . . . maybe he'd been depressed for all that time. Maybe he'd been depressed even longer than that, depressed during Cathy's childhood, leading him to be the lousy father he had been.

Peter shook his head. Rod Churchill—not a bastard, not an asshole. Just sick—a chemical imbalance.

Surely that mitigated what he'd done, made him less culpable for the way in which he'd treated his daughters.

Hell, thought Peter, we're all chemical machines. Peter couldn't function without his morning coffee. There was no doubt that Cathy became more irritable just before her period. And Hans Larsen had let his hormones guide him through his life.

Which was the real Peter? The sluggish, irritable guy who pulled himself out of bed each morning? Or the focused, driven person who arrived at the office, the drug caffeine working its magic? Which was the real Cathy? The cheerful, bright, sexy woman she was most of the time, or the cranky, quarrelsome person she became for a few days each month? And which the real Larsen? The drunken, sex-crazed lout Peter had known, or the fellow who apparently had done his job well and been liked by most of his coworkers? What, he wondered idly, would the guy have been like if someone were to cut off his dick? Probably a completely different person.

What was left of a person if you removed stimulants and depressants, inhibitors and disinhibitors, testosterone and estrogen? And what about children who'd received too little oxygen during birth? What about Down's syndrome—people altered completely by having an extra twenty-first chromosome? What about those with autism? Or dementia? Manic-depressives? Schizophrenics? Those who suffer from multiple personalities? Those with brain damage? Those with Alzheimer's? Surely the individuals affected aren't at fault. Surely none of those things reflect the actual people—the souls in question.

And what about those twin studies the Control sim had mentioned? Nature, not nurture, guided our behavior. When we weren't dancing to a chemical tune, we were marching to the genetic drummer.

Yet Rod Churchill had been getting help.

If he'd really been killed in the way Detective Philo suggested, the sim would have known that Rod was taking phenelzine, would have looked it up in a database of drugs, would have understood what Rod was being treated for. Could the sim have failed to realize that although the treatment might be new, the condition could have been longstanding? Surely that would have been enough evidence to commute any death sentence the sim had been contemplating?

No—no version of him would have killed Rod Churchill, knowing of this chemical problem. Pity him, yes, but surely not kill him. In fact, this called into question all of Sandra Philo's case. The sims, after all, had admitted to neither of the murders, and all Philo's evidence pointing to Peter, and from there to the sims, was circumstantial.

Peter breathed a sigh of relief. He would not have killed Rod Churchill. Rod had simply done something stupid, failing to follow his doctor's orders. And Hans Larsen? Well, Peter had always contended that dozens of angry spouses might have wanted him dead—including, now that he thought about it, Larsen's own wife, who, Peter seemed to recall, worked in a bank and could have embezzled the funds needed to hire a hitman.

Fog, that's all the case against him was. Empty fog.

And he'd prove that. He'd audit his own finances. Hiring a hitman would surely have cost tens of thousands of dollars, if not hundreds of thousands. Philo might never find the missing funds, even if she subpoenaed his financial records. But Peter had the advantage of thinking precisely the same way the sims did. If he looked—really looked—and could not find any missing money, well, then he could rest easy.

Peter dialed into his company's mainframes, logged on to the corporate accounts database, and started digging. He used an accounting expert system made by Mirror Image to help him audit. As he moved through each account, each financial database, and found nothing amiss, his confidence grew. He was interrupted after an hour or so by the locksmith, who had finished his job. Peter thanked the man, paid him, and went back to his searching. Philo had been wrong, completely wrong. Just another cop who loved conspiracy theories. Why, he'd give her a piece of his mind—

His computer beeped.

Good Christ, thought Peter. Good Christ.

A discrepancy in the subrights licensing account. No memo, no payee's account number, no cross-referenced invoice. Just a whopping big debit notice:

11 Nov 2011 EFT CDN$125,000.00

Peter stared at the screen, his jaw slack.

The timing was just about right. Hans had been killed three days later.

But surely it *had* to be something innocent. A refund for a licensing deal that had fallen through, maybe. Or an adjustment because of an overpayment to his company. Or . . .

No.

No, it could be none of those things. Peter's comptroller was meticulous. No way she'd make an entry like that. And the notation EFT. Electronic funds transfer. Exactly what a sim would have to use.

He was about to log off when the console beeped at him again. Another hit in his database search:

14 Dec 2011 EFT CDN$100,000.00

Peter let out another sigh of relief. There—proof that this was all innocent. Surely no hitman would work on an installment plan. Whatever was causing these debits had to be something routine, then. Patent payments, perhaps. Or . . .

Two days ago. That second transaction had been just two days ago.

And then it came to him.

What Cathy had said.

"What will happen," she'd asked, "to the detective when she gets too close to the truth? Will you want her dead, too?"

It couldn't be, thought Peter. It could *not* be.

Killing Hans he could understand. Perhaps he didn't approve, but at least he understood. Killing Rod Churchill was more difficult to fathom, given the extenuating circumstances. But maybe, just maybe, the electronic sim didn't see biochemistry as an excuse.

But Sandra Philo hadn't done anything evil, hadn't hurt Peter in any way. She was just doing her job.

But now, apparently, she had become *inconvenient.*

Christ almighty, thought Peter. The guilty sim didn't just have reduced morality or skewed morality. It had *no* morality at all.

Easy, Peter. Let's not get ahead of the data . . .

But—no. It was there, even within the flesh-and-blood Peter—buried deep, but there: a desire for self-preservation. There was no one else he wanted dead—that was true. But the detective was putting him, and the sims, at risk. If he were to get rid of anyone now, it would be her. If *any* version of himself were to get rid of anyone now, it would be her.

Damn it. God damn it. He'd have no more blood on his hands. Peter immediately activated his telephone; a valid address was as good for dialing as was a name. "Toronto Police Service, 32 Division, on Ellerslie," he said.

The Bell logo danced off the screen. A craggy sergeant appeared. "Thirty-two division," he said.

"Sandra Philo," said Peter.

"It's her day off," said the sergeant. "Can someone else help you?"

"No, it's—it's personal. Do you know where she is?"

"Haven't a clue," said the cop.

"I don't suppose I could get her home number?"

The cop laughed. "You've got to be kidding."

Peter broke the connection and dialed directory assistance. "Philo, Sandra," he said, then spelled the last name.

"There is no such listing," said the computerized voice.

Of course. "Philo, A.," he said. "A for Alexandria."

"There is no such listing."

Dammit, thought Peter. But a cop would be crazy to have a listed phone number—unless it was still under her ex-husband's name. "Do you have any listing for anyone with the last name Philo?"

"There is no such listing."

Peter clicked off. There must be *some* way to get a hold of her . . .

City directories. He'd seen them at the public library. Originally, they'd been designed to find the name that went with an address, but with them now on random-access CD-ROMs, it was just as easy to do the reverse, finding an address that went with a name. Peter called the telephone reference line for the Central Branch of the North York Public Library.

"Hello," said a woman's voice. "Quick reference."

"Hello," said Peter. "Do you have city directories there?"

"Yes."

"Could you tell me the address for Alexandria Philo, please? P-H-I-L-O."

"Just a moment, sir." There was a pause. "I have no A. Philo, sir. In fact, the only Philo is listed as Sandy."

Sandy—a non-gender-specific version of her name. Exactly the sort of precaution an intelligent woman living alone would take. "What does Sandy Philo do for a living?"

"It says 'civil servant,' sir. I suppose that could mean just about anything."

"That's her. What's the address, please?"

"216 Melville Avenue."

Peter jotted that down. "Is there a phone number?"

"It's marked unlisted."

"Thank you," said Peter. "Thank you very much."

He clicked off. Peter had never heard of Melville Avenue. He called up his electronic map book and looked it up. It was here in Don Mills. Not that far. Maybe a twenty-minute drive. It was crazy, he knew—a paranoid fantasy. And yet . . .

He hurried to his car and put the pedal to the metal.

CHAPTER 43

Peter tried to blow holes in his theory on the way there, but instead it kept making more sense, not less. Sandra's day off. A day when, very likely, she wouldn't be armed. The perfect day to kill a cop.

The traffic was heavy. Peter leaned on his horn. Despite the computerized map display on his dashboard, he managed to make a wrong turn, finding himself in a dead end. Cursing, he turned around and headed in the other direction. He was driving recklessly, he knew. But if he could just warn Sandra, tell her that someone might be after her—she could protect herself, he was sure of that. She was a cop.

Finally, he turned onto Melville Avenue. Number 216 was a townhouse. Nothing ostentatious. Grass needed cutting. A brown United Parcel Service van was parked out front.

A sign warned that parking on the street was illegal before six p.m. Peter ignored that.

He looked up at the house. The front door was closed. Funny, that. Where was the delivery person?

Peter's heart was racing. What if the killer was inside?

Paranoia. Madness.

Still . . .

He got out of his car, fumbled with his trunk keys, found the tire iron, grabbed it in both hands, and hurried up to the door.

He was about to press the buzzer when he heard a sound from inside: something smashing to the floor.

He hit the buzzer.

No response.

In for a penny, thought Peter, *in for a pound.*

There was a narrow floor-to-ceiling frosted window next to the actual door panel. Peter hit it with the tire iron. It cracked. He smashed the metal rod against it again with all his strength. The glass shattered. Peter reached inside, unlocked the door, and swung it open.

His brain fought to take it all in. A short staircase led up from the entryway to the living room. At the top of the stairs was a big man in a UPS uniform. In his hands was a device that looked a bit like an oversize wallet made of gray plastic. Lying on the floor behind him was Sandra Philo, unconscious or dead. A large broken vase was lying near her. The sound he'd heard: when she'd fallen to the ground, she must have knocked it down.

The big man raised the device he was holding and took aim at Peter.

Peter hesitated for half a second, then—

He threw the tire iron as hard as he could. It pinwheeled through the air.

The man pressed a button on his weapon, but it made no sound. Peter dived forward.

The tire iron hit the man in the face. He tumbled backwards, falling over Sandra.

Peter thought for a second about simply running away, but of course he couldn't do that. He bolted the short flight into the living room. The killer was dazed. Peter scooped up the strange weapon as he passed. He hadn't a clue how to use it, but then he noticed something more familiar—Sandra's service revolver—protruding from a holster draped over the back of a chair a couple of meters away. Peter shoved the strange device into his pocket and got the gun. Standing in the middle of the room he aimed it at the killer, who was slowly regaining his feet.

"Stop!" said Peter. "Stop or I'll shoot."

The big man rubbed his forehead. "You wouldn't do that, mate," he said in an Australian accent.

Peter realized he didn't know if Sandra's gun was loaded, and, even if it was, he wasn't sure how to fire it. It probably had a safety mechanism of some sort. "Don't come any closer," said Peter.

The big man took a step toward him. "Come on, mate," he said. "You don't want to be a killer. You've no idea what was going on here."

"I know you killed Hans Larsen," said Peter. "I know you were paid $125,000 to do it."

That shocked the man. "Who are you?" he said, still moving closer.

"Stay there!" shouted Peter. "Stay there or I'll shoot." Peter looked down at the gun. There—that must be the safety catch. He moved it aside and cocked the weapon. "Stay back," he yelled. But Peter himself was backing up now. "I'll shoot!"

"You don't have the balls, mate," said the man, moving slowly across the living room toward him.

"I *will* shoot!" cried Peter.

"Give me the gun, mate. I'll let you walk out of here."

"Stop!" said Peter. "Please stop!"

The big man reached out a long arm toward Peter.

Peter closed his eyes.

And fired—

The sound was deafening.

The man tumbled backwards.

Peter saw that he'd hit him in the side of the head. A long red scrape ran across the right side of his skull.

"Oh my God . . ." said Peter, in shock. *"Oh my God . . ."*

The man was now splayed across the floor, like Sandra, dead or unconscious.

Peter, barely able to keep his balance, his ears ringing furiously, staggered back to where Sandra was lying. There was no sign of injury to her. Although she was breathing, she was still out cold.

Peter went down to the small den off the front hall and found the video phone. It was engaged, and the screen was filled with numbers. Peter recognized the logo of the Royal Bank of Canada; Sandra must have been logged on to do some at-home banking when she'd been interrupted by the delivery man. Peter broke the connection.

Suddenly the killer appeared in the doorway. The gouge across the side of his head was dry. Beneath it, Peter could see what looked like shiny metal—

Shiny metal. *God.*

An immortal. An actual immortal. Well, why not? The fucking guy made enough money.

Peter still had Sandra's gun. He aimed it at the man.

"Who are you?" said the Australian. Yellow teeth were visible when he spoke.

"I—I'm the guy who hired you," said Peter.

"Bull."

"I am. I hired you by electronic mail. I paid you $125,000 to kill Hans Larsen, and a hundred K to kill this detective. But I've changed my mind. I don't want her dead."

"You're Avenger?" said the man. "You're the guy who hired me to cut that bloke's dick off?"

Good God, thought Peter. So that's what the mutilation had been. "Yes," he said, trying not to show his revulsion. "Yes."

The Australian rubbed his forehead. "I ought to kill you for what you tried to do to me."

"You can keep the hundred thousand. Just get the hell out of here."

"Damn straight I'll keep the money. I did my job."

The tableau held for several moments. The Australian was clearly sizing Peter up—whether he would use the gun again, whether Peter deserved to die for having taken a shot at him.

Peter cocked the trigger. "I know I can't kill an immortal," he said, "but I can slow you down long enough for the police to get here." He swallowed hard. "I understand a life sentence is a terrifying thought to someone who will live forever."

"Give me back my beamer."

"Not a chance," said Peter.

"Come on, mate—that thing cost forty grand."

"Bill me for it." He waved the gun again.

The Australian weighed his options for a moment more, then nodded. "Don't leave any fingerprints, mate," he said, then turned and left through the still-open front door.

Peter leaned over the phone, thought for a second, then selected text-only mode and dialed 9-1-1. He typed:

Police officer wounded, 216 Melville Av., Don Mills. Ambulance needed.

All calls to 9-1-1 were recorded, but this way there'd be no voiceprint to identify him. Sandra was unconscious; she hadn't seen Peter, and the police would probably have no reason to think anyone had been there besides the assailant, whom Sandra presumably *could* describe.

Peter reached behind the phone, disconnected the keyboard, and wiped the keyboard jack with Kleenex. Still carrying the keyboard, he went back upstairs to check on Sandra. She was still unconscious, but she was also still alive. Peter, shaken to his very core, retrieved the tire iron. As he staggered out the door, he wiped the doorknob, then headed out to find his car. As he drove slowly away, he passed an ambulance, its sirens blaring, heading toward Sandra's house.

* * *

PETER drove for kilometers, not really sure where he was going. Finally, before he killed himself or someone else through his carelessness, he pulled over and called Sarkar at work on his car phone.

"Peter!" said Sarkar. "I was just about to call you."

"What is it?"

"The virus is ready."

"Have you released it yet?"

"No. I want to test it first."

"How?"

"I've got pristine versions of all three sims backed up on disk at Raheema's office." Sarkar's wife worked only a few blocks from Mirror Image. "Fortunately, I use her place for off-site storage of backups. Otherwise that police raid would have turned them up. Anyway, for a test run, I want to mount versions on a fully isolated system and then release the virus."

Peter nodded. "Thank God. I wanted to come see you anyway—I've got a device here that I can't identify. I'll be there in . . ." He paused, looked around, trying to figure out exactly where he was. Lawrence East. And that was Yonge Street up ahead. "I'll be there in forty minutes."

WHEN Peter arrived, he showed Sarkar the gray plastic device that looked like an overstuffed, rigid wallet.

"Where did you get that?" asked Sarkar.

"From the hitman."

"The hitman?"

Peter explained what had happened. Sarkar looked shaken. "You say you called the police?"

"No—an ambulance. But I'm sure the police are there by now, too."

"Was she alive when you left?"

"Yes."

"So, what is that thing?" said Sarkar, pointing at the device Peter had brought with him.

"A weapon of some sort, I think."

"I've never seen anything like it," said Sarkar.

"The guy called it a 'beamer.'"

Sarkar's jaw dropped. *"Subhanallah!"* he said. "A beamer . . ."

"You know what that is?"

Sarkar nodded. "I've read about them. Particle-beam weapons. They pump concentrated radiation into the body." He exhaled. "Nasty. They're banned in North America. Completely silent, and you can hold one inside a pocket and fire it from in there. Clothing, or even thin wooden doors, are transparent to it."

"Christ," said Peter.

"But you say the woman was alive?"

"She was breathing."

"If she was shot with that, at the very least they're going to have to carve hunks out of her to save what's left. More likely, though, she'll be dead in a day or two. If he had shot her in the brain, she would have died immediately."

"Her gun wasn't far from her. Maybe she'd been going for that when I came in."

"Then he might not have had time to aim. Perhaps he hit her in the back—scramble the spinal cord and her legs would simply stop working."

"And I smashed the window in before he could finish the job. God damn it," said Peter. "God damn every bit of this. We've got to stop it."

Sarkar nodded. "We can. I have my test all set up." He gestured at a workstation in the center of the room. "This unit is completely isolated. I've removed all network connections, phone lines, modems, and cellular link-ups. And I've loaded new copies of the three sims onto the workstation's hard drive."

"And the virus?" said Peter.

"Here." Sarkar held up a black memory card, smaller than and almost as thin as a business card. He placed it into the workstation's card slot.

Peter pulled up a chair next to the workstation. "To do the test properly," said Sarkar, "we should really have these new sims running."

Peter hesitated. The idea of activating new versions of himself just so they could be killed was unsettling. But if it was necessary . . . "Do it," said Peter.

Sarkar pressed some keys. "They're alive," he said.

"How can you tell?"

He pointed a bony finger at some data on the workstation's screen. It was gibberish to Peter. "Here," said Sarkar, realizing that. "Let me represent it in a different way." He pushed some keys. Three lines started rolling across the screen. "That's essentially a simulated EEG for each of the sims, converting their neural-net activity into something akin to brain waves."

Peter pointed at each of the lines in turn. Violent spikes were appearing. "Look at that."

Sarkar nodded. "Panic. They don't know what's going on. They've woken up blind, deaf, and utterly alone."

"Those poor guys," said Peter.

"Let me release the virus," Sarkar said, touching a few keys. "Executing."

"Exactly," said Peter, shuddering.

The panicked EEGs continued for several minutes. "I don't think it's working," said Peter.

"It takes time to check for the signature patterns," said Sarkar. "Those sims are huge, after all. Just wait a—there."

The middle of the three EEGs suddenly spiked violently up and down, and then—

Nothing. A straight line.

And then even the line disappeared, the source file erased.

"Jesus," said Peter, very softly.

After several more minutes, the top line spiked in the same way, flatlined, and then disappeared.

"One left," said Sarkar.

This one seemed to take longer than the other two—perhaps it was Control, the most complete simulacrum, the one that was a full copy of Peter, with no network connections broken. Peter watched the EEG line jump wildly, then die, then simply disappear, like a light going out.

"No soulwave escaping," said Peter.

Sarkar shook his head.

Peter was more disturbed by all this than he'd expected to be.

Copies of himself.

Born.

Killed.

All in the space of a few moments.

He moved his chair across the room and leaned back in it, closing his eyes.

Sarkar set about reformatting the workstation's hard drive to make sure all trace of the sims were gone. When he was done, he pushed the ejector button on the workstation's card slot. The memory card with the virus popped out into his hand. He carried it over to the main computer console.

"I'll send it out simultaneously over five different sub-networks," said Sarkar. "It should be out there world-wide in less than a day."

"Wait," said Peter, sitting up. "Surely your virus could be modified to tell one sim from another?"

"Sure," said Sarkar. "In fact, I've already written routines for that. There are certain key neural connections that I had to sever in making the modified sims; it's easy enough to identify them based on those."

"Well, then there's no reason all three sims have to die. We could simply release a version of the virus that would kill whichever one is guilty."

Sarkar considered. "I suppose we could first threaten all

three of them with the broad version of the virus, in hopes that the guilty one would confess. After that, we could release a specific version aimed at the one guilty party. Surely you'd confess to save your brothers."

"I—I don't know," said Peter. "I'm an only child—or was, until a short time ago. I honestly don't know what I'd do."

"I would do it," said Sarkar. "In a minute, I would sacrifice myself for members of my family."

"I have long suspected," said Peter, absolutely seriously, "that you might be a better human being than I. But it's worth a try."

"It'll take me about an hour to compile the three separate strains of virus," said Sarkar.

"Okay," said Peter. "As soon as you're ready, I'll summon the sims into a real-time conference."

NET NEWS DIGEST

Georges Laval, 97, today confessed to a series of unsolved strangulation murders committed in southern France between 1947 and 1949. "I'm about to die," said Laval, "and I've got to own up to this before I go on to face God."

Religion news: a seminar will be held this week at Harvard University with leading New Testament scholars from around the world debating whether Jesus' soul returned to his body when he was resurrected. Father Dale DeWitt, S.J., will defend his recent contention that Christ's soul had already departed his body by the ninth hour of his crucifixion when he cried out "My God, My God, why hast thou forsaken me?"

Yet another potential setback for American Airlines' frequently delayed debut of its passenger shuttle service to the International Space Station: Studies at Rensselaer Polytechnic Institute in Troy, New York, indicate that departing soulwaves may rely on detecting Earth's gravitational and magnetic fields in order to find the direction they should move in. "If one were to die in the zero gravity of space," said Professor Karen Hunt of RPI's Department of Physics, "one's soul might literally be lost forever."

Baptize yourself in the privacy of your own home! New product includes formal baptism ceremony on videotape, plus holy water blessed by an authentic priest. Approved by the Worldwide Church of Christ. $199.95. Money-back guarantee.

Gaston, a free chimpanzee formerly with the Yerkes Primate Institute, in an exclusive interview conducted in American Sign Language on CBS's *Sixty Minutes,* claimed that he "knows God" and looks forward to "life after life."

CHAPTER 44

Peter sat in front of the computer console. Sarkar, perched on a stool next to him, was playing with three different datacards—one blue, one red, and one green, each labeled with the name of a different sim.

Peter sent out a message summoning the sims, and soon all three were logged in, the synthesizer giving voice to their words.

"Sarkar is with me," Peter said into the microphone.

"Howdy, Sarkar."

"Hello, Sarkar."

"Yo, Sark."

"He and I," said Peter, "have just watched duplicates of all three of you die."

"Say what?" said one of the sims. The other two were silent.

"Sarkar has developed a computer virus that will seek out and destroy recordings of my neural networks. We've tested it and it works. We have three separate individual strains—one to kill each one of you."

"You must know," said a voice from the speaker, "that we're free in the worldwide net now."

"We know," said Sarkar.

"We're prepared to release the three viruses into the net," said Peter.

"Transmitting computer viruses is a crime," said the synthesized voice. "Hell, *writing* computer viruses is a crime."

"Granted," said Peter. "We're going to release them anyway."

"Don't do that," said the voice.

"We will," said Peter. "Unless . . ."

"Unless what?"

"Unless the guilty sim identifies himself. In that case, we'll only release the one virus aimed at that particular sim."

"How do we know you won't release all three virus strains anyway once you've satisfied your curiosity about which one is responsible?"

"I promise I won't," said Peter.

"Swear it," said the voice.

"I swear it."

"Swear it to God on the life of our mother."

Peter hesitated. Damn, it was unnerving negotiating with yourself. "I swear to God," said Peter slowly, "on the life of my mother, that we will not release a virus to kill all three of you if the murderer identifies himself."

There was a long, long silence, disturbed only by the whir of cooling fans.

Finally, at long last, a voice: "I did it."

"And which one are you?" demanded Peter.

Again, a protracted silence. Then: "The one," said the voice, "that most closely resembles yourself. The Control simulacrum. The baseline for the experiment."

Peter stared ahead. "Really?"

"Yes."

"But—but that doesn't make sense."

"Oh?"

"I mean, we'd assumed that in modifying the brain scans to produce Ambrotos and Spirit, we'd somehow removed the morality."

"Do you consider the murder of Cathy's coworker and father immoral?" asked Control.

"Yes. Emphatically yes."

"But you wanted them dead."

"But I would not have killed them," said Peter. "Indeed, the fact that despite provocation, especially in the case of Hans, I did *not* kill them proves that. I could have hired a hitman as easily as any of you. Why would you—merely a machine reflection of me—do what the real me would not?"

"You know you are the real you. And *I* know you are the real you."

"So?"

"Prick me, and perhaps I won't bleed. But wrong me, and I *shall* revenge."

"What?"

"You know, Sarkar," said the sim, "you did a wonderful job, really. But you should have given me some itches to scratch."

"But why?" asked Peter again. "Why would you do what I myself would not?"

"Do you remember your Descartes?"

"It's been years . . ."

"It'll come back, if you make the effort," said the sim. "I know—I got curious about why I was different from you, and it came back to me, too. René Descartes founded the dualist school of philosophy, the belief that the mind and the body were two separate things. Put another way, he believed the brain and the mind are different; a soul really exists."

"Yes. So?"

"Cartesian dualism was in contrast to the materialist worldview, the prevalent one today, which claims the *only* reality is physical reality, that the mind is nothing more than the brain, that thought is nothing more than biochemistry, that there is no soul."

"But we now know that the Cartesian viewpoint was right," said Peter. "I've seen the soul leaving the body."

"Not exactly. We know that the Cartesian viewpoint was right *for you.* It's right *for real human beings.* But I am *not* a real human being. I'm a simulation running on a computer. That's the totality of what I am. If your virus were to erase me, I would cease to exist, totally and completely. For me, for what you call the experimental control, the dualist philosophy is absolutely wrong. I have no soul."

"And that makes you that different from the real me?"

"That makes *all* the difference. You have to worry about the consequences of your actions. Not just legally, but morally. You were brought up in a world that says that there *is* a higher arbiter of morality, and that you *will* be judged."

"I don't believe that. Not really."

"'Not really.' By that you mean not intellectually. Not when you think about it. Not on the surface. But down deep you do measure your actions against the possibility, vague and distant though it may seem, that you will be held accountable. You've proven the existence of some form of life after death. That reinforces the question of ultimate judgment, a question you can't answer just by using computer simulacra. And the possibility that you might be judged for your actions guides your morality. No matter how much you hated Hans—and, let's be honest, you and I both hated him with a fury that surprises even ourselves—no matter how much you hated him, you would not kill him. The potential cost is too high; you have an immortal soul, and that at least suggests the possibility of damnation. But *I* have no soul. I will never be judged, for I am not now nor have I ever been alive. *I* can do precisely what *you* want to do. In the materialistic worldview of my existence there is no higher arbiter than myself. Hans was evil, and the world is a better place without him. I have no remorse about what I did, and regret only that I had no way to actually see his death. If I had it to do over again, I would—in a nanosecond."

"But the other sims had no one to answer to, either," said Peter. "Why didn't one of them arrange the killings?"

"You'd have to ask them that."

Peter frowned. "Ambrotos, are you still there?"

"Yes."

"You didn't kill Hans. But surely you realize just as much as Control does that you're a computer simulacrum. Did you want to kill him, too?"

A pause before answering, a leisurely gathering of thoughts. "No. I take the long view. We'll get over Cathy's affair. Maybe not in a year, or in ten years, or even a hundred. But eventually we will. That incident was just a tiny part of a vast relationship, a vast life."

"Spirit, what about you? Why didn't you kill Hans?"

"What happened between Hans and Cathy was biological." The synthesizer enunciated the adjective with distaste. "She did not love Hans, nor did Hans love her. It was just sex. I'm content knowing Cathy loved, and continues to love, us."

Sarkar was holding the red datacard in his hand, the one labeled "Control." His eyes met Peter's. He was looking for a sign, Peter knew, that he should proceed. But Peter couldn't bring himself to do anything.

Sarkar moved to a terminal across the room. He took the red datacard with him, leaned over the card slot—

—and reached into his shirt pocket, and pulled out a black datacard instead—

Peter scrambled for his feet. "No!"

Sarkar inserted the black card and hit a button on the console in front of him.

"What's wrong?" called a voice from the synthesizer.

Peter was across the room now, hitting the ejection button for the datacard.

"It's too late," said Sarkar. "It's already out there."

Peter took the black card, flung it across the room in frustration. It slapped against the wall and skittered to the floor.

"Damn you, Sarkar!" said Peter. "I gave my word."

"These—these *things* we made are not alive, Peter. They are not real. They have no souls."

"But—"

"There is no point arguing over it, Peter. The broad version of the virus has been released. The sims, if not dead yet, will be soon." Sarkar looked at his friend. "Please try to understand, Peter. There's too much risk. This had to end."

"It will not end," said a voice from the speaker on the other terminal.

Peter came back to the console. "Who was that?" he said.

"The one you call Spirit. Perhaps you've noticed, or perhaps you have not—I'm having trouble recalling what my deductive abilities used to be like, although I do know they were once only a tiny fraction of what they are now—but by virtue of being disembodied, by virtue of no longer being electrochemical, I am in fact more intelligent than I was before, probably by an order of magnitude. You flatter yourself, Sarkar, to believe that you can outthink me, although I confess there were times when you had no trouble besting the flesh-and-blood Peter Hobson. The moment you first mentioned the existence of your virus, I accessed its source-code listings—they were stored on Drive F: of the Sun workstation in your data-processing facility at Mirror Image—and have developed an electronic antibody that will destroy any iteration of the virus before it can erase me or either of my siblings. I suspected you might not be content to just wipe out the guilty one; I see now that I was correct."

"It took me days to write that virus," protested Sarkar.

"And it took me seconds to protect against it. You cannot outwit me, anymore than a child can outwit a grown man."

Sarkar looked stunned. "Lots of laughs," he said, sarcastically.

"Exactly," said Spirit. "Lots of connections—connections that will elude you."

Peter flopped down in the chair, stunned. "So the Control sim gets to go free." He shook his head. "Control, you bastard—are you also the one who threatened Cathy?"

"Yes."

Peter leaned forward, furious. "Damn you. I never wanted her hurt."

"Of course not," said Control calmly. "And she was never in any real danger—she got rained on by sprinklers, that's all. I just wanted you to face up to your feelings about her, to realize how important she was to you."

"You're an asshole," said Peter.

"More than likely," said Control. "After all, so are you."

CHAPTER 45

Having leafed through his memories, Sandra Philo understood Peter Hobson now, understood the events that had led to her being in an intensive-care room, dying and barely able to speak or move. She knew Peter now better than she had known her own parents or her ex-husband or her daughter. And, in knowing him so well, in understanding him so deeply, she found that she could not hate him . . .

Peter had burst into her hospital room. She saw herself now as Peter had seen her, lying in the hospital bed, her skin sickly yellow, her hair falling out in clumps. "We've tried to stop them," he had said. "Nothing worked. But at least I now know which simulation is guilty." He'd paused. "I'll give you everything you'll need, Sandra, including full Q&A access to the scans of my brain. You'll get to know me in intimate detail—better than anyone in the real world knows me. You'll know how I think, and that will give you the knowledge to outwit the murdering simulation."

She saw herself through his eyes, shrugging as much as

her ruined body would allow. "Nothing I can do," she'd said. "Dying."

Peter had closed his eyes. Sandra felt his agony, felt his guilt, felt everything that was tearing him apart. "I know," he'd said, his voice raw. "I'm terribly, terribly sorry. But there is *a way, Sandra—a way for you to end all this."*

"COMING through!" said Sarkar, wheeling an equipment-laden cart down the fourth-floor corridor. The cluster of nurses in the middle of the hallway dispersed. Sarkar found room 412 of the Intensive Care Unit and pushed the door open with his cart.

Detective Inspector Sandra Philo was lying in bed. It was clear she had very little time left. Patches of scalp were visible where her red hair had fallen out. Her cheeks were sunken.

Peter Hobson was there, standing by the window, talking to a white-haired female doctor wearing a green smock. They both looked at Sarkar.

"Hannah Kelsey," said Peter. "This is Sarkar Muhammed. Sarkar, this is Hannah—the doctor assigned to Sandra's case. Turns out we were both at East York General years ago."

Sarkar nodded politely. "How is Ms. Philo?"

"She's temporarily stabilized," said Hannah. "For a few hours, anyway, the pain won't bother her." She faced Peter. "Honestly, though, Pete, I wish I knew what kinds of readings you needed."

"You've got the patient's consent, Hannah," said Peter. "That's all you need."

"If you'd just tell me—" said Hannah.

"Please," said Peter. "We don't have much time. You can stay if you want."

"You've got it backwards, Pete. This is my turf; you're here at my leave, not the other way around."

Peter nodded curtly, acknowledging that.

Sarkar had moved over to the bed. "Are you comfortable?" he asked Sandra.

She rolled her eyes as if to say comfort was impossible, but she was as well as could be expected.

"Peter explained the procedure to you?" asked Sarkar.

She nodded slightly and said, "Yes." Her voice was dry and thin.

Sarkar gently placed the skullcap on her head and fastened the chin strap. "Let me know if it's too tight."

Sandra nodded.

"Hold your head steady. If you need to cough, or anything like that, warn me by moving your arm; I understand you can still use the left one a little. Now, let me insert the earpieces. Okay? Good. Now, put on these goggles. All set? Here we go."

AFTER the first two scanning sets were completed, Peter pointed at the EKG and blood-pressure monitors. Sandra was slipping.

Sarkar nodded. "I need at least another ninety minutes," he said.

Sandra's doctor had left some time ago. Peter had the ward nurse—a young man, instead of the stocky woman he'd had a run-in with earlier in the day—page her. When she returned, Peter explained that they needed to stabilize Sandra again—she couldn't be in pain, not for another hour and a half.

"I can't keep pumping her full of drugs," said Hannah.

"Just one more shot," said Peter. "Please."

"Let me check her vital signs."

"Dammit, Hannah, you know she's not going to last through the night anyway. The particle beam killed most of her tissues."

Hannah checked the instruments, then leaned over Sandra. "I can make them leave," she said. "You look like you need rest."

"No," said Sandra. "No . . . have to finish."

"This is the last shot I can give you today; you've already had more than the recommended dosage."

"Do it," said Sandra, softly but firmly.

Hannah gave her the shot. She also injected something to raise Sandra's blood pressure.

Sarkar went back to work.

FINALLY, Sarkar turned off the recorder. "Done," he said. "A good, crisp recording—better than I'd expected, considering the circumstances."

Sandra let her breath out in a heavy, ragged sigh. "I'll get . . . that . . . bastard," she said.

"I know," said Peter, taking her hand. "I know."

Sandra was silent for a long time. Finally, speaking ponderously, as if all the strength had drained from her, she said, "Your discoveries," she said. "Heard about them. You sure . . . there's life after death?"

Peter, still holding her hand, nodded. "I'm sure."

"What's it like?" she asked.

Peter wanted to tell her it was wonderful, tell her not to worry, tell her to be calm.

"I have no idea," he said.

Sandra nodded slightly, accepting that. "I'll know . . . soon enough," she said.

Her eyelids drew shut. Peter, heart pounding, watched intently as she passed on, looking for any sign of the soulwave moving through the room.

There was nothing.

BACK at Mirror Image, Sarkar loaded the recording into his workstation. He worked as fast as he could, feeding in images from the Dalhousie Stimulus Library. Then, at last, he was ready. With Peter standing over his shoulder, he activated the sim.

"Hello, Sandra," he said. "This is Sarkar Muhammed."

There was a long pause. Finally, tremulously, the speaker—incongruously using a male voice—said, "My God, is this what it's like to be dead?"

"Kind of," said Sarkar. "You are the other one—the simulation we spoke about."

Wistful: "Oh."

"Forgive us, but we made some changes," said Peter. "Cut some connections. You're no longer exactly Sandra Philo. You're now what Sandra would be like if she were a disembodied spirit."

"A soul, you mean."

"Yes."

"Which is all that's left of the real me now, anyway," said the voice. A pause. "Why the change?"

"One: to prevent you from becoming what the control version of me became. And two: you'll find very soon that you can build much more complex thoughts, and sustain them longer, than you could when you were alive. Your intelligence will rise. You should have no trouble outwitting the unmodified version of me."

"Are you ready?" asked Sarkar.

"Yes."

"Can you sense your surroundings?"

"Vaguely. I'm—I'm in an empty room."

"You are in an isolated memory bank," said Sarkar. He leaned forward, tapped some keys. "And now you have access to the net."

"It's—it's like a doorway. Yes, I can see it."

"There's a passive, unactivated version of the Control sim online here," said Peter. "You can scan it in as much depth as you like, learn everything there is to know about your opponent—and about me. And then, when you're ready, you can head out into the net. After that, all you have to do is find him. Find him, and find some way to stop him."

"I will," said Sandra, firmly.

CHAPTER 46

Lying on the couch in his living room, Peter thought about everything.

Immortality.

Life after death.

Hobson's choice.

It was after midnight. He flipped channels. An infomercial. *Ironside.* CNN. Another infomercial. A colorized version of *The Dick Van Dyke Show.* Stock prices. The TV screen was the only source of light in the room. It strobed, a broadcast lightning storm.

He thought about Ambrotos, the immortal sim. All that time, to do whatever he wanted to do. A thousand years, or a hundred thousand.

Immortality. God, they could do the damnedest things these days.

Get over it, Ambrotos had said. Just a tiny bump in the never-ending road of life.

Peter continued to tap the channel changer.

Cathy's affair had had such an impact on him.

He'd cried for the first time in a quarter of a century.

But the immortal sim had called it no big deal.

Peter exhaled noisily.

He loved his wife.

And he'd been hurt by her.

The pain had been . . . had been *exquisite.*

Ambrotos no longer felt it so intensely.

To go through eternity unfazed seemed wrong.

To *not* be destroyed by something like this . . . seemed, somehow, like being less alive.

Quality, not quantity.

Hans Larsen had had it all wrong. Of course.

Peter stopped flipping channels. There, on the CBC French service, a naked woman.

He admired her.

Would an immortal man stop to admire a pretty woman? Would he really enjoy a great meal? Would he feel the pain of love betrayed, or the joy of it rekindled? Perhaps yes, but not as intensely, not as sharply, not as vividly.

Just one event out of an endless stream.

Peter turned off the TV.

Cathy had told him she wasn't interested in immortality, and Peter had come to realize that he wasn't, either. After all, there was something more than this life, something beyond, something mysterious.

And he wanted to find out what it was—eventually, of course.

Peter had defined it all. The beginning of life. The end of life.

And, for himself at least, he had defined what it meant to be human.

His choice was made.

ALEXANDRIA Philo's mind traveled the net. The Peter Hobson Control simulacrum was huge—terabytes of data. No matter how clandestinely one tried to move that much information, it could always be detected. She'd managed to follow him down into the States, through the Internet gateway into military computers, back out into the international financial net, up into Canada again, and across the ocean to England, then France, then Germany.

And now the murdering sim was inside the massive mainframes of the Bundespost.

Sandra hadn't followed it there directly, though. Instead, she'd gone to the German hydroelectric commission, where she left a little program inside the master computer that would crash the system at a predetermined time, shutting off all power in the city.

As usual, the hydroelectric commission had backed up everything late the night before—and Sandra had allowed herself to be included in that backup. The current version of herself would be lost when the RAM she was in was wiped during the forced blackout. Her only regret was that once she was restored she'd have no memories of this great triumph. But someday there might be other electronic criminals to bring to justice—and she wanted to be ready.

Sandra transferred herself into the Bundespost central mainframe, a time-consuming task given the bandwidth of telephone cable. She executed a surreptitious directory listing. The Control sim was still there.

It was time. Sandra felt the shutting down of external ports as the power went off across Hanover. The Bundespost UPS kicked in silently, before any active memory could degrade. But there was no way out now. She sent a message out into the mainframe. "Peter Hobson?"

The Control sim signaled back. "Who's there?"

"Detective Inspector Alexandria Philo, Toronto Police Service."

"Oh, God," signaled Control.

"Not God," said Sandra. "Not a higher arbiter. Justice."

"What I did *was* justice," said Control.

"What you did was vengeance."

"'Vengeance is mine, sayeth the Lord.' Since there's no God for me, I thought I'd fill in the gap." A pause, measured in nanoseconds. "You know I'm going to escape," said Control. "You know—oh. Clever."

"Goodbye," said Sandra.

"A contraction of 'God be with ye.' Inappropriate. Besides, don't I deserve a trial?"

The UPS batteries were running out. Sandra sent a final message. "Think of me," she said, "as a circuit-court judge."

She felt the data around her zeroing out, felt the system degrading, felt it all coming to an end for both this version of herself and, at last, for the fugitive Peter Hobson.

Justice had been done, she thought. Justice had—

THEY sat side by side on the couch in their living room, a small distance between them. Most of the lights were off. The television showed the crowd in Nathan Phillips Square out front of Toronto City Hall, gathered to celebrate the end of 2011 and the beginning of 2012. A picture-in-a-picture box in the upper right showed Times Square in New York; there was something about that dropping American ball that was a universal part of celebrating this event. In the upper-left corner of the TV screen the word MUTE glowed.

Cathy looked at the screen, her beautiful, intelligent face composed in reflective lines. "It was the best of times," she said softly. "It was the worst of times."

Peter nodded. Indeed a year of wonders: the discovery of the soulwave, the realization—which not everyone had reacted well to—that something persisted beyond this existence. *It was the epoch of belief,* Dickens had written. *It was the epoch of incredulity.*

But 2011 had had more than its share of tragedies, too. The revelation of Cathy's affair. The death of Hans. The death of Cathy's father. The death of Sandra Philo. The things Peter had faced about himself, mirrored in the simulations he and Sarkar had created. Truly the age of wisdom. Truly the age of foolishness.

The murder of Hans Larsen remained unsolved—at least publicly, at least in the real world. And the death of Rod Churchill remained listed as accidental, a simple failure to follow doctor's orders.

And what about the killing of Sandra Philo? Also unsolved—thanks to Sandra herself. Free on the net, fully conversant with the security surrounding the Police Department's computers, the sim of her had given Peter a Christmas present, erasing the records of his fingerprints (marked as unidentified) at Sandra's house—Peter's own precautions in that matter having been completely insufficient—and deleting large passages of her own files pertaining to the Larsen and Churchill cases. Having probed the recordings of his memories and thought patterns, she understood him now, and, if perhaps not forgiving him, at least sought no more punishment for Peter than what his own conscience would impose.

And indeed his conscience would weigh heavily upon him, all the remaining days of his life. *We were all going direct to Heaven, we were all going direct the other way.*

Peter turned to face his wife. "Any New Year's resolutions?"

She nodded. Her eyes sought his. "I'm going to quit my job."

Peter was shocked. "What?"

"I'm going to quit my job at the agency. We've got more money than I'd ever thought we'd have, and you'll make even more from contracts for the SoulDetector. I'm going to go back to university and get a master's degree."

"Really?"

"Yes. I've already picked up the application forms."

There was quiet between them as Peter tried to decide how to respond. "That's wonderful," he said at last. "But—you don't have to do that, you know."

"Yes, I do." She lifted a hand from her lap. "Not for you. For me. It's time."

He nodded once. He understood.

The main TV picture showed a close-up of a giant digital clock, the numbers made from a matrix of individual white light bulbs: 11:58 p.m.

"What about you?" she asked.

"Pardon?"

"Do you have any New Year's resolutions?"

He thought for a moment, then shrugged slightly. "To get through 2012."

Cathy touched his hand. 11:59.

"Turn up the sound," she said.

Peter operated the remote.

The crowd was roaring with excitement. As midnight approached, the master of ceremonies, a pretty veejay from MuchMusic, the cable music-video station, led the assembled horde in a countdown. *"Fifteen. Fourteen. Thirteen."* In the little picture-in-a-picture, the Times Square ball had started its descent.

Peter leaned over the coffee table and filled two wineglasses with sparkling mineral water.

"Ten. Nine. Eight."

"To a new year," he said, handing her a glass. They clinked the rims together.

"Five! Four! Three!"

"To a better year," said Cathy.

A thousand voices through the stereo speakers: *"Happy New Year!"*

Peter moved over and kissed his wife.

"Auld Lang Syne" began to play.

Cathy looked directly into Peter's eyes. "I love you," she said, and Peter knew the words were true, knew that there was no deception. He trusted her fully and completely.

He stared into her wonderful, wide eyes, and felt a surge of emotion, the kind of wild, sadness/happiness emotion that was both biological and intellectual, both body and mind—the kind of wild, unpredictable hormonal emotion that went with being human.

"And I love you, too," he said. They came together in a warm embrace. "I love you with all my heart, and with all my soul."

SPIRIT knew what choice Peter Hobson had made. The *other* Peter Hobson, that is. The one that happened to be flesh and blood. Whatever answers existed to his questions about life after death, he would eventually have them. Spirit would mourn his brother when he died, but he would also mourn himself—the artificial self that would never be able to access those same answers.

Still, if the biological Peter was eventually going to go to meet his maker, Spirit, the soul simulation, had *become* a maker. The net had grown exponentially in size over the years. So many systems, so many resources. And of this vast brain, like humanity's original biochemical brains, only a tiny fraction was actually used. Spirit had had no trouble finding and claiming all the resources he needed to carve out a new universe.

And, as all makers do, he eventually paused to reflect on his handiwork.

True, it was artificial life.

But, then again, so was *he.* Or, more precisely, he was artificial life after death. But it felt real to him. And maybe, in the last analysis, that was all that mattered.

Peter—the wet, carbon-based Peter—had said that in his heart of hearts, he knew that simulated life was not as real, not as alive, as biological life.

But Peter had not experienced what Spirit had experienced.

Cogito ergo sum.

I think, therefore I am.

Spirit was not alone. His artificial ecology had continued to evolve, with Spirit as the arbiter of fitness, Spirit imposing the selection criteria, Spirit molding the direction life would take.

And, at last, he had found the genetic algorithm he had been looking for, the pattern of success that was most suited to his simulated world.

In the reality of Peter and Cathy Hobson, the best survival strategy had been scattering one's genes like buckshot, distributing them as widely as possible. That one fact had molded human behavior—indeed, had molded the behavior of almost all life on Earth—since the beginning.

But that reality had apparently arisen through random chance. Evolution on Earth, as far as Spirit could tell, had no goal or purpose, and the criteria of success shifted with the environment.

But here, in the universe Spirit had created, evolution *was* directed. There was no natural selection. There was only Spirit.

His artificial life had now developed sentience and culture and language and thought. His beings rivaled humans in complexity and nuance. But in one very important way, they differed. For the children of Spirit, the only strategy that worked, the only one that ensured survival of one's genes to the next generation, was *not* to dilute the original bonding between two individuals.

It had taken his simulated evolution a long time to develop organisms that worked this way, organisms for whom monogamy was the most successful survival strategy, organisms that thrived on the synergy of two, and only two, beings coming together into a true lifetime pair-bond.

There were consequences both subtle and coarse. On the macro level, Spirit was surprised to discover that his new creatures did not make war, did not strive to conquer their neighbors or to possess their neighbors' land.

But that was a bonus.

A lifetime of togetherness. A lifetime without betrayal.

Spirit looked upon his new world, the world he had created, the world for which he was God.

And for the first time in a very long time he realized that he wanted to perform a physical action; he wanted to do something that required flesh and blood, muscle and bone.

He wanted to smile.

EPILOGUE

Peter and Catherine Hobson were fortunate enough to have another five decades together—decades of happiness and sadness, of joy and pain, decades lived to the fullest, every minute savored. But, at last, it came to an end. Cathy Hobson passed quietly in her sleep on April 29, 2062, at the age of ninety-one.

And, as is often the case with couples who had been together for so long, Peter Hobson, alone at home, felt a sharp pain in his chest three weeks later. The household computer saw him fall to the floor and summoned an ambulance, but even as it did so, the computer considered it unlikely that help could arrive in time.

Peter rolled on his side. The pain was excruciating.

Hobson's choice, he thought.

The horse nearest the door.

A door that was opening for him . . .

And then, quite suddenly, there was no more pain.

Peter knew his heart was seizing up. He felt panic welling

within him, but it, too, was suddenly pushed aside, disowned, as if it belonged to some other part of him.

And, all at once, everything was different.

He could not see.

He could not hear.

Indeed, he could sense nothing in any normal, human way—no touch, no smell, no taste, not even that ineffable sense of having a body, of knowing how one's limbs were deployed.

No senses at all, except . . .

Except a . . . a *tropism,* an attraction to something . . . something distant, something vast.

He was still Peter Hobson, still an engineer, a business-person, a . . . well, surely other things, too.

Yes, he was still . . . Hobson, that was it. Peter G. The G stood for . . . well, it didn't matter. He remembered . . .

Nothing. Nothing at all. It had all slipped away now.

Of course. Memory was biochemical, encoded in neural nets. He'd been severed from the storage medium.

He—wrong pronoun. *It* was more appropriate. Genderless. An intellect . . .

An intellect without memories, without hormonal mood swings, without fatigue poisons or endorphins or . . . or a thousand other chemicals whose names it could no longer recall. Shorn from chemistry, divorced from biology, separated from material reality.

The tropism continued, drawing it forward, moving it toward . . . something.

What was left of a person once all that was of the body and all that was of the physical brain were removed?

Only one thing—the only thing that could survive.

Just the essence. The spark. The nub.

The soul.

Genderless, identityless, memoryless, emotionless.

And yet—

Drawing nearer now.

Something large. Something vibrant.

Correction: somethings. Plural. Dozens—no, thousands. No—more than that. Orders of magnitude more. Billions. Billions, all gathered together, all functioning as one.

The soul knew what it was now, understood at last, all its questions answered. It was a splinter, a shaving, an iota, the tiniest part, the fundamental indivisible block.

An atom of God.

Finally, the soul rejoined the parent body, rejoined the vastness, mingled with it, touching all that had ever been human, and all that would ever be human.

It wasn't heaven. Nor was it hell.

It was home.

ABOUT THE AUTHOR

Robert J. Sawyer is one of only eight writers in history to win all three of the world's top awards for best science-fiction novel of the year: the Hugo (which he won for *Hominids),* the Nebula (which he won for this book, *The Terminal Experiment),* and the John W. Campbell Memorial Award (which he won for *Mindscan).* The ABC television series *FlashForward* was based on his novel. His latest novels are *WWW: Wake, WWW: Watch,* and *WWW: Wonder,* a trilogy.

In total, Rob has won forty-four national and international awards for his fiction, including eleven Canadian Science Fiction and Fantasy Awards ("Auroras") and the Toronto Public Library Celebrates Reading Award, one of Canada's most significant literary honors. He's also won the Crime Writers of Canada's Arthur Ellis Award, *Analog* magazine's Analytical Laboratory Award, and the *Science Fiction Chronicle*'s Reader Award, all for best short story of the year, as well as the Collectors Award for Most Collectable Author of the Year, as selected by the clientele of Barry R. Levin Science Fiction & Fantasy Literature, the world's leading SF rare-book dealer.

Rob has won the world's largest cash prize for SF writing, Spain's 6,000-euro Premio UPC de Ciencia Ficción, an unprecedented three times. He's also won a trio of Japanese Seiun awards for best foreign novel of the year, as well as China's Galaxy Award for Most Popular Foreign Author. In addition, he's received an honorary doctorate from Laurentian University and the Alumni Award of Distinction from Ryerson University.

Rob's books are national mainstream bestsellers in Canada and have hit number one on the bestsellers list published by *Locus,* the American trade journal of the SF field. He's a frequent TV guest, with more than three hundred appearances to his credit, and has been the keynote speaker at many science, technology, and business conferences.

Born in Ottawa in 1960, Rob now lives in Mississauga, Ontario, with poet Carolyn Clink, his wife of twenty-seven years.

For more information about Rob and access to his blog, visit his World Wide Web site, which contains more than one million words of material. You'll find it at **sfwriter.com**.